Praise for the novels of
JOHN R. MAXIM

"Dazzling."
Andrew M. Greeley

"Exhilarating."
Publishers Weekly

"Readers may need to take blood pressure pills."
People

"Just [a] few pages are enough to establish
Maxim's credentials as a pro."
Los Angeles Times

"Top-notch writing, great action, memorable
characters—what more could any
suspense reader want?"
Michael Palmer

"John Maxim is superb. And Bannerman is dynamite."
Iris Johansen

"Maxim does a great job."
Providence Journal-Bulletin

JOHN R. MAXIM

BANNERMAN'S GHOSTS

AVON BOOKS

An Imprint of HarperCollinsPublishers

This is a work of fiction. Names, characters, places, and incidents are products of the author's imagination or are used fictitiously and are not to be construed as real. Any resemblance to actual events, locales, organizations, or persons, living or dead, is entirely coincidental.

AVON BOOKS
An Imprint of HarperCollins*Publishers*
10 East 53rd Street
New York, New York 10022-5299

Copyright © 2003 by John R. Maxim
Excerpt copyrights © 1989, 1990, 1991, 1993 by John R. Maxim
ISBN: 0-06-000585-8
www.avonbooks.com

First Avon Books paperback printing: April 2004
First William Morrow hardcover printing: March 2003

Avon Trademark Reg. U.S. Pat. Off. and in Other Countries, Marca Registrada, Hecho en U.S.A.
HarperCollins® is a trademark of HarperCollins Publishers Inc.

Printed in the U.S.A.

10 9 8 7 6 5 4 3 2 1

For Thomas Christopher Maxim—
May the world you grow up in be a gentler place,
and may you help make it so

ACKNOWLEDGMENTS

I am constrained from naming those who've been so very helpful. To do so would probably cost them their jobs and, in one case, a likely prosecution. The Greta Kirch character is disguised, but quite real. She is brilliant; she is honorable; and, I'm proud to say, my friend. Another, now deceased, was the real John Waldo. Or rather, they tell me that he is deceased. I choose not to believe it, knowing Waldo.

BANNERMAN'S
GHOSTS

1

From the site he had chosen, the rebel commander could see sixty miles of coastline. The place was Angola on West Africa's coast. Its capital, Luanda, lay below him. Beyond was the shimmer of the South Atlantic Ocean, set ablaze as the sun neared the horizon.

The rebel commander was called Alameo. He was a tall man, somewhat gaunt, with an intelligent face whose normal expression was the hint of a smile, but many days had passed since he'd last smiled. He was dressed in green-and-brown mottled fatigues that bore no insignia of rank. His only distinguishing badge was his cap. It was a French-style kepi, flat on top, blue in color, with fabric that draped to his shoulders. He was known throughout Angola by that cap.

He had chosen this site, near the great waterfall, because it was easily defended. Only two winding roads snaked their way up the bluffs that marked the beginning of the inland plateau. Each road had a number of hairpin turns, all of which were within easy range of his mortars. An attacking force on the ground would be slaughtered. Nor did he fear an attack from the air. A canopy of forest protected his encampment from visual sightings by attack helicopters. And they would be within range of his missiles.

But his mind on this day was not on defense. When darkness fell he would descend the bluffs with only his captain and a few handpicked men. The Israelis, his advisers, had begged him not to risk it. Their leader, named Yoni, said, "You're not thinking straight. We can't afford to lose you over this."

Alameo answered, "He tortured her, Yoni."

The Israeli grimaced. "We know what he did."

"He cut Sara to pieces. He dismembered her, Yoni. And he kept her alive until the last cut. What she suffered was still on her face."

This last was not true, thought the man known as Yoni. He had seen her face himself. It was swollen, but vacant. She had indeed suffered greatly, but her face gave little sign of it. All they knew was that Savran Bobik had Sara for what must have been three terrible days. He then sent Alameo what was left of her.

The Israeli reached his hands to the taller man's shoulders. "Alameo . . . my friend . . . you must listen to me. I know that Sara was special to you. But she was one of us long before she met you. I trained her myself. And I loved her myself. Your claim is not greater than ours."

"Bobik sent her to me. Not to you."

The Israeli said, "Yes, but we sent her to him. Do you think I don't wish we never asked her to do it? I would give both my eyes to have her back."

"I want Bobik's."

The Israeli gestured toward the city of Luanda. Its lights had begun to blink on. He said, "Let us do this for you. We can move about freely. We're Mossad, but most of us have embassy status. The worst they can do if we're caught is expel us. You, they will shoot or much worse."

"You can have Savran Bobik when I'm finished with him. I intend to have him for three days."

The Israeli gestured toward a nearer set of lights. They came from a large biochemical complex surrounded by razor-wire fencing. It covered at least four kilometers square. Even so, only part of the facility could be seen. It was said to go four, perhaps five stories down. The main building bore the name VaalChem.

Yoni asked, "Is he there? That place is guarded like a fort. How can you hope to get out alive?"

Alameo shook his head. "He won't be at VaalChem. Not tonight."

"Then where?"

"At a warehouse that he uses. He'll be there in two hours. He's preparing another of his shipments of death. It will be his last. That, I promise."

"You are reliably informed?"

He nodded. "I am."

"By whom, Alameo? Who down there can you trust? Has it crossed your mind that this might be a trap? That he's waiting for you? That he's ready?"

"It has. He thinks he is. I'm not a stupid man, Yoni."

"If you take him," asked Yoni, "what then?"

"I told you. Three days. He will answer for Sara. And Bobik has much to tell us both about VaalChem."

"Well, do me one favor. Hold on to that thought. Savran Bobik is a sadist and an all-around pig, but VaalChem may have killed many hundreds to his one and they've died just as horribly as Sara."

"Not the same," said Alameo. "They all thought they were sick. They weren't strapped down while someone tore at their flesh."

A sigh. "Okay, agreed. Promise me I'll get to question him."

"You can have him on the third day."

2

Artemus Bourne had been expecting the shipment, but not for another few days at the least. The three red-and-white containers, resembling picnic coolers, bore the logo of one of the companies he owned, a biotech firm in West Africa. He would have Winfield's hide for this stupidity.

His instructions were explicit. They had all been ignored. The containers were to have been shipped most discreetly to another of his firms in Virginia. In plain language, they were to be smuggled. They were to have taken a circuitous route from Angola, to Lisbon, to Grand Cayman, to Virginia. They were then to be driven to Briarwood, his estate. Unopened, uninspected, and untraceable.

And yet here they were, expressed directly to his home, not only with those logos announcing their source, but with his name, in bold letters, emblazoned on the label and written in Winfield's own hand. The writing seemed a bit shaky, but definitely Winfield's. The damned fool must have fallen off the wagon.

By some miracle, however, the seals were unbroken. The

containers had made it through Customs unexamined. It was not that their contents were illegal per se. They were, for the most part, vaccines and antivirals that Winfield's researchers at VaalChem had developed. Nor was it that he wished to cheat Customs of the duty on the diamonds that he knew would be included. Bourne simply wished to avoid being asked why he was building a supply of vaccines for which there was no disease.

Most deliveries that seemed of a sensitive nature were normally taken through Briarwood's north gate. It was approached through woodlands by a winding dirt road and likely to be free of prying eyes. A guard stationed there had accepted the containers and had driven them up to the house. The guard apologized; he said he realized it was Sunday, but a Sunday delivery had been specified for some reason. The guard knew that Sundays at Briarwood were special and Winfield had surely known that as well. Sunday was brunch day. It had become an institution. In an hour, some two dozen guests would be arriving, two senators and a cabinet secretary among them. They would have a pleasant brunch and then get down to the business for which he'd helped put them in office.

But an hour is an hour and he might as well use it. Putting his annoyance aside for the moment, he hauled the three containers down the stairs to his basement. He would read the reports that had come with the vaccines. The clinical trials on humans had gone well, according to his last word from Winfield. This time all the subjects had survived.

And he'd look at the diamonds, unpolished, uncut. He'd been told that they were of exceptional quality, worth three times the value of comparable-sized stones that were mined in South Africa by De Beers. He didn't doubt it, given their source. Angola's diamonds were the best ever found. Even so, to his eye, they looked like ordinary pebbles of the sort that one might find in any streambed.

Truth be known, these stones were almost as worthless by any practical measure. He knew that diamonds were neither rare nor intrinsically valuable. The only functional quality of a diamond was its hardness. Its only real use was on the tip of a cutting tool. But De Beers had done an excellent job of not only hoarding and rationing their supply but in making them the sine qua non of romance. Diamonds are forever. A girl's best friend and all that. Never mind that the two-karat rock on her finger would be worth not much more than a good pair of shoes if De Beers' stranglehold were to end.

And it will, thought Bourne. It most deservedly will. Once we've solved certain problems in Angola.

In his basement, he paused at a floor-to-ceiling wine rack that was actually the door to Bourne's private world. It was an area off limits to household staff and unknown to all but a few close associates. He slid the rack open and carried the containers into what once had been a bomb shelter.

A former owner had added the shelter back in the Eisenhower era. It had been quite elaborate even then. It had two bedrooms, a pantry, a fully equipped kitchen, and its own ventilation and filtration systems. Bourne had since made a number of refinements. The largest of the bedrooms was now a laboratory. He'd installed all sorts of HazMat equipment including a chemical shower. This was at Winfield's request. The man liked to putter. But he also took the view that he'd like to survive should there ever be an accident with the bacilli. There was even a bolted-down cot with restraints and a stainless steel autopsy table. These latter two were there because Winfield had them on his wish list, but Bourne had forbidden their actual use. This was his home after all. One had to draw the line somewhere. No unwilling live subjects. No, not even monkeys. Monkeys scream even louder than humans.

Winfield also added the requisite electronics. Computers in the lab and in the smaller of the bedrooms. But Winfield's visits were occasional. Bourne was down there all the time. So Bourne added a bank of video monitors that surveilled all activity in the house and on its grounds.

The smaller bedroom was still that, a bedroom. He'd had it furnished to Winfield's taste so that Winfield could remain down there out of sight whenever he flew over to confer. Bourne also gave that bedroom a nice solid door that Bourne was able to bolt from outside. This wasn't done for any sinister purpose. It was simply to keep Winfield away from the wine racks that filled half the cellar.

And they'd added a freezer, actually more of a vault, of a size that many a small bank would envy. It already held several hundred thousand units of various vaccines and bacilli. And in a separate section, in a safe within a safe, were the little glass ampules that Winfield had devised to contain a most remarkable substance. There were four of these ampules, each three inches long, each partly filled with a superfine powder. Bourne had no plans for them; he simply liked having them. They were so exquisitely deadly.

He had almost come to think of these ampules as pets. He would never admit that. He knew it sounded insane. But the substance inside them would physically react every time he opened that safe. It was only the vibration; the stuff was so light and fine. It would do a little dance within the ampules. They were like wiggly puppies wagging their tails at the sound of their master's approach.

He had placed the three containers on a table in the kitchen. He cut the seals on all three and opened the one to his right. He let out a yelp and staggered backward. For there, looking up at him, was a human head, lips parted as if trying to speak.

Bourne took a moment to gather himself. He took several deep breaths to help quiet his pulse. He stepped forward again and looked down at the face. It was not one he recognized. A stranger. Under it, around it, he saw shattered glass vials and a puddling of the fluids that they had contained. They had all been intermingled and crushed. He used a kitchen spatula to open another, this time the one on the left. This time he had managed to prepare himself somewhat. The second head was less of a shock, but he recoiled all the same; this one stank. This one must have been dead some time longer.

Bourne pinched his nose as he took a closer look. Dark skin, quite dark, but a white man, no native. His features seemed, if anything, Slavic. He had a dense curly beard and a mane of black hair that would have been shoulder length if he'd had shoulders. Like the first, he was resting on a bed of broken glass. And he seemed to have a mouthful of diamonds.

Bourne felt sure he didn't know him, but he couldn't be certain. The face had been battered beyond ready recognition. He had the look of a man who'd died trying to scream, or trying not to choke on those stones. This one had undergone something special. The eyes were swollen shut to mere slits. His cheeks were doubled in size, their bones probably crushed, and his jaw was askew as if torn from its socket. This one seemed to have something carved into his forehead. Bourne couldn't make out what. The flesh had suppurated. Someone should have thought to add ice.

Bourne heaved a sigh. He put the spatula down. He opened the middle container with his hand. He'd expected, he supposed, to find another unknown face, but there was no mistake about this next one. This one wore bifocals in a tortoiseshell frame and had the same look of befuddled detachment that he'd worn since Bourne had first met him. The head had belonged to Sir Cecil Bonham Winfield, Chief Virologist and Director of VaalChem. This would tend to explain why Winfield's handwriting had suggested diminished capacity. He must have done those labels with a knife at his throat. And later, after his head was detached, someone must have decided to put his glasses back on. It seemed unlikely that they would have stayed in place as his head rolled across a floor somewhere.

Well, that's it, thought Bourne. So much for his brunch. He would have to disappoint them, turn all of them away. His mind would not be on business.

He looked for a note. Some sort of a message. Sending three heads did not seem the sort of thing that the sender would want to be obscure about. Not that he didn't have a pretty good idea as to who was most likely behind it. There was a man who'd become a considerable hindrance to certain of his projects in that part of the world. A man who had already cost him dearly.

But why this? Why now? What had brought it about? Perhaps a note had been included, underneath somewhere, amid the shattered vials and their former contents plus whatever other fluids had seeped from their heads.

Bourne wasn't about to go rummaging for it. He would summon Chester. He would let Chester do that. And whether or not Chester found such a missive, he suspected that Chester would be able to shed light on why his weekly brunch had been disturbed in this manner. Some months ago, he'd put Chester in charge of overseeing certain of his Angolan operations. An unpleasant place. Barbarous. But then, so is Chester. Wasn't Chester just over there? A week ago, yes. One assumes that Winfield had a head when Chester saw him. Otherwise, he'd have noticed something amiss.

"Amiss," muttered Bourne. "I think I've just made a joke."

Whatever the story, enough was enough. If the man he had in mind was the source of this atrocity, it was time that he learned that he was not beyond reach. Bourne knew just how to get him, how to make him rue this day.

He would say to Chester, "I have run out of patience. I want you to locate Elizabeth Stride. I want no more excuses. Go find her."

3

Bourne instructed the guards at the main gate of Briarwood to make his apologies to his guests. They were to radio those who would arrive by helicopter and say that the event had been postponed. They were told to cite a dangerous gas leak as the reason for the sudden cancellation. They were to say that Mr. Bourne would be calling them later to convey his sincere regrets in person. Bourne then summoned Chester Lilly through his pager.

Such a name, thought Bourne, for such an ungentle man. Bourne had wondered how Chester had survived his childhood. The name must have been a magnet for bullies. The answer, of course, was that Chester was a brute. He would almost surely have outbullied the bullies. If not, he would have revisited them later. He was not one to turn the other cheek.

It wasn't that Chester was especially large. He was, in fact, an inch shorter than Bourne himself, but of course much more solidly built. And, unlike himself, he had a head of golden hair, maintained by a Houston hairstylist named

Terrence. He would actually fly back to Texas for a trim. Chester wouldn't let anyone else touch it.

Chester's wavy locks were his only real vanity. He did not have much else to choose from. Chester had a face that could turn one's blood cold just by staring, often smiling, not saying a word. His smile held the promise of what he would do if only his employer gave the nod. And that expression was pretty much the only one he had. This was all well and good where intimidation was called for, but limiting, certainly, in other endeavors such as trying to meet women, for example. Not that Chester liked women. Not that Chester liked anyone. But he did like power and he liked being feared and he could be relied on to do as he was told. These qualities made him a valued assistant as long as one held his baser instincts in check.

He'd told Chester to enter through the north gate in order to avoid being seen by his turned-away guests. They would know that he does not repair gas leaks. He'd told Chester to park his car behind the stables and then come directly to the basement. He was not to pause to taunt any of the horses or to frighten the peacocks that wandered the grounds or to put a bullet through one of the beehives. He'd actually done that. The man had tried to shoot bees. It seems the bees mistook his hair for a mum and attempted to mine it of pollen.

This time he avoided them or they avoided him. Bourne watched him on the screen of one of his monitors as Chester approached without incident. Bourne waited, arms folded, by the three open coolers as Chester made his way down the stairs. He would let them speak for themselves. Chester appeared and greeted him with a nod, but his eyes quickly fell on the coolers. Chester stared, then almost smiled, and made a soft whistling sound.

He pointed. "In the middle . . . that's Winfield?"

"It was."

"Seems I'm not the only one who didn't like him very much."

"An astute observation, Mr. Lilly. And the others?"

Chester lifted his chin toward the cooler on the right.

"Looks like Kruger. Peter Kruger. Winfield's chief of security. Him I liked better than Winfield."

You would, thought Bourne, who now recognized Kruger. Good at his job, but despicable generally. While South Africa's apartheid was still in full flower, Kruger had been a Johannesburg jailer, fond of strangling black prisoners and then stringing them up so that their deaths would appear to be suicides. He'd later joined VaalChem, then based in South Africa. The firm was central to a project, later revealed, of using germs to sicken whole Bantu communities that were centers of revolt against apartheid. That ended when Nelson Mandela was freed. When Mandela came to power, he shut VaalChem down. Bourne then bought it for a song and moved the plant to Angola. Kruger managed to tag along with it.

Chester stepped closer to the first of the coolers. He reached a finger into the open mouth of the head that he had not yet identified. He asked, "What are these? Are these diamonds?"

"They should have been," said Bourne, "but I very much doubt it. I don't think that the sender would have been so considerate as to forward that part of the shipment intact. You're looking at a mouthful of gravel."

Chester abruptly drew his hand back. "Wait a minute. Those vials." He wiped the hand against his jacket. "Are you sure these were only vaccines they smashed up? Who says they didn't lace it with bugs?"

In truth, that possibility had failed to occur to him. If any of several bacilli had been added, they both had been infected already. But so would whoever had packaged this mess. Bourne doubted that he'd just been murdered.

He said, "They're only vaccines and one or two new antivirals. All those vials are color-coded with strips of Mylar tape. Even crushed, I know what was in them."

Chester accepted that uncertain assurance. Once again he reached into the head's open mouth. He took two of the stones and held them up to the light. "Yeah, they wouldn't have wasted real diamonds on this. Must be hundreds stuffed in there, maybe more that he swallowed. Unless they didn't know they were diamonds."

"They knew. I was only expecting a handful. And they're

letting me know that they knew that." And they're also letting me know, thought Bourne, that they know about Sunday being brunch day.

Chester's mind was elsewhere. He was poking the man's cheeks. He said, "See this? Makes him look like a chipmunk. This guy couldn't have fit one more stone."

"I suspect that his role in this was passive, Mr. Lilly."

"What's that on his forehead? Just cuts? Or a word?"

"A word. Perhaps a name. It seems to start with an S. In any case, who is he? Did he work for Winfield?"

"Not for Winfield, but he's done a few things for you. This one's that Ukrainian. He runs guns all over Africa. His name is Savran Bobik. Looks like he died hard."

"One does get that impression, Mr. Lilly."

"I mean harder than the others. Let me show you."

Chester seized the bearded one's head by the hair and lifted it out of the cooler. He then did the same with poor Winfield's matted locks. He held the two heads up to Bourne side by side, their noses almost touching each other.

He said, "Look at the necks. See the way the cuts go? Winfield's came from the back. Maybe two good chops. Winfield might have already been dead before they used the machete on him. But Bobik, in my opinion, was alive and awake. See his cuts? They're from the front. They wanted him to see it coming."

Bourne grunted. "That would seem to explain his expression."

"Him, they sawed before they chopped. See how the skin's torn? Him, they did an inch or two at a time. He was probably dead in a couple of minutes, but it must have seemed longer to him."

Bourne waved the dripping heads from his sight. He was glad that the floor wasn't carpeted. He peered into the container from which Bobik's head was taken, still hoping to find those reports. He saw what seemed to be a thick wad of papers, but these were not bound; they did not look like documents. It looked like some sort of a foldout.

He said to Chester, "Would you put those things down? They seem to have come with instructions."

Chester stacked the two heads on top of the third and reached in to withdraw the sodden mass. He shook it out and he opened it gingerly. Bourne saw that it was a single large sheet that had been folded several times upon itself. It opened up to about poster-size. In fact, it was an actual poster.

Though smeared, it showed a man in full length. The man was dressed in a uniform. The uniform was gaudy to the point of absurdity. It seemed more suitable for a Gilbert & Sullivan production than for use in the African bush. It was blue with red trim and dripping with braid, a gold star on each of the epaulets. It had a Sam Browne belt with two shoulder straps that crossed. They supported both a pistol and the sheath of a machete. The machete itself was in his hand. The hat was a kepi, flat on top with a visor, of the type that was worn by the French Foreign Legion. Fabric hung down from the sides and the back as protection against sun and insects.

The face beneath the visor was grim. The idea, Bourne assumed, was that he should look fearsome. But he didn't, especially. He looked almost embarrassed. It was as if he realized that the outfit was ludicrous, but had gamely agreed to pose in it. Whatever, thought Bourne. There he is and here we are. This delivery had come with a gift card after all.

Bourne said, "Well, this seems to remove any doubt. But the thought behind the gesture still escapes me."

"You know this guy?" asked Chester.

"That's our friend, Alameo."

"That's him? Oh, yeah. You said you met him once, right?"

Bourne nodded. "He showed up at a cocktail reception in Luanda, hosted by the Portuguese embassy. I assumed that he was in their employ. We chatted at some length about politics. He had crashed that reception. He was there to take my measure. Mine and several others who were in attendance. It was a brazen performance."

"That's why the bad blood?"

"For that ruse? Not at all. One had to admire it. Strolling into that assemblage of the venal and corrupt. He even offered a toast to their ultimate victory and to his own capture and death. If they'd only known. How they wish they had known. He's been quite inconvenient ever since."

Chester studied the face underneath the cap's visor. He said, "I thought he'd look tougher. This guy looks ridiculous. Do you think he's gone nuts? That wouldn't surprise me. They all seem to go nuts. Must be something in the air over there."

Bourne took this to be a sly comment from Chester. Bourne knew that Chester knew perfectly well what might be "in the air" over there.

Above the photo, there were lines of bold type. But their ink had run more so than the photo. Much of it was illegible. None of it was in English. Bourne asked, "What does that say? Can you read it?"

Chester pointed to an emblem, a stylized lion, that appeared at the bottom of the poster. "That's the symbol for Dumas Duganga. He took over as head of the rebels after Jonas Savimbi got killed."

"I know who Duganga is, Chester."

"Duganga and Savimbi go back a long way, but Duganga was more an administrator type. That's why they recruited Alameo."

"There's a good deal more to it than that," muttered Bourne, but he chose not to say anymore.

Chester studied the type. "Oh, wait. Now I get it. This poster's got to be at least a year old. It looks like these guys were using the poster as a way to introduce Alameo." Chester raised his finger to the top of the sheet and traced the first line of text. "See this? This part's Portuguese. This word *chefe* means chief. This word, *obedece,* I think, means obey. And here's the guy's name. You can see the last three letters. They're telling everyone to obey him."

"Who is 'everyone'?"

"All his troops, for openers. And I guess all the civilians. To make sure, this is written in three different languages. See the second line? That's Bantu. I only know a few words in Bantu, but I'd bet you that it says the same thing. The third line probably repeats it in Kikongo. Kikongo is like

Bantu, but it's pigeon Bantu. They speak it up in northern Angola."

"He'd have plastered this poster all over the country?"

"All over the rebel part, yeah."

"Telling everyone who sees it to obey this man. But why not just his face? Why that costume?"

"Because without it, this guy wouldn't last long," said Chester. "Some zoned out kid with an AK-47 might kill him on sight for his shoes. This way they'd know he's not someone to fuck with. That was then, though. I doubt he still needs it."

"Whatever," said Bourne. "He will have to be dealt with. But why has he sent me these heads?"

Chester had moved to the stainless steel sink. He was washing his hands with soap and water. Bourne said to him, "Chester, when you're quite finished, I have just asked you a question."

Chester searched for a towel. He seemed to be stalling. He wet his lips and said, "It could be revenge. I'm not sure, but I've heard certain things."

"And now I'm about to hear them. Will I hate this?"

"Not revenge against you. This would be mostly against Bobik. From what I hear, Bobik has done this himself."

"Done what, exactly? You mean cutting off heads?"

"And sending them, yeah. At least once. From what I hear."

"Now, Chester . . . I'm going to ask you straight out. Did you happen to hear whose head Bobik sent?"

Lilly squirmed. He gestured toward the figure on the poster. "It was Alameo's woman. This was three or four weeks ago. She came into Luanda; she got introduced to Bobik. This was at some night club. She came on to him, went home with him. A day or two later he found out who she was. Someone spotted her and tipped him, I don't know who. I guess Alameo sent her, maybe to pop him, maybe just to see what Bobik was up to. Bobik killed her and sent him her head."

Bourne gritted his teeth. "Her name? Do you know it?"

"Sara . . . Sara something. I think that was it."

"Then if I had to guess, that's what's carved in his forehead." Bourne closed his eyes briefly. He took a slow breath. "That would certainly account for Mr. Bobik's condition."

"You mean why he died slow? Yeah, but there might be more. Bobik sold a load of weapons to this other group of rebels. Not in Angola. In Sierra Leone. It's that bunch led by Colonel Mobote."

"The butcher of Kampala? The one who cooks people?"

"Yeah, that's the guy. And he doesn't just cook them. The guy collects recipes. He says the heart and the liver are the best for building strength, but a young female ass tastes the best; it's like veal."

Bourne stared for a moment. "Is this legend or fact?"

"Oh, it's true," said Chester. "Mobote made this videotape. Bobik had a copy. He showed me and Kruger. It's Mobote using ass to make veal piccata. This guy is a real Martha Stewart."

"You're saying, I take it, that he's totally insane."

Chester shrugged. "Yeah, he's nuts. I don't know about totally. Some of it's for juju. Juju's sort of like magic. Whatever part of a body you eat, a bullet can't hit you in your own body part. But it's also to scare the piss out of people. All this guy has to do is look at your ass and . . ."

Bourne rolled his eyes. "Let's move on."

"Okay, the weapons. Mobote was supposed to pay Bobik up-front with about two million in diamonds. Mobote sent his bagmen down to Angola, but the diamonds they brought were low-quality crap with even some industrials mixed in. Bobik told the bagmen to take a walk; don't come back unless the rocks were gem quality."

Bourne asked him, "How is this relevant?"

"It's background," said Chester. "It's . . . what's the word . . . context. A few days go by, Mobote's bagmen come back, and now they've got some very good diamonds. They'd ambushed one of Savimbi's mules who was smuggling them out of the country."

"Savimbi's?"

"Well . . . Duganga's. I still get them confused. Those two guys were joined at the hip. Anyway, knowing Bobik, I bet he tipped them on the mule and also got a cut on what they took. Then Duganga, I bet you, got word of the deal and . . ."

"Duganga? Or our friend Alameo?"

"I don't know. Either one. They both would have known that Bobik's on your payroll. Alameo could have figured that you owe him for his woman. Duganga would have figured that you owe him some diamonds."

"*I* owe them? Why? I had no role in either."

"But you do move weapons. It's a logical connection."

"No, Chester, it isn't. It's a leap to a conclusion. We may have used Bobik. Or rather *you* may have used him. But I never knew of this man's existence before he showed up here this morning."

Chester shrugged. "You can't know everyone. Some, it's better you don't. But they know who you are and they use your name sometimes. Your name opens doors. You'd be surprised."

"I've been surprised enough for one day," Bourne told him. "But I've a feeling that there's much more to come."

Chester gestured toward the pantry. "You got any instant coffee? I rushed over here; I didn't stop for coffee."

"You can wait."

Chester opened the fridge. "All the food for your brunch, is all that upstairs? I never had any breakfast either."

"You will not derail me, Chester. Have some orange juice and speak."

"I'm not ducking you. I'm trying to gather my thoughts. On an empty stomach, it's distracting."

"When we've finished," said Bourne, "you may wallow in Eggs Florentine. Please return to the subject at hand."

Chester said, "Look, if you're bothered by that arms deal . . ."

"I am not. It doesn't concern me."

"I'm just saying if you were, it's not too late to stop it. That shipment left Luanda, I think yesterday, maybe Friday, but Sierra Leone's way the hell up the coast. It could take, I don't know, up to a week."

"How is it that you know these particulars?" asked Bourne.

"I don't. Not exactly. But I can find out."

Bourne squeezed his eyes shut in an attempt to hold his temper. He said, "You are not to decide what I'm better off not knowing. Now I want you to tell me, no more bobbing and weaving, why we're looking at three heads, not one. The woman's head and stolen diamonds would account for Mr. Bobik. What part did Cecil Winfield play in this?"

"In those things? None. I don't think he knew."

"And yet, here he is. Why was this done to Winfield?"

"It . . . could be that some of the stuff Winfield makes has been tried out against Duganga's troops."

Bourne took another breath. "Could be? Or it was?"

"Could be because I'm not sure, but maybe so. Could be that Alameo doped out where it came from. Like you said, he met you. He knows you."

Bourne looked into his eyes. "I think you know more than you're telling me, Chester. Don't make me ask you again."

"Bobik and Kruger . . . they talked about it once. Trying some of these bugs on the rebels in Angola. That's what Kruger used to do in South Africa. They said all these diseases come from Africa anyway, so Duganga would think it was more of the same. I mean, they eat monkeys. They eat monkey brains. That's how AIDS and Ebola and all that shit started. Bobik says, 'Let's let them try something new.'"

Bourne's expression darkened further. He asked, "And you said . . . ?"

"I told them, plain English, I said, 'Don't even think it.' I said, 'Mr. Bourne has his own plans for testing those bugs and if you screw them up, you're dead meat.' But they might have done it anyway. I'm just guessing."

"Bobik and Kruger, you say."

"And maybe Winfield. Winfield might have gone along. He might have figured, 'What the hell . . . let's do a bigger field test.' Bigger than what he was doing for you."

"You say they did this on their own? You were in no way involved?"

"I thought it was just talk. You know how guys talk when they're having a few beers. Most times, that's as far as it goes."

"Most times, you say."

"This could be the exception." Chester sipped his orange juice from the bottle.

"And they thought that Duganga would never catch on. These three heads would suggest that he did."

Chester paused to think. He said, "More likely, Alameo. He found out when he got his hands on Bobik."

"And?" asked Bourne.

"And what?" Chester shrugged. "Here he is."

"Alameo finds Bobik. He takes his revenge. But all three heads have been sent here to me. There's a gap in my grasp of the sequence of events."

"You're asking why you? It's your company."

Bourne struggled to control his rising frustration. "I'll say it again. I'd never heard of Savran Bobik. I am innocent of the murder of Alameo's woman. Why did all this not end with Bobik's death?"

"I can make a good guess, but you get mad when I guess."

"Let's hear it. I will be the soul of patience."

"Like I already said, I bet they got Bobik first. I mean, smell him; he's the ripest of the three. Let's say that at first they didn't tie this to VaalChem. The woman he killed and the diamonds he stole were all the reason they needed. They probably would have started to peel off his face just to give him a taste of what was coming. In his place, what would you do? You'd try to deal, right?"

"Go on."

"He would have fingered Kruger and Winfield. He would have told them that VaalChem's the reason why so many of their troops were getting sick. So they pull a raid on VaalChem; they bring Bobik with them, or maybe they only bring his head."

"Um . . . VaalChem is a sizable facility, Chester. It must have a hundred security guards, to say nothing of a razor-wire fence."

"That's the plant. Winfield's office is outside the wire."

"And even closer to downtown Luanda, a capital crawling with soldiers," said Bourne.

Chester spread his hands. "So this couldn't have happened?"

A sigh. "It clearly did. Please continue."

"They hit the office, they get Kruger and Winfield. Say they hit just when Winfield is packing these coolers. They also see that he's packing those diamonds you're missing. They're a bonus. They think they're entitled. Winfield would have wet his pants in a second. He'd have told them anything they wanted to know including your address here at Briarwood."

"So this is what happened?"

"This is just my scenario."

"Before taking their leave, they would have rummaged, would they not? Winfield's clinicals should have been part of this shipment. They're missing. They've been taken. We must assume that a great deal more has been taken. This could be a catastrophe, Chester."

"Winfield didn't keep that much in his office. What was there, he kept in a safe."

"I'll point out that a little goes a very long way. And Cecil, no doubt, would have opened the safe in the hope of not emulating Bobik."

"Yeah, I guess," opined Chester. "Except they still wouldn't know what all that stuff was. Yeah, Winfield could have told them, but then they'd be scared to touch it. Winfield would have warned, one whiff, they all die. And they wouldn't have hung around very long anyway. Not after hacking off two more heads."

"They'd have dashed away, you think."

"I would. Wouldn't you?"

"Chester . . . they lingered. You are looking at the evidence. They took the time to pack them and ship them."

Chester stared at the containers. He said, "Yeah, they did. But you're looking for the worst case of what could have happened. I still think revenge was all they were after. I still think they wouldn't have taken the bugs. They'd need biohazard space suits to open that stuff. Winfield didn't keep any space suits in his office and I doubt that Alameo showed up equipped."

"That's your ray of hope?"

"Seems likely to me."

"Seems likely. My scenario," Bourne said to him icily. "You guess, you hear, but you never seem to know. My own guess is that you could have kept this from happening. How am I to have confidence in your judgment?"

Chester didn't answer. He looked at the stacked heads. He reached for the two that he'd piled on the third and put them back in their respective containers.

At last, he said quietly, "I'll fix it."

"You will? By what means?"

"I'll come up with something."

"You are to do nothing."

"We just let this pass?" Chester glanced toward the containers. "They hack off three heads and send them here to your house. Don't you think some kind of payback is called for?"

Bourne pointed to the heads. He said, "Chester . . . *this* is payback. You are talking escalation. I intend to respond, but in my way, not yours. I would prefer to defuse our situation over there before it gets any further out of hand."

"Like how?"

"By neutralizing our uniformed friend. I have asked you to locate Elizabeth Stride. I want and need her now more than ever."

"I keep trying to tell you," said Lilly, "Stride's dead."

"So you have," Bourne answered, "and I don't believe it. She'd be how old now?"

"Thirty-five . . . thirty-six. That's if she's still alive, and she isn't."

"Well, I think she is. And that she's somewhere in this country. I want you to find her, and quickly."

Chester Lilly sighed. He threw up his hands. "You've got the FBI . . . who owes you. You've got the CIA . . . who needs you. If both of them say that this woman is dead, the way to bet is that she's dead."

"You say you've personally seen their files?"

"At the CIA, I did. They let me sit at their computer. All the FBI had were some references to her that were three or four years out of date."

Bourne asked, "Did those files contain photographs?"

"The CIA's did. Except none were her. They were pictures of other Elizabeth Strides. All too young, too old, too ugly, wrong race. I looked at every one. Maybe twenty."

"And so no photos of her corpse, no dental records or the like. No DNA matches from a set of remains that would prove that she's no longer with us."

"They have other sources. All those sources say she's dead."

"Chester, she's been killed at least six times that I know of by people hoping to claim the reward. Now we're told that she died on an exercise bike the same year she came back to the States. An old bullet fragment worked loose. Is that the story?"

Chester nodded. "From a time when she got shot years before. It moved, cut into an artery, and killed her. Everybody I've asked says it happened that way. You're the only one who doesn't believe it."

"Too convenient."

"No one's seen her or heard from her since, Mr. Bourne."

"She came back to this country to get lost, to disappear. She must have had a plan and a place to go. That's why I think she's here somewhere."

Lilly answered with a shrug. "If you say so."

"Stride had a million-dollar price on her head. Try putting yourself in her place. Would you revel in the honor of being so valued or might you consider faking your death if being hunted grew to be tiresome?"

"I might," Lilly answered. "But I would have been smarter about it."

"Meaning?"

"Do you think she called some friends and said, 'Tell everyone I'm dead'? Do you think she's so dumb that she thought that's all it takes? Myself, I'd have done it so nobody would wonder."

"For example?"

"There are ways. I'd have planted a body."

"You have found one that's a perfect DNA match and with teeth that are identical to your own?"

Once more, Chester Lilly threw up his hands. "The whole

world says she's dead. You say she's alive. Say she is. What good is she to you?"

"Find her for me and I'll show you. Nothing from State Department Intelligence?"

"Same thing. Drew a blank. Our people there don't have a thing."

"Did you speak to Roger Clew?"

"I spoke to someone else pretty high up in Intelligence. I couldn't get as high up as Clew."

"You tried?"

"He wouldn't see me."

"He wouldn't? Even knowing that you work for me?"

"That cut no ice. He doesn't like you very much. That's why he won't come here for your brunches."

Bourne scowled. He'd forgotten. Twice now, he'd sent an invitation to Clew. In fact, he'd tried to get Clew there today, even offering an added incentive. Clew had not had the grace to respond. "Mr. Clew is in need of a lesson in manners. And a lesson on where his bread is buttered."

"You got something on him?"

"Not at the moment. But I shouldn't need to. His boss, for god's sake, the Secretary of State, is a regular attendee at my brunches. He was to have been here this morning."

"I know," said Lilly. "I saw his chopper turning back."

"And Roger Clew is one of hundreds of public officials who serve at the pleasure of the president. Does he realize that I could pick up the phone and . . ."

Chester shook his head wearily. "Mr. Bourne . . . don't even start. You can't touch Clew and the president won't either. The word is that Clew could make calls of his own. He's been at this too long; he knows too much shit. No one can even get into his files and those files are what everyone's afraid of."

Bourne suddenly turned thoughtful. "His files, you say."

"He has something on everyone. You included, I bet. Maybe nothing he could do much about, but enough that he's not about to party with you."

"Collected through his network of informants and such?"

"Other governments, too. He knows everyone."

"So if anyone could tell me where to find Stride . . ."

"Mr. Bourne . . . he wouldn't even tell me she's dead. Will you tell me what makes her so important?"

"That can wait. You can wait. I'm disappointed in you, Chester."

"Okay," he said, "I'm sorry. And okay, say she's alive. I still don't see what good she is to you. I know you don't care about the million-dollar bounty. It's not as if you're hurting for cash."

"She'd be worth more than that just in terms of good will. If I handed her over to the people who want her, no favor that I'd ask would be too great."

"So that's it? That's why?"

"I might do that down the road."

"But in the meantime, you want her to come work for you. Aside from why should she, why would you want her? Is it just because she's cut a few throats? There's no short-age of people who can do that, Mr. Bourne."

"Stride is special. Believe me. And it's more than a few."

"What's special is that Stride was a psycho, Mr. Bourne. She didn't work for hire. She hated those people. You heard what they did to her? You heard how she got started?"

"I'm fully aware of her history, Chester."

Again, Chester gestured toward the figure in the poster. "You think she'll take out this guy, Alameo? She'd do it for you? Is that what you think?"

You're getting warm, thought Bourne. But he said nothing.

"Say you found her," said Chester. "Why would you think she'd do it?"

"Trust me. She'd be put to good use."

"You'd send her over to Angola? Into the bush? Don't you think she'd stand out just a bit over there?"

"Stride would stand out just about anywhere, Chester. Which is why I can't believe that she's so hard to find."

"Same reason your wife hasn't been spotted lately. Same reason she's not doing much talking."

The remark angered Bourne. It wasn't the same. And he knew that he was being near-obsessive on the subject. It was possible, even probable, that Chester was right. But if Stride were alive, and if he could find her, oh, what an advantage he might have.

"It seems," he said, "that I must speak to Clew directly."

"You can try. But I don't think he'll see you."

Bourne stepped to the cooler that contained Bobik's head. "Oh, he'll see me," he told Chester. "I'll have something to trade. That's the business he's in, is it not?"

"Trade what?"

"The late Mr. Bobik has given me a thought. He's a major arms dealer, you say?"

"And drugs. Not your kind. The feeling-good kind. Chances are, that shipment includes a few kilos. Mobote likes to keep his top people addicted. It keeps them from getting ambitious."

Bourne sniffed. "Arms and drugs. Why not women while he's at it?"

"He does. But not this time. At least not for Mobote. Bobik also deals in slaves, but they're going somewhere else. A bunch of young girls from . . ."

"Chester . . . don't say it."

"Don't say what? From what I hear? I was not going to say that."

"Forgive me. From what, then?" asked Bourne.

"Not from what. It's from where. These young girls were supposed to be picked up in Cabinda, which is his last stop in Angola. Bobik has a dealer there who snatches them for him. They're all street kids and orphans, kids no one would miss and Cabinda's glad to get rid of them. Bobik sells them to plantations up the coast."

Bourne closed one eye, not sure that he grasped this. "You're . . . telling me that the arms ship is also a slave ship, not to mention a drug ship. What else might it be carrying?"

"Guys like Bobik will deal anything you want."

Bourne stared at Bobik's head. "What a loss to the world. A pig, but an undoubted entrepreneur. The slaves," he said, "might be just the right touch. They'll appeal to Mr. Clew's sense of outrage."

"You going to call him direct?"

"The sooner the better. In the meantime, there's the matter of these heads."

"I'll take them. I'll dump them where they won't be found."

Bourne nodded his assent. But then he seemed to change his mind. He said, "You know . . . this sending of heads . . . it's really quite an effective device."

Chester shrugged.

"These might come in handy. We'll freeze them."

4

Three days had passed since Bourne's aborted Sunday brunch. Roger Clew had begun his customary morning jog.

Dressed in a Notre Dame sweatshirt and shorts, he'd left his Georgetown apartment house a few minutes past sunrise. In past weeks, he'd been leaving through the basement garage in order to avoid being logged by the doorman. The building had several high officials in residence. The doorman was suspected of tipping reporters as to certain of their personal activities.

He'd had jogging partners, but not anymore. Too many saw it as a chance to have private time with him in which to advance some agenda of theirs. Clew saw running as his own private time. Fitness was part of it. He was forty-five years old. He'd reached the age at which most men become invisible to women who are twenty years younger. Until, that is, they'd find out who he was. Whoever said that power was an aphrodisiac knew what he was talking about. It certainly made for an active enough sex life, but not one that was long on romance. Lately, he preferred to be invisible.

Strapped to his waist was a fanny pack that contained his wallet, a few dollars in cash, his PDA, and his Beretta. The PDA was a new one, a prototype really. He had it on loan from its maker. It had a mini-computer that could download large files and among its features were a built-in cell phone and a recording device. He was able to speak into it and record any thoughts that occurred to him while he was jogging. Certain files and certain thoughts were of a sensitive nature. He never let it out of his sight.

He had reached the edge of the Tidal Basin and would make one circuit of its two-mile length. After that, he would stop for some bagels and coffee before returning to shower and dress. His driver-cum-bodyguard would be waiting.

Clew was approaching the FDR Memorial when he spotted the stretch limousine. It was illegally parked on the Tidal Basin path. It had left tire tracks across the lawn. The rear door opened and a man stepped out. Clew recognized him instantly. It was Bourne's man, Chester Lilly. He'd have known that head of hair a block away. And the figure still seated must be Bourne himself.

Clew turned, intending to reverse his direction when he saw that a second car had pulled in behind him. It had kept its distance, but it, too, blocked the path. Clew emitted a grunt of disgust.

He could scarcely believe that Artemus Bourne would have the gall to force a meeting in this manner. Or that Bourne, for that matter, would come all this way. The man almost never left Briarwood. Clew had thought that he'd made it abundantly clear that he had no interest in seeing him.

Lilly stepped toward him, raising his hands. He said, "There's no problem. Don't get bent out of shape." He then cocked his head toward the limousine door. "Mr. Bourne would like you to get in."

"Mr. Bourne can kiss my ass and so can you," Clew replied. "Now get the hell out of my way."

"See that?" said Chester. "And I'm trying to be nice. Bottom line is you're not getting past him."

*   *   *

Here's a man, thought Clew, who can't take no for an answer. First came those invitations to Bourne's Sunday brunches that some columnists called the hottest ticket in town. There were always one or two cabinet members and various congressmen and senators. The Secretary of State was a frequent guest. The secretary usually dropped in by chopper, joined once or twice by the president himself. The place was nearly as secure as Camp David.

Clew's most recent invitation was for last Sunday's brunch. The messenger who brought it was a striking young woman. She said her name was Claire, British accent; she was gorgeous. She had porcelain skin and lustrous red hair and a body to make a man weak in the knees. And she knew that damned well. And she used it. She said that Mr. Bourne was especially hopeful that he would be good enough to attend. She said that Mr. Bourne had been made aware that a certain animosity had risen between them. She said that he was hoping that a nice private chat would not only allay any misunderstandings, but perhaps even benefit them both. She offered to drive him down to Briarwood herself. She made it clear, not in words, but with her eyes, her inflections, that if he saw fit to accept Bourne's invitation, she in turn might see fit to fuck his brains out.

She left after handing him the formal invitation along with a card that bore her telephone number. But not before a final lingering handshake and a throaty, "If you don't, I'll be so disappointed. I would really like to know you better, Roger."

In the past, he'd returned Bourne's invitations unopened. This time he would not even bother to do that. He did, however, open the envelope. It contained not only the embossed invitation and directions to Briarwood by road and by air, but also a list of those who'd be in attendance. A few legislators, one appellate court justice, several business executives, all from energy firms. The president's Secretary of Commerce was listed, as were a couple of people from State. He noted with annoyance, but not with surprise, that one of the people attending from State was the man who headed the African desk. The henhouse was coming to the fox.

He'd been about to drop it into his shredder, but decided to keep it for a while instead. He wanted to remember those names. He did shred the card that held that young woman's number lest he ever be tempted to call her.

For a day or so he wondered whether he'd behaved rashly. Not so much about Bourne; it was more about Claire. If she was a gift, an incentive, whatever, she might well have been worth the trip. But on the Monday following last Sunday's brunch, he learned that it had been abruptly canceled. Bourne's guests had been turned away at the gate after driving two hours to get there. They probably had to settle for an Egg McMuffin somewhere. The world was a better place for it.

Whatever the reason for the cancellation, Clew assumed that Bourne had gotten the message that he, Roger Clew, would not have come. But Bourne himself called him at his office a day later. He asked for a face-to-face meeting, just the two of them, perhaps at some location midway. Bourne assured him that he would not come empty-handed. He had something of value to offer. Clew had told him, "Mr. Bourne, you have nothing that I want. I neither like you nor trust you; let's not waste each other's time. I have no wish to see you. Good-bye."

He'd regretted that somewhat. There was no need to be insulting. He also found himself thinking about Claire and wondering what the sweetener might have been this time around. And he had to admit that this sudden attention made him curious as to Bourne's motive.

On the Friday preceding the ill-fated brunch, he'd had a conversation with the Secretary of State in which the latter, Howard Leland, had urged him to attend.

"If you're uncomfortable, Roger, fly down with me. The moment you feel that your virtue is imperiled, I will whisk you to safety, I promise."

Clew declined and added, "You shouldn't go either. The man is a criminal, sir."

The secretary answered, "He's *our* criminal, Roger. As you know, using criminals is in fashion again. The playing field has been leveled considerably."

"All to Bourne's advantage. He's unindictable, right?"

"I consider that a small price to pay."

Clew didn't respond. He did not want this conversation. It wasn't about to change either of their minds. But the secretary pressed. He said, "Explain it to me, Roger. What distinction do you see between using Bourne and using such renegades as you have employed throughout your career in intelligence."

"You're referring to Paul Bannerman?"

"Bannerman, Harry Whistler, to cite two of the worst."

"You've just cited the two very best, sir."

"And you've used them even when it was illegal to do so. But of course I don't expect you to admit it."

Clew shrugged. "As you've said, they're in fashion again."

"And we've broken no laws in accepting Bourne's assistance. I'll ask again; what difference do you see?"

Clew answered, "Well, for openers, I trust them."

"You do? Where's their loyalty? Where's their patriotism? We need people who'll work to further strengthen this country. Not people who recognize no government but their own. They are outlaws, mercenaries, judge and jury."

"Um . . . what's Bourne?"

"An American," said Howard Leland. "First and foremost."

Clew blinked. "Just so I'm clear. You see Bourne as a patriot?"

"In his way. Yes, he is. His strength is our strength, and it's not just the oil. He's doing work that is vital to our national interest and could end up saving millions of lives. I'd convince you of that if I were free to discuss it. I'll remind you, however, that his help was invaluable after the September eleventh attack. It put some very evil people out of business."

"Yes, but who? Their financiers? An arms dealer here and there? He was thinning out his own competition."

The secretary sighed. "A most biased view, Roger."

"Sir, I think you know that I'm right."

The secretary said, "The point is, he delivered them. Did Bannerman? Did Whistler? If they did, where's the evidence? Those whom you've claimed that Bannerman took out seemed to vanish from the face of the earth. How are we to know that he actually found them? How were we to verify that he had the right people if he didn't deliver them for questioning?"

"They were questioned, I assure you. They'd have held nothing back. You would not have learned a thing from what was left of them."

"He's a torturer? You admit that?" the secretary asked Clew.

"Ask our widows and orphans how upset they would be upon learning that these people were not dealt with gently. I don't think you'd hear much of an outcry."

"The point is . . ."

"The point is," Clew told him, "that I'd trust him with my life. Would you say the same thing about Bourne?"

"I trust him to do what we need to have done. If his interests and those of our country coincide, that simply accelerates the process. Granted, we've had to turn a blind eye now and then. As you have. As you've just acknowledged."

"Let's . . . agree to disagree on this subject," Clew answered. "I'm not going near his damned brunch."

Our criminal, thought Clew. Situational ethics. Even so, if pressed, Clew would have to admit that "our criminal" was better at it than theirs. Bourne was definitely world class. Top ten. Off the charts. Right up there with the old robber barons.

He was also, according to *Forbes* magazine, the thirty-fourth richest man in the world. But those rankings were estimates, based on traceable wealth. If the true extent of his holdings were known, he'd be pushing Bill Gates for first place. His "holdings" included many public officials in any number of governments. In this country, over the past several years, Bourne's money had helped to elect, or reelect, at least fifteen key senators and congressmen. He did more than simply contribute to their campaigns. He had them coached on how to run, what to say, what to promise. And he'd focused on those who had something to hide, some transgression that could ruin them if published. He'd told them very clearly what he wanted in return for both his support and his silence.

Clew knew all this. So did everyone in Washington. Last election, Bourne had helped to put a president in office who not only was deeply beholden to him but who now echoed many of his views. It's the rich who have the power. It's the rich who've built this country. The worker bees have never much mattered. They vote, but they vote for the candidates we choose. The poor scarcely matter at all.

Bourne had made his first millions in oil—Texas oil. He had since seen it grow by the hundreds of millions when the government, in return for his generous support, had arranged that he be licensed the sole drilling rights off the shores of several West African countries where enormous new deposits had been found.

Bourne's company did no actual drilling because his was an "oil services" company. What that meant was that he brokered the drilling rights to those who did the work and took the risks. In so doing, his company collected commissions from big oil, and also from the African governments in question. Among his "services" was to help keep those governments in power until they were no longer needed. In the meantime, he would suck their countries dry.

Especially Angola. An astonishing country. It should be one of the richest on earth. Instead, it's one of the poorest. Its eastern half is littered with alluvial diamonds of the highest quality yet found. And they're laying on the surface. They don't need to be mined. But they're still in a war zone; they're still called "conflict diamonds." That's a label that De Beers has been trying to slap on them to try to keep them off the world market. Good luck, thought Clew. Half the world's in there buying them. Bourne's been trying for years to control that trade himself.

And all those diamonds, thought Clew, the best in the world, are still just a drop in the bucket. Angola's western half, its Atlantic coast, has been blessed with proven offshore oil reserves that are at least equal to those of Kuwait. The oil itself is light sweet crude, the most desirable grade. Add to this the most abundant fishing grounds on the planet.

Angola's people get to keep almost none of it, but try to find anyone who cares about them. They're only Africans, right?

Bourne would answer, "They are what they are. Show me one thing they've built, one resource they've developed. What claim do they have to what lies underfoot? All they're good for is labor and breeding more laborers when they're not busy hacking away at each other. I see the world as it is. I didn't make it that way. And if they've never had it, they won't miss it."

Except many of them did. They did not share that view. Bourne saw their objections, not as an inconvenience, but rather as a business opportunity. He made still more millions through the sale of arms to those governments that have the oil. They needed the arms to fight off insurgents who wanted what they thought belonged to them. And of course he sells arms to those insurgent groups as well, being paid, for the most part, with those diamonds again. He does so indirectly, through companies he controls, in order to keep them busy killing each other while his companies reap profits—once again—from both sides.

He either owns or controls several biotech firms specializing in tropical virology. A reporter had stumbled on Bourne's name in that connection. When asked, Bourne claimed to have no direct involvement. He said such firms were run by a charitable foundation that he had set up to honor his wife, who had died in a tragic boating accident. But his motives, he admitted, were not entirely unselfish. The work these firms are doing can protect oil workers from the perils of sub-Saharan microbes and pests. Clew doubted it. Those workers were already shot full of vaccines. They are also too easily replaced if they fall ill. Clew wondered what his real purpose was.

No one looks at him too closely because he is "our criminal." Here's the secretary actually saying so. Not that Clew was naïve about the realities of trying to do business abroad. Since the passage of the Foreign Corrupt Practices Act, U.S. companies were forbidden to bribe foreign officials. Very upright, very moral, and a crushing disadvantage. The result was that all of these American firms scrambled to sign up

foreign "consultants." If they couldn't offer bribes, they'd
hire people who could. It was the only way they could com-
pete.

The moralists in Congress didn't stop there. They decided
that the U.S. Intelligence services shouldn't work with foreign
agents who were outside the law. No assassins, of course, but
that was the least of it. No spies, no paid informants, no illegal hackers unless they've been specifically approved in advance and a clear mission statement is written. In effect, no
covert operations. If you seek that approval, you're then held
to account. If such a project goes wrong, your career's in the
toilet, especially if word of it appears in the press. No Intelligence service can function in that way. No Intelligence officer
who is in his right mind is going to put his name to a proposal
that might end up costing him his pension.

Those in government who were realists learned early on
that the services had been rendered impotent. They turned to
the Artemus Bournes of the world who were under no such
constraints. They knew that Bourne was already far ahead of
that game. He had long since developed a network of "consultants." He was better, and quicker, at getting things done
than any Intelligence service. He could deal both with criminal organizations and out-and-out criminal governments.

Deal with them? thought Clew. In some cases, he owned
them. At the least, he had his own people in them.

None of this was a secret. Everyone knew it. They knew
it because Bourne made sure that they knew it. He was the
man. The go-to guy. He got results and especially the oil.
The United States wanted that oil.

But the question at hand was, what does Bourne want?
Here was Artemus Bourne, in person, in the open. As far as
Clew knew, Bourne rarely left his home. His conglomerate,
Bourne Industries, was based in Houston, Texas, but Bourne
seldom spent any time there himself. He preferred being
closer to Washington, D.C., and the Briarwood estate became his base. The man almost never appeared in public for
fear that he might be kidnapped or killed. This was not paranoia. Clew would call it sound judgment.

Bourne had to be high on any number of hit lists. Those

who'd kill him were not those whose futures he'd made hopeless and whose countries he'd turned into killing fields. They wouldn't even know that he existed. Those who'd kill him were the people who were standing in line to take over and do more of the same.

And yet, here he was in the full light of day with only Chester Lilly and that chase car to protect him. Therefore, thought Clew, whatever Bourne wants must be vitally important to him. Clew knew that he ought to swing wide and jog on, but now that he'd wondered, he was curious. Ignoring Chester Lilly, he approached Bourne's limousine. Its rear door stood open. Bourne leaned forward, showed himself. He said, "Thank you for coming, Mr. Clew."

Clew ignored the sarcasm. "You're illegally parked."

Bourne said, "Mr. Clew, I intend to be civil. All I ask is five minutes of your time."

Clew gestured toward the car that had pulled in behind him. "That's your idea of civil? Fuck you."

"Hey," snapped Lilly. "Watch your mouth with Mr. Bourne."

Bourne said, "Chester! Be silent. Mr. Clew is quite right." He said to Clew, "If you'd turned, those men wouldn't have stopped you. They stay near for my protection, nothing more."

Clew replied, "State your business. Make it short."

Lilly said, "Hey, that's twice you got smart-mouthed with him. Now get in the car. Be a gentleman." As Lilly said this, he reached to take Clew by the arm.

Roger Clew, ordinarily, would have simply stepped back and told Chester not to touch him again. He certainly would not have gotten physical with him. But one gets to the point where enough is too much. He took Lilly's reaching hand and twisted it sideways, pulling Chester Lilly off balance. He swung his right foot against the back of Lilly's knee and Lilly fell hard against the pathway.

He heard Bourne shout, "No," but Bourne was too late. Lilly scrambled to his feet and, still in a crouch, lunged forward to grapple with Clew. Clew stepped into Lilly, smothering his rush. As Lilly raised both his hands and searched for a grip, Clew reached his hand under Lilly's right arm and seized him by the hair from behind. He jerked the bigger man's head sharply backward and downward. Lilly's throat was exposed; he was helpless. Clew jammed his right thumb under Chester Lilly's jawbone, pressing hard against the tender cluster of nerves that he knew would cause paralyzing pain. Lilly gasped and tried to break Roger Clew's grip, but all Clew had to do was shake Lilly's head to keep him from regaining his balance.

"Stop it," Bourne shouted. "Stop it at once." He said to his chauffeur, "You stay where you are." He scrambled from the limo while waving both arms at the men now emerging from the chase car. Clew saw both men hesitate, then ease back into their seats.

Clew released Lilly. He shoved him away. Lilly went reeling, tripping over his feet, before falling heavily to the grass. His face had turned red, almost purple with rage. With one hand, he covered his now throbbing jaw. He raised the other to his burning scalp and seemed horrified by what he felt there. With a squeal, he slid that hand inside his jacket.

"Chester . . ." Bourne stepped toward him. He said, "Don't you move."

Lilly hissed, "I'll kill him for that."

Bourne reached him. He slapped him. "Damn you, you will not. What you'll do is apologize to him."

Lilly had his Glock halfway out of its holster. He'd ignored the slap to his face. He snarled, "I'll do what? After what he just did?"

"Take a moment to notice what's in his right hand. Look slowly and carefully, Chester."

Lilly saw what he meant. Clew's right hand held a pistol. Clew was holding it low, hard against his thigh, his thumb on the safety and his finger on the trigger.

Bourne said to Lilly, "Do you see how he's holding it? It's against his leg so that you wouldn't have seen it. He's waiting for you to finish drawing your weapon so that he can put a hole in your head. I have just saved your life, you damned fool."

Lilly froze.

"See how calmly he waits? He really does want to shoot you. You've offered him a golden opportunity, Chester, but he doesn't actually care about you. In his mind, at this moment, he sees newspaper headlines. He sees my face, not yours, on a thousand front pages. He sees me embarrassed and compromised, Chester. He sees my influence shattered, my support diminished. Do you begin to understand this man, Chester?"

None of that, actually, had entered Clew's mind. His first thought was not to get shot. The sort of calm deliberation that Bourne had described would be second nature to Paul Bannerman and his people. In fact, it was one of Bannerman's women who'd taught him the moves he'd used on Chester. It was little Carla Benedict who'd taught him. Bannerman himself hadn't liked the idea. He'd said, "You're no Carla. You're not equipped for this, Roger. You've never had a gun pointed at you in your life and you haven't made a fist since about the tenth grade. You're better off walking away if you can. Never start a fight you can't finish."

"You're no Carla," was right. She would have thumbed out both his eyes. Still, there seemed no harm in letting Bourne think that his mind did indeed work that quickly. Clew's heart was pounding. He hoped that Bourne couldn't see that.

Clew said to Bourne, "That was not being civil."

Bourne said to Chester, "Mr. Clew is quite right. Take your hand off that weapon and get on your feet. Use those feet to take a nice calming stroll."

Chester parted his lips. He sucked in a breath. The veins at his temples were still pulsing.

Bourne said, "Not a word. Leave immediately, Chester. Be thankful that you're able to do so."

Chester showed his teeth, but he remained silent. While straightening his disheveled hair with both hands, he let his eyes say to Clew what he intended to do if he ever caught him alone. He turned and walked down toward the basin.

Bourne waited until Chester was well out of earshot. He said to Clew, "I must say that I'm impressed. I know that you have people who do this sort of thing for you, but I see that you're quite capable of doing it yourself."

Clew said, "I will give you two minutes."

"I do wish you hadn't messed up his hair. I think he'd almost rather have been shot."

"I said two minutes. You're going to use them on his hair?"

Bourne gestured toward the pistol that Clew was still holding. "We'll start the clock when you've put that away. It inhibits a full and frank exchange."

Clew twisted his fanny pack around to his side. He placed the Beretta inside, safety off. With his thumb, he probed for his PDA's recorder, hoping that he'd found the right button. He said to Bourne, "So, let's hear it."

Artemus Bourne drew an envelope from his pocket. "I need to find someone. I think you can help me. You won't do so out of the goodness of your heart, so I'm offering an exchange of information."

"I'm listening."

"This envelope holds details of an illegal arms shipment that is now on its way to Sierra Leone in defiance of a UN embargo. The supplier of the arms is a man named Savran Bobik. I am told that he's something of a horror. Do you know him?"

"Works out of Luanda? I've heard of him," Clew answered.

"The intended recipient is a rebel commander, not to mention a cannibal, named Colonel Mobote. That name is also not unknown to you, I'm sure."

Clew nodded.

"The shipment contains hundreds of Claymore mines with which he intends to mount a terror offensive against any and all residents of Freetown. It also includes thirty shoulder-launched missiles with which he intends to destroy any aircraft that try to use Freetown's Lungi Airport. If you've seen that airport, you know how easily he can do it. The arms, as we speak, are aboard a small freighter that is making its way up the African coast. They will be off-loaded fifteen miles at sea and taken ashore under cover of night."

"Explain to me why you would care," said Clew.

"I don't. I'm simply offering a trade. That shipment, incidentally, includes other goodies. A few personal luxuries for the colonel's comfort and assorted herbs and sauces to improve his cuisine. One crate will contain a quantity of heroin. It's intended to ease any of his troops' inhibitions where slaughtering the innocent is concerned."

"And why the sudden interest in Sierra Leone? You haven't finished looting Angola."

"I have interests in a great many places, Mr. Clew. Might we stick to the subject at hand?"

"You have the name of the ship?"

"I have everything, Mr. Clew, including the coordinates of the rendezvous point. If you'd had the grace to meet with me on Monday, you'd have had more time to make your arrangements. As we speak, however, you have less than eighteen hours. I assume that you'll want this done off the books and will not be involving our armed forces."

He was right, but Clew said, "That's a lot to assume."

"If a thing be done, then 'twere well it be done quickly," said Bourne, who was more or less quoting Macbeth. "Whomever you use, they should hit fast and hard. The freighter's crew may not resist, but Mobote's men will because they know that Mobote will hack off their arms if they should come home empty-handed." Bourne paused. He cocked his head. "Did I just make a joke?"

"Hacked-off arms? Empty-handed? No, that didn't quite make it."

Another pause. Bourne muttered that phrase to himself. He said, "No, you're right. Something missing there, correct?"

"Something missing was better. Now, if you don't mind . . ."

"Ah, yes. Where was I? We were taking that shipment. You should instruct whomever you use to wait until these people have headed back ashore and then blow them out of the water. You should insist that the cargo be sent to the bottom because . . . need I say it? You don't want it changing hands. And you don't want those drugs in circulation."

Bourne raised a finger. He'd had another thought. "Oh, be sure to tell them not to shoot at the freighter. It will have some twenty children on board."

"What children?"

"Slaves. All young girls, none older than twelve, all Angolan and some are quite comely. They were picked up in Cabinda for sale in Gambia where they'll be forced to work on some peanut plantation. The slave trade is still in full vigor, I fear. You don't want their little bodies washing up on the beach. That would make for bad press, even there."

"So what happens to them?"

Bourne did not seem to have considered their fate. He said, "I suppose I'd let them proceed on to Gambia. Board the freighter when it docks. Time enough to search it then. Have the Red Cross on hand to send them home."

"That's if they're still on board," said Roger Clew. "Slavers have been known to dump their cargo."

An impatient sigh. "So have your 'whomever' radio the captain. Let him know that they know he has children on board and that he mustn't drown them if he wants to live. When they're saved you can give them all scholarships to Harvard. There you have it, Mr. Clew. There's your plan."

Bourne paused. He waved a hand as if erasing those remarks. He said quietly, "I do not deal in children."

Clew had made no move toward the envelope Bourne was holding. "What is it that you want in return?"

"Do you know, or know of, Elizabeth Stride?"

"The Black Angel? Sure. What about her?"

Bourne stared. "You know her? You've actually met her?"

"Let's get to why you're asking, Mr. Bourne."

"I want only the answer to two simple questions. First, is Elizabeth Stride still alive? If she is, where can she be found? And I hasten to assure you that I mean her no harm. All I want is a meeting, nothing more."

"Just a meeting?"

"Only that. I'll make it quite worth her while."

Clew curled his lip. "Stride is an assassin. No one has 'just a meeting' with assassins."

"Stride 'is'? Present tense? Shall I take that to mean . . . ?"

"Take it any way you like. What do you want with her?"

"Even assassins have personal lives and this is a personal matter. I have no wish to hire her, if that's what you're thinking."

"Then, why?"

"I'll say it again. It's a personal matter. It is none of your affair, but this envelope is. I won't offer it twice, Mr. Clew."

On the matter of hiring her, Clew tended to believe him, but only because Stride was never in it for the money. Her motive was strictly retribution at first, and later to discourage those who hunted her. Clew couldn't imagine her working for Bourne, but he surely hoped to use her in some way.

As for the envelope Bourne was offering in trade, embargoed arms were being shipped all the time and this would be a drop in the bucket. On the other hand, he didn't want to learn next week that a plane full of some relief agency's personnel had plunged into the ocean off Freetown. He didn't want to know that he could have prevented it. Those kidnapped children were a wild card, of course. It was probably true that Bourne wouldn't deal in children, but he wouldn't have cared about freeing them either. Bourne was hoping that he, Clew, would care. Either that, or Bourne had some other reason for not wanting that ship attacked and sunk. Men like Bourne always have other reasons.

But the main thing Bourne wanted was Elizabeth Stride and Clew neither knew her, nor could he produce her. She'd been dead for three or four years. Her death, as he recalled, was more or less natural. He knew *of* her, sure. Lots of people knew of her. He'd never laid eyes on the woman himself. He knew her by reputation only. He was never quite sure how much of it had been earned and how much of it had been folklore. Whatever the mix, she was certainly deadly. And as for Bourne's claim of no sinister intent . . .

"I'm not sure I can help you, Mr. Bourne."

"That . . . sounds as if you can, but you won't."

Okay, thought Clew. We'll play *Let's Pretend.* "I don't know where she is at this moment."

Bourne's eyebrow went up. "And once again, that sounds

as if you know she's alive. Is she? Do you know that for a fact?"

"It's been more than a year since I've heard anything about her." This was literally true, but still a lie.

"And she was . . . and is . . . in this country, correct?"

"I had no reason to ask. I don't know."

"When you say you heard, from whom did you hear it? Was it from a reliable source?"

"Oh, indeed."

"Would this source have been Paul Bannerman, by chance? You are still his control, are you not?"

"I may have worked with Paul Bannerman. No one's ever controlled him. Anyway, he's pretty much out of the game."

Bourne snorted. "If you say so, Mr. Clew."

"The man has a life. He's trying to live it. You shouldn't believe all you hear."

"From what I *hear*, he got back in the game with a vengeance after the events of September eleventh."

"So did everyone else, Mr. Bourne."

"Has a life, you say. Just trying to live it. And yet he seems to know every assassin on two continents and surrounds himself with the cream of the crop. Is that what one does when one is out of the game?"

"In the first place," said Clew, "they are not assassins. They are, or were, highly skilled contract agents."

"Forgive me. My mistake. Freelance contract agents. They only kill when inconvenienced; is that right?"

"In the second place," said Clew, "those people are his friends. They look out for each other. Friends do that."

"Within the happy confines of Westport, Connecticut. So he's just a simple suburbanite now, doing violence only to crabgrass?"

"And moles."

"And these *friends* of his have all bought charcoal grills and have taken up golf, I imagine."

"I imagine."

Bourne snorted. "I'm told by my own friend, the Secretary of State, that no one seems to know how many they are. But you must know. Do you?"

"I do not."

"I think that's a fib. I'd bet that you know exactly."

Clew didn't. Bannerman's core group was less than a dozen, but at any given time there might be twenty more in Westport. Some stay, some pass through. Only Bannerman knows. Clew saw no use in enlightening Bourne. He said, "Mr. Bourne, you've run out of time. Either give me that envelope or don't."

But Bourne persisted. He said, "I've heard them referred to as 'Bannerman's Ghosts.' Is that why? Is it because they're especially elusive or is it because no one knows?"

Both, thought Clew, but that still isn't why, and, believe me, you don't want to find out. He said, "Have a nice day, Mr. Bourne."

"Or are they called his 'ghosts' because some of them, at least, are people who are widely believed to be dead?"

Clew grunted. "Now I see where you're going with this."

"Then I'll ask it straight out. Might one of his ghosts . . ."

"Be Elizabeth Stride? I don't know, but I doubt it."

"Will you ask him?"

"Waste of time. He'd want to know why I'm asking. I'd say, 'Because Artemus Bourne wants to find her.' It would be a very short conversation."

Bourne started to reply. Instead, he held up the envelope. "You'd be asking because you want to save lives. These arms will maim and kill a great many people if they are allowed to go ashore. You can keep that from happening. All I want is an address."

"So that you can kill and maim them with your own mines and missiles? Savran Bobik must be one of your competitors, correct?"

"There are always mines and missiles. Their source is irrelevant. There are thousands of suppliers of illicit arms. Your own government, as you know, is the biggest by far. Please spare me the holier-than-thou."

Clew had no rebuttal. He said nothing.

"As for Stride, you have my word that I intend her no harm. She'll be perfectly safe and fifty thousand dollars richer. She'll be free to melt away again with it."

Clew gestured toward the envelope. "I might see what I can do. First, I'll see whether that shipment checks out. If it does, I'll go into our database at State. If it shows a current location for this woman, I will ask her if she's willing to see you."

Bourne exhaled slowly. "Please don't take me for a fool. I know that there's nothing of use in those files. But those files are less than complete, are they not? Your own are said to be so much better."

Clew, with effort, concealed his annoyance. Speaking of moles, he had just been informed that someone at State had been doing some digging. It was probably Bourne's friend on the African desk. He had also been informed that Bourne was aware that Clew kept a set of files of his own. No harm there, however. His private files were no secret.

Bourne said, "Oh, don't pout. Yes, I've tried by other means. You are hardly the first person I'd have asked, Mr. Clew. I am perfectly aware of your feelings toward me."

"Does the FBI like you any better?" he asked.

"They don't have a file either. One is moved to wonder why. Even dead, she should still have a file."

"CIA?"

"They have files on several Elizabeth Strides, all of whom have claimed to be the Black Angel and none are the genuine article. And those people need me. They wouldn't have lied. So I'm reduced to coming to you, not hat in hand, but offering a nice quid pro quo. Do you want this envelope or not?"

"And if she can't be found? If she really is dead?"

"You would have to convince me of that."

"If I find her," said Clew, "and that's still a big if, why would Stride agree to see you?"

"You can give her this message. 'He isn't dead either.' Say those words and she'll know what you mean."

"Who is 'he'?"

"It's a personal matter, Mr. Clew."

5

Clew took the envelope. He resumed his morning jog. He glanced back only once to see Chester Lilly walking slowly toward Bourne's limousine. A loose cannon, that one. Not long on self-control. He saw Bourne, hands on hips, his lips moving, waiting. Bourne was clearly angry with Lilly. It wasn't an act. Chester Lilly, he thought, was about to lose some skin. Clew was pleased with himself. He jogged on.

As for the shipment of embargoed arms, Clew felt sure that Bourne's information would be accurate, but only as far as it went. Bourne's concern that no attack be made on the freighter leads one to suspect that he owns it. Or that one of his dozens of companies does. Bourne suggested that the freighter be allowed to proceed after the arms had been off-loaded. Bourne had not, however, made that part of the deal. The ship was a smuggler. Worse than that, it was a slaver. It was going to be put out of business.

Clew would ask the Liberians to handle this for him. Liberia borders on Sierra Leone and they've had their own problems with Mobote. The ship will be in their neighbor's territorial waters, but they won't lose sleep over that. He would ask them to wait for the arms to be off-loaded on the chance that there really were children on board. He would ask them to leave nothing floating, no survivors, whether the rebels resisted or not. He would tell them that if they tried to salvage those arms, they would do so at the cost of his friendship. He wouldn't mention the drugs. Too much of a temptation. The Liberians could then feel free to board the freighter and escort it back to their waters. As Bourne had suggested, whether seriously or not, he would have the Red Cross meet the ship when it arrived. The Liberians could keep the ship for their trouble, plus any other cargo it carried. They would probably hang the captain from a cargo davit and leave him there to rot as an example.

Then Clew would keep his end of the bargain. He would try to find Elizabeth Stride. He did not, however, promise that he would deliver her. But he'd look for her because now he was curious. Is it possible, he wondered, that she's really still alive? And what could make her so important to Bourne?

He would run a scan of his private files, but he doubted that they'd yield much about her. As deadly as Elizabeth Stride might have been, he did not recall that any of her activities were of direct interest to his office. Stride had worked the Middle East at the time when he worked Europe. A different cast of characters, for the most part. But he had known the man who was her partner, and her lover, from the time when she did show up in Europe. Was she on the run then? He couldn't recall. By that time, she'd long since had a price on her head and it hadn't seemed to slow her down a bit.

And nothing, for that matter, ever slowed Martin Kessler, the man she took up with in Europe. Kessler had already achieved near-mythic status long before he ever met Stride.

Bourne said to tell Stride, "He isn't dead either." It occurred to Clew that Bourne was speaking of Kessler. If so, Bourne has either been misinformed or he's dangling a lure that can't possibly get nibbled because Kessler was definitely dead. There might be some hint of a question about

Stride, but there was none at all about Kessler. And too bad, because Kessler was one of a kind. Kessler was technically the enemy back then. Well, not technically. Actually. But at least he was fun. He was nothing like the rest of those plodding, gray goons that East German Intelligence seemed to clone.

Clew couldn't recall how he and Stride got together. But it would be hard to conceive of a more unlikely couple. Stride, though not Jewish, worked for the Mossad. Clew had heard her described as a beautiful woman. With unusual eyes. They were her most striking feature. He'd heard her described as driven, no-nonsense, very cold and aloof, no soft edges. And there were those who thought that she was a lesbian, but that part, thought Clew, was probably horse shit. All a woman has to do to be tagged with that label is to let a few men make fools of themselves, hitting on her and getting blown off. Anyway, thought Clew, if that had been true, what was she doing with Kessler? More to the point, if she was a lesbian, what was someone like Kessler doing with her?

Kessler was an East German, a top Stasi agent, until the collapse of the system. The East German people hated the Stasi, but only the Internal Security Branch. They admired the Foreign Intelligence Service. They saw them as heroes, outwitters of the West, and they especially admired Martin Kessler. Good-looking, dashing, an Olympic bronze medalist. He won it in the Biathlon, skiing and shooting, and had very nearly medaled in the downhill. Kessler treated the cold war as he treated all else, as a game, as a merry adventure. The East Germans published comic books, actual comic books, that related, in color, his outrageous heroics, some of which weren't far from the truth.

Paul Bannerman, come to think of it, had known Kessler very well. Kessler had been assigned to try to turn Bannerman. Get close to him, work on him, try to recruit him. Kessler knew that attempt would be a waste of effort. Bannerman would see through it in an instant. He knew that Bannerman wouldn't work for a Communist regime. Not its leadership, anyway. But below the leadership there were some good people whom Bannerman had worked with on occasion. An exchange of favors. That sort of thing. Kessler realized that such an exchange was the most he could possibly hope for.

On a personal level, they enjoyed each other. Bannerman was an excellent skier himself, though not in the same league as Kessler. Clew remembered those two going head to head at Harry Whistler's lodge in Chamonix. Bannerman had a chance if they stuck to groomed trails, but not off-piste because he wasn't suicidal. He'd watch Kessler whip through a thick stand of pines as if he expected them to part and make room. He'd watch Kessler ignore posted avalanche warnings. Kessler wasn't showing off. He simply knew what he could do. But he was tempting fate in more ways than one. By going off-piste he was skiing through areas that weren't patrolled by Harry Whistler's armed guards. Harry's place was always filled with tempting targets.

Harry's lodge was the size of a small hotel. A spectacular setting, classic Swiss chalet construction, but more like a bunker beneath all that woodwork and with sensors at every approach. Bannerman and his people had an open invitation to take R&R there whenever they wished, as did Harry Whistler's own operatives. It was a place to relax and swap stories and gossip about people they knew in their trade. And between them, of course, they knew everyone.

They'd feed Kessler enough stories to keep his superiors happy. His superiors were sure that he'd pulled off an infiltration that the Stasi had been attempting for years. Kessler, however, was no double agent. No guest of the lodge would ever be asked to pay for his keep with information. All they had to be was interesting company and Kessler never failed to be interesting. He paid for his keep by giving ski lessons and by playing the piano after dinner. He taught a number of the women to ski, including some singularly dangerous women, some of whom he charmed out of their ski pants, so to speak. But this was before he met Stride.

Did Kessler ever bring Stride to Chamonix? Clew couldn't recall hearing, but it seemed likely that he would

have. He would have decided that she'd need some new
friends after she and the Mossad had parted company.

But what now? thought Clew. What to do about her?

He'd told Bourne that he wouldn't ask Bannerman about
Stride. But he might if his own files showed nothing. Bourne
must have some reason for believing she's alive. He's not a
man prone to wishful thinking. So *if* she's alive and *if* Bannerman knows where, he'll ask Bannerman *if* he's willing to
pass on Bourne's message. Three big ifs, thought Clew, but
there's no harm in asking.

And *if,* though unlikely, this resulted in a meeting, he
would want to have some time of his own with Stride to find
out why she's worth all this trouble.

Bourne was greatly displeased by Chester Lilly's performance. As Clew jogged off, he had reprimanded Chester. It
was all he could do not to slap his face again. But if he'd
slapped him, he realized, he might do so at his peril. Best to
wait until Chester gained possession of himself.

He reflected instead on the verbal sparring that he had just
engaged in with Clew. There weren't many light moments,
Bourne's two jokes notwithstanding. *Empty-handed. Something missing.* Clew wasn't amused. The man needs to
loosen up. But detached body parts seemed to come up often
lately. And Clew, to be fair, was at some disadvantage, not
having had the pleasure of seeing those three heads. That denied him a full grasp of the context. The best Clew could
offer was unbridled sarcasm. But Bourne thought he gave as
well as he got. One learns to embrace small satisfactions.

There was one brief exchange that still nagged at him a
bit. It was when Bourne observed, with sarcasm of his own,
that "Bannerman was just a simple suburbanite now, doing
violence only to crabgrass." What was Clew's rejoinder? He
said, "And moles." Was that a reference to the burrowing
garden variety or might Clew have possibly meant it as a
threat should Bourne decide to send some people up there?

No, it wasn't a threat. Clew would have said that straight
out. One can delve too deeply into off-hand remarks. Even
so, thought Bourne, it's an interesting idea. Perhaps it's time

we put some people in Westport. Not to penetrate, of course. A closed society, that one. But one likes to know the lay of the land.

Bourne's limo had crossed the bridge into Virginia. He glanced over his shoulder. The chase car was following. He asked Chester, "Those two. What sort of backgrounds do they have?"

Chester answered with a distracted "Huh?" His mind was occupied, no doubt, with revenge fantasies and would be for some time to come.

"Your two men. Would they be competent to work under-cover?"

"Who? Toomey and Kuntz?"

Well, he didn't mean Abbot and Costello, thought Bourne. He asked, "How are they qualified? You've hand-picked them, have you not?"

"Yeah, but just for work like this. They're muscle, that's all. They qualify by pounding on people or running them down with their car."

"Not deep-thinkers, you're saying."

Chester shrugged. "Maybe Toomey. A little. He used to be a cop. As for Kuntz, all he knows is busting heads and wrecking knees. He was one of those guys who did that Ul-timate Fighting. You know. Bare knuckles? Two guys locked in a cage?"

No, Bourne did not know. "There really is such a thing?"

"Oh, yeah. That's where I found him. Undercover like where?"

Bourne waved him off. "Never mind. Just a thought." And a bad one at that. Those two would be entirely too thuggish for Westport. But Clew might have given him a better idea. A couple of joggers might be ideal. No one ever looks twice at a jogger.

Bourne did not speak again until they'd reached Falls Church. He pressed the button that raised the soundproof glass panel separating them from the chauffeur. He said to Chester, "We need to talk. Let me know when you've gath-ered yourself."

Chester wet his lips. "That sneaky prick."

Bourne watched as Chester gently fingered his scalp, moving errant strands of hair back into place. He said, "Chester, I worry that you're out of control. I find that I'm in need of reassurance."

Chester lowered his hands. "I'm okay."

Bourne said, "I'll need to hear a bit more than that. Your behavior could have cost me very dearly."

Chester said, "He was being disrespectful."

"Even so . . ."

"You said it yourself. He needs a lesson in manners. He's shit compared to you. You're a great man. A giant. That prick ducked you one time too many."

"Chester, we deal with 'shit' every day. When we've finished, it is easily scraped off our shoes. Until then, we try not to antagonize people, especially when we want something from them."

"Yeah, I know."

"In any case," said Bourne, "it isn't just your tiff with Clew. I meant this whole business in Angola."

"I told you. That was Bobik. I never thought he'd really do it. Was that Bobik's whole shipment that you just gave to Clew?"

"I've a feeling that he won't be complaining."

"And, hey, those girls Bobik has on that ship? I only heard about that maybe two weeks ago. Like you said, the guy's a pig. I didn't like that part myself."

"And you gave him a good talking to, I've no doubt."

"Well, no. I mean I might have." Chester tried to sound convincing. "The thing is, though, I didn't hear it from him. I heard it from this guy Bobik sends with his shipments. A Nigerian. Name's Moshood. He's this fat little fuck; his breath smells like a sewer. He was bragging that he might pork his way through all twenty during the trip up the coast."

Bourne grimaced in distaste. "Why are you telling me this?"

"So you know there are places where I draw the line. First of all, I made sure they weren't going to Mobote for him to try one of his recipes on. They're not; they're really going to pick peanuts. Second, I knocked the little prick on his ass when he made that crack about porking them."

"Are you saying you wish you'd prevented the shipment?"

"The slave part? Yeah, I wish. But I couldn't have stopped it. Mostly I'm saying that's the first I heard. I'm saying that a lot of things happen over there that I'm not necessarily in on."

"Then perhaps I need to find someone else who can keep a tighter rein on events."

Chester darkened. "Don't say that. You don't have to worry."

"We'll see."

"You shouldn't say that either. I've always delivered, except maybe for Stride. What makes you think Clew will do better?"

"He'll try," said Bourne. "He was not entirely forthright with me, but that was, of course, to be expected. He'll do his best because I've now aroused his interest. If he does locate Stride, he'll attach a few strings. I'll deal with that when it happens."

"If he doesn't, can I have him?"

"No, Chester, you cannot. What I want you to do is fly down to Houston and have Terrence work his magic on your hair."

It's like sending him to a therapist, thought Bourne. It also puts some distance between Chester and Clew until Terrence can make him feel whole.

Bourne asked, "Have you spoken to VaalChem again?"

Chester nodded. "A couple of times. They're still pretty strung out, but they're mostly back to work. They never even realized that Winfield was missing until I told them to break into his office. They got rid of the two bodies and cleaned the place up."

"Winfield's and Kruger's. Still no sign of Bobik's?"

Chester shook his head. "No one's going to find Bobik. He was already dead by a couple of days. The rest of him is probably rat turds by now. They just brought along his head to freak Winfield. I've got Winfield's staff taking inventory now to find out what else is missing. They said it might take a few days."

"That's too long. I need to know what our vengeful friend may have taken and also what Bobik may have taken before that. You said they ran some tests in the rebel-controlled area?"

"I only said there was talk. I never heard that they did."

"Oh, depend on it. They did. That's why we have all three heads. I'll need to know what they used and the effect that it had."

"Yeah, but how?" asked Chester. "This is Africa, remember. Like Bobik said, it's where most of these bugs come from. Say you hear that Duganga's troops are dropping like flies. How are you going to know that it isn't, like, normal? How are you going to know that it's yours?"

"We'll know which virus by its symptoms, of course. We'll know it's one of VaalChem's by its DNA signature. But to run that test, we'll need the blood of a victim."

"What, go in and get one? Who's going to do that?"

"Aid workers, Chester. Doctors Without Borders. They'll either go in or the victims will come out. We don't need a body; we only need the blood. VaalChem will offer to assist the Red Cross. That is how we'll get a sample of the blood."

Bourne said this, then paused as a troubling thought struck him. He'd been thinking strictly in terms of Angola. He asked, "Might Bobik have been selling these viruses elsewhere?"

"Who to?"

"To anyone. To Mobote. He'd sell anything, you said."

"I'll find out," Chester answered. "That's if anyone knows. Could be, the ones who'd know are in your freezer."

"What about this Nigerian?"

"Moshood? Hard to say. You think there could be some in that shipment?"

Bourne paused to consider that disturbing possibility. "Unlikely," he said, "but not out of the question. It won't matter, however, if Clew handles this properly. That shipment will never reach Mobote. All the same, have someone question Moshood the moment they can get their hands on him."

"Whatever he knows, we'll get it out of him," said

Chester. "I got people who can grab him when that ship docks in Gambia."

Bourne wrinkled his nose. "He rapes children, you said?"

"He won't anymore when we're done with him."

"Yes, see to that after Terrence has healed you. Go from his salon to our offices in Houston and meet with our personnel people. You will need to select a reliable successor to our unlucky friend, Sir Cecil Winfield. Who's that Russian biologist that Winfield brought in? Nikolai something. Very highly regarded."

"He brought in lots of Russians. Half of them are named Nikolai."

And he'd had to outbid several countries, thought Bourne. Syria, Iraq, and, of course, the Israelis. A dozen countries had been eager to recruit these researchers after Russia's bio-weaponry program went bust. And that's to say nothing of South Africa's program, the most gruesome, in its way, of them all.

"You'll know the one I mean. His face is all pockmarked. It seems he got too close to his work at one point."

Chester nodded. "That's Shamsky. Okay. Him I'll try first. But he might not be so hot for the job after what happened to Winfield."

"Greed overcomes fear. Pay whatever you must. That done, make arrangements for a new unsullied shipment. I want those vaccines and I need the reports that should have accompanied this batch. I've no doubt that Winfield's files were ransacked, but see what they can find all the same."

"Do all this by phone? I should fly to Luanda."

"Your last visit, Chester, was not without incident. I think I'd like you closer to home for a spell. Be back here by this time tomorrow."

"What are you going to do? Sit and wait for Clew to call you?"

"Clew or whomever. I have other sources. If Clew disappoints me, I may take more drastic action. But first I must have those vaccines."

Chester asked, "You still won't tell me why you want Stride?"

"One thing at a time. Get this done."

"How about what all these vaccines are for? Any reason why I can't know that?"

"To keep certain people healthy, should there be an epidemic."

Chester turned in his seat. "An epidemic of what?"

"I haven't decided as yet."

6

Clew had stopped a block away from his Georgetown apartment to pick up two coffees, one buttered bagel and another with cream cheese and chives.

The one with cream cheese was for Alex Rakowsky. Alex had been assigned as his driver and bodyguard and was also his personal assistant. Clew's past bodyguards had never liked the idea of allowing him to go jogging unescorted. They had usually run along with him. Alex, though qualified, was older, had a paunch, and was content to let Clew sweat for both of them. He was also nearing retirement. Clew decided not to mention his encounter with Chester. Alex might feel duty-bound to accompany him thereafter and Clew doubted that the man's heart could take it.

Alex was waiting outside the garage entrance. He seemed unusually anxious; he was pacing the sidewalk and he seemed greatly relieved when Clew came into view. Clew understood why. He was almost thirty minutes behind schedule.

Alex asked, "You okay, sir?"

"I'm fine. Here's your bagel. Come on up while I shower."

Alex stepped to the Lincoln that he'd parked at the curb. The engine was running. He reached in to shut it off. He said, "I was about to go looking for you."

"Sorry. Lost track of the time."

They walked down the garage ramp to the basement elevator. As the elevator rose, Clew turned to him and asked, "Who else knew where I'd be jogging this morning?"

Alex asked him, "Why? Did something happen?"

"Nothing much. But have you told anyone where I'd be?"

Alex spread his hands. "How would that be news? You've been doing the same thing for a year, am I right? Same days of the week, same time, same route, which, by the way, I've asked you to change. I've asked you not to be so predictable."

Predictable. Exactly. Alex was right. That was how Bourne knew when and where he could be found. The doorman hadn't seen him leave, but he knew his routine. Someone must have slipped him some cash. Clew had almost found himself wondering whether Alex could be among Bourne's inside sources. But that didn't seem likely. Paranoia creeping in. Rakowsky had no access to the files at State. Or at least he wouldn't know how to decrypt them.

Alex sat in the living room with his coffee and bagel while Clew went to shower and dress. Clew emerged from his bedroom knotting his tie. He told Alex to relax; he'd be just a few more minutes. Clew went into his den where he kept his home computer to see what, if anything, he had on Stride. As he'd thought, there was no specific file on Stride. He did a search of her name in several others.

Her name popped up as part of Martin Kessler's file. Only bits and pieces there. It only mentioned her in passing. The most fruitful source was the Israeli media. There were dozens of newspaper stories about her, all breathless accounts of the Black Angel's forays against the terrorists who had killed Israeli children. She'd become by then a national heroine. But many of those stories were either inventions or someone else's acts that were attributed to her. They had her

doing things she couldn't possibly have done unless there
were at least three or four of her. But Clew found enough
that seemed more or less reliable and a bio began to take
shape. Nothing recent, but a good deal of background.

There was one photo of her. Or believed to be of her. The
notation on it read, "Almost certainly Stride." It had to be at
least ten years old. He found it in his file on another old
friend, the Israeli Yitzhak Netanya. Netanya, who now
headed up the Mossad, was with the Shin Bet when the picture was taken. She was in the photo with him, as were several other people. It was a candid shot, not posed. No hint of
when or where. Tel Aviv, most likely. Perhaps some diplomatic function.

Stride easily stood out; she was an elegant young woman.
The photo showed her full length and in profile. Tall and
lean, athletic-looking, and yet very feminine. Yes, feminine,
thought Clew. That surprised him. She also had a warm and
easy smile on her face. He'd never thought of Stride as ever
smiling. In the photo she was speaking to an elderly gentleman, her right hand lightly touching his chest as she spoke.
The man clearly seemed to like her; he seemed comfortable
with her, which meant that he probably didn't know who she
was.

The reason for the "Almost certainly Stride," was that she
was disguised on this occasion. She had dark hair, dark eyes,
and dark skin in this photo, but none of that darkness was
genuine. She wore wigs and tinted contacts when she
worked for the Israelis, the better to pass as an Arab. The
original Elizabeth was fair-haired and fair-skinned. Her
eyes, Clew now recalled, required those contacts because of
their unusual color.

He remembered being told that they were amber, almost
yellow. They'd been compared to the eyes of a stalking cat.
Those of a cheetah, locked on to its prey, a cheetah getting
ready to pounce. Clew wondered if anyone would have
made that comparison if she'd never gone near the Middle
East and had never become the Black Angel. If, as a girl,
she'd had the sense to stay home, those eyes would have
been simply pretty.

Clew hit several keys to combine all he'd found into something approaching a chronology. "Hello, Elizabeth," he said under his breath. "So let's see who you were and how you happened."

Home, to his surprise, had been Houston, Texas. Clew blinked when he read that. Coincidence? Maybe. That was also the home of Bourne Industries. But Stride hadn't been born there. She wasn't even born American. Elizabeth was born in Saudi Arabia, but of European parents, not Arabs. Her birth parents had made the fatal mistake of traveling to that country unmarried, her mother pregnant. Both were arrested, her father was deported. Her mother was thrown into Az-Zahran prison where Elizabeth was born four months later.

An American couple got wind of her birth. The Americans, Richard and Hannah Stride, were over there working for Aramco Oil, he a geologist, she a nurse. Hannah was unable to bear children of her own and had jumped at the chance to have this beautiful blond infant. She'd been urged to adopt her by some righteous Saudi friends. These friends told her that she'd also be rescuing the baby because the non-Muslim infant would otherwise have been sold. She'd be somebody's little blond sex toy.

Soon afterward, they moved with her back to the States where Elizabeth grew up quite normally. She knew early on that she'd been adopted, but she'd been protected from knowing the truth about the circumstances of her birth. Her adoptive father died when she was fifteen. Her adoptive mother lived to see her graduate from college, but then she, too, passed away. Elizabeth found some papers in her mother's effects that named her biological parents.

She felt compelled to travel back to her birthplace and learn what she could about her parents. The story is that she learned more than was good for her. Her search took her to the same Saudi prison in which her birth mother had been confined. She was promptly arrested. She was never told why. She was held in that prison for more than a year, repeatedly beaten and raped by the guards. Her disappearance eventually led to inquiries by the American consular staff.

The Saudi warden decided to get rid of her. He could have killed her and buried her in an unmarked grave, but he decided for some reason to let the sun do it. He had her dumped, half dead, in the searing desert up near the Jordan border. She was found and nursed by an Arab woman who herself was later murdered for that act of kindness. She was rescued again by Amnesty International, or at least that's who her saviors said they were. In fact, they were Mossad. They were Israeli agents. They ended up recruiting and training Elizabeth and putting her hatred to work.

"Mr. Clew?" It was Alex. He said, "Sir, we're running late."

Clew said, "Just another few minutes."

The Israelis had told her that they'd used their sources to find out what became of her real parents. They were Romanian nationals from the north of that country, both of ethnic Germanic descent. Her father had been a star soccer player. Her mother was a medical student who traveled with his team as a trainer and masseuse. The team was in Saudi Arabia for a match at the time when they were arrested by the Mutawain, the Saudi religious police. Her father, deported, bribed his way back in and set about searching for her mother. He was betrayed, caught, and hung within days. His body was left dangling for a week.

The warden of Az-Zahran prison, meanwhile, had taken a fancy to her mother. Even before Elizabeth was born, he offered her a more comfortable cell if she, in return, would accommodate him. She rebuffed him, he beat her, lashed her face with a strap. She was badly scarred, no longer so attractive. The warden gave her to his guards who raped her repeatedly, just as they later raped Elizabeth.

Clew knew that rape was commonly practiced in many Middle East prisons. It is used to humiliate, break the spirit. The warden dropped by to see how well it was working. He told her that her baby was to be sold. She attacked him, spit at him, raked his cheek with her nails. This time he beat her to death.

Clew wondered how the Mossad could have known this. He supposed that a guard might have witnessed these events and then told tales out of school. But he wouldn't have put it past the Mossad to embellish or even invent. He didn't doubt that Elizabeth's birth parents had been killed, but describing their deaths in vivid detail seemed to him a motivational tactic.

If so, the tactic certainly worked. She became their avenger all over that region. What made her effective as an instrument of vengeance—aside from her personal hunger for it—was the fact that she was a woman. Dressed in an abaya, fully veiled, fully covered, she could come and go on the streets of any city attracting no more notice than a shadow.

She did get that warden. She cut his throat to the bone while he sipped an orange fizz at a sidewalk café in Riyadh. She found two of his guards and cut off their right hands. In the Arab world, this was a terrible fate. The left hand is considered unclean. It is used for ass-wiping and aiming to piss. The right hand is used for all polite contact. Never touch another Arab with the left. Never hand him something with it, never wave to him with it. A man who has had his right hand cut off is doomed to a life of humiliation, ostracism. That was why she didn't kill them outright.

When Elizabeth's personal scores had been settled, she went on to dispatch any number of known terrorists and anyone who happened to be with them. She found one who'd bragged of bombing an Israeli school bus and had killed or maimed many children. She left that one alive, but with no eyes, no tongue, and without the means of siring his own offspring.

The newspaper story that related that incident remarked that she had strong feelings about children. It said that she couldn't have any of her own as a consequence of her treatment in prison. But two later stories said she couldn't have children because she'd been shot outside a hotel in Bucharest. She'd gone there on a mission of mercy.

She had traveled to Romania with an Israeli delegation. They'd gone there to buy Jews who wished to emigrate. This was during the Ceausescu regime, or rather, just at the end of it. The regime was willing to release all such Jews, but only at a price of so much per head. The average going rate was four thousand dollars, payable in either gold or diamonds. Elizabeth had asked to be part of this mission because she hoped to learn something about her roots and whether she might still have relatives there.

Martin Kessler had also turned up in Bucharest. It seems he was there doing much the same thing for ethnic East Germans who wanted to emigrate. No honor among fellow Communists, thought Clew. The greedy Ceausescus made everyone pay. Kessler might or might not have known Stride by reputation. More likely, he spotted her with the Israelis and began asking questions about her. Fascinated by her looks and by her bloody history, he contrived to meet her at a relocation conference hosted by the Swiss Red Cross. Kessler tried to charm her, but she wasn't much interested. She did not regard him as a serious man because he didn't seem to believe in much of anything, least of all the system he worked for. He was also too much of a swashbuckler for her taste. He was gleefully reckless. An adventurer. Kessler, however, knew his way around Romania and he offered to help her trace any blood relatives who were surely still living in that country.

The regime, at this time, was on the verge of collapse. There were popular uprisings everywhere. Stride and Kessler, during their search, happened to turn up at a couple of the hot spots. The Romanian secret police had been watching them and concluded that they must be up to no good. They could not be arrested—they had diplomatic passports—so the secret police found another way to teach the Israelis a lesson.

The regime, always looking for a new source of income, had set up a training camp just outside Bucharest for Hamas and Hezbollah fighters. The base had been funded by Iran. The secret police alerted Hamas to the presence of the woman who was called the Black Angel. It was Hamas, in fact, who'd put the price on her head, with payment guaranteed by the Saudis.

Stride and Kessler arrived back in Bucharest. A team of gunmen had set up an ambush outside the Excelsior Hotel.

Kessler spotted them, too late: he did push her aside, but Elizabeth took three of their bullets.

It took Stride almost a full year to recover. Kessler stayed with her, protected her, cared for her, except when he and the other Israelis were tracking down the people responsible. He found the man who had given the order, a colonel in the secret police. Kessler threw him out of a window. He went to Geneva with the Israelis because that's where the regime had stashed all the diamonds that they'd been paid for thousands of émigrés over the years. The Romanians were also racing to Geneva to grab that stash for themselves. There was, as Clew recalled, a good deal more killing, but the Israelis did get their diamonds. They carried off bags of them, all superior gem quality, all cut and polished and assorted by weight. A few weighed as much as five karats. The collection was worth almost forty million dollars. They gave Kessler a bag worth over two million. All two karats or less. They were the easiest to sell. They called it a finder's fee.

Kessler and Elizabeth stayed in Europe together. Kessler had no job to go back to. East Germany was imploding by that time as well. Elizabeth never went back to Israel. But in Europe they had to stay on the move because Elizabeth was still worth a million dollars dead, twice that if delivered alive. As if that wasn't enough to make their lives less than restful, word had somehow got out that Kessler had kept the entire forty million in diamonds. There were several attempts to capture one or both and coerce them into giving up the stones. It turned out that the Israelis had spread that story in order to avoid having to account for the diamonds they had recovered. They weren't thieves. They didn't keep them for themselves. They did the same thing the CIA used to do before Congress passed another of those moralistic laws that effectively castrated that agency. They used them to fund other sensitive operations for which there could be no formal budget.

If Kessler did take her to the lodge in Chamonix, this would have been a good time to do it. She'd certainly be safe there and she was probably still healing. But they couldn't stay forever and it wasn't a life. It must have been their last stop before they decided to leave Europe and try to get lost in America. They tried to settle down in one place or another, but either someone managed to track them down or Kessler would get bored and get himself into trouble.

Kessler had found, in an American drugstore, a brand of cigarillos called Swisher Sweets. He thought they were something that gay people smoked. Elizabeth told him that they had no such connotation, but Kessler was still amused by the name. Kessler only smoked cigars, hand-rolled, good Cubans, but he bought some Swisher Sweets all the same. Stride may have wondered what he wanted with them, or perhaps she knew that it was useless to ask. By that time, she'd probably given up trying to understand the workings of his mind. So unknown to her, at least in the beginning, Kessler would go out and look for a saloon in a blue-collar section of town.

He'd flounce in, affecting an effeminate manner. He'd put his Swisher Sweets on the bar and order a frozen daiquiri. This was guaranteed to elicit some comment from one or more other patrons. Inevitably, some cowboy or biker would insult him. He would respond meekly, which invited more abuse, until the bully went too far and either crowded him or touched him. Kessler would take him apart. Bannerman said that Kessler didn't always leave unscathed, but that it would take at least three men to defeat him. Kessler didn't seem to mind an occasional defeat. It was worth it as long as he got in his licks. He felt that it kept him in trim.

For Elizabeth, however, this was one straw too many. She was grateful to him and she knew that he loved her, but finally enough was enough. She moved out and said it was over. He stayed in touch all the same and continued to watch over her, presumably hoping that she would relent. But then she died on that exercise bike, this time for real, a few months later. Kessler, disconsolate, went back to Europe where he wandered, aimless, for a year or so. Nothing was the same. He sank into a depression. He checked into the same Bucharest hotel where he had first stayed with Elizabeth. He ordered a bottle of room service champagne. He drank it and then Kessler shot himself.

Clew had found that hard to believe at the time. Kessler was nothing if not resilient. He had never seemed the type to feel sorry for himself. But the champagne part rang true. A final toast to Elizabeth. And his suicide had been reliably confirmed by the new Romanian government. They'd shipped his body back to his home town of Leipzig where Kessler was still a hero to many. They put up a statue over his grave. Clew had heard that children still come to his grave. They leave flowers and sometimes a yellowed copy of one of his old comic books.

"Mr. Clew?" He heard Alex Rakowsky behind him. "We're already a half hour late."

Clew looked at his watch. Alex was right. His staff would soon be gathering for his regular morning briefing. But that briefing would have to be delayed a bit longer while he put a call through to Liberia. He reached for his fanny pack, took out his Beretta, and clipped it onto his belt. He drew out his PDA and said, "One more minute." He pressed the Rewind button on its recorder. He hit Stop, then Play, but for only a few seconds. He heard his own voice say, "Have a nice day, Mr. Bourne," followed by Bourne asking why they're called "ghosts." Their voices had been muted by the fanny pack, but the quality was adequate. He hit Stop again. He placed the PDA into its cradle, which sat at the side of his computer. He downloaded several files into the device, including the one with that photo. He'd reread them when he wasn't so rushed.

Alex asked him, "Did you find what you needed?"

"Not entirely. But more than I expected."

"If you don't mind my asking, how secure is that computer? I mean, what if someone hacked into it? Could they?"

Clew nodded. "They could, but they wouldn't get anything. They'd need the encryption code to begin with. It's got a firewall system that will destroy all the files if they try to get in some other way."

Alex asked, "Destroy them? Where would that leave you?"

"Inconvenienced. For ten minutes. There are more where these came from."

Clew had reached to shut down his machine when a light flashed to show that he had mail. Not ordinary e-mail. It was specially encrypted. He'd need to type in another code to read it.

Alex said, "Bet that's your office asking why you're still here."

"Encrypted? I don't think so. That's what telephones are for."

As if to prove it, he hit several keys, taking care to block Alex's view of the board. A message dropped down. It was still encrypted. But he recognized the six-character code of the sender. Clew smiled. He muttered a name to himself. He added, "Speak of the devil."

"Problem?" asked Alex.

"Oh no. Just a friend."

The code was Paul Bannerman's. Clew shook his head bemusedly. His first thought was that Bannerman must be reading his mind. Calling him this morning. Today of all days. Was he calling him to ask, "What's all this about Stride?" But there was no way that Bannerman could have heard about his encounter with Bourne. Or at least he didn't think so. Not this quickly. It had to be on some other subject.

He decrypted the message. All it said was, "Please call me. I might need a favor. And Susan asks whether we'll see you next week."

Clew understood the last part of that message. It was asking whether he would be coming to Westport for a gathering that Bannerman was hosting. The occasion was the birth of his and Susan's second child. It was due, well . . . now. Any time now, thought Clew. The gathering had started as close friends and family. Clew hadn't thought that he'd be invited. But the guest list seemed to be growing by the day. There were people coming from as far away as Moscow. It was looking more like a convention.

Clew would call Bannerman from his office on the scrambler. Regarding the gathering, he'll say, "Sure. Wouldn't miss it." Then he'll ask Bannerman what favor he needs. And as long as we're talking favors, thought Clew, he'd ask Bannerman what he might know about Stride. He wouldn't wait for that slave ship to be seized.

Clew hit a key and the message blinked off. In its place were the notes on Elizabeth Stride, including that one photo that he'd found. He paused to take another close look at it. He enlarged it so that it filled the screen.

A remarkable woman. Now he wished that he had known her. He had a hunch that she would have been just as remarkable if she'd lived a more conventional life. A top athlete, perhaps. She seemed to have that kind of body. Her tenacity, her resiliency, would have served her well in just about anything she tried. And she would have found a man who was good enough for her. Not a wild man like Kessler. Someone steady.

Okay, he thought. Say it. You mean someone like you?

Yeah, well, maybe. Who knows? And even later, after all the hurt and the damage, someone like him could have helped her to heal. He'd have protected her. Been proud of her. He'd bet he could have saved her.

He heard Alex ask, "Who's the babe? Do you know her?"

Clew muttered a curse. He felt a blush on his cheeks. He quickly shut off the machine. Alex mistook his reaction for anger. Alex said, "I'm not peeking. I couldn't help seeing." He was standing well back from the screen.

Clew said, "She's no one special." He gathered his things.

He'd been caught indulging himself in a fantasy. He could have handled her? He could have saved her? What next; he'd become the only love of her life? Domestic bliss forever more? Get real.

Even so, thought Clew, he wished that he'd known her. He really wished that he could have known her.

7

On the evening before Clew saw Bannerman's message, a small dinner party had taken place on an island off the Carolina coast.

The hostess of that party had been running late. Her three guests were due to arrive very shortly and she still hadn't showered and changed. The meal that she'd prepared was almost ready, however. All that remained was to light her gas grill. After that, she could be dressed in twenty minutes.

She'd stepped onto her patio to fire the grill when she heard police sirens in the distance. She paused to listen, as most people would, to determine where the sirens seemed to be headed and to wonder what might have happened. She then went about her task, as most people would. She had felt no sense of alarm.

That in itself was remarkable, she supposed. It was not so long ago that the sound of sirens would have triggered a less passive response. She would have gone to the closet where she kept her blue duffel. It was always packed and ready, well hidden. It held cash and weapons, and two changes of clothing plus the loose-fitting black she used for night work. It contained two wigs and two sets of contact lenses, one set tinted dark brown, the other blue. It contained two sets of false documents as well and about a million dollars' worth of diamonds.

Within seconds she would have been out of her house. She would have been walking, not running, toward a spot she'd selected from which she could watch unobserved. If the sirens passed her by, nothing lost; she'd go back home. If they'd converged on her address, she would simply have vanished, never to be able to return.

But on Hilton Head Island, where she'd made her new life, and especially in Sea Pines, her gated community, all that a siren usually meant was that some older resident had fallen ill and that someone had called 911. There was crime on the island, but not much and mostly petty. Almost none of it took place within the gated communities. They were wealthy, therefore tempting, but not worth the risk. Most had only one exit, easily blocked, and all were well guarded and patrolled.

True, there was that episode two years ago when the bounty hunters came to the island. To her surprise, however, they had not come for her. They had come for two people who were strangers to her then. A young girl and her guardian, both Muslims. It was Martin who'd spotted the three bounty hunters. He had recognized the Englishman who led them. It was the Englishman's turn to be surprised when he saw the Black Angel standing over him that night. Martin fed what was left of him to the crabs.

She had hoped that was the end of it. It was wishful thinking. Those who sent them sent others, three Algerians this time. The Algerians came by boat, across the Atlantic, to do what the bounty hunters had failed to do. But this time they came not to kidnap, but to kill. The Algerians were fanatics, out of control. Their intention was to kill on the grandest scale possible. They brought with them the warhead of a nuclear device. They did not have the means to detonate the device, but they did have the means to release its radiation by exposing its plutonium core. It was a very near thing. They had almost succeeded. They would have turned this island into a desert for a thousand years into the future.

The federal authorities had gone to great lengths to keep this event from the public. No one knew what sort of device they had brought or how easily they had reached these shores with it. The actual damage to the island was minimal. A few yachtsmen whose boats were near that of the Algerians did suffer from radiation poisoning. They were told that they had scarlet fever, an isolated outbreak; they were whisked away for treatment. And thousands of others never knew how close they came. They never knew that Martin Kessler had stopped the Algerians. They never knew that he gave his life for them.

The authorities had decided to keep their names out of it. Especially her own. It might invite more attacks. The man who saved this island could not have been Martin Kessler because Martin Kessler had been dead for some time. The authorities had contrived a romantic fiction that he, the year before, had put a gun to his head because he could no longer live without her. And if she, Elizabeth, had predeceased Martin, she could not have been part of this either. The problem there, however, was that she was in fact here. Her name was in the phone book. E, period, Stride. Her last name was even on her mailbox.

"Very dumb, Elizabeth," Martin said more than once. "God forbid that those who hunt you should be inconvenienced. This way they can send you a bomb through the mail and save a fortune in travel expenses."

He would not have understood. She wanted to be real again. She wanted to live like everyone else and to try to find the person she'd been before all the hatred and the killing. But, of course, he was right. That was pushing it. That was dumb.

The authorities solved that problem through a simple device. They created a file on the Elizabeth Stride whose name was in the Hilton Head phonebook. The photo in that file was of her next-door neighbor, a woman almost eighty years old. That file showed that she was a widow who'd moved here from Warren, Ohio. Clearly not the Black Angel. Look elsewhere, not here. There was no Martin Kessler here either.

She lit the gas grill. She felt her eyes growing moist. She muttered to herself, "Damn you, Martin."

He hadn't died to save all these people. That was a romantic fiction as well. He died because to him, this was just one more adventure. He died because it probably never occurred to him that one day his lunatic luck might run out. He died because he didn't have the sense that God gave him. He should never have come to this island.

She'd told him not to come. She'd told him not to try to find her. She'd told him, "No, Martin. I don't love you. I don't."

She'd told him, "What's more, you bring nothing but trouble. If it doesn't find you, you find it, and I'm tired. I'm tired of living with a price on my head. You're as hunted as I am, but with you it's a game. You don't avoid them; you entice them. You revel in outwitting them. And when we've outdistanced them, at least for a while, you'll get bored and go looking for some dive of a saloon that has two or three Harleys parked out front. You with your damned Swisher Sweets."

She'd told him, "I've had it. I want a life, Martin. I want to have friends. Normal people. Women friends."

She'd said, "I want to do the things that normal people do. I want to go shopping, play tennis, have a garden. I want, for a change, to walk into a restaurant, not having to check out the exits in advance and not having to scan every face in the room."

She'd said, "I don't love you. You don't love me either. What we are is a habit and a bad one at that."

She'd said all these things to him. And other things just as hurtful. She'd thought that most of them were true when she said them.

Did she love him? Well, yes. But she didn't know it then. Was she grateful to him? Sure. He'd saved her life more than once. He'd stayed near her bedside for a full three months after she had been shot in Romania. And later, much later, he'd gone back to Chamonix and spread the word that she'd died in the States. She should have thanked him for that. She never did. Instead, she got angry when he turned up again. "Just checking," he said. "Just to see you're all right."

But by that time, she was seeing a man with whom she could take quiet walks on the beach. And go to the movies, go to dinner, go dancing. He was a nice man, a doctor; she liked being with him. Except for her reluctance to let him see her naked, she might very well have had a sex life again. But he'd have known bullet scars when he saw them.

In the end, though, she was grateful that Martin had come. She was grateful, above all, that he'd saved the life of the girl who had become like a daughter to her. Young Aisha was the one the bounty hunters wanted most. Aisha was the heir to considerable property in and around Cairo, Egypt. She had an uncle who was desperate to gain control of that property because it was worth many millions to him. The uncle, and the people with whom he did business, were willing to kill anyone who stood in their way. But under Egypt's law, it couldn't be touched unless Aisha could be found and brought back to Cairo where her uncle would become her legal guardian. Or unless it could be proven that she's dead.

The bounty hunters did find her, they took her, they hid her, until they could arrange to have her flown out. But Martin had found them. She and Martin got her back. The bounty hunters died where they stood. Then her uncle's associates sent in the Algerians with instructions to kill her and be done with it. Instead, every one of them died on this island or in the waters around it. Even the uncle and the uncle's associates. They all died. But Martin died with them.

Aisha was fourteen years old when this happened. Very brave, but still very young. She'd been living here, in hiding, sent here with false papers by her parents who had reason to fear for her life. They saved Aisha, but they could not save themselves. Both her parents were soon to be murdered.

How well she had accepted that terrible loss. Aisha's strong Muslim faith had sustained her. It was a faith that Elizabeth had at one time despised and, later, a faith she almost wished that she shared when she saw how it had comforted Aisha. It was Aisha, in fact, who had comforted her in the weeks after Martin Kessler died.

Damn him.

Damn you, Martin.

Tears ran down her cheeks.

But she dried them and forced herself to shake off the memory. She did not want to think about this anymore. She did not want to think about Martin. She went into her bathroom and turned on the shower, stripping out of her clothing as it ran. She avoided looking at herself in the mirror. She did not want to see her scars either. She stepped under the spray and lathered herself thoroughly before rinsing hot and then cold. Cold showers were a habit. She thought they heightened her senses. And, not least, they seemed to tighten her skin.

She patted herself dry and returned to her bedroom where she'd laid out the dress and the shoes she had chosen. The dress was oriental, full length, a soft yellow, with an embroidered ivy vine at one shoulder. Very soft, very cool, very feminine, she thought. She had just the right bracelets to go with it.

She still heard the sirens. Perhaps more than before. And they did seem to sound more urgent than usual. She could hear the whooping sounds that police cruisers make when they want other vehicles to get out of their way. And now the harsh bleat of a fire truck. They were nevertheless headed in the opposite direction. They grew farther and farther away.

Her three dinner guests were now a few minutes late. They were probably held up by that activity. Just as well. She could use the time to touch up her hair and to do a final check in the kitchen. She'd set a table for four on her screened-in porch, which looked out on a tidal lagoon. She saw that there were just enough clouds in the sky to promise a colorful sunset. She had prepared a nice salad of fresh fruit, mostly citrus. The main course, from the grill, would be a butterflied lamb that had been marinating most of the day. Dessert would be a blueberry cobbler that she'd made. She'd never tried one before and she'd burned it just a bit, but a sprinkling of brown sugar would hide the charred edges. In any case, the sun would have set by that time. They'd be eating it by candlelight. Perhaps no one would notice.

She had chosen a wine, a nice Chardonnay, even though her guests would probably decline it in favor of iced tea or Pepsi. All three were Muslims, but not equally devout. There was Jasmine, who'd converted to Islam while in prison, but had yet to fully embrace those teachings that related to dietary laws. Jasmine, or Jazz as she was generally better known, saw little harm in an occasional Jack Daniel's and even less harm in a pork chop.

Elizabeth had never asked why she'd been in prison. But she knew that Jasmine, who was black and had grown up in Brooklyn, had once been a drug addict and probably a dealer and possibly a prostitute as well. Not that it mattered. Nor did her real name. The person she'd been before she became Jasmine was a person who no longer existed.

Well, perhaps not entirely. She had not lost her street smarts; the hard edge was still there. She could still, in her thirties, have done well as a hooker. Good body, chiseled features, and a big easy laugh. She would still have no trouble stopping traffic.

Nadia Halaby, the second of her guests, had been a Muslim from birth. She was born in Algeria to a well-to-do family, but educated in France. Nadia was a graduate of the Sorbonne and still kept an apartment in Paris. She'd grown up playing tennis, stayed with it through school, and eventually won several amateur titles before briefly turning professional. She was now an instructor at a tennis academy where talented young hopefuls came to train.

Nadia, however, was much more than that. And her tennis academy was much more than that. While in France, she had set up a safe house of sorts for Muslim women who had fled from their homelands. That first one was attacked and under constant threat. Nadia fled to this country, flew those women here with her, and set up a much larger safe house on this island. These were women who had fled the oppression of their sex in their various Islamic homelands. Some wanted education that had been denied them. Some ran from marriages that had been arranged for them. A few had talents, artistic or otherwise, that they had been forbidden to pursue. They were, in the eyes of those Algerian terrorists, no better than whores and already lost to God. Such women, if found, were to be stoned or burned and so should those who'd given them shelter.

Young Aisha was no runaway. Aisha's mother had known Nadia and was one of her supporters. When it became clear that Aisha's life was in danger, Aisha's mother knew where to send her because she knew that Nadia would protect her with her life. But the bounty hunters tracked her and, later, the fanatics. When the Algerians realized that it wasn't just Aisha, when they were told that all those runaways were living here as well, not to mention the notorious Nadia Halaby, it seemed that Allah himself must have led them to this island. The Koran, according to their reading of that book, enjoined the faithful to "make wide slaughter in defeating the enemies of God." Those words are in there, but they refer to invaders. Foreign armies, for example. Not women. And not children.

Elizabeth, again, tried to push this from her mind. This was not a time to indulge in old sorrows. This was a bright and lovely occasion. Aisha had turned sweet sixteen. Elizabeth dearly wished that her parents could have lived to see the splendid young lady that their daughter had become. But they would not have been surprised. They had raised her after all. And, according to Aisha, they were still around anyway, so make that five guests instead of three.

Nadia says that Aisha is the image of her mother and she says that Aisha's mother was stunning. The same enormous dark eyes, the same raven's wing hair except that Aisha wore a much shorter cut now. The same skin coloring under her tan; it was somewhere between olive and gold. The same ultra-wide smile, the same perfect complexion, and, according to Nadia, the same heart.

Aisha's only fault, thought Elizabeth, was her tennis game. She was getting frustratingly good. They played a few sets of singles at least once a week, but Elizabeth hadn't beaten her in months. Not legitimately, anyway. Sometimes

Aisha would have the final set in her pocket and she'd suddenly start double faulting and such to let Elizabeth back in the match. And of course she denied that she was just being kind, but she does that with other opponents as well. No killer instinct. She should work on that. Save the kindness for after the match.

Perhaps the new racket she'd bought Aisha for her birthday would encourage her to go for the jugular more often. It had a good name for that. The Wilson Sledge Hammer. She'd seen Aisha admiring it in the pro shop.

Suddenly, Elizabeth felt an unwelcome chill. What if Aisha and Nadia and Jasmine were late because they were the cause of those sirens? Someone after them again? No, don't even think it. Those sirens had seemed headed more toward the main gate than toward the tennis academy. Even so, Elizabeth stepped out onto her driveway. She waited and worried for another ten minutes until at last she saw Nadia's car coming.

"I'm sorry Elizabeth," Nadia told her. "We couldn't resist going to see what was happening. I guess we're still sensitized to sirens."

As Nadia spoke, she had opened her trunk and was gathering wrapped birthday presents. She was handing some to Jasmine, who was wearing a dress. So was Nadia. So was Aisha. Along with high heels. Elizabeth had never seen them in heels. They looked very nice, all primped and accessorized, but when one has only seen them in more careless attire, the effect is something like being costumed. They would look more Islamic at sundown, however, when the three of them covered their heads with hijab and knelt side by side on her oriental rug to say their evening prayers before dinner.

Jasmine said to Aisha, "No peeking at the presents." She said to Elizabeth, "Doesn't Aisha look hot?"

Nadia frowned. "The word is 'lovely,'" she said.

Jasmine winked at Elizabeth. "Muslims aren't supposed to say 'boobs' or 'bod' either. But that doesn't mean she don't have them."

Elizabeth glanced at Aisha, expecting a blush. But Aisha was still looking toward the sound of the sirens, a faraway expression on her face.

Elizabeth asked Nadia, "Well, what happened? Do you know?"

"A shooting," Jazz answered. "In a bar outside the gate. A place called Jump & Phil's. Do you know it?"

Elizabeth nodded. "I've had lunch there."

"We couldn't get very close with the car, but I spoke to one of the security guards. He said that several people were down."

"It's pretty awful," said Aisha. "Three inside the bar and three more in the parking lot. At least four of them are already dead."

Nadia's lips had tightened again. She said to Elizabeth, "She knows that because she jumped out and ran over there. She's lucky it's her birthday or I'd spank her."

"I . . . needed to see," said Aisha weakly.

"What you needed, young lady, was to do as you're told. If you ever . . ."

"Wait a minute," said Elizabeth. "What kind of a shooting? A robbery? Or did someone go berserk?"

Jasmine shook her head. "Neither one. It wasn't postal. The security guard said it looked like a hit. A man walked in, pulled a gun from his jacket, shot a guy who was sitting having dinner with his wife. The victim's still alive, but the shooter is down. Some guy who was sitting at the bar took him out. He stuck the shooter in the head with a knife. Not a real knife. A table knife. But it was enough. The guy did a lobotomy on him."

Nadia added, "Well, it wasn't *quite* enough. The man with the knife in his brain went into spasm. His hand kept twitching and he sprayed half a clip while people were diving for cover. At least two more were hit before this man from the bar could finish the job with that knife."

Elizabeth's eyes narrowed. "A bystander did that?"

Jasmine, too, was skeptical. "If that's all he is. Could be he's a bodyguard. The first man who got shot has his own TV show. Never heard of him myself, but they tell me he's famous."

"An actor?"

"Commentator. Political stuff. The kind where people call in. Those guys always have someone mad at them."

Perhaps so, thought Elizabeth. Some nut acting on a grudge. It did not have the sound of a professional hit. She said, "Or maybe it was personal. An old boyfriend. An ex-husband."

"Pissed-off boyfriends," said Jazz, "don't usually have a getaway driver waiting outside, especially one with a shot-gun. It seems this . . . bystander . . . picked up the shooter's pistol and put a few holes in the driver's windshield when he tried to take aim with the shotgun. The bullets missed him but the flying glass didn't. The driver got away after plow-ing through pedestrians and bouncing off a couple of cars. He's in a banged-up blue Buick with the windshield shot out. They'll catch him. He can't get it off the island."

"Where's this bystander now?"

"Still at the restaurant. Talking to the police. Aisha says he was there with a pretty young woman. She got a good look. She's never seen him before. I had guessed that he might have been an off-duty deputy, but she says the other deputies didn't seem to know him either."

Elizabeth looked at Aisha. Aisha wouldn't meet her gaze. Elizabeth was beginning to understand why Aisha felt the need to get a look at this man. It did sound like something that Martin might do if he'd happened to be in that bar. They would need to have a talk, but that could wait. Whoever he was, he was no off-duty deputy. She felt sure that he wasn't a bodyguard either. Bodyguards go armed. They don't rely on restaurant flatware. They don't count on using the shooter's own weapon when more shooting needs to be done.

All in all, however, an uneven performance. Parts were impressive. Cool and professional. The man had done this before. But he'd failed to kill quickly, not once, but twice, and more people were hurt or killed because of it. He was more than a little bit reckless as well. Any professional who had just *happened* to be there should have lowered his head and stayed out of it. Especially when the victim had already been shot. This man didn't hesitate. He jumped right in. Most professionals would not have. Martin certainly would have. And that was why she wouldn't be too hard on Aisha for wondering if it might have been Martin.

Aisha had never fully accepted that Martin Kessler was dead. Martin had telephoned her from the boat, the one that the Algerians brought over. It was on a reef twenty-five miles out and surrounded, at a distance, by Coast Guard patrol boats. They couldn't get closer. The boat was too hot. The radiation was such that no one could survive it. Martin knew full well that he hadn't long to live, but Martin was Martin and he couldn't resist making it a game even then. He was already planning a little surprise for those who would eventually board the boat.

He'd said to Aisha, "Don't worry about me. If they tell you I'm dead, make them show you my body. If they can't, then you shouldn't believe it." He'd said, "Ask Elizabeth. I'm like a bad penny. You can never get rid of bad pennies." He was lying through his teeth. He knew he had no chance. Aisha knew it as well, but she knew it in her head. She just couldn't accept it with her heart.

As for who that man was, the mysterious bystander, they could read all about it in the morning papers and find out who did what to whom. The best proof, thought Elizabeth, that it wasn't Martin Kessler was that Martin would know better than to show up on this island with a new and younger girlfriend in tow. She'd have shown him where to put that table knife.

Elizabeth forced a smile. She put an arm around Aisha. She said, "Our birthday girl is here. We have presents to open. Let's go in and enjoy ourselves, shall we?"

Aisha asked Elizabeth, "Are you going to serve wine?"

"Well, I've chilled some for myself. And for whoever might like some."

"Could I have just a taste? I'd like to know what I don't drink."

"Over my dead body," said Nadia.

8

The morning paper came. It was full of the shootings. Among the dead were a tourist from New Jersey and a local real estate broker, a woman. They were the ones who'd been hit by random bullets. To Elizabeth's surprise, the assassin still lived, although in a vegetative state. His accomplice, with the shotgun, still hadn't been caught. Neither of the men had been identified.

Their intended victim, the talk show host, had undergone emergency surgery. His name was Philip Ragland. His show was called *The Ragland Report*. She had never seen the show or heard the name. Ragland, it said, was in guarded condition, but he was expected to survive. The man who interceded was one Adam Wismer. The paper identified the young woman with him. It gave her name as Claudia Kelly. The news report, oddly, minimized Wismer's role. It suggested that several of the patrons were involved in subduing the man with the gun. Someone had stabbed him. It wasn't clear who did. Some witnesses said that the knife had been thrown. Some thought that this Claudia Kelly had thrown it.

Others said that it was already in the man's skull before Kelly or Wismer had reacted.

The young woman threw it? Impossible, thought Elizabeth. No one makes a killing throw with that sort of knife. She knew a little something about knives.

Elizabeth didn't know quite what to make of this confusion. She had given mixed reviews to this mysterious Wismer, but it now seems that he'd had a lot more to contend with than polishing off the two shooters. From what she'd heard earlier, there hadn't seemed to be much doubt that Wismer was central to all this.

She'd understood that Wismer had finished the knife job, even if he hadn't started it. The paper did mention that he fired some shots through the plate-glass window at the getaway car. But that element of the story seemed almost incidental. He shot, he missed, and that seemed to be that. It said that he and Miss Kelly were visitors to the island. They lived on a yacht at the Palmetto Bay Marina. It said they'd only been here for two or three weeks and were in that restaurant purely by chance. This much had been gleaned from the police reports only. Mr. Wismer, apparently, could not be reached for comment. He and Kelly were in seclusion.

It seemed to Elizabeth that if she were a reporter, she would damned well have reached him for comment. Was he being protected? If so, by whom? How could a man do what he'd apparently done and be allowed to fade into the background? But she put the thought aside. It was none of her business. Except that it had made her friends late for dinner, it did not touch their lives in any way. She had shopping to do, then a golf lesson later. After that, she would spend some time at the gym to work off the effects of last night's feasting.

Her day did not go as planned because the island went crazy. She heard sirens all afternoon. She ignored them at first, but then Nadia started calling. Nadia kept a police scanner in her office. She'd acquired it after the terrorist attack along with several other early-warning devices. First she'd heard on her scanner that a woman had been kidnapped. The victim was the young woman who'd been tending bar when the shooting erupted in that restaurant.

Nadia said, "There's got to be a connection."

"One would think so," Elizabeth answered, "but what?"

"Well, she was a witness."

"So were forty other people. And that's why the newspaper account seems so muddled. No two people saw quite the same thing. It never fails."

"Well, the people who saw her get kidnapped all agree. She was walking toward the dock. Three men snatched her in broad daylight."

Elizabeth raised an eyebrow. "The dock? What dock is that?"

"At Palmetto Bay Marina."

Where the man with the knife keeps his boat, thought Elizabeth. Coincidence, probably. She chose not to comment. This still wasn't any of her business. She said, "Let me know what develops."

Nadia called again about two hours later. She asked, "Elizabeth, is Aisha there with you?"

"No, she isn't. I haven't seen her."

"She took off on her bike. I don't like her being out. I hope she didn't ride down to that house. I can see all the smoke from my window."

"Um . . . what house is that?" asked Elizabeth.

The house in question was in North Forest Beach and the scene of a new round of violence. The house had gone up in flames and exploded. This was only within the past hour. Someone, according to what Nadia had heard, had driven a fuel truck through the front wall after some sort of bomb had gone off. The fuel truck, she said, had been stolen earlier from its depot at Hilton Head Airport.

Elizabeth felt the hairs on her neck start to curl. Aviation fuel? Someone used an airport truck as a battering ram? Once again, thoughts of Martin entered her mind, but Nadia said the driver was a woman. She was described as having red hair, cut short, and as being very petite. Neighbors reported that shots had been fired before, as well as after, both explosions. Several people, men and women, were seen running from the house just after she drove the truck into it. A van ripped its way out of the burning garage. It was followed by an older green Pontiac. The redheaded woman then emerged from the flames. She was carrying what looked like an automatic weapon and seemed in no particular hurry. She climbed into a car that was waiting for her. That car was a light brown Ford Taurus. Another man and woman were in the front seat. They drove off before the fire trucks arrived.

A redhead, thought Elizabeth. Petite. Cool and deadly. And as reckless as Martin if not worse. Elizabeth's mind gave the redhead a face, the face of a woman whom she'd known by reputation before meeting her, sort of, in Europe. She had come to Chamonix with Paul Bannerman's crew. But no, she decided. That's too much of a leap. That was not Carla Benedict in that fuel truck.

She had enough trouble envisioning the scene that Nadia had been trying to describe. It was hard because Nadia had pieced it together from the squawking reports on her scanner. A Taurus, a van, and a green Pontiac. All being hunted by too few police cars, half of which were still at that burning house. Elizabeth had almost expected to hear that an older blue Buick had been there as well. One with its windshield shot out.

She said, "I'll go out and see if I can find Aisha."

"Bring your cell phone," said Nadia. "Let me know."

Elizabeth drove up to the Tennis Center. From there, she took the route that Aisha would have taken if she'd ridden her bike toward Forest Beach. She followed the still-rising smoke. All streets leading to that house were blocked off by police cars. She doubted that Aisha could have gotten through even if that had been her intention. The police were letting cars and bikes out, but not in.

Elizabeth called Nadia. "I don't think she's here."

Nadia said, "Keep looking, okay? I know that she's not likely to have been kidnapped, but it's happened once and now that other young woman has been snatched . . ."

"I'm sure Aisha's fine. We're going to find her."

"Have you heard what just happened at the airport and the hospital?"

"How would I hear? You've got the scanner."

"You should get one. Another bomb went off at the hospital. They just made another try for that talk show host, Ragland. What's the name of that real hot explosive? It sounds like the name of a bug."

"You mean thermite?"

"Thermite. Right. It cooked the man who tried to use it. They think it's the getaway driver from last night. They're not sure yet because all that's left are his feet. But they'd already identified both of those men. They're wanted for a series of bomb attacks and murders. They're terrorists, but they're yours for a change."

"They're mine?" asked Elizabeth. "What does that mean?"

"Well, sort of yours. They're fundamentalist Christians. They belong to something called the Reconstructionist Church. These two have fire-bombed a number of abortion clinics and at least one gay bar as well. Last night's shooter had stoned his ex-wife to death after catching her with some other guy. The theory is that they went after Ragland because Ragland had blasted their church on his program. You want to hear a hoot? Ragland called them Shiite Christians. Sort of blasphemous, maybe, but it's funny."

"Ragland's safe?"

"Just wet. The bomb set off the sprinklers. On top of all this, a private jet has gone down after taking off from Hilton Head Airport. They think the jet is registered to a government agency, some Washington think tank or other. I don't know whether it's connected to the rest of this mess, but that fuel truck that came from the airport makes you wonder."

It did make her wonder. "What brought it down?"

"Not another bomb, if that's what you're thinking. Witnesses say it nosed over and dropped like a stone as soon as it got over the ocean."

Elizabeth took a breath. "I'll keep looking for Aisha. I have an idea where she might be."

It was only a hunch, but it seemed worth a try. Last evening, Aisha had felt compelled to get a closer look at Jump & Phil's. She did not see, of course, what she hoped she would see. Even so, she'd acted strangely for the rest of the evening. Not withdrawn, exactly. She'd certainly gushed over her birthday presents and mugged for the camera when the snapshots were taken. She'd held up her end of the dinner conversation, but the effort did seem forced from time to time. And she also got just a tiny bit looped on the one glass of un-Islamic wine that Jasmine gave her.

They'd had their talk about Martin at the end of the evening. She'd taken Aisha aside and Aisha knew what was coming. Aisha asked, "Elizabeth, don't you feel him near you sometimes? I mean, aren't there times when you're sitting by yourself and you find yourself talking to him?"

"I try not to, but I do. And then I can't shut him up."

She smiled. "You admit it. So you don't think that's crazy."

"It's not crazy at all. It's perfectly normal. But I know that I'm talking to a memory, Aisha. I know that I'm not really hearing him."

"You're sure?"

"It's the same as when you talk to your parents."

She said, "No, that's different. They're in heaven, but they're real. I know that they can't be just a memory, Elizabeth, because they know all about you."

"I see."

"No, you don't. You think I'm only talking to myself. But they tell me lots of things that I couldn't have known. Especially when they come to me in dreams."

"Such as?"

Aisha hesitated. "I'm not sure I should say."

"And why not?"

"Because you won't believe it. Or you'll try to explain it. Or you might even think I've been poking through your closets if I tell you things that you don't think I know."

"I . . . guess I'd like to hear one example," said Elizabeth. "For the record, though, I know you wouldn't poke."

Aisha hesitated. "Do you still have your blue duffel? The one with your weapons and things?"

"What about it?"

"Elizabeth, I was with you when you threw it away. You carried it out back and threw it into the lagoon. Did you change your mind about not needing that stuff? Did you go back and fish it out later?"

Elizabeth stared. This did sound like poking. "Have you seen it since I tossed it? Tell the truth."

"No, I haven't. It's my mother. I told her that you got rid of it. She was sure that you'd have second thoughts about that. She said you might want it to be over, and it might be, but that you'd want to be on the safe side."

Intuition, thought Elizabeth. Strictly Aisha's. Not her mother's. But she said, "Yes, I did change my mind."

"I don't blame you."

Elizabeth asked, "What else has she told you?"

Another hesitation. "She thinks you'll get bored. She thinks you're not the type to live quietly."

"Well, she's wrong."

"And she told me that Martin . . ." Aisha stopped. "Never mind."

"She told you that Martin's still alive?"

"Um . . . no. Well, not exactly. In one dream she was telling me what heaven is like. She says it's pretty much the way it's described in the Koran, but only for Muslims and only at first. It changes once the Muslims get used to the idea that they're not in Kuwait anymore."

"Kuwait?"

"Mom was making a joke. Like in *The Wizard of Oz*. Like when Dorothy said, 'We're not in Kansas anymore.'"

"Nice to hear that she's kept her sense of humor," said Elizabeth. "Nice to know you can still have some fun there."

Aisha started to speak. She seemed to think better of it. Elizabeth said, "Don't stop now. You're on a roll."

Aisha lifted her chin. "You won't make fun of this, will you?"

"And now I can't wait. Spit it out."

"She says Martin's not there. I had asked her to look. She says she'd have found him if he's there."

Elizabeth had to smile. "We're talking Martin? In heaven?"

"Uh-huh. And see? You're already making fun."

"No, I'm not, sweetie. It's just hard to envision Martin Kessler with wings. But maybe there's some sort of halfway house system. Maybe Martin is stuck there for a while."

Aisha shook her head. "Martyrs go straight to heaven."

"Even the lunatics?"

"Martin wasn't a lunatic."

Elizabeth softened. "I . . . didn't mean him." Well, she did, but it was not the thing to say. "I meant religious fanatics. Suicide bombers."

"They're not martyrs. And they're in for an unpleasant surprise."

"I take it that your mother hasn't seen them around."

Aisha chewed her lip. "I'm being serious, Elizabeth."

"I'm sorry. I just wondered . . ."

"I did ask her about that. Heaven's only for those who have love in their hearts. Martin had love in his heart."

"Yes, he did."

"Then he'd be there, Elizabeth. But my mother hasn't found him. I'll believe that he's dead when she finds him."

And that, thought Elizabeth, turned out to be that. It's a fairy tale, of course, but try telling that to Aisha. These talks with her mother are dreams, nothing more. But they're good dreams. They're nice dreams. No harm in them, probably. There's a very thin line between faith and delusion, but Aisha isn't likely to cross it.

Elizabeth's car rounded Sea Pines Circle. She turned off on the exit that led to Jump & Phil's. It was at the end of a group of low buildings that housed other restaurants and shops. The front door and front windows were covered with plywood. Employees were still sweeping up glass from the driveway. Boarded up or not, it was open for business. There were several outdoor tables in a patio area and all of those tables were occupied. An outdoor bar had been set up as well.

No surprise, she supposed. It was a neighborhood tavern. Its regulars had probably been stopping by all day to hear details of the shoot-out from the owners and staff. But speaking of staff, one of them had been kidnapped. One would think that these locals would be worried about her, but most of them seemed in high spirits.

And there was Aisha. She was standing with her bike. She

was talking to one of the young waitresses. She wore shorts and a tank top, also very un-Islamic. Tilted back on her head was a western-style hat with a pair of large feathers curling out of the band. It was the hat she'd been wearing when Elizabeth first saw her.

Back then, her name was Cherokee Blye. Aisha needed an alias; Nadia came up with that one. The idea was to pass her off as an Indian. The Cherokee tribe was indigenous to this area so it didn't seem that much of a stretch to make her an Indian princess. Language was no problem. She spoke English with barely a trace of an accent. If, on occasion, she were to lapse into Arabic, anyone who overheard her would probably assume that Aisha was speaking in Cherokee. And, in fact, she did learn a little Cherokee.

New name or not, the bounty hunters found Aisha. But they're dead and so are the people who sent them. The need for the alias had passed. And that, thought Elizabeth, was too bad in a way. Aisha did look like an Indian princess. And while Aisha Bandari was a perfectly good name, it wasn't quite as snappy as Cherokee Blye. But at least she still had the hat.

Aisha had spotted her. She acknowledged her presence with a smile and wave. The smile did not immediately extend to her eyes. Her eyes had an, "Oops, am I in trouble?" sort of glaze. But they brightened quickly. Nadia would be trouble. This was only Elizabeth. And Elizabeth could be wrapped around her finger.

Oh, really?

Well, I wouldn't press your luck if I were you, thought Elizabeth.

Aisha pushed off and coasted over on her bike. She asked Elizabeth, "Have you heard what's been happening?"

"The hospital, you mean? And the plane? Yes, I've heard."

"And Leslie's okay. She called. She got away."

"I . . . assume you mean the woman who was kidnapped," said Elizabeth.

"Leslie Stewart. The bartender. She just called her boss, Jump. She told him she's fine, just a little beat up, but she didn't want to say where she is yet."

Elizabeth asked her, "How would you know this?"

"Jump made the announcement a few minutes ago. She's mostly why all these people are here. They started coming right after she was kidnapped."

That announcement would account for the crowd's relaxed mood. "Why wouldn't she say where she is?"

"A female thing, maybe? She wants to clean herself up?"

"It sounds more like she wants to avoid the police. But why would she if she says she got away?"

"The FBI agents asked Jump the same thing. He could only repeat what she told him."

"The FBI was here?"

"They're all over the island. They were after the two who did that shooting last night, but now they're looking for a whole bunch of people. They were showing some photographs around."

"Did you see them? The photographs?"

Aisha nodded. "We all did. Several men and two women. No one here recognized any of them."

"None were of the couple that was in here last night?"

"No, but his name isn't Wismer, by the way. The paper got it wrong. His name is Adam Whistler. And the woman who was with him is named Geller, not Kelly. Jump knows them. They've been in here several times."

Elizabeth wondered; did the paper get their names wrong? Or did this couple deliberately misspell them, mispronounce them when they gave their names to the police? That wouldn't have fooled the police for very long, but the media would be slower to catch on. She wondered because that's what she would have done. It might have given her an edge, time to vanish. And she wondered because this new name was familiar. She knew it from Europe, from her stay at Chamonix. But that Whistler, Harry Whistler, a formidable man, would be in his early sixties at least. She shook off the thought. Coincidence. Nothing more. There must be thousands of Whistlers in the world.

"These photographs," said Elizabeth, "do you remember any names?"

"They wouldn't give us their names. They wouldn't tell us much of anything. But one of the women looked a little like you. Not a lot, and not as pretty. Just something about her."

"A redhead?"

"Uh-huh."

"Very small?"

Aisha nodded. "She looked pretty tiny in the photo. Oh, wow. Elizabeth, don't tell me you know her."

I just might, thought Elizabeth, but she chose not to say so. She told Aisha, "The police were broadcasting that description in connection with that Forest Beach explosion. Are any of those FBI agents still here?"

"They got a call and they left, but one said he'd be back. Is it okay if I stay here for a while? It's not as if this happens every day."

Elizabeth shook her head. "Nadia's worried about you. Throw your bike in my trunk. I'll take you back."

"She's not going to worry if she knows I'm with you. Can I buy you a Coke? I've got money."

"I'd . . . rather not see any FBI agents."

Aisha made a small grimace. "I forgot about that. You're afraid they might recognize you?"

"Not likely," said Elizabeth, "but there's no need to risk it. I'll buy you a Coke back at my place."

As Elizabeth drove back to her house on Marsh Drive, she called Nadia to say that she had Aisha with her. It was nearing six o'clock, it would be dinnertime soon. Perhaps Aisha could stay and have some leftover lamb? Perhaps she could even sleep over?

Nadia answered, "I should really say no. That's twice now that she's taken off on her own in the midst of all this mayhem that's been happening."

"She won't be on her own. And we'll be staying close to home."

"Very well," said Nadia. "I'll chew her out tomorrow. Anyway, it seems to have quieted down. They're broadcasting a ten twenty-one on the scanner."

"What's a ten twenty-one?"

"It means 'return to base.' They're calling in all cars except for a couple that are still at the house that blew up. Oh, and some that are still at the hospital."

"Does that mean they've rounded up everyone involved?"

"Well," said Nadia, "that's what's odd about this. Some of the policemen asked the same thing. The dispatcher wouldn't answer them. All she'd do was repeat the ten twenty-one. When two or three of the policemen complained, she gave all the cars a ten-three code. Ten-three means 'stop transmitting.' In other words, 'shut up.'"

"What exactly were they complaining about?"

"The FBI taking over. Telling them to break off. They said the FBI only has jurisdiction where those two federal fugitives are concerned. They said they think there's a lot more than that going on. The dispatcher said, 'You've been given an order. You are not to make any arrests.'"

Elizabeth shrugged. She said she wasn't surprised. The FBI has a history of grabbing the limelight, especially in cases that are likely to make headlines. But Nadia had a feeling that there was more to it. She said, "The feds can't just say, 'We're here now. Get lost.' They certainly can't say, 'Don't make any arrests' when this much local damage has been done."

"Sure they can," said Elizabeth. "They did that two years ago. They put a tight lid on what happened down here. It's as if it never happened at all."

"That was different," said Nadia.

"It always is," said Elizabeth.

"That time it took someone pretty high up."

"It always does," said Elizabeth. "Look, we're almost at my house. This is none of our business. Agreed?"

"I suppose," Nadia answered. "But aren't you curious?"

"A little. Not enough to stick my nose in."

"Well, make sure that Aisha gets to bed early. She's playing in a tournament tomorrow."

"I will."

"And make sure she eats light. No dessert. And no wine."

"Nadia . . . she had a few sips on her birthday. It probably tasted like brake fluid to her. I don't think she'll turn into a lush."

"Well, she shouldn't have had any. We're still Muslims, remember."

"I'll try not to corrupt her, I promise."

9

Yes, she was curious. Yes, she'd try to get over it. But that didn't seem to be working. She and Aisha fixed dinner. After that they played backgammon. Her mind wasn't on it. She lost three straight games.

Her mind was on the names, Whistler and Bannerman and especially on the redhead who'd driven that fuel truck. If Harry Whistler was involved, so, most likely, was Bannerman. Harry wouldn't have come here from Europe without letting Bannerman know. And if Bannerman was in this, that redhead was Carla. She knew Carla to be one of Bannerman's deadliest. Cold as ice, no nerves, many thought her insane. The only part that did not seem to fit was the automatic weapon that she was seen carrying while walking out of that burning house. Carla Benedict was known to work with a knife. Or a set of keys. Or the rat tail of a comb. And sometimes with only a thumb.

Her mind was also on something that Nadia had said. She'd remarked that these people seemed somehow untouchable no matter how much damage they'd done. Bannerman might not have that kind of clout by himself, but no matter, he'd know the people who do and that's the best kind of clout. She understood that someone very high up must have ordered the police to stand down. And the FBI as well? Someone high up indeed. That might explain why the role of that man in the bar was minimized in the newspaper accounts. And if that man, Adam Whistler, is untouchable as well, he must be related to Harry. His son? She couldn't recall Harry ever mentioning a son, but much of that period was a blur.

As for the people in those FBI photos, the way to bet was that they've scattered by now. Professionals don't linger. They hit and they vanish. They were probably no longer on the island. Except Adam Whistler and the woman who was with him. They'd come on a yacht and yachts don't move quickly. They might have left it, of course, but perhaps they did not. Perhaps they're still down at the marina. If they are, perhaps some of the others stayed with them. She was tempted to go and see for herself, to get a firsthand look at who's here. But she wouldn't because she was going to be sensible. She was going to leave well enough alone.

She glanced up at her wall clock. She said to Aisha, "It's your bedtime."

Aisha looked up as well. She said, "It's only nine o'clock."

"You've had a busy day. You'll need your rest for tomorrow."

Aisha said, "I'm wide awake. One more game."

"Um . . . actually," said Elizabeth, "I need to run out. I won't be long, but I want you in bed first."

Aisha looked at her oddly. "Why don't I come with you?"

"It's a private matter. I just need to see someone."

Aisha lowered her eyes. "I think I should come with you."

"Did you hear me say it's private?"

She answered, "Yes, I did. May I say something now?" She didn't wait for Elizabeth to answer. She said, "You've been quiet ever since before dinner. I think I know what's been on your mind and I think I know where you're going. Elizabeth, I think you know who they are. I think you're going down to that boat."

There's such a thing, thought Elizabeth, as being too damned perceptive. But okay. "I . . . might take a quick look."

"Will you be taking your blue duffel?"

"There's no need for that. I'm just going to look. Nothing more."

"There are lots of boats down there. Do you know which one they're on?"

She said, "If it's still there, I'll find it."

"You'll find it quicker if you take me with you. I know how big, what color, and the name on the transom. I heard Jumpy telling those FBI agents."

"So tell me."

"I'll point. I'll go with you and I'll point."

Elizabeth raised her finger. She said, "I'll do the pointing. And right now I'm pointing at your bedroom."

Aisha did come with her. Elizabeth had yielded. Aisha had reminded her that she'd seen the photos that those FBI agents were passing around. The ones with no names, only faces. That was why she might need Aisha's eyes.

That argument, however, was not what persuaded her. She felt sure that she'd recognize at least one of those faces whether she'd seen the photos or not. What did persuade her, although against her better judgment, was the thought that the two of them were less likely to be noticed than if she had gone by herself. A mother and her daughter, out for a stroll. Well, not that perhaps. She'd never pass as Aisha's mother. Not that anyone would look at them that closely.

On reaching the complex at Palmetto Bay, she saw that quite a few people were coming and going. Aside from the marina, there were three busy restaurants and a number of shops in the area. She would not have stood out after all.

Elizabeth cruised the lanes of the parking lot looking for any of the cars that had been mentioned, especially the light brown Ford Taurus. She found a brown Taurus, but she saw two more just like it. A waste of time, she realized. They were probably all rentals. They were exactly the sort that a professional would choose, ones that looked like a few hundred others. She found a parking slot near the narrow roadway that led to the launching hoist and the slips. She killed the engine and switched off the lights. "We'll take a walk down there. Try to act like a tourist. Don't act as if you're looking for someone."

They took their time. They stopped twice at shop windows. A few real tourists, a few boaters, passed going or coming. When they had gone beyond the lights from the storefronts, Elizabeth began to point out several stars, as if that was why they'd walked down there.

They reached the twin ramps that led to the slips that were on either side of the launch ramp. In the moonlight, they could see the entire marina. There were a hundred or more boats of all types and sizes, but only a few showed any sign of activity. There were owners in their cabins, watching TV. Others sat on their decks sipping cocktails.

Two older men were standing near the top of the ramp, both wearing floppy hats, baggy jackets, and shorts. The larger of the two men was fishing for crabs, lowering a four-sided trap. He was chatting with the other man who stood farther down. The other one was busy filleting a fish at a table built into the railing for that purpose. He was chuckling at something that the bigger one had said. All seemed perfectly normal. People fished there all the time.

Elizabeth asked, "Now, what kind of boat is it? Are we looking for power or sail?"

"It's a sailboat. Tan hull. The name is *Last Dollar*."

"If you see it, just say so. Don't point."

Aisha tilted her head. "I think I already have. That big one way down to the right."

Elizabeth shifted her eyes in that direction. The boat Aisha meant was tied up at the fuel dock some three hundred feet from where they stood. It was lit inside and out. She could see movement in the cabin. But the transom was in shadows. She could not make out the name.

Elizabeth shook her head. She said, "That doesn't seem likely."

"Bet it is. It's the only one that fits the description."

Elizabeth remained doubtful. That could not be the one. Not that lit up. And not at a fuel dock. Not unless its owner is awfully sure that he didn't have an enemy in the world. No professional, for that matter, would get caught dead on a sailboat. No speed, no mobility, a thin fiberglass hull. If she were the enemy, that boat, with those on it, would be a lump of melted plastic by now.

Aisha said, "Well, we're here. Don't you want to check it out?"

But as Aisha spoke those words, her voice had trailed off. She had turned to look at something behind them.

"What is it?" asked Elizabeth.

Aisha kept her voice low. "That man with the crab trap. He was staring at us. Now he's speaking into a cell phone."

"Is he watching us now?"

"No, he just turned away. He said something to that other man, the one cleaning the fish. Now the other man is looking at us sideways and . . . uh-oh."

"What is it?"

"The second man. The smaller one. He's one of the men in those FBI photos."

Elizabeth didn't turn because her eyes were on the boat. She saw a woman's figure climbing up through the hatch. The woman was dressed in a dark business suit and she was holding a cell phone to her ear. She stood with one hand cupped over her eyes as if to shade them from the glare of the shore lights. She was looking directly at Elizabeth. Now a young man, or a boy, came through the hatch and joined her. Elizabeth took a breath. No, it wasn't a boy. It was a small, slender woman with red hair.

She said, "Aisha, right now. Walk back to the car."

"What's happening?"

"Just do it. I'll be two steps behind you."

"Oh, boy. I'll try. But I think we're too late. Those two men came over. They're blocking the ramp."

Elizabeth turned. She saw that they had. And that they weren't so old after all. Now she saw that the woman with the cell phone was coming. She had gestured to the redhead, telling her to stay on board. The redhead objected, but she obeyed. The one with the cell phone was approaching the ramp. Her eyes were still locked on Elizabeth.

Aisha took her hand. "How much trouble are we in?"

"I want you to leave. They won't stop you. Go now."

"Leave you here? I won't do that. Who are they, Elizabeth?"

The two men heard Aisha say Elizabeth's name. The big one said, "See? Did I tell you? I told you." The other answered, "I'll be damned."

Elizabeth sighed. "Hello, Billy. Hello, John." Then she cursed herself under her breath.

More of Bannerman's people. She'd ignored her own hunch. And she should have known that if that boat were still there, someone would have been posted to guard its approaches. She'd been living in peace for too long.

The man who said, "I told you" was Billy McHugh. Back then, he was known as Bannerman's monster. A frightening man, unnervingly silent. Come to think of it, she'd never heard him speak before this. But here he was, speaking. He said, "Next time listen," to the smaller man with him. The smaller man repeated, "I'll be damned."

Not only had Elizabeth never heard McHugh speak, she'd never seen a change of expression on his face. But his face now revealed not only surprise but what might pass for pleasure at seeing her again.

John Waldo, the one who kept saying "I'll be damned," had been only slightly more talkative when she knew him. Unremarkable in appearance, you'd never look at him twice. But Waldo, it was said, could move through a darkened house without so much as stirring a curtain. No security system, it was said, could defeat him. No border patrol either. No minefield. His hair was white, but it was white then as well, except when he needed to be someone else. Some other nationality. Even some other sex. Like her, he had worn an abaya in his time. As with her, it had made him invisible.

Billy said, "Hello, Elizabeth. Except weren't you dead?"

Waldo added, "That's what I thought. Good to see that you're not. Except what are you doing down here? Are you part of this?"

When one of them spoke, the other's eyes and head kept moving. Between them, the two men missed nothing. Billy stood with his massive arms folded, one hand probably resting on the butt of a weapon that was slung underneath his left shoulder. Waldo stood with his hands clasped behind him. Waldo's weapon, no doubt, was at the small of his back. Baggy jackets, thought Elizabeth. That alone should have alerted her. They were too covered up for this warm evening.

She answered, "I live here. And I'd like to stay dead. I wish you'd forget that you've seen me."

"You live here? No kidding?"

"And no, I have nothing to do with all this. I want to keep it that way."

Waldo seemed doubtful. "So you're just passing by?"

"Um . . . guys . . . you've been busy. I was curious. Wouldn't you be? What if someone did all this where you live?"

Billy said, "Well, for starters, this wasn't all us. We just got here today. A friend needed a favor. We'll be gone before sunrise tomorrow."

"Was that friend Harry Whistler? Might that be his son's boat?"

"Those are . . . pretty good guesses for someone just curious."

"Forget it," she said, "I'm sorry I asked. Now excuse me; we have to be going ourselves. It's way past this young lady's bedtime."

She took Aisha by the arm, but Aisha resisted. Elizabeth would have thought that she was frozen with fear were it not for the look on her face. Her expression was a mixture of relief and fascination. To Elizabeth's dismay, she extended her hand. She said, "I'm pleased to meet you. My name's Aisha."

John Waldo took her hand, but he used his left. He kept his right hand near his weapon. "Like you heard, my name's John; this is Billy," he said. He looked up at Elizabeth. "So she knows who you are?"

He was asking, of course, how much Aisha knew, and therefore how much he could say in her presence. He was also asking her what name she was using. She had answered to Elizabeth, but Elizabeth what? He expected an alias. She chose not to enlighten him. She'd have preferred that they hadn't heard Aisha's name either. Too uncommon. Too easy to find.

Elizabeth answered, "She knows more than enough. And we really have to be going."

Aisha said, "But, Elizabeth, if these men are old friends . . ."

"They're not friends. They're simply men I once knew. And they know that I mean no offense."

Neither man had made room to allow her to pass. "I'm offended," said Billy. "You're not being nice. Here's a girl with good manners. You could learn a few things."

Elizabeth groaned. She could scarcely believe this. Here's Bannerman's monster pretending to sulk. Here's a world-class killer, gun, knife, or bare hands, telling her that she's being antisocial.

"Stay a minute," said John Waldo. "Molly's coming. Say hello."

Elizabeth turned. She saw that the woman who had stepped off the boat had slowed midway to the ramp. She was tapping out a number on her cell phone as she walked. Elizabeth knew of only one Molly. She asked, "That would be Molly Farrell?"

"Yeah, you met her?"

"Just that once."

"Oh, yeah," Waldo nodded. "In Chamonix, right? You holed up there with Kessler for a couple of months."

"It was where I met most of you, yes."

Elizabeth had especially liked Molly Farrell. Very young back then. Even younger than she was. Sad eyes, but warm-hearted. They had had some long talks. She had seemed not at all like the rest of that crowd, but Elizabeth had learned that she was every bit as lethal. She was Bannerman's expert in electronics, explosives.

She asked John Waldo, "Who is she calling?"

"Bannerman, most likely."

"About me? Damn it, John . . ."

"No harm to you. She's just touching base. We won't mess up your life, I guarantee you."

"Is he here on the island?"

"We didn't need him for this. Molly's Bannerman's right hand; she's been calling the shots. She wants a few words. Don't rush off."

Molly must have asked them to hold her. Very well. She would stay for another five minutes. Aisha, in the meantime, had lost any sense that these might be dangerous people. She was asking John and Billy, "So this Bannerman is your boss?"

Billy rocked a hand. "We don't think of him that way."

Waldo squinted. "We don't? Then what is he?"

"You say 'boss' and people think, like, a Mafia thing." He turned to Aisha. He said, "He's more like a coach. Except coaches yell sometimes. He never yells."

Aisha smiled. "I have coaches who yell."

"Oh, yeah? You play sports? You look like you play sports."

"Not another word, Aisha," said Elizabeth.

Waldo scowled. "Here's a kid who knows how to converse with adults and here's you telling her to shut up. Don't you know what that does? That arrests her development." He said to Aisha, "Your age, I played stickball. Down here, you can't do that, I guess. Too many trees."

Elizabeth glowered. "John, what are you doing?"

"Catching up. Making small talk. Hey, come on. It's been years."

"And giving Molly Farrell time to finish her call. By the way, when did she become Bannerman's right hand? Anton Zivic had that job last I heard. Is he dead?"

"So now you're asking questions. It's okay for you?"

"Keep this up and I'll arrest *your* development."

A smile. "Zivic's fine. You want to hear this or not?"

She had met Anton Zivic. An interesting man. He'd been a KGB colonel, stationed in Rome. Once Bannerman's enemy, then an ally, then a friend. An elegant man. Cultivated. Well read. More a planner and a strategist. More like Bannerman himself for that matter.

Waldo said, "He's still in Westport, but he had to slow down. He needed two new hips and a rod up his spine. He got car-bombed. You never heard?"

Elizabeth shook her head. "No, I hadn't."

"It was when he went back to Rome for a visit. Some old grudge. We took care of it. Anyway, Anton gets around pretty good. He runs this fancy antique shop in Westport. You ever get up there? Stop in. He'd like to see you."

Billy said, "You should. You'd get a discount, I bet."

"I don't travel so much anymore."

Billy said, "He gave my wife a good deal on two lamps. These were Tiffany lamps. You know, like church windows. And he got us a whole rack of old copper pots that my wife has hung up in the kitchen."

"And she uses them," said Waldo. "Hell of a cook. She's Italian. Best cooks in the world."

"The secret's fresh vegetables." Billy patted his stomach. "I grow them myself. I got a garden."

This newest revelation was almost too much. Billy McHugh has a woman? An actual wife? And he's growing tomatoes and peppers in his yard? Next she'll hear that he shops the garage sales and bakes casseroles for new neighbors.

Waldo saw her surprise. He found it amusing. He said, "Billy's been housebroken some since you knew him. He was living in this rooming house, run by a widow. One thing led to another. You know how it is."

No, thought Elizabeth. She couldn't imagine it.

"Bannerman, too," Waldo told her. "He's married."

"That I knew," said Elizabeth, "but as I recall, some of you were against it at the time."

"Some of us, yeah, but only at first. Susan, that's her name, came to Westport to snoop. She was a newspaper reporter. Worse than that, her father, he's this ex-cop named Lesko, didn't want his daughter near Bannerman either. Damned near killed him after someone else tried to kill Susan. That's another long story, but it worked out okay. He's part of the family. He got married himself."

"That's nice," said Elizabeth. She was still watching Molly.

"Got his own kid," said Billy. "Hey, you know who he

married? Elena Brugg. You heard of her, right? The Brugg family? Zurich?"

"Not off-hand," said Elizabeth.

"The family's worth about nine zillion dollars. But she falls in love with this ex-New York cop who's as ugly as Billy and almost as scary. It's funny how it happened. That's another . . ."

"Long story?"

"Maybe when you're not so rushed," said John Waldo. He paused, then brightened. He said, "Hey, you know what? Bannerman and Susan have a six-year-old daughter and another kid's due any time now. The whole crew's flying in to get a look at the baby. We'll talk some business, but a lot of it's social. It's like when we all went to Chamonix."

"I'll send a stuffed animal," said Elizabeth.

"You ought to come up. Bring Aisha here with you." He asked Aisha, "Would you like that? We're more fun than you think. Don't listen to Ms. Stride here on that subject."

Cute, thought Elizabeth. He'd just confirmed her last name. Aisha had shown no confusion on hearing it. But she knew that it was pointless to have tried to keep it from them. After this, if they wanted to find her, they'd find her.

Aisha said, "Sure I would. If Elizabeth goes. But she doesn't seem crazy about the idea. Could I ask . . . who's that woman who stayed on the boat?"

"There's three," said Waldo. "Which one do you mean?"

"The one with red hair. The one who's pacing the cockpit."

Waldo looked. "Oh, her? She's one of our friends. She flew down with Molly this morning."

"Is she, like . . . a killer?"

"Just a little bad-tempered."

"She's the one I've been hearing about all afternoon." She looked up at Elizabeth. "So, you know her after all."

"I wasn't sure then."

"Can I meet her?"

"You may not."

Waldo let out an exaggerated sigh. "See that?" he said to Aisha. "Antisocial again. You, you're willing to meet some

new people. She doesn't even care about seeing old friends.
You'd think she would have asked who else is here."

Elizabeth said, "I already know. That *is* Carla Benedict on
that yacht, is it not?" Molly had told her to stay put for some
reason. "It was Carla who blew up that house with a fuel
truck. It was probably Carla who took out that jet. Nice to
see that she's learned to calm down."

"She didn't do the plane. And she's calmer than you think.
Did you know that she owns a bookstore in Westport? Sells
a lot of Harry Potter. She does readings for kids."

This was more than too much. "I am . . . happy for her."

"Her bookstore's right near Anton's. Nice restaurant in
between. And she has a boyfriend. I don't think you'd know
him. She's had bad luck with boyfriends, but this one has
lasted."

"That's what you call bad luck?" asked Elizabeth. "She
kept killing them."

Billy said, "Nah, that was just that Italian. Before him was
Doc Russo, but she didn't kill the Doc. The same people
who tried to kill Susan got him, but with Carla some people
just assume."

"The new guy," said Waldo, "is a Russian, like Zivic. Like
Zivic, he's ex-KGB. Carla met him in Moscow and, yeah,
she did shoot him, but they got along better after that."

"Good story," said Billy, "but it's not for young ears."

"Those young ears," said Elizabeth, "have heard quite
enough."

"No, I haven't," said Aisha. "They got along *better*?"

Waldo said to Elizabeth, "Hey, you brought it up. The
point is . . ."

"The point is," said Elizabeth, "that you're all peaceful
citizens except when you're killing each other."

Waldo frowned. "Not each other."

"You know what I'm saying."

"Yeah, I do. And I think you know how it is. Carla's still
Carla when she needs to be Carla. Bannerman's still Bannerman. We're all who we are."

She said quietly, "Not all of us. I'm out of it, John."

"I hear you. But you better talk to Molly."

"What about?"

"Someone's looking for you. Some guy name of Bourne. Here she comes. Let her tell you about it."

10

Artemus Bourne had dined alone in his study. He did not look up as his maid cleared the dishes and his butler placed a brandy on his desk. His attention was focused on a large well-thumbed atlas that he had been perusing through dinner.

No one, he reflected, seemed to have much use for a big heavy atlas these days. It's all on computers. CD-ROM discs. Nothing ever seems quite as real on a screen as it does in a handsomely bound volume. The world is not a video game.

He enjoyed, of an evening, tracing his fingers over those countries whose economies he had influenced. Twenty-two, to be precise. Spread over three continents. In a few, he damned near *was* the economy.

In its margins he had jotted the key industries he owned, the commodity markets he had cornered. He had penned the names and titles of a hundred officeholders who were, inextricably, in his pocket. Not named, but envisioned, were the thousands of workers who trudged off to their jobs every morning. Tens of thousands. A million. He'd never troubled to count them. All secure in the conceit that their lives are their own. Well, they're not, thought Bourne. They are mine.

Megalomania? No. Megalomania is delusional. There was nothing delusional about it. Hard-hearted? No. It was realistic. Even honest. He was not among those hypocrites who claimed to act for the good of the common man, the employee, and certainly not the stockholder. They're the worker bees. They exist to be used. All that fuss in the media about Enron et al., as if it were news that investors get fleeced. Of course they get fleeced. It has been ever thus. Instead of whining about it, they should count their blessings. They're lucky to be living in this century.

In ages past he would have been a duke ten times over. Owning castles on the hill. Conscripting armies of peasants. Sending them off to battle to enlarge his holdings. Executing any laggards among them.

These days, we field armies of lawyers and accountants. Not traditionally a criminal class in themselves, but a distinction that's becoming increasingly blurred. We still need to augment them with more overt malefactors such as our Chester Lilly and his ilk. Those dukes, no doubt, had their own Chester Lillys to deal with any who became inconvenient. They also had bishops to persuade all the peasants that suffering is good, the more brutish, the better. Each stroke of the lash adds a brick to the palace that awaits you in heaven, so shut up.

We've lost the romance of that era, thought Bourne. We still confer knighthoods, but we call them vice presidents. We no longer have dungeons, torture chambers, the rack; we've replaced them with unending litigation. Where that fails, we still execute the occasional upstart. That's the only part left that's exciting.

Oh, not true, thought Bourne. It's *all* exciting. It's a kick. Even the annoyances like this business in Angola. They distract, but they do wonders to stir up the blood. No, the world is not a video game, but it is a great game nonetheless.

Among his amusements, sipping brandy with his atlas, was to contemplate national borders. Those on the African continent in particular, and its neighbor next door, the Middle East. Every border was either a political fiction or the product of somebody's whim. Most were drawn by this or that colonial power. Whole countries created with the squiggle of a pen. Winston Churchill once created at least five that Bourne knew of within the space of about fifteen minutes.

Churchill said, "You want borders? There they are. Let's move on." And those lines were drawn with utter indifference to the wishes and the claims of the people who lived there. On the other hand, the people, the tribes that were affected, were utterly indifferent to those lines as well. "Call the country what you will, but it isn't *our* country. Place your borders where you will, but they aren't our borders. These are our ancestral lands and you can't have them."

It was a recipe, certainly, for eternal tribal conflict. All loyalties are tribal, not national. Territorial disputes would have tribe fighting tribe when they weren't fighting a central authority that they rightly saw as having no legitimacy. And when one group takes power by fair mean or foul, they'll give all the best jobs to their fellow tribesmen because that's where their loyalties are; that's who they trust. Inevitably, everyone else feels left out and, *voilà,* we have the seeds of civil war.

The European powers saw this coming, of course. It was wonderful news for their arms industries. The central authorities would need lots of weapons. They wouldn't last a month without the wherewithal to keep the disenfranchised at bay. The rebelling tribes would need modern weapons because without them all we'd get is a lot of wholesale hacking as we've seen in Rwanda and elsewhere. We really don't mind them shooting each other. But we do tend to squirm when they hack.

The main thing, however, is to keep them all busy fighting and fearing each other. For all the pious mouthings about peace and stability, no interested foreign government wants either. Most African governments certainly don't. Almost all are administered by minority tribesmen who would soon be sent packing by an honest election. Every Arab regime along with them. Give them peace and stability and the first thing you know, they'll start noticing that they're being plundered.

Roger Clew had made a snide remark to that effect. He'd asked, "Why the interest in Sierra Leone? You haven't finished looting Angola."

Hmmph! Roger Clew. A fine one to talk.

Clew's government was happy to back Jonas Savimbi when the coastal one third of that country was Marxist. So, in fact, was Savimbi, when it suited his purpose. Clew's government switched sides when the Soviets imploded. All that lovely oil. Let's rethink our ideology. We'll dump Savimbi, but let's not let him be defeated. We need him so that coastal Angola needs us. Let Savimbi keep them busy while we pump their offshore oil and while our fishing fleets gobble up their seafood.

We won't be piggish about it. They'll get their fair share. Or at least a few hundred of them will. If they didn't, they wouldn't be able to buy all those guns and tanks and land mines that we sell them. They'd need them to fend off Mr. Savimbi, who seemed to feel betrayed for some reason. And we certainly can't sell U.S. weapons to Savimbi. That might strike our coastal friends as duplicitous. So we'll have someone else sell him someone else's weapons. The Israelis, for example. Let's let them make a buck. This way everyone comes out ahead.

Very sensible, thought Bourne. Make sure nobody wins. Each side wants it all, but they can't get it; it's a stalemate. Oh, the Coastals did manage to knock off Savimbi, whose behavior was becoming increasingly bizarre. Burning witches. That sort of thing. Savimbi, just as likely, was betrayed by his own for the sin of getting bad press. Betrayed by Duganga, his old comrade in arms? No, not by Duganga. He would not have had the spine. If anyone, it would be Alameo.

With Savimbi gone, things did settle down. They still send out patrols and they ambush each other, but they also do business with each other. Smuggling is rampant. It employs tens of thousands. Deals are made by cell phone, by radio, and even in person by groups that slip in through their porous lines of battle. The two sides must maintain close radio contact in order to arrange safe passage for the smugglers lest they blunder into a minefield. Also for Red Cross aid workers and such.

Bourne could pick up his phone and call Luanda right now and get patched straight through to Duganga himself at one of his shifting headquarters. He wouldn't, of course. Deniability, you know. Best to stay several layers removed. But he would call Alameo. He would do so with relish. He had, many times, rehearsed in his mind the words he would say to that man on the day when he finally had Stride in his grasp.

Where were we? thought Bourne. He had lost his train of thought. Ah, yes. Mr. Clew. The annoying Mr. Clew. And Clew's naïve scruples re: Angola.

Long before the oil, the diamonds, the seafood, Clew's government helped itself to its populace as well. Very well, not the government. The landowners. Same thing. Three out of every ten African slaves were taken from that one coastal region. They were always the strongest, the biggest, the healthiest, all the better to survive an ocean crossing. Name a top black athlete and you'd get good odds that his forebears were snatched in Angola.

What made them so hearty? No one seems to be sure. It is one of those mysteries of genetics. It certainly couldn't have been what they eat. The cassava root appears to have been their staple ever since they walked on two legs. It's the Angolan equivalent of Ireland's potato except that practically no one else eats it. All cassava is used for in the rest of the world is to make tapioca for puddings. And the damned stuff is poison if not properly prepared. One must leach it to get the cyanide out. Leach it and dry it and then God knows what. But how in the world did they discover the process? By trial and error? That sounds terribly incautious. Unless their taste-testers were their *own* slaves or captives. Or perhaps they tried recipes on the old and the weak.

Of course, thought Bourne. The old and the weak. The deformed and the short and the stupid. In the long run that would certainly strengthen the gene pool. The testers must have also included the ugly because they're a handsome people as well. Fine-looking women. Beautiful children.

Malnourished on the whole, but the bone structure's there. Those twenty young girls that Bobik was transporting should be quite a treat for that . . . what's his name? . . . Moshood . . . during the trip up to Gambia.

Which reminded him . . .

Bourne thumbed his atlas to the page that showed the entire west coast of the continent. He traced a finger from Angola to Sierra Leone. Let's see, he thought. It's eight o'clock in Virginia. It's four hours later in Sierra Leone. That freighter of Bobik's should just about be there for their rendezvous with that cannibal's men. Bourne wondered what arrangements Clew decided on making, not that it mattered very much. The main thing is that Clew is keeping his word. He is looking for Elizabeth Stride.

Bourne's informant was Clew's driver, one Alex Rakowsky. Well, no, that's not accurate either. Clew's paunchy driver was not on the payroll. He had simply been tasked by another of Clew's colleagues to observe and report on Clew's behavior. The driver had been told that Clew was suspected of running some rogue operation. Secret files, clandestine contacts, and the like.

"Keep your eyes and ears open, keep us informed. It's an additional duty, so we'll up you a pay grade. That will make for a nicer retirement check. No harm to Mr. Clew. We assure you of that. You might even help to save him from himself."

The driver was talked into it. He must not be very bright. He would not have made the cut in Angola. Thanks to him, however, we knew of Clew's jogging habits and were able to have our private chat. And we learned, although too late, that Clew carried a recorder along with a pistol in that belted thing he wore. We know that he recorded our conversation because the driver heard him test his machine after he'd gone home and showered. That was unexpected. And an annoyance. Who'd have thought that Clew would go out jogging wired? A few parts of that discussion had potential for discomfort should they find their way into the media. And Clew's recorder, according to the driver, seems to be a sophisticated piece of equipment. It records, it makes phone calls, and it downloads computers.

Damned gadgets. There's a new one every time you turn around. He was glad that he stayed out of that business.

On returning home, Clew had gone to his computer and called up several files on Elizabeth Stride. The driver says that one bore her likeness. Great news. We'd been told that no photographs existed. Clew downloaded it into his sneaky machine in order to take it to work with him. This must be a good thing. It means that Clew is on the hunt. We also know that Clew must have called Paul Bannerman, probably using that same machine and probably on his way home from our encounter. We infer this because, according to his driver, Bannerman replied with an encrypted message. We don't know what it said, but whatever it was, the message seemed pleasing to Clew. According to the driver, as reported back at State, "Clew smiled and he got a little dreamy about it." Is that how he'd respond upon hearing that she's dead? Of course not. Therefore, she's alive.

Bourne thumbed forward again to the map of Angola. He ran his fingers over the eastern two-thirds, the part once controlled by Savimbi, now Duganga, and of course by our friend Alameo. It was also the half that would not be worth having were it not for the fact that it was littered with diamonds. Control those diamonds, the best in the world, and you hold the world's diamond trade hostage. The South Africans, the Belgians, the Israelis would come begging. And he'd almost done it. At one point, he'd almost done it. And he would have were it not for Alameo's interference.

"Alameo?" he murmured. "We really must talk."

It won't be in anger; I'll be perfectly civil, your recent behavior notwithstanding. Oh, it's true that I was miffed when I saw those three heads, but I've come to appreciate the grandeur of the thing. In fairness, you must come to appreciate me. I intend to persuade you that you're on the wrong side. I intend, very soon, to have something you want. I'm assured that it is something that you value most highly, more than life itself by all accounts.

I intend to have Elizabeth Stride.

11

"Give me a minute with her first," said John Waldo. He broke off to intercept Molly.

Elizabeth waited as the two of them huddled. She saw him gesture toward Aisha, explaining her presence. He took longer on the subject of Elizabeth's resurrection, recounting, no doubt, how much she'd been told. Molly's lips said, "Let me speak to her privately."

She approached with a smile and offered her hand. She shook hands with Elizabeth and with Aisha in turn. She studied Aisha's face. She said, "Aisha. That's a Muslim name, isn't it?"

Aisha nodded. "Yes, it is. Hello, Molly."

"The name of Mohammed's favorite wife, am I right?"

"Uh-huh. But it's pretty common now."

"On this island?"

"Not really. But we have lots of others."

"Other Muslims?"

"Mostly women. But some of them use English names now because . . ."

"Aisha," said Elizabeth, "that'll keep."

Molly looked at Elizabeth. "No end of surprises." She said to Aisha, "Could I ask you a favor? Take a short walk with Billy. I need a few minutes with Elizabeth."

Aisha looked at Elizabeth, who said, "Go. It's all right."

Molly said to Waldo, "John, I'd like you to stay." Billy placed a hand, lightly, on Aisha's shoulder. "You want to go look at the boat?" he asked.

Elizabeth said, "I'd rather she didn't."

Billy leaned toward her. "Let's lighten up, okay?"

For an instant, as he said it, Billy's eyes turned cold and dead. She was getting a glimpse of the Billy she remembered. It didn't frighten her exactly, but it did give her pause. Billy used that hesitation to turn Aisha toward the ramp. Elizabeth did not try to stop them.

Molly Farrell watched them go. She said, "Lovely girl."

"She is. She's very special," said Elizabeth.

"I wouldn't worry about her meeting Carla. Carla's better with kids than you'd imagine."

"Harry Potter," said Elizabeth. "I just heard."

"Carla's nose is out of joint because I made her stay on post. You can say hello later. She's a big fan of yours. She never realized that you were the Black Angel until after you and Kessler had left Chamonix. She thought you were just Kessler's woman."

"I'm not the Black Angel anymore," said Elizabeth.

"And what about Aisha? Does she know about you?"

"She does, but it no longer matters."

Molly seemed bemused. She was shaking her head. "Well, someone has to say it. It's a very small world. Six degrees of separation and all that."

Waldo wasn't sure that he followed. He asked, "What's that 'six degrees' part?"

"It's a theory," Molly told him. "It means we're all linked. We know hundreds of people. Each of those knows hundreds more. In the end, we know people who know everyone."

Waldo wasn't so sure. He said, "We know our own kind. That's a lot more important, I think."

Elizabeth added, "And most of us seem to be here."

Molly answered, "Well, a few. You've heard some of it from John. Harry Whistler's son, Adam, got involved in that shooting. He's a good man. You'd like him. He's very much Harry's son. He would have tried to mind his own business, but Claudia, his . . . friend, forced the issue."

"In what way?"

"She threw the knife. She's an unusual young woman." Molly threw a glance toward the boat. "She's aboard. We're just getting to know her ourselves. The third woman is her mother. She flew in today, too. The mother and Harry, it seems, have grown close. She's been widowed even longer than he has."

"I'm . . . glad for Harry," said Elizabeth to Molly. She said to Waldo, "Is that true? With a table knife?"

"Twenty feet, moving target. Some throw. Could you do that?"

"Not on purpose."

"Even Carla said she couldn't. You know why? You're both human. This Claudia, however, goes you one better. It turns out that she's also an angel."

Molly said, "He's not kidding. She does think she's an angel."

"Not your kind, either," said Waldo. "A real one. A year or so ago she got shot, almost died. She had a . . . I forget . . . Molly, what do they call that?"

"A near-death experience," Molly answered.

"Right," said Waldo. "So she's pretty much dead. Not breathing, no heartbeat, no nothing. Then she meets this white light I keep hearing about. It's St. Peter? God? I don't know. She doesn't either. Whatever it was said she's being sent back as young Adam's guardian angel. I'm not saying I believe it, but I'll tell you, she believes it. You might, too, when you hear a few things she's done since. Adam says she talks to birds and the birds talk to her. That plane that went down? She might have done that with birds."

I'm so glad that Aisha's not hearing this, thought Elizabeth. *I hope she's not hearing it on that boat.*

Molly said to John, "Let's not get into that now." She said

to Elizabeth, "Let's get back to why we're here. There were some people hunting Adam. He's been trying to lie low. But that shooting forced his hand and . . . well it's not important how . . . but the people who were after him saw this on the evening news and decided to come down here and finish him. His father knew that Adam was in danger. Harry and his people jetted over from Geneva, but he realized that they couldn't get here in time. So he called Paul Bannerman. We were down here in two hours. All we wanted to do was get Adam off the island, but things got a bit out of control."

"Is Harry here now?"

"As we speak, he and Adam are down at Jump & Phil's. It's all boarded up, so it's private. Harry brought the twins with him. Do you remember the twins?"

The Beasleys, thought Elizabeth. Donald and Dennis. Murderous, paunchy identical twins. Both would now be in their fifties. Been with Harry for years. "I saw one of them," she said. "At Chamonix."

"They were both there," said Waldo. "You just didn't know it. See one, and the other one's behind you."

"In any case," said Molly, "they're still settling a few things. But the trouble seems done with. We'll all be gone soon. Harry's thanking a few locals who've been a great help, including that girl who was kidnapped."

"You must have had more help than that," said Elizabeth. "Who got the local cops to back off?"

"Roger Clew. Paul called him early this morning before we left Westport to fly down here. Clew got the FBI to keep the law off us if we should run into problems. Have you ever met Roger, Elizabeth?"

"I haven't, but I know who he is."

"Which brings me back to my 'small world' remark. It turned out that Roger was about to call Paul because he had a request of his own. Roger is pretty sure that you're dead, but he's asked Paul to confirm it."

Elizabeth frowned. "And now Bannerman knows I'm not."

"Paul won't compromise you. Don't worry about that. Clew was asking on behalf of Artemus Bourne. Does that name mean anything to you?"

"I've seen it in the papers. Worth billions? Big oil?"

"Big a lot of things," said Molly. "Bourne thinks you're still alive, but Roger says he's not sure. If you are, he wants to meet you; he wouldn't say why. But he promises to make it worth your while."

"Do you know him?"

"We know of him. We can't help being impressed. He makes the old robber barons look like bicycle thieves. So Paul wonders what makes you this important to him. The message is that he'll meet you at a place of your choosing. There's fifty thousand dollars in it for you."

"But you have no idea what this Bourne wants from me?"

Molly shook her head. "Nor does Roger. Roger, by the way, has no use for Bourne. He agreed to ask, but only because he got something in exchange. Bourne tipped him on some sort of arms deal."

"So it's all the same to him if I decline?"

"That's my take."

"Then that's it," said Elizabeth. "I'm not interested, Molly."

"There's more to the message. Bourne asked Clew to tell you, '*He* isn't dead either.' He told Clew, 'She'll know who I mean.'"

Elizabeth closed her eyes. "I said the answer is no."

"Would that 'he' be Martin Kessler, by chance?"

A deep sigh. "Probably." She glanced down toward the boat. Aisha and Billy were standing in the cockpit, Carla was sitting on the railing. A middle-aged woman had come up through the hatch followed by another, very pretty, much younger. The younger one . . . that would be the angel, she assumed. Wonderful, thought Elizabeth. That's all Aisha needs. A new friend who thinks she's been to heaven.

She said, "Listen, Molly . . . I want to stay dead. But Bannerman won't lie to Clew, will he?"

"No, he won't lie. But he'll say that you're dead as far as Bourne is concerned. He'll ask Roger to leave it at that."

Elizabeth asked, "He won't tell Clew where I am?"

Molly shook her head. "Not without your permission. He did say that Roger's hot to meet you himself if you should turn out to be alive."

"Let's . . . not open that door, okay, Molly?"

"It's your call."

"I'd be grateful."

"Then it's done," Molly told her. "So where's Martin Kessler? Is he here?"

"Martin's dead."

"As you wish."

"No," she said softly. "In his case it's real. This was not the first trouble we've had on this island. I won't take the time to go into it now, but we stopped it, Martin mostly, and it cost him his life. Martin's been dead for two years."

Molly and John exchanged curious glances. Elizabeth felt sure that she knew what they were thinking. She said, "No, he did not shoot himself in Romania. He staged it so that both of us could be dead. He showed up back here a few months later."

"Wait a minute," said Waldo. "Let me get this straight. You died on an exercise bike. When was that?"

"A little more than three years ago."

"And the Bucharest hotel thing was when?"

"Less than a year later. But as I've said . . ."

"We heard you," said Waldo. "Bucharest never happened. Fact is, we knew that story was bullshit because too many people saw Kessler after that. Except now you're saying he's been dead for two years. He's been seen since then, too, from what I hear."

"That's not possible."

"Well, tell that to Harry Whistler," said Waldo. "Harry, or I guess it was one of the twins, spotted Kessler in Switzerland . . . I don't know . . . eighteen months ago. He was walking down the street in Davos dressed like a Davos ski instructor."

"A ski instructor?"

"Red jumpsuit with badges."

Elizabeth made a face. "Next you'll tell me he spoke to him."

"From what I hear, he would have, but he wasn't sure at first. But then Kessler must have spotted him, too, because he saw Kessler glance over his shoulder as if he knew that the other twin must be near. Only someone who knew them would do that."

"And?"

"That's it," said Waldo. "Kessler crossed the street and ducked him. The twin figured he had reasons, so he left them alone."

"John . . . people 'glance' when they're crossing a street. Very few of them are checking for identical twins." She paused. "Wait a minute. You said 'them'?"

"He was with some woman. She had regular ski clothes. She was probably signed up for a lesson."

"Attractive?"

"Hey, Elizabeth . . ."

She grimaced. "I'm sorry. Stupid question. Forget it."

She had found herself envisioning a beautiful young woman, tailored ski suit, splendid body, hugging him as they walked, Martin nuzzling her, grinning, on their way to some hotel room. Look at me, she thought angrily. Getting jealous. It's insane.

"It could not have been Martin," she said firmly.

Waldo shrugged. "Suit yourself. But that wasn't the first time." He turned to Molly. "Where else did we hear?"

"Tel Aviv, as I recall."

"Yeah, that's right. Tel Aviv. That was more like a year ago. We heard he hooked up with the Mossad."

"Well, he didn't."

Molly squinted as if she were trying to remember. She said to Waldo, "Some job involving Africa, wasn't it?"

"Something like that. Let me think."

"And diamonds," said Molly. "It was something about diamonds."

Waldo brightened. "Yeah, diamonds. Him and the Israelis. The Israelis are into a whole lot of things; they don't spend all their time fighting Arabs. The Israelis are big in the diamond trade lately. West African diamonds. Best in the world. But the Israelis have to smuggle them out because of this boycott that De Beers, I think, started. The boycott's on those countries where the rebels mine the diamonds and sell them to buy guns and drugs."

Molly shrugged. "Some boycott. It's not going to work. Once a diamond has been polished and cut, there's no way to tell where it came from."

Waldo said, "That's my point. Get them out and then cut them. Maybe Kessler's doing some smuggling for them."

"I don't know," said Molly. "He'd have to know Africa. I don't recall that he'd ever been there."

"Maybe not," said Waldo, "but it's still about diamonds. Tel Aviv's already a big cutting center. In five years, they want to be bigger than Antwerp. Anyhow, that's twice someone saw him."

Elizabeth sighed. This was getting ridiculous. First a Swiss ski instructor, then an Israeli agent, and now maybe a smuggler of West African diamonds. Next we'll hear that he's in partnership with Elvis. All of this, to Elizabeth, was absurd on its face. She said as much to Molly and Waldo.

It was she, to begin with, who had worked with the Mossad and someone must have gotten them mixed up. And even if Martin had survived by some miracle, he would never work with the Mossad. He'd always said they're too tricky, too devious for him, aside from always being too serious. He'd worked with them once, but that was for her and only because she'd been shot. They'd both set out to track down the people who shot her. They both had their own sources; it made sense to work together lest they end up putting holes in each other. In the end, in fact, it was one of Martin's sources who helped them to recover the Ceausescus' cache of diamonds.

Those diamonds, thought Elizabeth. That must be it. Someone had confused an event years ago with some more recent rumor about Martin.

She said, "Aside from Martin not trusting the Mossad, why would they want to work with Martin Kessler?"

Molly shrugged. "They did once. You just said so."

"They had no choice; they needed each other, but that wasn't a match made in heaven. I mean, Martin's father served in Hitler's Counter Intelligence Service. Martin, himself, had been Stasi."

"Elizabeth," said Molly, "they wouldn't have cared. It's

not as if his father ran Auschwitz. Anyway, Martin hadn't even been born until after that war had ended."

Elizabeth shook her head. "Add the difference in temperament. The Mossad's a deliberate, no-nonsense service that thinks in terms of long-range objectives. Martin was nuts. He didn't think past next week. He would have been nothing but trouble."

Elizabeth paused. She raised her fingers to her temples. She remembered what Martin had said to Aisha. "*I'm like a bad penny. I'll keep turning up.*" She said, "Damn it, why am I talking about this? Martin's dead. There's no question about it."

Molly asked her, "You say he died on this island?"

"Just off it." She gestured toward the ocean.

"I guess I have to ask how and when."

Elizabeth saw that Aisha and Billy were returning. Aisha waved a farewell to the three still on the boat after shaking each of their hands. As she walked up the dock, she met Elizabeth's eyes, her head cocked to one side, an odd expression on her face. Aisha couldn't possibly have heard Martin's name, but she looked the way she'd look if she had. Elizabeth dismissed the thought as it formed. Perceptiveness is one thing; reading minds is another. Or maybe Whistler's angel sent a seagull up to listen and the seagull flew back to report. Is that crazy? Why crazy? It would make as much sense as Martin Kessler's resurrection. Now we even have the Holy Land involved.

She'd talked about Martin enough for one day. She didn't need another discussion. On the other hand, she thought, let's put an end to this subject and not hear about any more sightings.

She said, "Aisha, come up here and listen to this. I'm going to go through this just one more time and then never talk about it again."

She turned to Molly and began telling the story of the terrorists who had come to the island.

"Aisha's hearing this," she said, "because it's her they came to kill. It was the second attempt on her life here. Aisha's uncle was behind it; he'd already killed her parents. You don't need to know why, but that's the essence."

Molly reached to touch Aisha. She whispered, "I'm sorry." To Elizabeth, she said, "Please go on."

"The second attempt was with a nuclear device. It was the warhead from a Russian artillery shell. They only had the warhead, not the trigger mechanism. They couldn't detonate it, but they could and did leak it. It might have killed every living thing within miles if Martin hadn't reached it in time."

Waldo looked at Molly. "Did we know about this?"

Molly shook her head. "It's news to me. And if Paul knows, he's never shared it."

Elizabeth explained why it had been suppressed. A special antiterrorist task force created by the National Security Council had enshrouded the event and its participants. They had done the same thing with several other failed attacks that had no connection with this one. "The policy was to keep them quiet, avert panic, but this was before the nine/eleven attack and the so-called war we're in now."

Molly said, "Then I would think that Roger Clew should have known."

"Clew sits on the council?"

"No, but his boss at the time did," said Molly. "That was Barton Fuller. He and Roger were close. Fuller surely would have briefed him on this."

Elizabeth agreed. "On the big picture, yes, but not about me and Martin. Not about Aisha and some friends of ours either. The man who headed the task force had made a decision to keep all of our names out of this. He knew that if he didn't, someone else might try for us. That would have put us back where we started and this island might not have been so lucky."

"He would have kept your names from Roger?"

"Unless Roger asked."

Molly understood. "And why would he?" she said. "He would not have expected a name that he'd recognize. But how did you get involved in the first place?"

Elizabeth waved a hand. "Let's just get to how it ended. Martin had taken a bullet in the belly, but he managed to get to the terrorists' boat. He'd caught Aisha's uncle; made the uncle come with him. Martin took the uncle and the yacht out to sea. By the time Martin got them a few miles out, they had all been fatally exposed. Neither one could survive and Martin knew that. With police boats and Coast Guard patrol boats in pursuit, he kept going until he was out of sight of land. He found a reef and ran the boat aground on it."

She said, "The Navy was called in. They used divers to surround it with floating booms and helicopters to drop some sort of dome on the boat. Next they pumped a thick foam through that covering. They did that in order to contain the radiation until specialized equipment could arrive the next morning. Until then, they kept their distance, but the boat was surrounded. Martin had sealed himself in the main cabin when they started pumping the foam. He had Aisha's uncle with him and he gave him a choice between dying hard and dying easy."

She said, "The uncle spilled his guts and provided the names of everyone else who was behind this. Martin put him on the radio, made him tell the authorities. Then Martin threw him out. He suffocated in the foam. Having done that, Martin asked to be patched through to me. They couldn't find me, so he spoke to Aisha and asked her to take care of me. He told her that he was about to sit down, have a drink, put his feet up, and relax. He said the bar was well stocked; no use wasting it."

"Sounds like Kessler," said Waldo. "I remember one time . . ."

Molly said, "Hold that thought. Let her finish."

"The next morning," said Elizabeth, "they boarded the boat and cut their way through the hardened foam. They found Aisha's uncle where Martin had left him. Martin, however, was nowhere to be found."

"He swam away," said Aisha.

Molly asked, "Um . . . swam to where?"

"Well, I know that he couldn't have swum back to shore. There must have been another boat that picked him up."

Molly seemed confused. "While the Coast Guard was watching?"

"Exactly," said Elizabeth. "It couldn't have happened. He did get off the boat, but he went nowhere but down. He had to have left the boat just after dark because the foam, we heard later, would be starting to harden. After sundown, the boat was lit up with floodlights. So he had a period of a half hour, tops, when he could have slipped into the water unseen, but he would have been spotted if he surfaced. He didn't surface. He swam underwater with an outgoing tide. He swam until he drowned. The tide took it from there."

Molly said, "I still don't get it. What would have been the point?"

A sad shrug. "You knew Martin. This was typical Martin. He might have thought that it would make a better comic book."

"You think he did this on a lark? With a bullet in his belly?"

Elizabeth sighed. "Not a lark. Not exactly. Martin didn't want his body to be found because he'd promised Aisha that he wouldn't die. And you see where that's got us. She believes him."

"Except what if she's right? What if someone picked him up?"

Elizabeth took a breath. "Don't you start."

"But you weren't there. This is all secondhand. Why isn't it possible that he had some help?"

"From the Coast Guard? The Navy?"

"They both obey orders."

"And their orders were to entomb that boat and not let anyone near it before morning. He was quarantined, Molly. They did not want him off. They'd measured his exposure at a thousand rads. They'd confirmed that he couldn't survive it. Add to that internal bleeding from the bullet he took. Add drowning and he's dead three different ways."

"You still can't be sure," said Aisha in a whisper.

"Honey . . . you're not listening. He wanted it that way. He was trying to spare you."

"And you?"

"I suppose."

"Then don't talk as if he was playing some game. If he's dead, he died bravely. You should honor him, Elizabeth."

"She's just hurting," said Molly. "She's still mad at him for dying."

John Waldo grunted. "That's assuming he's dead."

Elizabeth glared. "You're not listening either."

"Yeah, I was. But what's the harm in you talking to the twins to ask them about that time in Davos? And as for the Mossad, you still have connections. Why wouldn't you just pick up the phone and ask them what they know about this?"

"Because that story is ridiculous. And then they'd know I'm still alive."

"Then if you want," he said, "we could check that out ourselves in a way that would leave your name out of it, okay?"

"You'd be wasting your time."

"No, they wouldn't," said Aisha.

Molly told her, "We'll see what we can do."

12

Shortly before midnight, West African time, a Liberian patrol boat had put to sea bearing extra fuel and ammunition. In addition to its crew, it carried eight well-armed troopers of the second Liberian Commando.

It would rendezvous with a helicopter gunship near the coordinates their commander had been given. The gunship was fitted with pontoons. There, as the American, Clew, had insisted, they would wait in the darkness five kilometers distant until the off-loading was completed. They would wait facing into the wind so that the soft wop-wop of the gunship's idling rotors could not be heard from the freighter.

The officer put in charge of this interception was a major whose troops called him Scar. The major's true name was Thomas Mitchell. It was an Irish name, a white man's name, but the major was African to the roots of his soul. There were many such names in Liberia.

The major was a man of very personal experience with bands such as the one he intended to ambush. He had once been a student who had hoped to be a doctor. Then a gang of bandits who called themselves rebels mounted a raid on the suburb of Monrovia in which he and his young wife were living. There was little of value for them to take, only some food, a few watches, no weapons. What they wanted most of all were the women.

He and his wife had almost escaped amid all the shouting and shooting. They had nearly reached a thick stand of trees on the edge of a rubber plantation. He was struck by a bullet; it may have been a stray. It entered from behind him just below his right eye and it tore his cheekbone away. His wife screamed as he fell; she was calling for help even though he tried to tell her to be silent. Soon there were men with guns standing over them. They pulled his wife off him and looked at his face. He heard one of them say, "This one's finished." Another one seized his wife by her blouse and threw her onto the ground. He heard that one say, "This one's mine."

That one raped her. He beat her when she tried to resist. Major Scar would always remember her cries, but he could do nothing to help her. He remembered trying to pull himself up. He could barely raise his head by that time. His wife's cries were of fear but they were not for herself. She was begging them to stop long enough for her to help him. A man who was awaiting his turn with her said, "Shut up. He's no good to you now."

They were not speaking English. Their language was Ibo. They wore combat fatigues with all patches torn off. Nigerian soldiers. Deserters. Now bandits. One of them saw that he was still moving. He said to another, "Go finish him off." The other one started to pull out his machete, but just then more shooting erupted in the distance. Army troops from the capital were coming. They crouched for a moment and readied their rifles. One said, "Take the woman and let's go."

That was all he remembered. He must have passed out. He later learned that their men raped nearly all of the women. Some they killed when they were done. A few, they took with them. His young wife was among those they forced to go with them for their further entertainment as long as she lasted. He never saw her again.

When his wound had healed, although it left him disfig-ured, he joined the army of Charles Taylor. Charles Taylor had been a rebel commander himself, then president, then deposed by new rebel commanders. The new ones, like the old ones, had American names. Their descendants, freed slaves, had been offered this new homeland long before the American civil war. Liberia was Muslim, but they came as Christians. It had been the faith of their former owners and of those who had paid for their passage. Many wore cruci-fixes pinned to their clothing. It was a good way for them to recognize each other and to set themselves apart from the tribes. The new commanders quickly came to terms with Major Scar lest his unit become the next rebel army. One day, perhaps, the cycle would end.

The major's men addressed him by his proper name and rank, but they called him Major Scar, or simply Scar, among themselves. He didn't care for that at first. It seemed less than courteous. But his sergeant assured him that no insult was intended. On the contrary, said his sergeant, the men were quite proud to be able to say that they served with Major Scar. Had the major not noticed how many of the men in the Second Commando had scars on their cheeks? These were all self-inflicted. They were better than medals or col-ored berets for letting people know that they were the tough-est. This was good because a soldier with that reputation is always looking for the chance to prove that he is the bravest of the brave.

The sergeant was right. They had many such chances. And during his years with the Second Commando, he hunted the men who had taken his wife, their faces burned into his memory. He never found even one. They had melted away. Or more likely, they hadn't lived very long. Most such bandits lasted only a matter of weeks. Drugged or drunk, and very often diseased, they would soon fall to killing each other or be ambushed by more disciplined troops.

But others just like them would soon take their places. There was never a shortage of young men who had nothing. No land, no work, and no education. No cause to believe in and therefore no hope. The bandits tell them, "You have nothing because 'they' take everything. It is right that we take back what they have stolen." They're given guns and they're given life and death power over any who happen to have anything they want. In short order, any vestige of humanity is lost. That was why Major Scar saw no point in taking prisoners. Any who surrendered were questioned, then shot, even those who tried to claim that they were forced into service. If that was true, it was true for one day at the most. Until they were given a gun.

He did not see himself as a brutal man, however. He was good to his troops; he'd had them all learn to read, and each got a share of any contraband they captured. Those shares fed their families. They received little pay. And each was given land that would be theirs forever. That had been his idea and the president embraced it. It gave them a sense that, unlike most other Africans, they had a real nation of their own to defend. Not just tribal lands that are always in dispute. A real nation with real borders, not colonial borders. The oldest true nation in Africa.

He required them to show due respect to civilians and never to bully or rob them. They knew that if they did so he would punish them with fines. They knew that if they raped he would hang them. Barring that, however, they had no cause to fear him. On the contrary, they made fun of him sometimes, but it was always a good-natured joshing. They made fun because he doted on his beautiful new wife and never stopped bragging about her. Especially now that she was with child. But he had good reason to be proud of her.

When he met her, she was a Red Cross volunteer who had helped so many families out of misery. She didn't mind the scar, the big dent in his face, because she had seen so much worse. To this day, she still worked for the Red Cross part time. Full time, she was a teacher at the secondary school that the Red Cross had helped her to set up. The school had a piano and she taught herself to play it. She had tried to teach him, but he had no gift for it. So now she was teaching the children.

Not a brutal man at all, but he still took no prisoners. He knew that was why he'd been given this assignment. That,

and the fact that there were said to be children on the
freighter that was bringing these weapons. His general knew
that he would see to their safety until the Red Cross could
take them.

His general held the rank of Army Chief of Staff, but he
was in command of all the services. His general's name was
Abednego Tubbs and he always wore wonderful uniforms.
He wasn't christened Abednego. His real name was Herbert.
Once during a battle he climbed into a tank that had been hit
by a rocket and was burning. He used the tank's guns to
drive the enemy off and then he climbed out without so
much as a smudge. The no-smudge part was the hardest to
believe because he knew burning tanks to be sooty. But
something like this had also happened in the Bible. The
original Abednego was one of the three who some king
threw into a fiery furnace. An angel not only kept them from
burning but got them out with their clothes neatly pressed
and the king gave all three of them promotions. The general
says his soldiers started calling him Abednego. More likely,
he came up with that by himself. It sounded a lot more
heroic than Herbert and it suited the painting that he later
commissioned of himself on top of that tank.

He was vain, but a good man. Not especially corrupt. Or
at least he didn't try to enrich himself beyond what seemed
reasonable for a man in his position. He would take his
proper share, but no more than was fair, of whatever that
freighter and its cargo might bring. But not of the weapons.
They were not to see land. The general, however, had wa-
vered somewhat at the thought of such profligacy.

"One is tempted," said the general, "to capture them intact. We, meaning the army, could either use them ourselves
or sell them back to the Americans."

"We could, but you've given your word, sir."

"My word? You speak of honor? Where's the honor in
this? I have agreed to an act of piracy, Major."

"Piracy, sir? It's no cruise ship. It's a smuggler."

"You see? You always need the high moral ground. I admire
that in you, but we're not missionaries. Try to leave a little
room for give and take."

"This man, Clew," asked the major. "He is powerful? Important?"

"He has been a valued friend on occasion."

"Is it not better, therefore, to nourish that friendship? You can do as he asks or you can do as you wish. Go the one way and this Clew will be in your debt. Go the other and that friendship may be lost."

The general grumbled. "Even so, such a waste."

"We'll still have the freighter and its cargo," said the major.

The general shrugged. "That is something, I suppose. But those missiles are worth a half million each. We're to feed them to the fishes? And Mobote's men with them? This seems more than a little extreme, does it not?"

"Not extreme, sir. Simply final. Your friend Clew has asked that this matter be handled as quickly and as quietly as possible."

The general was still brooding. "It could be more than weapons."

"Sir, my orders are to send it all to the bottom, not to start opening crates."

"Think a moment," said the general. "This is Savran Bobik's shipment. Bobik deals in many things. Mobote and his men like their stimulants, you know."

The major understood. He was referring to amphetamines. First heroin to keep them from thinking too much, then amphetamines to wake them from their torpor. "I've seen what they do under stimulants, sir."

The general nodded gravely. "I know that you have. But such drugs also have a medicinal function. And they were not part of the agreement."

"Sir, if you order it, I will search for narcotics. But there will be a fight, and I'm going to have losses. I would need to have that order in writing."

The general waved him off. "We're just thinking aloud." He said, "Go ahead. Do it your way. Make it final. But when you take that freighter, have it searched top to bottom. List everything you find so that nothing disappears when our own customs officers come aboard."

"And if I find other drugs in the rest of the cargo?"

"Call them medical supplies. I'll be there to receive them. They'll be put to good use, I assure you."

Major Scar had thought it best to say nothing more. His general, perhaps, intended to sell them. Perhaps the money from the sale would be put to good use or perhaps it would simply disappear. The major decided to spare his general what might be too great a temptation. If he did find drugs, he would bring them in as ordered, but he would first call ahead and speak to his wife. He would see to it that she was on hand to claim them. She and her Red Cross representatives.

However . . . first things first. Down to business.

Mobote's men appeared in a high-powered trawler that could probably do twenty knots. It was the property, no doubt, of one of many smugglers who trafficked up and down this stretch of coast. The trawler came without lights, but it surely had radar. The radar would pick up the major's patrol boat, but because it was a full five kilometers distant, it should seem to be one of a great many fishing boats that would normally be working these waters at night. To that end, he had the patrol boat rigged with the same working deck lights that the fishing boats used. If the pontooned gunship bobbed in line with the patrol boat, its signature would resemble the rigging for the netting that was common to most of those fishing boats.

The trawler had slowed almost to a stop before approaching the freighter. They were, no doubt, making radio contact and getting an assurance that all seemed to be well. The major's radioman searched for the frequency they were using. By the time he found it, it was no longer needed. The trawler had moved forward and tied up to the freighter. In its shadow, the trawler was no longer visible. But soon deck lights came on. The off-loading began. While a crane lowered two heavy pallets of weapons, several boxes were being carried by hand by way of the ship's boarding ladder.

The off-loading was efficient. It took less than fifteen minutes. The major watched as the trawler fell away from the freighter and turned its bow toward the coast. When it reached a point more than a kilometer from the freighter, the major gave the signal for the helicopter to rise and to blind the trawler's crew with its searchlight. His patrol boat sliced through the water, full speed.

Mobote's men heard the sounds of both engines before they were able to spot either source. The major saw them scramble, looking this way and that. Most had automatic weapons at the ready. When the searchlight blazed on, most covered their eyes. The major gave the order to fire. His deck gunners started raking the hull with two fifty-caliber machine guns. They aimed at the rudder and the waterline. The helicopter's gunner began sweeping the decks. Several of Mobote's men returned fire. Some aimed their weapons at the blazing white light and some at the muzzle flash of the deck guns. Their own fire exposed them. Most were quickly cut down. Several leaped overboard and tried to swim beyond the reach of the searchlight. The trawler was already sinking stern down and was listing sharply to one side.

The major ordered his patrol boat to circle it slowly. He ordered his gunners not to shoot at the swimmers. They could see to them later. Concentrate on the trawler. He ordered the helicopter crew to break off and proceed to illuminate the deck of the freighter before anything could be thrown into the sea. Only when the trawler began to roll over did he order his men to cease firing. He used his own spotlights to pick out the men who had managed to get off the trawler. He counted seven upturned faces in all. Some were fearful, some defiant, at least three had been wounded. Of the seven, four were dressed in camouflage fatigues. The other three were either shirtless or in mufti. The latter three would be crew. He looked closely at the faces of those who were in uniform on the chance, however slim, that God would be so good as to let him avenge his first wife.

As before, as always, there were none that he recognized. One of them, with some sort of tattoo on his forehead, did not seem to grasp his disadvantaged situation. He was shouting dire threats using very strong language. He was one of the wounded. He belched blood as he shouted. He tried to raise a pistol, but it slipped from his hand because a bullet

had taken his thumb off. He only realized it now. He paused
to stare in disbelief. The major's sergeant raised his weapon;
he was ready to shoot him, but the major said no, it's a
waste. Let him cling to some wreckage. Let them try to
swim to shore. The sharks, by now, would have picked up
the blood scent. The sharks would be coming from all sides.

His radioman said, "Major, the chopper's reporting. The
pilot saw children being dragged out on deck. He says that
their hands are tied behind them."

"He's stopped it?"

"Yes, sir. He fired a burst. But the captain threw something else over the side. It's a red-and-white container. He
says it's still floating."

"What about the freighter's crewmen?" he asked. "Are
they armed?"

"The pilot says some were, but they now have their hands
up. Their captain was trying to get them to fight, but they
don't seem so eager to die for him."

The major said, "Have the chopper hold its station. Tell
the pilot that we'll board in ten minutes."

The freighter's boarding ladder was still down from the off-
loading. The major's patrol boat eased alongside. Five
armed soldiers and their sergeant raced up its steps. They
preceded the major and a harbor pilot who'd been brought to
see the freighter back to port. The soldiers quickly secured
the crew that was on deck. They forced them to kneel at the
rounded stern railing and gathered the weapons that they'd
dropped. They positioned themselves to cover all hatches,
sealing in whatever crew that might remain. They gathered
the children under one of the lifeboats well away from any
likely line of fire.

Major Scar appeared on deck. His face frightened the
crew, and that was well, but he saw that it also frightened the
children. Most were trembling, some were crying. A few had
dropped to their knees in despair or perhaps out of weakness.
They were all very thin. Some of the young girls had soiled
themselves. Two of them showed signs of having been
beaten. He felt sure that they'd endured more than beatings.

He ordered a soldier to untie their hands. He told the harbor pilot to proceed to the bridge and asked him to take the children with him. "Search the bridge and the captain's quarters," he said. "Find the ship's log and its manifest. Give these children the means to clean themselves up and give them any food that you find."

As the soldier cut their ropes, the major tried to soothe them. Gently, he assured them that no harm would come to them. Those who wish it would soon be returned to their villages. Those without family would be fed and sent to school and would live with other children like themselves. He asked one of the girls, one whose lips had been split, to identify the man who had done this to her. She was too afraid to speak, but another girl wasn't. The other girl stepped forward and pointed. She had gestured toward the captain and another man, a fat man, who wore the cap of a first mate. "It was that one and that one," she said.

"Only two?"

"Only those, but they came every night." As she spoke she wiped her mouth with her hand as if trying to cleanse herself of them.

The captain was white, but not European. His accent seemed Algerian, Moroccan perhaps. The captain had managed to screw up his courage and was making demands of the major. He protested the boarding, citing maritime law. He was ordering the major to get off his ship at once. The major seized him by his hair and bent him over the railing. He looked up at the gunship still hovering above them and asked the pilot, through gestures, whether he could still see the package that the captain had jettisoned. The pilot swung his spotlight to a point off the stern. It lit the small container, still bobbing. The major, still holding the captain by the hair, reached down to his crotch and lifted him bodily. He threw him over the side.

He waited for the captain to struggle to the surface. He called to him and said, "Now swim to that box. Don't come back without it. If you hurry, you might beat the sharks."

Only seven of the crew remained on deck. These included the mate whose turn was soon coming. He had expected a

crew of perhaps ten or twelve. He sent two of his men to
search belowdecks and gather any who might be hiding.

"Question them," he said. "Ask them what this ship is carrying. It won't all be listed on the manifest."

Next, the major approached the first mate. This was a
black man, very short and very fat. More than fat, he was
filthy and he stank. But he was not a poor man; he was wearing much gold. He wore rings and a watch, gold chains and
a crucifix. The crucifix was three inches long. It was flanked
on its chain by animal bones and charms that were thought
to be magic. This was a man who liked to cover all bases in
case the Christian teachings were mistaken. The man
guessed what was coming. His eyes went wide. He attempted to bargain for his life. He said, "I know the cargo.
I'm the only one who does."

A Nigerian, thought the major, on hearing this man's accent. Probably Ibo. One more mark against him.

"You've known some of it quite well," the major answered.

The mate said, "Those girls lie. Don't listen to them. But
I know which crates are marked falsely on the manifest. I
know what is hidden. I will help you."

"We'll manage," said the major as he drew his sidearm.
He aimed it five inches below the mate's belt. The mate
moved to cover that spot with his hands while shouting for
the major to wait. The roar of the pistol cut him off. The bullet's impact lifted the man to his toes before he folded over
and fell on his face. It had exited under the base of his spine,
exploding the Nigerian's anus. The Nigerian bucked and
writhed on the deck, his smashed hands still trying to press
against the hole that had been drilled through his center of
pleasure.

The major heard gasps from the crew that remained. He
said to them, "None of you will be shot as long as you give
us no trouble." Your captain is, of course, another matter. He
said to his sergeant, within the mate's range of hearing, "As
for this one, let him lie in his blood for a while. Soon
enough, he'll get the bath that he needs."

He was not a brutal man, he reminded himself. But some

things leave no room for mercy. The men he'd sent below came back to report. The only others, they said, were two firemen and the cook. They said they told the firemen to stay with their engines. If they do their jobs they would both be released when the ship has put in at Monrovia. They'd marched the cook to his galley and set him to work preparing hot soup for the children.

"Well done," said the major. "What cargo did you find?"

"A Mercedes, lots of motorbikes, most not new; they must be stolen. Also some computers and cellular phones, all in crates with aid agency markings. And a great many crates we couldn't take the time to open, also with similar markings."

"No idea of their contents?"

"Some said food," he answered. "Some said medical supplies. All of these are addressed to distribution facilities in ports where this freighter had already been."

The markings were probably genuine, thought the major. Tons of aid goods, all stolen. All intended for black market sale up the coast. This was, he realized, a disappointment to his soldiers. If those crates contained what their stencils indicated, his soldiers would get no share of their value. The Red Cross would surely reclaim them. But they'd share in the ship and they would each get a motorbike. They would get a share of whatever else they might find, with the single exception of drugs as agreed. The major felt sure that he would find drugs. They were probably bobbing in the ocean.

The captain had managed to swim to the box that had preceded him over the side. Using it for flotation, he'd paddled around the stern to the port boarding ladder where the patrol boat still waited. The patrol boat's crew snared the box with a hook as the captain pulled himself onto the platform. There, the captain stiffened. He was hearing distant screams. The screams were coming from Mobote's men, who were still treading water in the darkness. The sharks had wasted no time. An armed crewman prodded the captain with his weapon. The crewman forced him to carry the box as he staggered, exhausted, up the steps.

The captain almost fell into a swoon when he saw the

condition of his mate. The mate was still rolling and
writhing on the deck on a great smear of blood that kept
widening. This time, the armed crewman had to keep him
from falling as he led him toward the stern and Major Scar.

The major said to him, "So you, too, like little girls."

The captain stammered, "I never . . . I did not . . ."

The major's eyes turned cold. "That's a lie. Don't tell another."

The captain's chin quivered. "I . . . at least didn't beat
them."

"Oh, good. That will make all the difference."

"This is true," whined the captain. "You can ask them.
Please ask them. It was not me who beat those two girls."

You're a dead man, thought the major, but he said, "You
might live. You might live if you don't lie again."

The captain went limp as if greatly relieved. "I won't lie,"
he said. "Ask me anything."

The major gestured toward the hatch that led to the hold.
"What else are you carrying beyond what we've seen?"

"I don't know. This is true," said the captain, his eyes
wide. He pointed at the mate. "Only he knows."

"Why so?"

"He's not really a seaman. He is Savran Bobik's man. His
name is Moshood. The rest of us are seamen. We move
cargo port to port. In between we must mind our own business."

The major asked, "Are there drugs in the hold?"

"There are medicines. Many medicines. All kinds."

"I mean drugs of the kind that affect one's behavior."

"Not in the hold. Only those with the weapons. I know of
no others. This I swear."

The major asked, "Are there other weapons?"

"I don't think so. I think only that shipment."

The major sniffed. "You don't know very much. But you
did know enough to throw this overboard." He reached to
pick up the container.

The captain gestured toward the mate once again.
"Bobik's man said, 'Hide it,' but there was no time. I thought
this must be trouble so I threw it."

The major studied the box he was holding. It had been tightly sealed with reinforced tape, but the tape underneath had already been cut. Someone had used fresh tape to reseal it. The box itself resembled an ice chest. On one side, it bore a corporate logo. The name on it sounded South African.

He asked, "What is VaalChem?"

"They make different medicines. That's all I was told."

"Why would a medicine be thrown overboard?"

"Because this was supposed to go to Mobote. When we left Luanda and got out to sea, Bobik's man opened one of the crates. Not the crates with the weapons. A small one. He found drugs and special foods for Mobote to cook with and he found this container inside. I heard him say, 'What is this? Why is this here?' He pulled it out so he could get at the drugs. He helped himself to some of them. Three bags. Next, he took out his knife and he opened this container. When he looked inside he seemed very surprised. I asked him, 'What have you found?'"

"Well?" asked the major. "What was it?"

"I don't know," replied the captain. "All he said was, 'Don't touch this; don't open it; don't go near it.' He put the drugs that he stole into that container and he took it down to his cabin. That is the last I saw of it until you attacked. That is when he told me to hide it."

So, thought the major, what have we here? The Nigerian was not only cheating Mobote, he was stealing from Savran Bobik as well. Whatever surprised him that he found in that container must be of considerable value. The major said, "Well, let's both see what it is." He reached for the clasp knife that he carried in his pocket. He slit the new tape and he pried off the lid. He flinched as fumes rose to his face.

The fumes, however, were only dry ice. He could think of no narcotic that would need to be kept cold, but narcotics were the first things he saw. White powder wrapped in plastic, almost sure to be heroin; the quantity looked to be half a kilo. The major picked it up to examine it closely and then tossed it into the sea. There were two smaller packages of a crystalline substance. Methamphetamines, probably. They went over as well. He poured the dry ice onto the deck to get at the rest of the container.

At its base he saw a jar that was imbedded in green foam. The foam had been molded to accommodate its shape in order to protect it from breakage. He saw that there were spaces for two rows of jars, but only that one space was used. The major reached in and removed the jar. It was small, about the size of a woman's fist. It was made of very thick glass. Its top and its base had been further protected by dipping it into a plastic substance such as that which he'd seen on the handles of tools. The jar's middle section, however, was clear except for a yellow paper band wrapped around it. A label, perhaps, but there was no writing on it. Perhaps the color by itself had a meaning.

The jar was only about one-third filled. Looking past the yellow label he was able to see that the jar contained some sort of powder. More heroin, perhaps? No, not packaged this way. Besides this powder wasn't white; it was pink. And the powder was much finer than any that he'd seen. More like talc, but even finer than that. So light, so fine that it almost seemed alive. The slightest movement of his hand would cause it to jump. It seemed to creep up the sides of the jar.

He turned and walked toward Bobik's man, the Nigerian. As he did so, he slit the rubber seal with his knife. Bobik's man had curled into a fetal position, as much as his girth would allow. The helicopter's prop wash had fanned his blood into a smear almost three meters wide. He saw the major coming. He begged the major, "Do not shoot me again. You are Christian. I am Christian. Do not shoot me."

But then he saw that the major wasn't holding his pistol. He saw that the major was holding a jar and that the major was trying to open it. A new kind of fear washed over his face. He cried out, "No, no, no! What are you doing?"

The major stood over him. "What is this?" he asked.

The Nigerian gasped, "Do not open it. Don't."

The major was startled by the vehemence of his plea. This man was swimming in blood; he had been emasculated, and yet suddenly those seemed to be the least of his problems.

"What is this?" asked the major. "Why are you so afraid?"

Bobik's man didn't answer. He bit his lip. He tried to back away from the jar. The major said again, "Tell me what it is."

"It is poison," the man croaked. "Throw it over the side."

"What kind of poison?" asked the major impatiently. "Perhaps you'll know better if you see it up close."

"No, no. Do not open it. Do not let it fly out."

The major understood that the powder must be dangerous. He no longer intended to open the jar. All he'd meant to do was to loosen the cap in order to loosen this man's lips. But the cap came free sooner than he had expected and some of the powder did indeed seem to fly. It wasn't much. No more than dust blown off a book. Were it not for the helicopter's powerful searchlight, it would not have been visible at all.

The little cloud of pink powder quickly dispersed, but it did so in a very odd way. Its particles seemed to dart away from each other as if searching for a means of escape. This was all the more odd because they seemed to resist both the breeze and the prop wash, both of which were behind him. But only for an instant. Then they chose a direction. It was as if they had reached an agreement.

The Nigerian had clamped his ruined hands to his face and had tried to roll out of their path. What was left of the cloud drifted back toward the stern where the captain and his crew were being held. Halfway there, it was no longer visible.

The captain and his crew had been watching the mate. Unlike him, they did not seem greatly alarmed. The major heard a crewman ask the captain what was happening. The captain only shrugged. He truly didn't seem to know.

The Nigerian's hands were still pressed against his face. He had reached the railing and was trying to stand. He seemed intent on throwing himself over the railing, but the strength of his legs had deserted him. His whole body wilted. He collapsed onto the deck. His eyes held an expression of utter despair. With one bloody hand, he made the sign of the cross before joining both hands at the tip of his chin. He began to recite a Hail Mary.

"The Holy Mother can wait," said the major. "Talk to me."

The Nigerian ignored him. He kept praying.

"First me," said the major. "Then I'll let you make your peace."

The Nigerian croaked, "Go make your own peace. You're as dead as the rest of us now."

13

Elizabeth, with some sadness, had said her farewells and, with Aisha, drove away from the marina. She hadn't wanted to be found, but she was glad that she'd gone there. She'd never really seen herself as one of them before. She was, in her own mind, just a guest passing through during her time in Chamonix. But they'd seemed to have embraced her as one of their own. She couldn't help but feel warmed by the thought of it.

From what Elizabeth had heard about Westport, their good will wasn't limited to their own tight-knit circle. It applied to their neighbors and friends as well although she doubted that many were aware of that fact. But anyone who tried to hurt a neighbor or friend was likely to end up in the trunk of a car. Not dead, necessarily. Given time to reflect. Given time to consider moving elsewhere.

Her route back to Sea Pines took them past Jump & Phil's, the bar where all this had started. She took her foot off the gas as she coasted by its entrance. The bar was also where it ended, according to Molly. Harry Whistler was still in there behind all that plywood, as was his son, Adam, and the two Beasley twins.

Correction, thought Elizabeth. Only one of the twins. The other would be, as John Waldo had explained, somewhere in the shadows outside. She resisted the temptation to slow down a bit more and see if she was able to spot him. She knew that she wouldn't. He'd been doing this too long. He wouldn't even be where she'd expect him to be. Much more likely, the twin would spot her.

Aisha asked her, "Aren't you going to stop in?"

Elizabeth shook her head. "Let's just get home."

Aisha asked, "Don't you think you should at least say hello? Mr. Whistler is going to know that you're here as soon as he talks to Molly. She's probably called him already."

"I'm sure that she has," said Elizabeth.

"Well . . . wouldn't it be polite to . . ."

Elizabeth stopped her. "You're saying that you'd like to meet more of them, right?"

"Well, sure. But if you'd rather, I can wait in the car."

Elizabeth curled her lip. "I wish you'd waited in your bed. I'm not going in because the owners are in there and, apparently the bartender, Leslie, as well. I don't need them to know that I know Harry Whistler. My quiet life here would be over."

Aisha nodded. "I guess I see what you mean."

"Harry knows that. Believe me, he won't be offended." They were almost at the gate. "Let's just get home."

Aisha said, "Well, at least you can tell me what he's like."

"Who, Harry?"

"Uh-huh. And Paul Bannerman, too."

"I . . . didn't really know them that well," said Elizabeth. "Martin knew them much longer than I did."

"But you spent some time with them. You must have formed an impression. And Martin must have told you what they were like."

"He did, and Harry was about what I expected. I suppose it was Paul who surprised me the most. I'm not sure I've ever met the real Paul Bannerman."

Aisha looked up. "I don't get you."

"Harry is Harry. There's a range, but it's all Harry. With Bannerman, it's more like he's two different people. If I'd met him somewhere else and knew nothing about him, I'd have thought, what a gentleman; what a nice-looking man. Attentive, a good listener, very kind."

"Until you get to know him?"

"That's my point. I never did. I never got to see the other side of him."

"So you're saying he's like a Jekyll and Hyde."

"No . . . that's not right either. Martin used to say it's his eyes and his voice. Martin said when he's angry, you'd think they'd go hard. But they don't. Not like Carla's or Billy's, for example. His eyes take on a shine and he gets very quiet. He said that's when you want to be on his side because you don't want to be on the other one."

Aisha squirmed in her seat. She said, "He sounds scary."

"I imagine that he has his moments."

Elizabeth began to reconsider what she'd said. "On the other hand, I'll tell you how Molly described him. She said he looks like, and acts like, the sort of man who mothers wish their daughters would marry. But their daughters never do because they think he'll be boring. Reliable and steady, a good provider, but boring."

"His wife's name is . . ."

"Susan."

"She mustn't have thought so."

"She might have when that's what he needed her to think. But over time, he must have grown to care about her, probably despite his intentions. And I guess he felt the need to try to live normally. I suppose that most of us do at some point. He'd have had to tell her who he is and what he's been, but by that time I'm sure she had a pretty good idea. It must have taken her a while to adjust to all that. But they gave it a chance. They worked it out."

Elizabeth felt Aisha's hand on her knee. She felt Aisha give it a squeeze. She realized how wistful she must have sounded. Living normally. Loving someone. Working it out. Elizabeth drew a breath. She shook off the thought. They were passing through the guarded Sea Pines gate.

Aisha said, "Mr. Waldo said some people tried to kill her. He mentioned it twice. A long story, he said."

"Someone tried. It was before they were married. They saw killing her as a way to hurt him."

"So you do know that story?"

"Almost everyone does. By that I mean everyone who lives in our world. You don't, so please don't ask me to repeat it. As John said, it's not for young ears."

"The story's so awful?"

"He . . . made sure that no one would try that again. Let's get off the subject, okay?"

"Well, we can't," said Aisha. "Well, okay, maybe that one. But I can't pretend that I never met all those people. I mean, that was pretty exciting."

They were waved through the gate. "You made a hit with them yourself."

"You know what surprised me? They don't seem very tough."

"They aren't. Except when they are."

Aisha asked, "What about Harry Whistler? Is he anything at all like Paul Bannerman?"

Elizabeth had to smile. "That's a tough one. Yes and no. Think of Bannerman as the neighbor who comes over to help you when . . . I don't know . . . say your furnace goes out. Nice guy, good neighbor, and you have no idea. Think of Harry as the neighbor who throws roaring parties and you always see a line of stretch limos out front. Paul likes to live quietly. Harry likes to live big. They're both big, but in their own way."

"What does he look like?"

"Harry? He's a great genial bear of a man. He has a beard, sort of square, an Ernest Hemingway beard. And like you he always wears western hats. It's been several years, but that look was his trademark. I doubt that he's changed very much."

Aisha smiled. "That's not how I'd have pictured him either."

"You envisioned a more shadowy, nondescript look?"

"Well, you'd think he wouldn't want to stand out in a crowd. You'd think he'd want to be more like Bannerman."

"It's the only way anyone's ever seen him," said Elizabeth. "If he ever felt the need to be harder to find, he could change that look pretty easily."

"Like you with your wigs and black outfits?" she asked.

"Same thing."

"Except I wouldn't call you genial." Aisha touched her knee again. "I mean, you're great with me and I love being with you, but you're not exactly bubbly with most people."

A grunt from Elizabeth. "I'm working on that."

"Those people we met . . . you say they're all pretty dangerous?"

"Not to you. Not to anyone you'd know."

"You know what I liked? I liked the way they would rib you every time you got snippy. They wouldn't do that if they didn't like you."

Elizabeth shrugged. "I suppose."

"You know who really likes you? The little one, Carla. Mr. Waldo said that she was bad-tempered, but she was pretty friendly when I met her. You should have come down. Carla likes you a lot. She told me that I'm in very good hands. She said that you're one of the best with a knife."

Elizabeth blinked. "Carla said that? To you?"

"No, not exactly. At least not straight out. She just said the best, but not at what. But then she said that Claudia's pretty good, too. That's when I thought she meant good with a knife. And right then, Billy said, 'Let's get off that, okay? Let's talk about something nice.' And Carla said, 'Sure. Why don't we talk about birds?'"

Never should have let you meet her, thought Elizabeth.

Aisha said, "Claudia thinks she's an angel."

"Who said so? Claudia? She announced it just like that?"

"No, Billy brought it up. He was changing the subject. Then it was Claudia who asked both of them to stop. She was a little embarrassed, I guess, but she never said it wasn't true."

"It's probably true in her mind," said Elizabeth. "Oxygen deprivation. I've seen it before. Hallucinations can seem very real."

"Like with me? Do I hallucinate when I talk to my mother?"

"We've discussed this. You dream. It's not the same thing at all."

Aisha sighed. She said, "You'll see. You just wait."

"Let's talk about something else, shall we?"

"Um, now that you mention it . . ."

"Something else besides Martin."

Aisha shook her head. "I was thinking of Nadia. She'll probably ask me what you and I did tonight. I'm going to have to tell her, but how much?"

"Tell her everything," said Elizabeth. "There's no reason not to. Except that she'll want to skin me alive and she won't be too happy with you either."

"I'll make sure Jazz is there to get between us."

"Good thinking."

"One more question," said Aisha. "Mr. Waldo said someone was looking for you. That doesn't mean *after* you, does it?"

She'd almost forgotten. Artemus Bourne. "It's nothing. Some guy wants to meet me. It won't happen."

They continued on. Elizabeth said little. As she turned the car on to Plantation Drive, she said, "Listen, Aisha. All that talk about Martin . . ."

"I know. You don't have to say it."

"It's just that I don't want you getting your hopes up."

Aisha said, very softly, "We'll just wait."

14

It was the next day, early morning. It was not a jogging day. Clew had gotten to his office by 7 A.M. in order to catch up on assorted correspondence before being bogged down in meetings. Most of his mail had come through his computer. Most of it was encrypted, but instantly decoded at the touch of a series of buttons.

Since last night, he'd heard nothing more from Paul Bannerman and that, in itself, was good news. Bannerman's people must all be off that island by now. He'd have heard right away if they'd had problems. The other good news was that Bannerman now owed him. Clew had done him a considerable favor.

Clew scrolled through his messages. He saw nothing else marked "Urgent." He came to one from his contact in Liberia, the usually reliable Abednego Tubbs. The language of the message was deliberately vague. It said that the matter was being attended to in accordance with their discussion. It said that the package was already wet and that further inspection was about to take place.

Clew understood this to mean that the arms had been destroyed and, Clew assumed, their recipients with them. It seemed to say that the freighter had not yet been boarded, but that the general's men were ready to do so. This message had been sent at two o'clock in the morning, Liberian time. Allowing for the four-hour difference, that meant that the message had been sitting in his machine since ten o'clock last night, Washington time. Clew glanced at his watch. 7:40 A.M. The interception, therefore, had taken place a full ten hours ago.

Clew scrolled down the page looking for a later message. He saw nothing new from General Tubbs. He thought it odd that the general sent an interim report, but nothing more detailed after that. The boarding, Clew assumed, must have gone without incident. The ship was probably docking in Monrovia by now. Perhaps the general had decided to wait until a search of its hold could be conducted.

At half past eight, Clew shut down his computer and proceeded down the hall to a conference room where the first of his meetings was already under way. Clew's driver and assistant, Alex Rakowsky, intercepted him. Alex said, "You're late, but so was everyone else. They know it's going to be the same old bullshit."

"Give me an hour, then call in a bomb threat."

Rakowsky chuckled. "You got it."

This morning's topic was the need for increased cooperation among the Intelligence services. An end to the turf wars. More Intelligence sharing. Even after all this new Home Security business, such meetings were an utter waste of time. Clew could no longer count the number of sessions that he had sat through on that subject. They usually followed some Intelligence failure, some senator asking, "Why didn't we know this?" Or they followed a memo signed by a new president who still thought that just because he gave an order, the various services would obey it.

The same proposals would be made. The same assurances would be given. A few crumbs would be traded, a few files swapped. But soon human nature would kick in again because each of the services was made up of people. They deal in information. What they learn makes their careers. They don't advance by making some other service look good. Clew thought it naïve to expect that they'd share without getting something better in return.

The FBI's representative yawned and stretched as Clew entered. He was already bored, but he gave Clew a wink. He and Clew had already held their own private meeting and had agreed to a small exchange of favors. The official had seen to it that Bannerman and Whistler had a twelve-hour window to get their people off that island. What he'd wanted in return, to Clew's quiet amusement, was Clew's help in locating Elizabeth Stride, or else in confirming that she's actually dead. Here's that agency still trying to score a few points with the powerful Artemus Bourne, having come up empty on its own. The FBI man obviously had no idea that Clew had already met with Bourne. If he had, he would have asked for some other favor. Clew had gladly agreed to the deal.

At a quarter to ten Alex entered the room holding a slip of notepaper. He made his apologies to the others in the meeting and said, "Sorry, sir. You need to see this." Clew read the message that Alex had written. It said, "No bomb scare. Just a call from Paul Bannerman. You've been in here more than an hour." Clew feigned a grim expression and rose to his feet. He said, "Please keep going. I'll try not to be long." No one ever seemed to question grim expressions.

Once outside, he asked Alex, "Is he still on the phone?"

Alex shook his head. "He said there's no rush. He said he'd be in his office all morning. That was really him, right? That was Bannerman?"

"Guess so."

"He sounds like . . . I don't know . . . I don't know what I expected. Yeah, I do. You remember Sydney Greenstreet from the old Bogart movies? That's who I thought he'd sound like. Sydney Greenstreet."

Clew smiled. "That's how you pictured him? Old and fat? Hooded eyes? I love it. Now I can't wait to tell him."

"More the voice. A little creepy. And stroking a cat. But he sounded like a regular guy."

"He is. He's a sweetheart. Wouldn't step on a bug."

"With respect, sir, I think you're full of shit."

No rush meant that Bannerman was just checking in. It confirmed that his people were extracted without incident. Bannerman and Whistler had both used their own planes. They both had pilots who were well experienced in snatch and go operations. In this case, however, they were under no pressure. They probably could have hitchhiked off that island.

Clew returned to his office. On his desk were two telephones, one secure and one open. The one that was secure was fitted with a mute that covered his mouth when he used it. It was fitted with a scrambler as well. He lifted the receiver and punched out the number of Bannerman's office in Westport. It was a private line, also very secure, within the travel agency that Bannerman owned. The agency actually did book some travel, but it was, primarily, the communications center of Bannerman's near-global network. The computers in most of Bannerman's cubicles had never so much as looked up an airfare. One of those terminals was said to have access to the NSA's Echelon surveillance system. Clew doubted it himself. Echelon was untappable. Nor would Bannerman say one way or the other. And his silence, of course, encouraged the belief that his people had managed to crack it. As in diplomacy, as in any negotiation, what the opposition thinks you know is often more useful than the knowledge itself.

Bannerman, in fact, was busy booking some travel when told that Roger Clew was on his private line. He was making an assortment of dummy arrangements for some of the people who'd be coming to Westport. The dummies were intended to disguise their destinations. A few of them were doubtless under surveillance by someone's intelligence service somewhere. He showed most of them flying into Washington, D.C. They would certainly be followed if they actually showed up there, perhaps even rounded up and detained. But they wouldn't be there; they'd be in Westport.

He was dressed in a faded sweatshirt and jeans, sipping

coffee that he'd picked up at Starbucks. His normal dress at work was a suit or a blazer, but he'd promised Susan he'd be home by late morning to finish wallpapering the nursery.

Bannerman took the call in his conference room. "Good morning, Roger," he said brightly. "Well done. Molly and the others are back here in Westport. Harry and his group flew out before dawn. They'll be landing in Geneva in an hour."

"He took Adam and his lady back with him?"

"Both Adam and Claudia and two or three others. They've left Adam's boat. They'll send a crew for it later."

Clew asked, "Will Harry Whistler be coming to Westport?"

"He was coming all along. I have some business with Harry. But now it seems that both Adam and Claudia will be joining us. You've heard about Claudia?"

"Yeah, she thinks she's an angel."

"I'm developing an interesting circle of friends. What about you? Are you a definite?"

"Barring some crisis," said Clew, "absolutely."

"The guest list seems to be growing by the day. I'm starting to wonder if it's such a good idea. So many of us in one place."

"Except for the ghosts," Clew reminded him.

"The trouble is," said Bannerman, "they don't want to miss it either. They haven't seen some of these people in years."

"Yeah, but no one's going to know who's there and who's floating. If you're doing this over two or three days, you can rotate a few of them at a time. Either that or postpone if you're uncomfortable about this."

Bannerman had already set up a rotation. He said, "No, I know that a raid isn't likely. And Susan's looking forward to seeing her father. So, absent any kind of a realistic threat, I'm reluctant to disappoint everyone."

"They tried you twice," said Clew. "You made it expensive. I'm not saying that they're any more comfortable with you, but as long as you tread lightly and don't rub their noses in it, I think they're inclined to live and let live."

"You agree with that precept? Live and let live?"

"Within limits," Clew answered. "Um . . . why are you asking?"

"Because I have some news, but before we get into it, have you found out what Bourne wants with Stride?"

"Not yet, but I mean to. And I will."

Bannerman took a beat before speaking again. "Roger, the news is that Stride is alive. She's been told of Bourne's offer. She has no interest. As far as Bourne and the rest of the world are concerned, Elizabeth Stride is still dead."

On Clew's end, stunned silence. Then he managed, "You've found her?"

"She had mixed feelings about the encounter. But we've promised that we will respect her wishes. That 'we' includes you, of course, Roger."

Clew's voice took an edge. "You did not have to say that."

"No need to take offense. I've said the same thing up here. She's dead until she tells us differently."

"Okay, none taken. But just so I know . . . someone actually met her and spoke to her, right? We're not talking hearsay. This was face-to-face with Stride?"

"Face-to-face. No mistake. It was Elizabeth Stride."

Clew asked, "You've confirmed it with more than one source."

"Be assured. There were multiple sources."

Clew paused to absorb this. "Are you going to tell me where?"

"Roger . . ."

"Roger, what? I don't need to know? It would really piss me off if you said that to me."

"Will you stop? It's her wish. This is not about you. I said we'd tell no one. I've given my word."

Another brief silence. "Is she there? Is she in Westport?"

"No, Roger, she isn't. She's never been here. And that has to be your last guess."

"I'd still like to meet her."

"I . . . don't see that happening."

"Your decision?"

"Her request. It's not up to me. If it were, we'd have you both over for drinks. I wouldn't mind seeing her myself."

"Well, what *can* you tell me? Is she working? What's she doing?"

Bannerman said, "Working? Not the way that you mean it. She's made a new life and it seems to be a good one. She has friends. She has a home. She feels safe. She's overdue."

"Married? A boyfriend?"

"That's none of our business."

"Paul, give me a break. This has come as a shock. I've been reading about her, thinking about her; I've had trouble getting her out of my head. I was probably in prep school the last time that happened."

"A crush?"

"Oh, fuck you."

"Okay, an attraction."

"An interest," Clew insisted.

"Hey, Roger . . . listen. I don't blame you a bit. I found her extremely attractive myself. A little hard to know, hard to like at first, but if someone had put three holes in your belly, you might be a little standoffish yourself."

Clew asked, "Where was this? At Chamonix?"

An affirmative grunt. "Just before they left Europe. She and Kessler, I mean. They stayed for something like six or eight weeks. I was there for part of that time."

"Kessler didn't find her so hard to like."

"Well, she wasn't a walk in the park for him either. She'd get in a black mood and threaten to leave him and ten minutes later she'd be crying in his arms. I'm making her sound unstable and maybe she was. I assume that you know what she'd been through."

"As I've told you," said Clew, "I've been reading."

"Then try to sound pleased that she's put it behind her."

"Is she over Kessler?"

"Um . . . Roger . . ."

"I'm just asking. It's a reasonable question. After all, the guy shot himself over her."

"That's personal, Roger. Let's leave it alone."

"So you're saying she hasn't put that part behind her. You know more than you're telling me, don't you."

"If I do, it's not much. And what I do know is private. It is simply none of our business."

Clew was annoyed. "Hey, come on, we're just talking. It's not as if Stride could take up with just anyone. You say she'd break into tears. Who would understand why? It would have to be someone like, well . . . you or me."

Bannerman took a long sip of his coffee. "How's life treating you otherwise, Roger?"

"Okay. Subject closed. Except for Artemus Bourne. Do you care if I tell him that Stride is alive, but that she said she does not meet with scumbags?"

A sigh from Bannerman. "Roger . . . why push it? You've heard that she's alive, but you can't find out where. It's the truth. Why not leave it at that?"

"He's had someone at State trying to get at my files. For that alone, I'd like to shit on him a little."

"Bourne would have tentacles almost everywhere, Roger. I'm sure that didn't come as a surprise."

"I bet I know where to look. I'd guess the African desk. Bourne's been pretty busy in Africa."

Bannerman blinked. "Anyplace in particular?"

"Angola. Oil and diamonds. You just hesitated. Why?"

"I took a sip of my coffee."

"Then you took a few sips when I was talking about Kessler. I'll ask you again. Do you know something I should know?"

"I'll tell you what. I'll stop sipping. That way you'll stop reading some deep hidden meaning every time I pause long enough to swallow."

"If you have something on Bourne . . ."

"Will you get off this? I do not."

Clew grunted. "Okay. But if you ever do, tell me."

"Word of honor. You'll be the first."

"By the way, I knocked his goon, Chester Lilly, on his ass. I don't think we're destined to be friends."

"You?" asked Bannerman. "You got into a fight?"

"He came at me. I handled it. And yeah, damn it, me."

"Was this in Bourne's presence? Bourne saw it?"

"Front row seat. I messed his hair. He's got a thing about his hair."

"Roger . . ."

"I know. You told me. Never start one I can't finish. I don't know where you got the idea that I'm some kind of a wimp. I can handle myself better than you think."

"What I said was never start one that you *don't* finish, Roger. That's especially true if you've humiliated someone. No one ever forgets being shamed."

"He won't try for me again. Bourne didn't like it either. Bourne spanked him and sent him to his room."

"And now you're looking forward to insulting Bourne." Bannerman took a breath. "Look, I have an idea. Come up early. Like tomorrow. We'll whack a tennis ball around or maybe go sailing. Give this a chance to settle down."

Clew said, "Now you want me to hide."

"Bourne probably had his wife murdered. Did you know that?"

Clew paused. "I've heard whispers. What do you know about it?"

"It's a matter of record that she'd filed for divorce and was asking for his Briarwood estate. It's a matter of record that the lawyer she hired had an accident of his own on the same day as hers. The point is . . ."

"I know. He's not someone to mess with," said Clew. "But maybe it's time someone did."

Clew hung up the phone and sat back in his chair. He said beneath his breath, "*What a prick.*" That's two insults from Bannerman in one conversation. Bannerman had said, without actually saying it, "Back off. Bourne's out of your league." He had also said, without actually saying it, that if he, Roger Clew, thought he'd have a chance with Stride, he had best get a grip on himself. And the bastard is so calm, so smooth, and so reasonable, you hardly feel the knife going in.

He closed his eyes and muttered, "No, you're doing it to yourself."

You were making a fool of yourself over Stride and now you're trying to blame Bannerman. You reacted to the news of her being alive in a way that Bannerman could not possibly have expected. Hell, you would not have expected it yourself. Stride's alive after all? Glad to hear it. I'm pleased. That's all you had to say. You don't start doing cartwheels. You don't say, "I'd like to call her. Maybe dinner and a movie."

Well, he hadn't gone that far. Damned near though.

And another thing, Roger. Be honest with yourself. You're not only annoyed at what Bannerman won't tell you, you're annoyed at how easily he found her. Here's Bourne putting three federal agencies on her trail and Bannerman locates her in less than a day.

But how? And where? Okay, let's think about this.

Clew went into his computer to the file that he'd downloaded containing the photo, "Almost certainly Stride." Next he opened a blank window beneath it. The window was a file that he had named *Doodlings*. His thinking process seemed to work better when he could type out his thoughts as they came. The first words he typed in were STRIDE IS ALIVE. Underneath, he wrote BANNERMAN, also in caps. On the line after that, he wrote HOW AND WHERE?

Bannerman said face-to-face. But he said not in Westport. He said it's someplace where Stride has built a new life. And she'd asked whoever found her to be quiet about it.

Clew suddenly brightened. He thought, I'll be damned. On the keyboard, he typed the words HILTON HEAD ISLAND. That's it, he realized. He added four exclamation points. Sure, he could be wrong, but the timing's too neat. He'd bet they found her when they went there to help Adam Whistler.

But hold it. Steady, Roger. That's one hell of a coincidence. For that to be the case, she would have to be living there. And out of all the thousands who live on that island, she'd have to have been spotted by Bannerman's people. It's possible, of course, that she spotted them first. But if she had, would she have approached them? Not likely. I mean, here's a woman who has worked at being dead. Would

Stride have walked up to them, out of the blue, and said, "Hi, guys. Long time no see. Let's do lunch sometime when you're not quite so busy blowing up half of my fucking island."

No, he thought. Hilton Head Island might be where they saw her, but it wouldn't be where she lives. She had to have flown in with Harry Whistler.

That's it, he thought. That begins to make sense. He tapped the return key a couple of times. He typed in the words "From Chamonix."

There was a knock on Clew's door. He ignored it. A second knock came and the door opened partly. Alex stuck his head in. He said, "Mr. Clew? They say they need you back in that meeting."

He did not look up. "I'll be in when I can."

Alex asked, "There's a problem? That phone call from Bannerman?"

"I'm handling it," Clew told him. "Ten minutes."

"You want your coffee?" Alex asked him. "I brought it."

Clew nodded absently. Alex came in. He set the mug on Clew's desk. Clew raised a hand to the monitor's screen to block what he had just written. Alex asked, "Any way I can help?"

"Thank you, no," said Clew. "Close the door if you will."

Rakowsky left the room. He closed the door, but not fully. Clew rose from his chair. He pushed the door shut himself. He sat again and stared at the screen. He murmured the word, "Chamonix."

Chamonix, he thought. Of course. She'd been there with Kessler; she'd been Harry's guest. After that, we know that they came to the States. If we all know that, so would those who were tracking her. She kept moving around with them nipping at her heels. She needed a place where she could settle, be safe. Where would that place be? Wouldn't she have called Bannerman? She and Kessler certainly knew about Westport. One would think that they'd have opted for Westport.

Except Bannerman said no. He said that she'd never been there. And assuming that Kessler had a vote in where they'd go, he would probably not have liked the idea of settling in some yuppie suburb. Kessler's choice would have been Chamonix. Harry Whistler was his friend long before he met Stride and probably before he met Bannerman. He must have been to Harry's lodge a dozen times. He knew every inch of the village below it. But then . . . oh, wait . . . why would Kessler blow his brains out? What had happened with them in between?

She'd dumped him once. It was that Swisher Sweets business. And Bannerman had said that she kept threatening to leave him. So she probably dumped him once and for all. Even so, it still was hard to imagine that Kessler would pop himself over that. Okay, he loved her, but this was Martin Kessler. Women have probably been hitting on him from the day he started to shave. He'd have found all the solace he could handle.

But he did shoot himself. It could have been for something else. It could have been any number of things. Bannerman didn't seem to want to talk about Kessler. In fact, he specifically avoided the subject. So Bannerman must know. And it must have been ugly. Why else would Bannerman duck all questions about him?

Stride stays in Chamonix under Harry's protection. Harry takes her to parties, loosens her up. His friends become her friends. In time, she settles in, buys a house, takes up needlepoint. But Stride is still Stride and she owes Harry Whistler. She can't just sit when young Adam is in trouble. She flies over with them and it's suddenly old home week. And Bannerman had to have known right along that she was alive and with Harry.

He'd as much as said so. Wait, what did he say? He said that Harry flew home with Adam and Claudia and, he said, two or three others. If it's three, two of those would have been the Beasley twins. Harry doesn't go anywhere without them. The third one had to have been Stride.

Thanks a lot, Paul, thought Clew. Thanks for the trust. I'll remember this the next time you need me for something.

An icon on the screen of his computer began flashing. Another cryptogram had come in. He hit a few keys to see who it was from. General Tubbs again. This one was flagged "Urgent." He hit another key and a window appeared in the middle of his file on Stride. Its heading was a shout, nine words, all in caps.

It read, *"DAMN YOU, YOU HAVE SENT US A PLAGUE SHIP."*

15

Clew read the short account with growing confusion. The general seemed to be saying that the ship was infected by some kind of virulent disease. His best officer, he said, was probably doomed along with all the soldiers who had boarded the freighter. They'd been told that none of them could hope to survive, the ship's crew and the children included. They'd been told this by a man in the pay of Savran Bobik.

Clew didn't understand. Calling it a plague ship seemed to suggest that the ship was diseased before the general's troops got there. And who was Bobik's man? Was he already on board? Clew had to assume that he probably was. He must have been escorting the shipment. And if Bobik's man said they were all going to die, it follows that he had to know what was killing them. The general's last lines were, *"The freighter must be burned and sunk so that it cannot reach land. But why should I have to give such an order? This should be on your head, not on mine."*

Clew readied himself to type out a response. His fingers

wanted to write, "Will you fucking calm down?" but he forced them to use gentler language.

Clew wrote in reply, *"I need more specifics. What did Bobik's man say? Ask him what plague. Bubonic? What kind? Are you saying it was part of that shipment to Mobote? What is the condition of your men at this moment? Is the ship still at those coordinates?"* He hit the encryption key and sent it. Clew sat back and stared at the screen.

Alex knocked again and opened the door. "Mr. Clew, they're starting to get pissed in that meeting. They say they have better things to do."

"Let them go," said Clew. "I'll apologize later." He muttered to himself, "I don't need this."

"Same problem as before?"

"Huh? No," he said distractedly. "No connection."

"You need more coffee? Let me get you more coffee."

Alex, too quickly, stepped into the office and reached for the mug on Clew's credenza. Clew tapped a key and his screen went blank before Alex could get a clear view of it. He looked up at Alex, into Alex's eyes. Those eyes had dropped, but not soon enough. He knew that Alex had tried to read the screen.

Clew said to him, "Alex, I do not need more coffee."

Alex blanched. He said, "I'm . . . just trying to be helpful. I'll be outside if you need me."

Clew saw that once again Alex failed to shut the door. Clew did not get up this time. He stayed at his monitor. He knew that he would have to give further thought to how *helpful* Alex was trying to be. And who he was actually helping.

The icon flashed again. The general was responding. This time he seemed more in control of himself. Clew read the message as it scrolled down his screen.

It said, *"The ship is under way. It is headed out to sea. Major Scar had ordered it turned into the wind in order to keep the infection from spreading. He believes that this substance cannot go against the wind. Those already infected are kept at the stern. All others, including the children, are forward. He has a helicopter gunship and a patrol boat, but he says that neither of these craft were exposed. He has ordered them both to stand off. Major Scar informs me that no one shows symptoms, but Bobik's man said they will soon be very sick. First sign will be bloodshot eyes and bad headache. It is not bubonic. Bobik's man said it's Marburg. Do you know Marburg? Even worse than Ebola. Bobik's man said that they cannot survive. He is dead now himself. Loss of blood. He'd been shot. And yes, this container was part of the shipment. Who would send such a thing to such a lunatic as Mobote? Please stand by. Major Scar is reporting again."*

Clew waited. Major Scar? He assumed it was a nickname. Whoever he was, he seemed refreshingly competent. This major was all that was keeping his general from killing a few dozen people.

The next message came a few minutes later. *"I have also consulted a virologist here. He confirms that Marburg is fatal, no question. A very bad death comes within seven days. There is no vaccine, no treatment, no hope for any who have been infected. It only dies when it has consumed the host and no other host is available. That is why isolation is required. The host becomes liquid; he is nothing but blood. Our virologist says this blood is a river of virus. Get some on you and you are a dead man. But blood also dries; it gets blown by the wind. You can be far away and it will find you. This is why I tell you that the ship must be sunk using napalm, I think, so that none can escape.*

"Major Scar accepts this. Also the blame. He confesses that he opened the jar after Bobik's man warned him not to do so. He says that the contents rose up like pink smoke, very fine, very light, and the smoke was alive. He believes that he is most probably infected, as were all who were gathered downwind of his position. Not so, perhaps, all those who were upwind. He suggests quarantine, but this seems too big a risk. I trust that you will make the right decision."

My decision, your ass, Clew said to himself. He leaned forward to make his reply, but he stopped. Like smoke? Very fine? Scar said it was alive? The phrase "weapons-grade" flashed into Clew's mind. Only weapons-grade toxins behave in that way. The pink would be from tissue or chicken blood, the mediums in which they are grown. What would Bobik be doing with weapons-grade Marburg? Where could he have possibly gotten it?

Clew took a deep breath. One thing at a time. He resumed typing out his response.

He wrote, *"Too big a risk? I see almost none. That freighter is at least fifteen miles at sea and you say most aboard are to windward. Quarantine is right. You have nothing to lose. You say that Scar has isolated those who might be infected. Keep them isolated for the full seven days. Give it a month if you must. His chopper and patrol boat can escort and observe and keep all other vessels from approaching. I will not, repeat not, cause that ship to be destroyed until you've given quarantine a chance."*

Clew waited again. Several long minutes passed. Impatient, he opened a window to search for a source that could advise General Tubbs. World Health in Geneva was the logical choice, but he'd never get them to keep this quiet. South Africa, however, had a major facility that might be more inclined to be discreet. The National Institute of Virology, Johannesburg. Clew composed an additional message.

"I think you must also confirm that it's Marburg. You have only the word of a smuggler, now deceased. The jar must be retrieved; it must be examined. Your virologist must know how to handle it safely. If he doesn't, he must enlist someone who does. Have him call Johannesburg now."

Clew waited for a good fifteen minutes this time. He hoped that the general was taking his advice. He hoped that the general wasn't on another phone dispatching a Liberian bomber to that freighter. The icon flashed. Roger Clew bit his lip.

The message read, *"The major agrees with your suggestion of quarantine. He hopes to live to see his wife and baby. True, we only have the smuggler's word that it is Marburg but the major thinks he knows what he is talking about. The smuggler recognized the jar because he'd seen others like it when they were in Bobik's possession. But he swore he didn't know one was part of the shipment until he found it*

*himself while he was stealing. He said that Bobik would
never sell these to Mobote because Mobote had no means to
disperse them. One cannot simply spill them into the wind
and hope that the wind doesn't swirl. Is Bobik's man right?
Is he truthful? We don't know. But why were they going to
Mobote?"*

The message, a long one, continued.

"A part of the problem has been solved," wrote the general. *"Those held at the stern were the captain and crew. I
am informed by Major Scar that they are no longer aboard.
He says that they have chosen to sacrifice themselves by
leaping into the ocean. This happened only minutes ago. He
says that his men are now hosing down the deck. Some must
have started bleeding already."*

Bleeding already? Not this soon, thought Clew. More
likely, they had just been machine-gunned. Way to go,
Major Scar. You're a good one.

"Major Scar," it continued, *"will remain near the stern
until serious symptoms appear. Any others who begin to experience symptoms will join him and stay with him there. If
they become sick, they too will go swimming. I am assured
that Marburg cannot survive after passing through the belly
of a shark."*

Clew took a breath. That did seem the way to bet. But assured? Assured by whom? Had they placed that call to Johannesburg yet? Clew hit the scroll button. He read further.

*"Our government does not wish to consult with Johan-
nesburg. Their white scientists once made similar poisons to
use against opponents of apartheid. Even now, we would not
trust Johannesburg. However, we are seeking advice from
Angola. Our virologist is contacting the Angolan firm whose
name is on the container in question. Major Scar gives the
name of that company as VaalChem. Our government will
also be interested to hear why they have developed such a
terrible substance and why it was going to Mobote."*

As Clew read this he said, "Fuck." And then louder,
"Fucking Bourne." You own VaalChem, don't you, you son
of a bitch? Your own government is damned well going to
ask those same questions.

Clew entered his reply. *"I want that container. I want it as evidence. I believe that if you pack a virus in ice it is dormant and cannot seek a host. Ask your virologist; I believe he'll confirm. Then order Major Scar to find a larger container—an oil drum should do—put that one inside and surround it with ice. Have him seal the drum, place the drum in a lifeboat. Lower it and tow it with the longest line he has. I'll need a few hours to arrange a pickup by a reliable vessel."*

He hit "send" and sat back and waited.

Clew was shooting from the hip and he knew it. The ice part was right. The freighter would have ice. But he was not at all sure what that vessel would be or how he could handle this quietly. The U.S. embassy in Monrovia was bound to have a chopper. Sure, it does, he decided. They all do over there. They're kept on alert and ready to evacuate for whenever the next civil war breaks out. The trick will be to get them to pick up that drum without telling them what is in it.

He was also itching to pick up the phone and start shitting all over Bourne. He muttered, "I've got you, you arrogant bastard. If that's Marburg, you're definitely going to prison. Especially if it's weapons-grade Marburg."

The general's reply came more quickly than expected. It was also very brief and to the point. *"Ice idea is correct. Lifeboat is sensible. But the jar is evidence. We will retain possession. Evidence has been known to become lost in such cases. And this freighter, as payment, is no longer sufficient. After seven days have passed, you and I will renegotiate. You might have many families to compensate."*

Clew cursed, but he wasn't really surprised. The freighter could still end up being sunk. Liberia was already out of pocket on the raid and would probably suffer more losses. Clew hoped that twenty children would not be among them. Bourne was right about that. It would make for bad press. And he hoped that Major Scar would not be among them. He seemed to be an excellent officer. General Tubbs, either way, was going to ask for the moon. If Clew knew General Abednego Tubbs, the general already had a pen in his hand and was putting his wish list together.

Clew slipped his PDA into its cradle. He downloaded all of the decrypted messages. He transferred the originals to a graphics program and then he deleted that program. Not impossible to restore but very difficult. His *Doodlings* box was still on the screen. His notes about Stride and where she'd probably been seen. And that photo: "Almost certainly Stride." He had a lot more than Stride on his mind at the moment. He almost erased it along with his Doodles. He had that photo in his files at home and at two other backup locations. His finger, however, paused over the key. Stride and Bourne, he thought. Bourne wants to find Stride. And now suddenly here's Bourne popping up once again in a context that seems unconnected. Coincidence? Maybe. But it does make one wonder.

Clew downloaded his notes and the photo as well. As before, he erased what remained. He went back into Search and typed in the word *Marburg*. He'd do an hour or so of homework on tropical virology. After that, he'd scan some Foreign Intelligence Files to see how much he could learn about VaalChem. Normally he'd try the FBI and CIA, but he'd bet that those services would be a dry hole. They seemed a little too cozy with Bourne. By lunchtime, he'd be ready to get into his car and do something that was probably unwise. But what's the good of being a political untouchable if you can't have a little satisfaction now and then?

He reached into his desk and found Bourne's invitation to the brunch that had been aborted. He opened the envelope and withdrew the little map that contained the directions to Briarwood. He was going to take a ride to the Shenandoah country. He was going to drop in on Bourne unannounced.

He was going to make Artemus Bourne sweat.

16

Artemus Bourne had been neglecting his bees. The past week had produced some unnerving distractions, but that certainly wasn't the fault of the bees. He should not have left his hives unattended.

He suited up in his Chilly veil and gloves and proceeded to the area in back of the stables where he kept a neat row of ten hives. They weren't ordinary hives; he'd had them specially designed. Their architecture matched the scheme of his house. Rustic-looking, mostly wood, with wide overhanging eaves to protect the actual hive inside.

Nor, in fact, were they ordinary bees. These were African bees, better known as killer bees. Extremely aggressive in defense of the hive. Especially the females; they're the ones with the stingers. The early Romans used to raise them. They would keep them on their warships. They would catapult the hives at enemy ships with the aim of distracting the oarsmen and the archers. All that flapping and swatting as the Romans closed in. It must have been a sight to behold.

Half an hour earlier, he'd received a call warning him that

he might have a visitor. The caller could not be certain of it. All he knew was that Clew had left his office at State after being heard to mutter, "Fucking Bourne." His caller had added, "I'm not sure about this either, but I think he's confirmed that Stride is alive. And I think he might know where she is."

"Excellent," said Bourne. "But I need you to be certain."

"I've got someone at his computer right now. Nothing yet. He's built in some blind alleys."

"If Clew's coming here, you have several hours. Exceed yourself this time. Get it done."

Bourne wasn't sure whether to feel pleased or annoyed when a guard at the main gate announced Clew's arrival. He said that both Clew and his driver were armed, but they wouldn't check their weapons at the gate. Bourne said, "I doubt that he's planning a drive-by. All the same, lead them up here and stay close."

There seemed no end to Mr. Clew's bad manners. Clew had twice ignored his invitations to brunch. Now he shows up unbidden, unfrisked, and in a snit, contemptuous of the house rules. Nor has he arrived in especially good humor if his "Fucking Bourne" is any indication. However, thought Bourne, this intrusion will be tolerable provided that he's kept his end of the bargain and has in fact located Stride. If the news is as promised, all will be forgiven.

Well, not all. But at least this interruption.

Bourne glanced at his watch. It was a quarter past two. Chester could be showing up here any time, his business in Houston completed. We don't need any further unpleasantness, thought Bourne. Bees do best in a tranquil environment. Of course Chester, by himself, still upsets the bees, having traumatized them in the past. In any case, thought Bourne, we'd best keep this meeting brief. A response, an address, then off you go.

Bourne watched as Clew stepped out of his Lincoln. Clew had not bothered to make himself presentable. Shirtsleeves, no jacket, no necktie. The guard who had escorted him gestured toward Clew's lower back and mimed the location of his weapon. Bourne nodded to show that he understood. He said to the guard, "Wait by your car."

Roger Clew's driver had also stepped out, but he stayed at the door of the vehicle. The driver was an older man, jowly, thick-set. That would be Mr. Rakowsky, no doubt. Something less than a genius, he'd been told. He looked as if he wished he were elsewhere. For all of that, however, he did seem alert. His eyes moved constantly, attentive to his duty, and he'd left his engine running at the ready.

Clew's own eyes were locked on the object of his visit. He hesitated, not expecting the bee garb, or, for that matter the hundred or so bees that had alighted on Bourne's head and shoulders.

Clew kept his distance. "Is that you under there?"

Bourne sighed. No greeting. No addressing him by name. Clew seemed even less civil than the last time they spoke. Bourne answered, "Move slowly, and you needn't fear the bees. I gather you know nothing about bees."

"I know that they're bugs. And bugs are right up your alley."

Bourne didn't quite know what to make of that comment. It had the sound of a double entendre, but perhaps Clew was mocking his hobby.

"If you knew the first thing, you would not call them bugs. They are a fascinating species, highly specialized, efficient. They are the perfect model of a Communist Utopia. Lenin kept bees. Did you know that?"

Clew said, "I didn't come here to talk about bees."

"The organism, you see, is the hive, not the bee. The bee has no independent existence. By itself, you'd be correct; it's a bug, just a bug. It's only the big picture that matters."

Clew's hands went to his hips. "Are you through?"

"Very well. Let's have it. I'll just stand here in silence. That way I won't worry about being recorded."

"I'm not wired," said Clew. "I don't need to be wired. We can both strip down naked if you like."

"I . . . um, think that I'd rather be recorded," said Bourne as he gently brushed the bees from his body. "But I accept you at your word. You seem upset. Is there a problem?"

Clew nodded. He said, "Yes. I think you could say that. It came in a red-and-white cooler."

That response startled Bourne. Could Clew mean those heads? How could he possibly know about the heads? He was glad that he hadn't yet removed his hooded veil, lest Clew see that he was at a disadvantage.

Clew said to him, "Weapons-grade Marburg, Mr. Bourne. In a VaalChem container. In that shipment of arms. Why are you producing weapons-grade Marburg?"

Bourne was now doubly startled. Even aghast. His expression, he realized, must be one of confusion. And of ignorance, innocence, total surprise. So why waste it, he decided. He took off his hood.

He said, "I've not the foggiest. What the devil do you mean?"

"I need to say it again? We have the evidence, Bourne. Most of that freighter's crew is already dead. It will probably kill everyone on board."

"Everyone being . . . ?"

"The raiding party and those girls, those kidnapped children just for openers. And God knows how many if that ship should reach land. The Liberians are going to be after your ass, but they're going to need to stand in line."

Bourne raised a staying hand. He said, "I wish you'd go slowly. With more grace, if possible, but more slowly; I can't follow. I take it that the freighter has been intercepted by some sort of force from Liberia."

"It was. Why weapons-grade Marburg?"

"No, no," said Bourne. "More slowly than that. Was that shipment destroyed or was it not?"

"The shipment went down, Mobote's men with it. It went down except for a VaalChem container that had held a lab flask full of Marburg. Bobik's man on board stole it along with some drugs and along with the VaalChem container it came in. It's your bad luck that Bobik's man is a thief. Without him we might never have known."

Bourne affected a pained, yet patient expression. "Known *what*, for heaven's sake. Exactly what are you asking?"

Clew showed his teeth. "I have to say it again? I think you're producing weapons-grade Marburg. If you're making it, it follows that you're selling it."

"Mr. Clew," he said calmly. "It's quite clear that you dislike me. But you must try to keep that from coloring your judgment. First of all, that shipment was Bobik's, not mine. I promise you I've never met the man. As for selling it—to whom? Do you think to Mobote? Why then would I have urged you to sink it?"

"Because it was evidence. You wanted it destroyed."

Bourne threw up his hands in a show of dismay. He said, "Very well. Let's take these things in order." But he stopped himself when another thought struck him. He said, "I've just been threatened with the wrath of Liberia. Did I understand you correctly?"

"You did."

"Liberia, Mr. Clew, is not a world power. Its government is barely a Liberian power. You might as well tell me that I'm in disfavor with some gang from the South Bronx or Watts." He raised his hand again. "But I digress."

Bourne said, "Let's take this box. This VaalChem container. Those containers are shipped all over the world. They're *containers,* you see. They are *shipping* containers. Most are discarded when they've served that purpose. Some, I don't doubt, end up being reused. I wouldn't be surprised if people pack their lunches in them even though they sometimes carry human organs. The container that you speak of could have come from nearly anywhere. It has no evidentiary value."

Clew started to speak. Bourne said, "No, hear me out."

He said, "VaalChem, as you know, is a biotech firm specializing in tropical virology. They make vaccines, Mr. Clew. Vaccines of all kinds. Although my grasp of that process is limited, I know that one cannot develop a vaccine without studying the virus that one hopes to defeat. Does VaalChem have Marburg? I would assume that they do. I would assume that they have cultures of smallpox as well. And Ebola, Lassa fever, HIV . . . the whole spectrum."

Clew blinked. "You said smallpox? Where would you get smallpox?"

"I think you know that it's readily acquired."

Clew shook his head. "Not legally, it isn't."

"In that case, I must be mistaken."

Bourne snorted inwardly. Not legally, he says. Clew was just being annoying. The popular notion is that no one has smallpox. No one except the CDC in Atlanta and a similar facility in Russia. Small samples, kept frozen, entirely safe. In truth, that story is a comfortable fiction. The Defense Department knows perfectly well that at least six other countries have it. As for the Russian supply, their so-called "small samples," they've actually made twenty tons of the stuff. They've tested it repeatedly in ICBM warheads. They've tested it in special refrigerated warheads to keep the heat of reentry from cooking it.

"This 'whole spectrum,'" asked Clew. "Is it all weapons-grade?"

"You've used that term. I haven't. Who *says* it's weapons-grade?"

"I told you," Clew answered. "Bobik's man had some. He'd seen it before. A Liberian virologist confirmed it."

"This virologist was on board?"

"He was in radio contact. He confirmed it based on its physical description."

Bourne smiled almost gently. He shook his head slowly. He said, "Now I wish you'd recorded all this. That way you'd be able to play it back later and hear just how ludicrous it sounds. Confirmed? By radio? By a *Liberian* virologist? Next you'll tell me that he's the top man in his field. His field has how many in Liberia? Two? I know that sounds elitist, if not racist, but so be it."

Bourne went on.

He said, "Your other expert witness is some piglike Nigerian who's not only a smuggler, but you say he's a thief. That's Bobik's man, correct? Some clown named Moshood? And yes, I knew that this man would be on board. I didn't mention him among the particulars I gave you because he should not have been significant. If you want to get to the bottom of this, I suggest that you track down Bobik himself. Ask *him* your questions. I'm sure you'll get better answers. You might find that he has a better head on his shoulders than the errand boy he sent with that shipment."

Oh, my, thought Bourne. A better head on his shoulders? What Freudian principle caused that to pop out? Never mind. Doesn't matter. Clew won't get it.

"Let me summarize," said Bourne. "We had an agreement; I've done my part; you've stopped that arms shipment. Something went wrong; you'd love to blame me, but you can't, so go deal with it yourself."

"Yeah, we had an agreement. But you're lying through your teeth. Now you want me to tell you where to find Stride. What does she have to do with germ warfare, Mr. Bourne? What connection does she have to all this?"

"None whatever."

"Oh, really?" said Clew. "As it happens, I know better."

"No, you don't. If you did, you wouldn't have asked. And you don't because the two are not related."

Bourne waited for some rejoinder from Clew. None came. He'd been right. The man was bluffing. Bourne said, "You're either fishing or you're looking to renege. Please excuse me for a moment. I have to pee. I'll remind you that you have given your word. When I come back, I expect you to keep it."

Bourne stepped behind a shrub at the rear of the stables. An indelicate ruse, but he needed a moment. Clew had said something that had caused a stirring somewhere deep within the wiring of his brain. What connection? There was none. At least not directly. Elizabeth Stride and this shipment of arms? They should not have been related, but were they?

The shipment was Bobik's. In the works for some time. He'd asked Chester whether Bobik might be selling VaalChem's wares. Chester couldn't be sure, but Bobik certainly had access. And we know that Bobik might have "tried them out" against Alameo and that bunch. But would Bobik have sold Marburg to a lunatic like Mobote? It would be vastly more likely to kill Mobote and everyone within a few miles of him. Could killing Mobote have been his intention? No, certainly not. If it were, he could have simply poisoned those condiments that Chester said had been included. A dose of strychnine in Mobote's barbecue sauce. A dash of hemlock in his paprika.

But suppose that Bobik really did ship the Marburg. And that's *if* it was Marburg. We're not sure of that yet. We'd be sure if Clew had mentioned the color of the label. If the label was pink, it was certainly Marburg. If the label was yellow it was Marburg and then some. It was Marburg grafted to smallpox. Clew may not even know and we can't ask him, of course. We're not supposed to know such details.

Bourne's urine stream had reduced to a trickle. But he held his pose. He wanted more time to think.

Very well, he decided. Say the flasks contained Marburg. Say that Bobik did in fact get his hands on that material. Say he did ship some to Mobote. Would Bobik have shipped them in a *VaalChem container*? He could not have been so stupid. It's not possible.

At that moment he felt the same stirring again, but this time it was rising in volume. This time it seemed to be shouting at him. It was asking him, *"When did Bobik die?"*

What had Chester said? Bourne was trying to think. They'd got Bobik first. He was the ripest of the three. They may have only brought his head to Winfield's office. They'd shipped all three heads on the Friday or Saturday preceding their arrival here at Briarwood. But the arms for Mobote hadn't left by then, had they? According to Chester, they hadn't. And Alameo, according to Chester, had wrung Bobik dry before detaching his head from his body.

Oh, damn, thought Bourne.

Alameo. He did this.

Among the things he had wrung out of Bobik must have been the details of this shipment. He found the crates before they were put on that freighter. But wouldn't he simply have taken the weapons? No. Too heavy. Too much to haul off. Or too much to get past army checkpoints in Luanda. So he booby-trapped the shipment in such a way that the virus would be traced back to VaalChem. That would have been his motive, not Duganga's stolen diamonds. He sent that lab flask in a VaalChem container like those in which he sent the three heads. Mobote was to open it, probably sniff it, and decide that it didn't seem flavorful enough. He and everyone around him would be dead within days.

Alameo sent one, but he must have kept others. Not just Marburg. All those different strains of smallpox. He might or might not have a plan for their use, but something will doubtless occur to him. And if he found all those toxins in Winfield's safe, he probably found the corresponding vaccines and Winfield would have told him which is which. One assumes that he'd have Winfield inject himself first to be sure that Winfield was not being sly. That done, would he not have injected himself? Against everything? All of it? Bourne wondered. Can one do that? If he could, he's now immune and so is Duganga. So are all of Duganga's key people.

Oh, my, thought Bourne. This gets worse and worse.

Roger Clew called out, "Um . . . I don't have all day."

Bourne muttered, "Prostate problems. One moment."

He shook himself off. He zipped himself up. He repeated, Oh, my. This is not at all good. Finding Stride grows more essential by the hour.

He took another moment to gather himself. He said to Clew, "No more fencing. I think you've found Stride. I think you've delivered my proposal."

Clew stared at him hard. "A little bird told you? That same little bird back at State?"

"Informed intuition. I can see it in your eyes. And you're going to try to tell me she's dead."

He saw that Clew was vacillating. He was making up his mind. Clew surprised him by saying, "No, I won't. And yeah, I have."

Bourne's heart leaped. "Well, where is she? What did she say?"

"She said that you're full of shit about VaalChem. Oh, wait. That wasn't her. That was me."

Bourne darkened. He repeated, "You've given your word."

Clew gestured toward Bourne's feet. "You know you've pissed on your shoes?"

Bourne narrowed his eyes. "I will ask you one more time."

"And you got a few drops down your pants leg."

"Mr. Clew . . ."

"She did get your message. That's all I agreed to. Her answer was no; she does not want to see you. And I'm going to shut VaalChem down."

"Do your worst," said Bourne. "You gave her the whole message?"

"What? That you'd pay her? She isn't for sale."

"You were to say to her, *'He isn't dead either.'"*

"Either she didn't know who you're talking about or she didn't care either way," replied Clew.

Bourne blinked. "You're a liar. That cannot be true."

"Sticks and stones, Mr. Bourne, but I'll spell it out for you. If your 'he' is Martin Kessler, she knows better; he's dead. If your 'he' is someone else from her past, that's where he's going to stay. In her past."

As Clew spoke, Bourne looked deeply into his eyes. He realized that Clew wasn't toying with him. Clew actually believed what he was saying.

Bourne wanted to say, *"You damned fool,"* but he didn't. He said with forced calm, "You may leave now."

"Oh, I'm going. I'll be busy. I'm going to hurt you."

"With that? You have nothing. Good-bye, Mr. Clew."

Clew started toward his car. He looked back over his shoulder. He said, "I'm also going to get you for killing your wife. One way or the other, you're finished."

"Please get off my property, Mr. Clew."

That last part, the wife thing, had barely registered with Bourne. It was a dead issue, so to speak. And gratuitous. Clew had already managed to make him lose his temper. He had very nearly said far too much.

Stride knows he's dead, does she? She's certain? You damned fool. Stride might believe it and you might believe it, but she doesn't know any such thing.

Bourne wanted to say, *"You don't think he's alive? Take a walk with me down to my freezer. I'll show you three more of those VaalChem containers. I'll show you the calling card that came with Savran Bobik's. It's a poster. Here, let me unfold it."*

He'd like to have said, *"See? Does it begin to sink in? Alameo is Kessler. Kessler is Alameo. 'Alameo' is Portuguese. What it means is 'the German.' He's alive and, I assure you, he's kicking."*

But Bourne couldn't say that. Not now. Not in this context. If Clew were to realize that those two men are one, he would quickly put the rest of this together. Clew's antipathy may have been clouding his judgment, but that only made the man stubborn, not stupid. Those heads, and especially Savran Bobik's remains, would do violence to one's claim of noninvolvement.

And truth be told? That claim was largely true. He was innocent of almost every part of this.

Damn Bobik, thought Bourne. He had brought all this on. If he hadn't tortured and beheaded that woman, we wouldn't have Kessler seeking vengeance in kind. What was her name? Sara. She was Kessler's *new* woman. That tidbit alone might have been of use in pulling the strings of his former love, Stride. Kessler's been less than faithful. How would she respond to that? She would not have required him to be faithful if dead. But *pretending* to be dead? And then dallying with Sara? It seems imprudent to cheat on an assassin.

We'd best keep that to ourselves if she's to be of any use. And we're getting off the subject, thought Bourne.

If Kessler had simply killed Bobik and been done with it, he might never have learned that VaalChem was testing certain of its creations on the rebels. But he did question Bobik. Duganga might have insisted. Duganga would have wanted to know what became of his stolen diamonds. That would have led to Bobik telling them about Mobote. Ratting him out, as they say. Kessler learns of the shipment; Kessler booby traps the shipment, never dreaming that it might be intercepted. And but for Bobik's greed and Kessler's revenge, VaalChem's useful work might have gone on unnoticed. All that would have remained would be to neutralize Kessler through his one Achilles' heel, namely Stride. Neutralize him, control him, and through him, Duganga. Through Duganga, we control all those excellent diamonds. We control the entire world market.

But now we have Roger Clew, more annoying than ever, threatening to cause even more disruption. How much does he know and how much of it is bluff? We'd best know the answer, and quickly.

Bourne placed another call to his contact at State. He was careful not to use the man's name. On reaching him, he asked, "What success have you had?"

"Getting into his files? Not much, I'm afraid. If our other friend is right and he has found that woman, he's buried his notes somewhere in his system and he seems to have downloaded some. We found one early message from some general in Liberia. It looks like it should have been the first of a series, but we don't see anything more recent."

"Downloaded them?" asked Bourne. "To another computer?"

"If he hasn't, he will. He has one in his apartment. From that one, apparently, he spreads them around. As you know, he is tight with a certain friend up north. I'd bet he parks copies up there. He is, incidentally, going up there next Tuesday. He's marked off three days on his calendar. The word is, there's some sort of . . . I don't know . . . some summit meeting."

Bourne paused. "Well, never mind then. It's really not worth the trouble."

"It isn't? Mr. Bourne, I was under the impression . . ."

The man sounded piqued. He had risked his career. Never mind that he'd been well rewarded.

"It's no longer a concern," Bourne told him. "But I thank you."

Bourne had lied to him, of course. He was more interested than ever. And Clew won't be attending any meetings. But it was better to have his friend at State think that nothing more was to be done. If questioned under oath, he could say that's where it ended. Artemus Bourne had shown total indifference.

Bourne looked at his watch. Lilly must be on his way. Bourne took his cell phone from the pocket of his overalls and punched out the number of Chester's device. Chester answered on the third ring.

Bourne asked him, "Where are you at this moment?"

"On my way from the airport. Just got in from Houston. Look, I have to tell you, the news isn't good. There's some scary stuff missing over there."

"I am not surprised. And you don't know the half of it. Where are Toomey and Kuntz? Can you reach them?"

"Sure, why?"

"Do you recall asking me whether you could have Clew? I've had a change of heart. You may have him."

Chester hesitated. He said, "All these names. Are you using the cell phone I got you?"

"I am."

"The Nokia, right? The GSM digital?"

"Very nearly impossible to eavesdrop," Bourne answered. "You've explained that. I took it to heart."

"Okay, but you still shouldn't say too much more. I'll be there in fifteen minutes. You can tell me when and where."

"This evening," Bourne answered. "Before he gets to his apartment. I will tell you exactly what I need you to do. You are not to deviate from it."

"Mr. Bourne . . . I got the picture. Fifteen minutes."

17

"That looked pretty ugly," said Alex to Clew at the start of their drive back to Washington.

Clew didn't reply. He stared ahead.

"I could see his face after you walked away. The guy was not having good thoughts."

Still nothing.

"I'd say he looked like he had a bee in his bonnet, but that would be beating this to death. Except, from all I hear, Bourne's not someone to mess with. I bet you that he's on the phone right now, trying to get you reassigned to some shit hole, maybe embassy duty in Kabul."

Clew took a breath. "I need to ask you a question. Is there anything you think you should tell me?"

"Like what?"

"Like whether you've had business with Bourne."

Alex turned in his seat. "Where'd that come from?"

"It's a simple question, Alex. Yes or no?"

Clew was watching to see whether Alex turned pale. He didn't. His color was rising. "You're asking me whether I have been bought. Is that what you're asking, Mr. Clew?"

"Consider this practice for a lie detector test. I'm going to need you to take one."

"About me and Bourne? That's the question you'll ask? Back then was the first time I ever saw him. What, you think I'm a regular at his brunches?"

"With his people, then. Have any approached you? Have you ever met with anyone in his employ?"

"Mr. Clew . . . this is getting me mad."

Clew chewed on his lip for a moment before speaking. "Bourne does have someone on the inside at State. He knows things he shouldn't have known."

"You're saying he has sources." Then sarcastically, "You *think*? We're State. This guy's world. Of course he has sources. He probably has hundreds. That doesn't mean anyone's bought."

Clew started to speak. Alex held up a hand. "In the first fucking place, I have taken an oath. I do my job; I follow orders; no one buys me. Second, just for practice for my lie detector test, I admit that I have met two of his people and that one of them did tempt me a little."

"Who and when?"

"The first one was what's-his-name . . . Chester. Chester Lilly. I met him when he came to State to see you. You recall that I sit outside your door, do you not? You recall that you blew him off, do you not? This is how it came to pass that I met him."

"Not since?"

"Never seen him, never heard from him, never again. Negative. *Nada*. No more after that. No time, no way, not fucking ever."

"Lose the attitude, Alex. I do have to ask. Who's the other one? You said you were tempted."

"I'm not sure I should tell you. Maybe I should take the Fifth."

"Alex . . . I'm really in no mood for jokes."

"Yeah, well I'm in no mood to have my loyalty questioned. The other one was Claire, the English babe who brought you Bourne's invitation. I showed her in, remember? I could hear every word. I could see she was ready to give you a blow job if that would have got you to go to Bourne's brunch. I suspected that I could have got one myself if I promised that I'd try to talk you into it."

Clew almost smiled. He didn't respond.

His driver asked him, "You happy? Are we through with the questions?"

Clew answered, "One more." He paused for a moment. "Alex, who else do you report to at State?"

"I report to security. You know that."

"I mean on my activities. And you know what I'm asking."

"Like . . . does anyone get curious?" asked Alex. "Sure they do. All the time. It's not news that you make people nervous. Do I answer their questions? That depends on their rank. It also depends on whether I know. And most of the time I know zip."

"Who in particular?"

A brief pause. "No one special."

Clew folded his arms. "Very well."

"You don't believe me?"

"I believe there might be something that you wish you had told me. Take your time. Let me know when you think of it."

Neither man spoke much for the rest of the trip. Clew thought it best to give Alex some room. As Alex had said, he took an oath; he follows orders. But it's not always clear whose orders to follow. And sometimes all you're asked is to do a small favor. It seems harmless; you do it; you want to be a team player. Except that there are teams and there are teams.

They got back to the State Department building on C Street. By then it was almost four o'clock. Clew spent the next two hours on his computer, gathering all that he could find about VaalChem and especially about Artemus Bourne. A lot of it was blocked. Clew wasn't surprised. He would find out exactly who blocked it, but for now, he downloaded those files that he found.

There were no further messages from General Tubbs. It was ten o'clock at night in Liberia. On Bourne's death ship, Clew supposed, there was nothing to be done. Nothing but wait. Steering into the wind. That major hoping that he'd live to see his wife and child, but knowing that he probably wouldn't.

Alex had knocked on his door only once. It was shortly after they had returned. He said he'd missed lunch; he was going to grab a sandwich in the sixth-floor cafeteria. He didn't ask whether Clew wanted anything for himself. That was unusual. Alex normally asked. It made Clew wonder where Alex was actually going. Very probably, he thought, to some other office to tell someone that he might be in trouble.

At half past six, Clew loaded his briefcase with the day's unread mail and with his PDA, which held all the files he'd downloaded. Briefcase in hand, he stepped out of his office. Alex was back at his desk.

He said to Alex, "Long day. Let's go home."

Alex rose, but he did not meet Clew's eyes.

18

Chester Lilly waited with the woman named Claire in a car a block and a half from Clew's building. It was twilight. A light rain was falling. Clew's car would approach by one of two routes. Chester's car was positioned so that he could see both of them as well as the entrance to the building's garage. Claire had already learned from the doorman that Clew almost never went in through the lobby. Almost always the garage and almost always on foot. He was usually dropped off at the ramp.

Chester's muscle was already in the garage. Toomey and Kuntz had entered on foot because access by vehicle required a card that would raise the cantilevered wooden barrier. Toomey, the ex-cop, had jammed the arc of one of the two surveillance cameras. Its sweep would now stop short of a space directly in front of the elevator. Anyone watching the monitors in the lobby would probably not notice the shortfall.

The cage fighter, Kuntz, had broken into a van that had been parked there unused for some time. The van was covered with a month's worth of soot and the layer on its wind-shield had not been disturbed. Its owner, Kuntz decided, was not likely to appear. They would wait in the van unseen by other residents who might enter the garage before Clew.

Both men wore Baltimore Orioles jackets. Both men had knitted orange ski masks in their pockets and each had a pair of leather gloves. The jackets and the ski masks were the first items that any potential witness would be likely to de-scribe and possibly all that any witness would remember. They were easily disposed of after use.

Chester kept his cell phone flipped open and ready so that he could alert them when Clew's car appeared. He'd told Claire that she could go, that he no longer needed her. "Go get yourself a drink and relax."

She said, "No. I'll stay. Mr. Bourne wants me with you."

He answered, "You'll do what I tell you."

She said, "A man with a woman is less likely to be noticed than a man would be sitting by himself. We're an innocent couple. We're sitting here chatting. I'll pretend to be chat-ting. All you need to do is nod."

Claire stopped pretending when Chester announced, "I'm going to want to see this myself."

Claire straightened. She said, "Don't even think it."

He said, "Clew won't see me. He'll be out cold by then. I just want to see what Kuntz does to his face."

"You've seen what he does. And Clew has seen both of us. It's not worth the risk of being made."

"He hit me. Did you know that? Right in front of Mr. Bourne. That little prick grabbed me by the hair."

Claire closed her eyes. She said, "Your hair looks just gor-geous. That's the first thing I noticed when you picked me up. I think Terrence is an absolute genius."

Chester growled, "Now you're stroking me. Quit it."

"No, it's the truth. You have beautiful hair. I could pick you out from a block away, which is why we're at a block and a half."

"Don't get smart."

She said, "Okay, let's review why we're here. Job one is to get Clew's PDA so Mr. Bourne can see what is on it. Job

two is to make it look like a mugging, which means they
take his watch and his wallet. Job three is to beat the shit out
of Clew because he was rude to Mr. Bourne. All three jobs
can be done in two minutes flat. Let's not make this a spec-
tator sport."

"Just one look," said Chester. "I'll bring an umbrella. That
way my hair's dry and nobody sees it."

"Chester, if Mr. Bourne heard you right now . . ."

He reached for her hand. He dug his fingernails into it.
"Say one word, it's your ass. Do you understand me?"

"And if you don't let go," she said wincing, "it's your
balls. Chester, get your fucking hand off me."

He released and pointed. "There's his Lincoln," he said.
He tapped out a number on his cell phone. "We're rolling."

Alex pulled the Lincoln up to the ramp. He said, "Look, Mr.
Clew . . ." But he didn't finish. He said, "Never mind. Good
night, sir."

Clew asked, "Alex, why don't you come up for a drink?
Maybe watch a little basketball. We'll talk."

Alex sucked on his lip. He wasn't quite ready. He said, "I
would, but my wife . . . we play bridge on Friday nights. I
promised her I'd be home by eight."

"In the morning then," said Clew. "Stop by; we'll get
some breakfast."

"Yeah, breakfast. I'll see you tomorrow."

Clew opened his door and stepped out onto the sidewalk.
He said to Alex, "You have a good night."

Clew walked to the ramp and had nearly reached the bottom before he heard the Lincoln pull away. He also heard the
squeak of a car door's hinge from somewhere deep in the
garage. He thought nothing of it. Some other tenant. His
mind was more on Alex, who had seemed a decent man.
Good record, no black marks, decorated in Vietnam; he'd
put three daughters through college. If he'd somehow gotten
in over his head, Clew felt sure that he'd come clean in the
morning.

He switched his briefcase from his right hand to his left in
order to fish for his keys. One of the keys was a tubular de-

vice that allowed residents to use the garage elevator. As he inserted it, he felt a small chill. It occurred to him that no engine had started after he'd heard that one squeak. He released his keys, left them dangling in the panel, and slipped his hand under his jacket. His fingers found the butt of the pistol he carried. He wasn't greatly alarmed. He did not draw the weapon. But he turned, protecting his chest with his briefcase because muggers had been known to work garages like this one.

They had seemed to come from nowhere. They were on him at once. Two men wearing ski masks, baseball jackets. One of them turned sideways, aimed a kick at his groin. Clew blocked it by lowering his briefcase to that region, but the force of the kick slammed him backward. Clew's shoulders and head hit the elevator door. He tried to draw his pistol, but another kick came. The impact crushed his fingers against it. The second man grabbed him by his right arm and spun him. Clew's face hit the elevator door. He felt a hand groping for the pistol through his jacket. Clew managed to work the safety catch with his thumb. He gritted his teeth. He squeezed the trigger twice.

He felt a shock of pain as the bullet creased his buttock and he heard a cry of "Shit" from the man who'd tried to grip it. The man backed away; he was clutching his fingers. The man hissed, "Fucker shot me. Take him out."

Clew had partly turned; he almost had his gun free when a blow to his kidneys lifted him off his feet. His briefcase fell. He had no strength to hold it. The fingers holding his weapon turned flaccid. He could see a fist poised. It was aimed at his face. He tried to use his thumb to attack that man's eye, but his arm would not obey his brain's command. The man with the fist took Clew's arm, almost gently, and lowered it out of his way. Clew saw the fist coming. It chopped downward at his eye. Clew heard a popping sound as his cheekbone shattered, but he felt little pain, only numbness. The fist came again. It struck the same spot. This time he saw only flashes of light. When the flashes cleared he realized, although now only dimly, that his eyes were looking in two different directions. One must have gone out of alignment. With his good eye he saw that the man who'd cried "Shit" had his hand to his mouth and was sucking blood from it. Clew could see, again dimly, that the man had Clew's pistol. He heard the man snarl from inside his knitted mask. He saw the pistol come up. It was coming at Clew's mouth. The man jammed it through his lips. Clew heard his teeth snap. He heard the other man say, "We don't shoot him. Give me room."

Clew saw, in slow motion, another fist coming. It was all that he saw. He saw nothing more. After that, there was only a dull thumping sound and the crunch of more bones in his face.

Rakowsky had made a left turn, passed in front of Clew's building, then only got two stoplights farther. It was Friday night gridlock in Georgetown. The falling rain deepened his already dark mood. Now he wished that he'd taken Clew's offer. Go up to his apartment, have two or three vodkas, and get a few things off his chest.

Yeah, he'd told Clew the truth; he'd had no contact with Bourne. But, yeah, he'd become an informant. There were nicer ways to put it, but that was the word. A goddamn backstabbing informant.

The man at State who approached him was Henderson Quigley. He was bureau chief on the African desk. Used to be U.S. Consul to Angola.

Quigley said, "As you may know, Clew goes his own way. A good man, don't mistake me, but not a team player. Moreover, he has antagonized a man whose activities are vital to our nation's interests." He asked, "Alex, are you a team player?"

Alex had told him, "Hey, I'm not your guy. You got problems with Clew, talk to Clew."

But then the things Quigley asked him, they were always so small. Alex threw him a tiny little bone now and then just to keep this guy off his back. Quigley asked, "What are his habits? Who does he see?"

"That's your question? Clew sees fifty people a day."

"I mean anyone . . . remarkable. Anyone you thought odd."

"Clew works, eats, and sleeps. He gets up and he jogs. Maybe two nights a week he goes out on a date. Don't ask me how often he gets laid."

"Oh, I wouldn't. Of course not," said Quigley. "Unless . . ."

"Don't start with 'unless.' I won't touch it."

"Fair enough. Nor should you. I understand. I have just one other small question."

They were always small questions. But they start to add up. He went in to tell Quigley, "That's it. No more," but then Quigley dangled a promotion. The promotion meant an extra two hundred a month for the rest of his life when he retired. That two hundred would just about cover the payments on some college loans that were still strangling him. Quigley said, "It's no gift. I think you're way overdue. You can take the raise in pay in good conscience."

But it wasn't in good conscience. It bothered him. It ate at him. He knew that he'd been bought cheap.

"Screw this," said Alex, as he flipped his turn signal. "I'm not waiting till the morning. I'm telling Clew now. I'm telling him about fucking Quigley."

Chester, with Claire, had moved his car to within a hundred feet of the building's garage. They were on a one-way side street, not much traffic, no pedestrians, but some could appear at any time. With the car's engine running, they sat and waited for Toomey and Kuntz to emerge and climb in. They heard two muffled and echoing shots. Chester spat an obscenity. "I told them no guns. Oh, shit. Do you think that's Clew shooting?"

He reached for his umbrella. Claire said to him, "Don't."

"Two shots; they could be down. I gotta go look. You get behind the wheel. You be ready." He opened the door and he unfurled his umbrella before stepping out into the rain.

She said, "I'll wait for one minute, not one second more. You three bozos will be on your own."

She watched as Chester trotted up to the entrance. He crouched, peered down the ramp, turned, and gave her thumbs-up. She revved the car's engine in response. Sec-

onds later, Toomey and Kuntz both appeared. She saw that
Toomey was cradling his left hand with his right. She could
see that the hand was bleeding badly. Kuntz stripped his ski
mask from his melon-shaped head. He had Clew's briefcase
under his arm. Kuntz, too, was massaging the knuckles of
one hand. No doubt, he had bruised it on Clew.

She saw Chester gesture toward Toomey's ski mask. Get
it off. Look normal. Keep your head down. Chester pushed
them toward the car, but Chester wasn't following. He held
up one finger. He mouthed, "One minute." She leaned her
head out the window, hissing, "Don't. Don't go down there."

But that was exactly what Chester was doing. He couldn't
resist. He had to see. Toomey and Kuntz reached the car and
climbed in. Toomey was in pain. He said, "Son of a bitch.
He blew off part of my finger. It's squirting blood. You got a
towel?"

Claire told him, "Use your jacket. Don't get it on the
seat." She tapped her horn angrily, three times.

Chester found Clew where the other two had left him. Clew
had slid down the elevator door. Chester saw that Clew's
keys still dangled from the panel. He decided that he might
as well take them.

He still held the umbrella; it was still fully open. He squat-
ted over Clew to make a closer inspection. He felt something
crunching under his foot. He looked. It was one of Clew's
teeth. He saw with satisfaction that Clew's face was raw
meat. From the middle of his brow to his now crooked jaw,
Clew's face was a mass of blood and swelling. Clew didn't
seem conscious, but his eyes were partly open. One more
than the other. It bulged out of its socket. Clew suddenly
gagged. He was choking.

Chester said softly, "You still feel? Glad to hear it."

He leaned closer. He said, "You like to pull hair? Well, for
that, I'm going to scalp you, you little shit." He reached into
his pocket for his clasp knife.

Claire saw the headlights coming up the street behind her.
She said, "You two get down. Duck your heads."

She averted her face as the vehicle passed, but she looked up again when its brake lights came on. She saw, to her horror, that the car was Clew's Lincoln. It was turning into the garage. "Damn you, Chester," she muttered. "You two stay here." She climbed out of the car and walked quickly toward the ramp, her hand reaching for the gun in her purse.

Rakowsky stopped to use his card in the cantilevered barrier. It raised up; he drove into the garage. His eyes were on the space that was reserved for Clew's car, but he saw a sudden movement ahead and to his right. It was a man. With an umbrella. It was opened indoors. The man was behind the row of parked cars. He was trying to squeeze between the cars and the wall while hiding behind the umbrella. It was only then that Rakowsky noticed the shape that was crumpled by the elevator door. He saw blood on the door, streaks and splatters.

In almost the same motion, he threw the Lincoln into park, opened the door, and drew his weapon. He swept the Beretta over half the garage before dropping its sights to the umbrella. He steadied his aim on the roof of the Lincoln and called, "Hold it. Right there. One more step and I shoot."

The man froze, but Alex could not see his hands. He said, "One chance. You're going to close up that umbrella. Use both hands to do it. Do it slow."

The man shifted his weight. He seemed to lean toward the ramp. Alex knew that the man was measuring his chances, deciding whether he should risk running. But Alex was deciding whether to shoot. It could be a resident who stumbled on something and decided that he wanted no part of it. Except not with the umbrella. The umbrella was wrong.

Alex decided. "I'm shooting on three. Here's one; here's two . . ."

"Take it easy. Don't shoot."

"Close the umbrella. Hold it straight up. I want to see both your hands all the way."

The man still hesitated. Alex said, "Okay, three." Taking careful aim, he put a hole through the umbrella. The man jumped. He lowered the umbrella part way.

Alex saw the face, the wavy blond hair. He said, "Lilly? Chester Lilly?"

Lilly didn't respond.

Alex blinked. He felt a knot form in his stomach as he realized who the body by the elevator must be. He said to Lilly, "Is that Mr. Clew?"

Lilly's hands were at his shoulders. He shrugged.

"Get on your knees," said Alex. "Do it now."

Lilly obeyed. Very slowly.

Alex kept his gun on him as he reached for his cell phone. He punched out 911. He waited, then spoke. "My name's Alex Rakowsky." He gave his location, side door, garage entrance. He cited his State Department ID. "My boss has been bushwacked, I think shot, maybe dead. I need EMS, police. Make sure they know I'm armed. I'm holding the bastard who . . ."

Alex felt three blows against his ribs and his hip. He heard the three shots being fired. At first he didn't realize that he had been shot because the shots sounded more like loud slaps. Lilly darted. Alex fired. Lilly yelped, but kept going. Alex swung his pistol toward the source of the slaps. He saw the woman. He knew her at once. The one who gives blow jobs for Bourne. She was backing away, telling Lilly to move. The gun in her hand was a small one, small caliber. He realized that was why he wasn't knocked off his feet, but he felt himself sinking, sliding down the Lincoln's fender. He felt the strength draining from his arms and his legs. His head was beginning to swim.

He heard Lilly bark, "Finish him. Kill him. He knows us."

She snapped back at him, "Get out of here. *Now!*"

Alex raised his Beretta. It was terribly heavy. He jerked off two shots in the direction of Lilly, but the bullets went wild, making sparks against concrete. He heard another slap. A bullet pinged off the Lincoln.

Lilly shouted, "Get closer with that popgun. A head shot."

The woman shouted back, "I hear sirens. Get out." Alex saw that she was now coming toward him.

He raised his gun hand with the aid of the other. He fired. He missed. She fired. She hit him. Two more slaps, one hit his throat, the other his cheek. Alex couldn't see. There were only shapes and shadows. Nor could he hear except for dull echoes and a steady ringing sound that came from inside his head. He felt pain, also dull, in his chest and in his head. He remembered, dimly, that he had been shot, but his brain told him no, it's a dream; you're only dreaming. That's why you can't see. It's not real.

One of the shadows grew much larger than the others. It was the shadow that had started where he'd last seen the woman and it was advancing on him. It seemed to him that he knew her, that he'd recognized her, but his mind was unable to recall who she was. He leaned farther back as the shadow approached him. He saw his hands rise as if of their own will and he saw two brilliant red flashes. His Beretta had bucked and tumbled onto his chest. He heard an echoing roar that seemed strangely distant. And a fountain had erupted. It was a fountain of red; it spurted upward and arced downward. He could feel its warm rain on his face. In that instant, however, the shadow enveloped him. A weight fell across him. It covered his face. It caused his head to slam backward against a hard surface. But the weight wasn't hard. It was soft.

His mind tried to grasp what was happening to him. All was silent. All was dark. He tried to feel what was on him. He felt softness; he felt fabric; he smelled scented flesh. A woman was on him. She was lying on top of him. A part of his brain thought he had to be dreaming. A fantasy dream. He'd had them before. He liked having such dreams; he would readily admit it, although perhaps not to his wife. But they're the dreams that a man has a right to enjoy. It's no sin because they're not voluntary.

This dream woman's breasts were covering his face. He brought up his hand to try to touch them, to feel them. His groping was awkward. She must not have liked it. She began to move away. She slid down him a little and then off him. She settled into the crook of his arm. That's okay, he thought. We'll just lie here together. His hand crept to her cheek. Her hair had fallen across it. He tried to be gentle as he brushed it away. He stroked it. It was wet. She must be crying.

Suddenly it came to him. He knew who she was. He thought he knew why she was crying.

He whispered, "Elizabeth? You're Elizabeth, aren't you."

She didn't answer. Nor did she move. He realized that his voice sounded bubbly and scratchy. He thought that maybe she couldn't hear him.

This began to feel more and more like a dream. He knew that Mr. Clew had been trying to find her. He knew that she must have come here to see him. But now Mr. Clew wasn't able to see her because . . . because . . .

Now he couldn't remember. He couldn't think why. But he thought that must be why she was crying.

He said, "Don't feel bad. He does want to see you. He'll be so glad that you aren't dead."

He wasn't sure that she could hear him. There was too much other noise. There were sirens, car doors slamming, people running, men shouting.

He said to her, "Elizabeth? Do you hear me, Elizabeth?"

She didn't answer. He caressed her face again. It struck him that the shape of it was wrong. His hand was on her cheek; his thumb should have felt her nose, but her nose wasn't where it should have been. And his fingertips found something very rough, very jagged. He reached farther past her temple toward the hairline on her brow. Beyond the hairline, there was nothing, no top to her head. She was missing the top of her head.

He tried to ask her what happened. His voice sounded like gargling.

Anyway, she couldn't answer. She had fallen asleep.

All those men shouting. He wished they would be quiet. He heard, "Holy shit" and "This one's breathing" and "Jesus!"

He moved his hand to cover her ear. He said, "Elizabeth, it's okay, you just rest. In the morning, Mr. Clew will buy us breakfast."

19

Molly Farrell was at home, in her attic workshop, using her roof-mounted night-vision camera to scan the immediate neighborhood. It was not surveillance. She was testing her systems. She did so at least once a week, in late evening, when most of her neighbors were at home.

Her attic resembled an electronics repair shop. Six monitors, ten keyboards, two satellite phones, and an electrically operated dish that rose up through a skylight when needed. The night-vision camera showed only soft greens except for the blinding white glare from lit windows. The screens of three other computers were flashing. An unusual spurt of messages had begun coming in while she was only halfway through her checklist. She'd go through them as soon as she was finished.

The camera paused on Paul Bannerman's house. It was four houses down from her own. Paul and Susan had bought it when Cassie was born. He had lived much more simply before he met Susan, but still within this well-protected compound. The Bannerman home, made of stone and split timbers, overlooked the waters of Long Island Sound in a section of Westport known as Greens Farms Estates.

It was one of some twenty homes in the complex. No two architectural styles were alike. All were pleasant in appearance and tastefully landscaped, but none were so grand as was implied by the name. No three-car garages, no colonnaded fronts, no gatehouses manned by private guards. They were the sorts of homes bought by the moderately successful. They blended in to Westport unnoticed.

Some of Bannerman's neighbors were doctors and lawyers and others owned various businesses in town. Most of his neighbors were only that: neighbors. But some of those who ran businesses were Bannerman's people. They had come to Westport with him and they'd stayed. Those businesses, for the most part, were entirely legitimate. Among them were a popular restaurant, an antique shop, a bookstore, and a quaint bed-and-breakfast. There was a firm that installed home security systems and another that serviced computers. Bannerman himself had his travel agency in a double storefront on the Boston Post Road.

Molly had once run the restaurant, called Mario's, but she'd turned it over to Billy McHugh, who enjoyed tending bar there most evenings. The bed-and-breakfast belonged to his former landlady, who had since become Mrs. McHugh. The bookstore was Carla Benedict's project. She owned it jointly with her partner, Viktor Podolsk, with whom she also shared a modest Cape Cod just inside the pillared entrance to the compound. Podolsk, the handsome former KGB major, was thought to be the only man, ever, with whom Carla Benedict had been seen holding hands.

Such intimate displays had seemed as alien to Carla as a salad would be to a piranha. But Carla, in his presence, was unfailingly soft-spoken and bordered upon being amiable. She had been so, in his presence, ever since he recovered from the bullets that she had put in his chest in the lobby of a Moscow hotel. It had been inadvertent. She had fired at movement. Viktor, as it happened, was trying to protect her from two other gunmen who'd appeared in the lobby. Carla, who'd grown fond of Viktor by then, and who'd already lost one lover to a shooting and had carved up another with a broken wine bottle, very nearly had a breakdown, convinced that she was cursed. The black widow syndrome, someone called it.

But Viktor had survived with Carla's encouragement. That encouragement consisted of "Don't you fucking die," as Carla kept pressure on his bubbling chest until medical help could arrive. Since that day, it was assumed, they had mated many times without Carla, ever once, trying to eat him.

Molly's own home was two houses farther in, a Victorian, the oldest in the complex. It was furnished with period antiques. The antiques had been gathered by Anton Zivic, the other and more senior former KGB agent. Zivic shared the house with her, but they kept separate quarters. John Waldo used her living room couch on occasion but he was always gone before breakfast. He had broken in sometime during the night, but there was never any sign of forced entry. He would leave a note telling Molly that he'd been there. The note would suggest some additional refinement to Molly and Anton's security system. Molly would promptly install that improvement, but Waldo always managed to subvert it.

This frustrated Molly in the extreme. She would very much like to have responded in kind, but she couldn't because Waldo had no home of his own. He slept here and there, one night here, one night there, and had done so as long as she'd known him. His penetration was all the more galling because the security system was of her own design. It was Molly who ran the computer store and the firm that installed home security systems. Every house in the complex had one of her systems. They'd come highly recommended by Bannerman himself after Greens Farms Estates had a series of burglaries. Nothing much was ever taken because the burglar was John Waldo and Waldo was merely making a point.

All the neighbors seemed to like Paul Bannerman and his family although several had wondered and gossiped about him. They had often seen visitors come and go at odd hours. Even odder than the hours was the range of his acquain-

tances. Some were well dressed, some were scruffy, some
were men, some were women. Several spoke with thick foreign accents. A few stayed with Bannerman for days at a
time in the apartment that was over his garage.

Molly knew that they'd wondered because they'd asked
her about him. She'd explained that the visitors were tour
operators mostly. Travel agents host their colleagues all the
time. The odd hours were explained by the distances they'd
traveled. It wasn't a nine to five business. She knew that
these answers satisfied most of them, but that many still gossiped among themselves, especially when a visitor seemed
Middle Eastern in appearance. They, like many, had been
sensitized to any stranger whose features were suggestive of
Islam.

Molly also knew what they said to each other because she
had wired nearly all of their homes while installing their security systems. All the neighbors had computers. Some had
multiple computers. Because these were tied to their security systems, the computers were easily compromised as
well. She'd installed a highly sophisticated implant that resembled the FBI's Carnivore system. In addition, she'd developed a simpler version of the FBI's Magic Lantern. The
former allowed her to read all their e-mail. The latter
recorded all keystrokes. By reading those keystrokes she
could read all their passwords. She could also read any encryption codes that their owners might have employed.
These implants, unlike hidden video cameras, were virtually
impossible to detect.

She drew the line at installing video cameras. Security
was one thing, voyeurism another. These people were her
neighbors; some were friends. Nor did she eavesdrop as a
matter of course. That would have consumed too much time
for too little purpose. It was only when a neighbor seemed
unduly curious about all those comings and goings. And, as
Molly would freely admit, she did it because, well . . . she
could.

She'd especially enjoyed developing the system that she'd
installed in the Bannerman house. It was overkill, really,
much more than he'd asked for. There were motion detec-

tors, external video cameras, and pressure plates on each set of stairs. There was an arrangement of different-sounding alarms depending on the nature and location of the threat. But Bannerman had told her that enough was enough. To begin with, there had never been an intrusion, not even an attempt, at least not at his residence. The various alarms had gone off several times. The greatest threats that they'd detected were some door-to-door evangelists who were alerting Westport's residents that Jesus was coming.

The alarms weren't klaxons; they were musical tones. The thought at the time was that musical tones would be less distressing to his daughter. Nor were they all alarms. Some were simply signals telling Paul and Susan that this or that friend was on his way. The signals had no real purpose. Paul and Susan didn't need to be warned, for example, that Carla was about to stop by. Molly simply thought they were fun. The musical tones that signified Carla were the tum-TUM-tum cello notes from *Jaws*. Billy's was a fee-fi-fo-fum. John Waldo was announced by "Tiptoe Through the Tulips." None of them were greatly amused by those choices, but, as Molly explained, it was too late to change them because Cassie had learned them all by heart.

John Waldo has asked, "Okay, smart-ass, what's yours?"

"Just a theme from some movie."

"What movie?"

"Pretty Woman."

"A hooker," exclaimed Waldo. "I feel better."

She completed her checklist, retracted the camera, and closed up the motor-driven skylight. She sat down at the first of the flashing computers and opened the first of the messages. She muttered "Oh, my God" as she read the text. She wet her lips and began opening the others.

They were all from different sources. All were on the same subject. Roger Clew had been attacked in his building's garage. Some said shot, some said bludgeoned, one said both. Several said that his condition was grave and that he was not expected to live. Clew's driver, who was with him, suffered multiple gunshots and died on his way to the hospital. A second victim, a woman, was dead at the scene.

The woman was thought to be one of the assailants. Clew's driver and the woman had apparently shot each other. The woman had seemed to be known by the driver. He'd been conscious long enough to give his own name and Clew's. When asked about the woman, he called her "Elizabeth." He said the words, "Elizabeth tried."

Tried? thought Molly. Or was he trying to say *Stride*?

She inserted a disk. She copied all of the messages. She slid her chair to another workstation. She recalled that on the morning before this, Roger Clew had downloaded a number of files to be stored within Bannerman's system. She inserted a new disk. She copied those as well. She slid back across the floor to still another workstation and clicked to a list of music titles. She moved her cursor up the list. She clicked on "Pretty Woman."

It told Bannerman that she was on her way.

Cassie was still up. She'd been waiting for Molly after hearing the tones. Cassie met her at the door and greeted her in French. She exclaimed, *"Ma tante jolie. Bonjour, bonjour."*

Susan's voice called out, "She's learning French. Don't get her started." She said, "Anyway, honey, it's *bonsoir,* time for bed. Ask Aunt Molly if she'd like to tuck you in."

Molly saw that she and Paul were busy clearing dinner dishes. Susan asked, "Have you eaten? I can heat up a plate. Paul makes a terrific osso bucco."

"I've had dinner, thanks. And you shouldn't be standing," said Molly to the hugely pregnant Susan.

"I'll be lighter on my feet any day now," said Susan. To Cassie she said, "Come give us a kiss. And say good night in English if you don't mind." She said to Molly, "The world already has enough problems without six-year-olds speaking French. First grade. Do you believe it? Computer science, too. The Little Bo Peep days are over."

Molly lifted Cassie, pretending to groan, and carried her to her mother. She got her kiss and her hug and then a kiss from her father. Her father, smiling softly, looked questioningly at Molly. He saw that her eyes had flashed hard for an instant. Molly handed him the disks that she'd copied and said, "Look at these, then turn on the TV."

Molly said to Cassie as she walked toward the stairs, "I know a very old lullaby in French. It guarantees the nicest kind of dreams."

Cassie said, "After French, I really want to learn German. That way I'll know what you're all talking about. Even Grandpa Lesko speaks German."

They did often speak German when discussing certain subjects while Cassie was within earshot. And Lesko had to learn it by total immersion after moving to Zurich with Elena.

She said, "Tell you what. I'll teach you some German. That way you can surprise him when he gets here next week."

"Will you teach me something nasty?"

"What for?"

"It's fun to tease him."

"Ahem," came Susan's voice from the dining room.

CNN Headline News already had the first reports. They were sketchy. The story was "developing." Bannerman had gone through the first of the discs by the time that Molly had rejoined them. Susan had been looking over his shoulder as he scanned the eight separate reports. She said, "It looks as if they've rushed to be the first one to tell you. But I guess it's good to have friends."

Bannerman answered, "They're not friends. They're just people I know. This one woman is a judge who lives in Roger's building. This next one is a captain with the D.C. police who says that we met a few years ago. None of them would have our home number."

He'd no sooner said it when their phone started ringing. He made no move to answer. The answering machine recorded a message. The call was from an assistant to the Secretary of State. He said, *"Sir, Mr. Leland has just heard the news. He's anxious to speak to you. He's saddened and shocked. You can reach him at either of these numbers."* He listed a home phone and a cell phone.

Bannerman walked over. He shut off the ringer. He said, "That phone will be ringing all evening. Let's let the machine take their messages for now. I'm going to call that Washington policeman."

Bannerman had been on the phone for ten minutes. He ended the call saying, "Thanks, Greg. I owe you." He still couldn't put a face to that police captain's name, but they had indeed met at some function years before and the captain seized the chance to be "owed one."

He said to Susan and Molly, "Roger's alive. He's at the Georgetown University Hospital. He's in surgery now. He's in critical condition. They thought at first that he'd been shot in the face, but the X-rays only showed blunt force trauma. He'd tried to get his gun out, shot himself, just a flesh wound, but that bullet also hit whoever did this to him. They know this from the blood and the tip of a man's finger that they found on the concrete near Roger."

"The dead woman," said Molly. "Tell me that wasn't Stride."

"It does sound as if Clew's driver was saying her name, but the dead woman wasn't Elizabeth. Whoever she was, she looked nothing like Stride. This woman was about ten years younger, not as tall, and her hair was dark brown, worn shoulder length. They've already run her prints. They have not found a match. She carried a purse, but no ID."

"And she did shoot Roger's driver?"

Bannerman nodded. He said, "The driver's name is Alex Rakowsky. Five hits, but small caliber, not much punch. Rakowsky managed to kill her after he had gone down. His shots pretty much took her head off."

Bannerman paused. He looked at his wife. He asked, "Should you be hearing this, Susan?"

"I'm okay," she answered, "but I'd better sit down." She eased onto a sofa. She was cradling her stomach. "Who's this Stride? Who's Elizabeth Stride?"

Molly tossed a hand. "She's just someone we know. I jumped to a conclusion. No connection."

Bannerman said to Susan, "You don't look so okay. Should I get you to . . ."

"No."

"Well, at least let me get you upstairs to lie down."

She said, "This baby will either come early or it won't. Your friend Roger is the one who's in trouble."

"Yes, but . . ."

"Please finish," she said firmly. "I'll deal with it."

He hesitated before saying, "This part won't be on the news. One of them tried to scalp Roger with a knife. No other knife wounds. Just that one."

Molly was staring into his eyes. She'd seen something there. She'd seen a lack of surprise. Her eyes were asking, "What is it that you know?" He stared back with the message, "We'll talk later. Not now." Susan saw the exchange. She asked, "What's going on?"

He pretended distraction. "I'm just trying to get it straight. I mean as the captain described it."

Roger's driver, he told them, dropped him off at his garage, but came back a few minutes later. Maybe Roger had left something in the car; we don't know; but the doorman saw him pass and then return. He pulled in and must have seen Roger being attacked. Figure two men. They'd been waiting for him. When they jumped him, Roger managed to squeeze off two shots even though he had not cleared his weapon. The bullet casings were still in his pants.

The doorman, at this point, heard what seemed to be shots. They were muffled and he couldn't tell their source. He stepped out on the street, looked up and down, but saw nothing. He then went back inside to check his video monitors. This is maybe a minute after he heard the shots. By that time, Rakowsky was back in the garage. The doorman saw him on one of the monitors. The doorman said that he had his gun drawn and he had a phone to his ear. He was calling 911. He never finished that call.

"But that call was recorded," said Molly. "Any names?"

"Just a call for assistance. Stay with me."

Bannerman resumed the D.C. captain's summation. "The doorman saw Rakowsky pointing his gun at a man who was holding an umbrella. The umbrella was open even though he

was indoors. He was coming, said the doorman, from between two parked cars. It looked as if he'd been trying to hide
there. The doorman said he couldn't see the man's face. He
saw that he was wearing a dark business suit and that he
seemed to have a knife in his hand. Rakowsky must have told
him to get down on the floor because right then he started to
kneel. At this point the doorman made his own 911 call, but
cars had already been dispatched."

Molly asked, "That's all he saw? One man? Both hands
full?"

Bannerman said, "I agree. There had to have been others.
They had to have already gone out. The doorman didn't see
them, but they might be on the tape. They must have taken
Roger's briefcase out with them. The umbrella man didn't
seem to have it."

Susan said, "That's what they wanted? His briefcase?"

"It would seem so," said Bannerman. "And his watch and
his wallet. Someone wanted this to look like a robbery."

Susan asked, "So they got them. Why hurt him so badly?
And why take the time to do that to his hair?"

He said, "I have no idea."

Once again, however, he felt Molly's eyes. Once again, he
knew what she was thinking. She was thinking, "You know
a lot more than you're saying. Let's talk when we're alone.
And then let's fix this."

Bannerman cleared his throat. "Let's get back to the doorman. While he was calling 911, he heard more shots being
fired. On the monitor he saw the umbrella man get up and
start to run toward the ramp. He saw Rakowsky, who'd been
hit by that time, shooting in that man's direction. We know
he winged him because there was new blood on the floor. No
trail leading to it, so it must have happened there."

"So now we have two who were wounded," said Molly.
Her eyes added, "They'll be easier to find."

Bannerman nodded. "Two wounded, two dead. Right
about here, the woman appeared and she began shooting at
Rakowsky. I say 'appeared' because this is where the camera's sweep caught her. Clew's driver was, by then, shooting
wildly. That sweep, incidentally, had been jammed to fall

short of covering the spot where they got Roger. That's how the captain knew that this was preplanned. The camera moved on and by the time it came back, both Clew's driver and the woman were down. He'd killed her before she could finish killing him."

A red light had been flashing on Bannerman's phone. Molly walked over to it. She scanned its Caller ID. There had been sixteen calls in the short time they'd been speaking. She said, "Most of these are from our own people. And it looks like the news has reached Europe already. Here's one from Harry Whistler and one from Susan's father. The others are all local. All our people want to know."

Bannerman said, "Okay, let's have them meet at my office." He said to Susan, "I should brief them myself. Will you be all right for an hour or so?"

She nodded. "I'll be fine. But let's talk before you go."

Molly said, "I'll wait outside. I'll start calling them."

"I won't keep him," said Susan. "Two minutes."

"Do you have any doubt that I can handle this?" Susan asked him.

"The shock about Roger? Well . . . given your condition . . ."

"Never mind my condition. I'm pregnant, not blind. I think you know who did it. So does Molly. And I think you're about to go killing over this. I know that look you get, Paul."

He said, "Susan, I get *that look* when I'm thinking. And by the way, we don't rush off to 'go killing' every time a friend has been harmed. Roger's a friend, but he's not one of us. And he might have brought this on himself."

"Which makes it all right?"

"It means we'll think before acting. We don't swing at every pitch. But you're right, there's more to this than you've heard. I'll tell you all about it, but later."

"Paul, why don't you just let the cops deal with this? And the State Department. The Justice Department. Roger wasn't one of us, but he's sure one of them. They're going to be all over this."

"That's one of the things we'll discuss," he replied. "One option will certainly be to sit tight, depending on how this attack touches us. Believe me, we won't go off half-cocked."

"Molly didn't look so deliberative," said Susan. "She looked ready to run with this now."

"She won't. She knows better."

"Without orders from you?"

He said, "And I think you know better than that. I do not give them orders. This isn't a gang."

She replied, "I do know that. You never give orders. You either ask or you tell them what you're going to do. You know perfectly well that they'll say, 'Sure, let's go.' When has it been any other way?"

"Lots of times."

"Listen . . . I'm about to give birth to your son."

"Susan . . . I know that. Nothing matters to me more."

"Then whatever you decide, I want you to promise that you won't go after them personally. Our children need a father and I need you right here."

"And I love you and Cassie more than you can imagine. I won't take foolish chances. That I'll promise."

She squinted at him. "Did I just hear a hedge?"

"No, you heard a firm promise from your husband."

"Understand me," she told him. "I know that Roger is our friend. Whoever did this should pay and if we need to get involved, I'm simply asking you to let Molly handle it."

He said, "Let me talk to her. We'll see."

Molly was standing outside, her cell phone to her ear. She snapped it shut as Bannerman approached.

He asked her, "Molly, will you do the briefing? I think I'd better stick close to Susan."

She nodded. "I will and you should."

"You're sure you don't mind?"

"What I mind is going there stupid," she said. "I've just called Anton. He's gathering all the others. Do I get to hear what you wouldn't say inside? Who did this? And don't say you're not sure."

"I'm not," he said, "but I can make a good guess. My

guess is that Artemus Bourne is behind it. If that's true, the umbrella was Bourne's man, Chester Lilly. The thing is that Lilly might have acted on his own. He had his own grudge against Roger."

"Personal?"

"Roger hit him."

Molly blinked in surprise. "Our Roger had an actual fight?"

"I know. We've already had that conversation. There was some hair-pulling too. It might account for the scalping. It seems that Chester Lilly . . ." He paused. He added, "And it isn't just Lilly. It could also have been personal with Bourne."

"Why with Bourne? Because Roger wouldn't tell him where Stride is?"

"No, because Roger wouldn't leave it at that. He wanted to grind it in with his heel. I warned him, but I'm not sure he listened." He asked, "That second disc. Is it all about Stride?"

"It is. He's been researching her. Kessler as well. But I didn't see anything worth all this."

"When did Roger send those files?"

"Yesterday morning. I don't normally read them. I only opened them after I heard."

"Well, I think he's been busy since yesterday morning. Let's assume that there were some more in his briefcase. Could Roger have learned where Stride is living?"

Molly shrugged. "He could have guessed. But just because we were there? It might have crossed his mind, but that's an awfully big stretch. And even if Roger did vault to that conclusion, he'd know better than to put it in writing."

"He clearly had *something* in his briefcase that was worth this. Would Clew have confided in his driver?" asked Bannerman.

"I'd doubt it. He would surely know better than that."

"Well, we both know that Rakowsky said her name before he died. I didn't want to get into it in front of Susan. Roger knew that Bourne had informants at State. So if Roger never talked to his driver about Stride, his driver found out on his own."

"But why *would* he say her name?"

"We might never know. Roger seemed to have a thing for her. Perhaps Rakowsky did as well. Let's put that aside for the moment." Bannerman grimaced before speaking again. He said, "Listen, Molly. There are things I haven't told you. I couldn't because I had given my word. It was also because it was none of our business until you ran into Stride."

"You've known she was alive?"

"Well, I knew she hadn't died. I knew that she'd been living on Hilton Head Island. I knew about the trouble that they had there two years ago. I would not have expected her to stay after that. I didn't realize that she was still there."

Molly put her hands on her hips. She said, "I'm waiting."

"Beg pardon?"

"For the other shoe to drop. What else did you know?"

"Martin isn't dead either. He was taken off that boat. Last I heard, he's in Angola. Bourne has interests in Angola. I have reason to suspect he's been a thorn in Bourne's side, but only because of something Roger said this morning. It was only then that it started to dawn on me why Bourne was so eager to find Stride."

"Whoa," said Molly. "Back up a few pages. Who took him off the boat? The Israelis, by chance?"

"They . . . were part of it, yes. Look, I'll fill you in later. I'll go in and make some calls to get an update on Kessler. In the meantime, are you able to contact Elizabeth?"

"Believe it or not, she's in the telephone book."

"By name?"

"E. Stride. Waldo looked it up. He showed me."

He said, "Molly, she trusts you. Call her right now. We have to assume that Bourne knows where she is. Tell her not to pack a bag, just walk out the door. It should look as if she'll be coming right back. Tell her . . ."

"I know how to do this," said Molly. "So does she."

"She does? You just told me her name's in the phone book."

"I guess I meant aside from that lapse."

"Just get her out. She's going to want to know why."

"She'll get out first," said Molly. "Then she'll ask."

"You and Carla go get her. No, wait. Not Carla. They haven't started rebuilding from Carla's last visit. Fly down there with Billy. Leave right after the briefing. Have Elizabeth here in Westport by morning."

"And if she refuses?"

"That's why you're bringing Billy."

"Can I tell her, positively, that Martin's alive?"

He nodded. "Only that. Let me tell her the rest of it."

"John and I already told her that we heard he'd been seen. I said I'd check it out. I guess I just have. Why was I left in the dark?"

He said, "Molly . . . that whole business wasn't pleasant for me either. I'll tell you what I can when I can. Have Anton put together a package on Bourne, his Angolan interests in particular. I want a list of all his political connections. Don't worry about accuracy; rumored payoffs will do. I need his habits, where he lives, what sort of security. And tell Anton that he needn't be discreet about this. Let the word get around. Let's see who gets nervous."

"So you are going after him?"

"I don't know yet. We'll see. For now, though, will you please go get Elizabeth?"

She was no less annoyed. She said, "Sure. I'll bring her back. But Elizabeth was utterly convinced that he's dead. Why would she believe it this time around?"

"You can say that Paul Bannerman gives her his word, even though I've just broken it by telling you this much. You can now tell Anton. I don't think he'll be surprised. But you needn't tell anyone else yet."

Molly opened her phone. She tapped out a number. "You know that she's going to carve you up for this, don't you? All this time, you could have told her. You let her think he's dead."

"Kessler wanted it that way. He made me promise."

20

Bourne sat at the computer in the basement room that he'd furnished for the late Cecil Winfield. He knew little of computers. He mistrusted them.

The disastrous Chester Lilly had downloaded the files from that PDA thing that Clew used. He was furious with Chester, now more so than ever. But at least Chester did get Clew's briefcase.

Bourne glanced over at Chester, who sat on Winfield's bed, a towel wrapped around his right thigh. He was compressing it to stop the seeping of blood where Clew's inconvenient driver had shot him, a flesh wound. He'd been a veritable study in self-justification ever since he'd limped back to Briarwood.

He'd said, "I had no choice. Who would have figured on the driver? Never once in the past has he gone and come back. How could I know he'd come back?"

"Even so, my instructions were explicit, were they not?"

"Make it look like a mugging. I told them ten times. Jump him, take the briefcase, give him a pounding, and get out of there in one minute flat."

"That would *seem* to be the formula for a competent mugging," said Bourne as he scanned through Clew's messages. "But now I wish you'd recruited some urchins off the street. They are no doubt more practiced than Toomey and Kuntz."

"Now you're dumping on those two." Chester rose to their defense. "Except for Toomey getting part of his finger shot off, I thought they were doing pretty good. You wanted Clew hammered; he got hammered good. You wanted the briefcase; you got it. They were out of there before the driver showed up and it would have gone great except for Claire."

"You say you couldn't stop her?"

Chester spread his hands. "I mean, who would have thought? Claire . . . I don't know what got into her head. She jumps out of the car; she runs down the ramp. I yelled, 'Don't.' I tried to catch her. Ask Toomey."

"She ran in and started shooting? For no reason you can think of?"

"It was like she went crazy. I had to go in after her. Claire and Clew's driver are blasting away. It was nuts," said Chester. "That's when I got this." He winced in pain as if for punctuation.

Bourne doubted that he'd heard an unedited account. There was probably no use in asking Toomey or Kuntz. By now, they'd have been well rehearsed.

He asked Chester, "You're certain that she won't be identified?"

"Who, Claire? I don't know how from what's left of her. She never carried an ID while on a job. She caught at least two nines in the face, so no one's going to recognize her picture if they show one. She's never been busted, so she's never been printed. The only dental work she had was done over in England. A damned shame that she's dead, but she blew it. She fucked up. This is what you get for using women."

Bourne ignored this last. He said, "Fingerprints? What of Toomey's?"

"From what they find on the floor? They'll get some DNA, that's all. The part with the print is where he took the bullet. Besides, it's all mixed with the leather from his glove. They'll never get a match off what's left."

"They've found part of a finger. Toomey's missing such a part. That would seem a useful clue, would it not?"

"He'll lay low until he's healed and this blows over."

He'll lay low, thought Bourne. He might lay lower than you think. This cannot be traced back to me.

Before sitting down to peruse the stolen files, Bourne had scanned the news channels for reports of the episode. He had contacts in Washington whom he could have asked directly, but they'd surely have wondered why he'd care. The news accounts he saw were more or less similar to Chester's version of the event. One oddity, however. One station reported that the woman with no face had been tentatively identified as "Elizabeth." It seems that Clew's driver had been heard to say her name before the police pried them apart.

Elizabeth? As in Stride? Why would he call her Elizabeth?

A dying brain. Confused. Disoriented, surely. But something, thought Bourne, must have planted the seed. Stride must have been on his mind. He and Clew must have been talking about her. Perhaps Clew had told him that he'd found her.

One found, but one lost. Claire will be sorely missed. Capable, reliable, always pleasing to look at. Not a few of his brunch guests were enamored of Claire. Not a few will regret that she's no longer available as, if they've earned it, their dessert. He among them, of course. They'd had many a diversion. She was too acrobatic for his tastes on the whole. Men his age no longer bend as they used to. But she was often considerate. One appreciates that. She'd say, "Lie back. Be still. I'll do everything myself. I'm going to make you purr like a kitten."

Missed, but not irreplaceable, thought Bourne. He'd have Houston look for one even better. His personnel people are aware of his requirements. Like Claire, she must have the sort of looks that turn heads. Like Claire, she must be British with a proper British accent. It makes them seem cultivated, even if they are not. A few months of tutoring smooths any rough edges. And of course she must be willing to do as she's told.

But of course one mustn't be inflexible, thought Bourne. The right American might also do nicely. Wouldn't it be wonderful if Elizabeth Stride could be enticed by all this money and power. She'd do more than make him purr. She'd be the lioness; he'd be the lion. Well . . . after they've had time to get acquainted.

"Did you find it yet?" asked Chester. "Anything about Stride?"

The question interrupted his reverie.

"Nothing current. Not yet. Not about where she is. I hope she's not planning to be in Westport next week. That would complicate matters considerably."

Chester asked, "Why in Westport? What's next week?"

"Clew was planning to be there. Some sort of conference."

"How'd you know that? That's on Clew's PDA?"

"No, Quigley told me. He didn't know the agenda, but I don't like the timing. Clew might well have intended to enlist their support. I've sent two people up there to keep their eyes open and to preempt, if need be, any problems from that quarter."

"You sent *what* people? Mine? Without going through *me*?"

Bourne said, without looking up from the screen, "They are not your people. They are my people, Chester. Your fiefdom is limited to my African affairs. You'll recall that I do have interests elsewhere."

Now Bourne did raise his eyes. Chester actually looked hurt. This brute's lower lip was protruding. "You still could have told me," said Chester.

"My bad, as they say."

"And what's this preempt? That makes it sound like you'll hit him. Two guys to take out that whole bunch?"

"They are well equipped, believe me. But there might be no need. One likes to plan ahead. You should try it some time. Now please let me finish my reading."

Now he looks like a boy who's been sent to his room. Very well. We'll try to brighten his mood.

"At the moment," said Bourne, "I'm on an old freighter somewhere off the coast of Sierra Leone. You'll be pleased to know that those slave girls have been rescued. They'll be reduced to bloody puddles in a week or ten days, but at least they may have died with their virtue intact. Your Moshood, however, has been fed to the sharks, bleeding, but alive and fully conscious."

"Had it coming," said Chester. "Wish I could've watched."

"Quigley says that Clew erased these exchanges with Liberia. Once erased, could they be recovered?"

"Normally, yeah, but not on that system. If Clew wanted to deep-six them, they're gone."

Bourne grunted. This whole business might yet be contained. Some inducement toward this Tubbs might be helpful. "Do you know anything of this general? Abednego Tubbs?"

"The Liberian? Yeah. He's a doofus."

"How about a Major Scar of the Second Commando?"

"The Second Commando is their army's top unit. I don't think I ever heard of a *Major* Scar, but all the soldiers in that unit have scarred faces."

"More magic? More juju?"

"No, they don't do that shit. It's an identity thing. It's so everyone can see they're in that unit." Chester dabbed at his wound as he said this.

"There are no other units like this Second Commando?"

"Hardly any," Chester answered. "They're also all Christians. Lots of Christians in Liberia. I think I heard they all wear gold crosses."

"Each to his own brand of magic, I suppose."

"That doesn't mean that they're choirboys, though. I heard they never take any prisoners."

Bourne found himself wondering whether they might be for hire. Especially their commander, this major called Scar. He certainly has seemed to keep his head on that freighter. It's too bad that he isn't very likely to survive. Bourne might have made him an interesting offer. He might have said, *"Major? I'm planning some changes. I think I need an African who knows about Africans to oversee my African holdings. Right now I have Chester, but that's not going to last. One blunder too many. Downsize him for me, will you? You're a Christian, so you probably won't cook him and eat him. Just as well. There's a saying: 'You are what you eat,' and believe me, you don't want to be Chester."*

No matter. It won't happen. But I wish you weren't dying. I wish you'd found some juju that works against Marburg. I assume you've already tried prayer.

Juju, thought Bourne. Bulletproof troops. There's no end to the nonsense that some people will believe. It's no different, he supposed, from being persuaded that seventy-two virgins await martyrs in paradise. Personally, he'd have settled for Claire.

"Damn," he exclaimed. The screen had suddenly changed. Clew's exchanges with Tubbs had shrunk to nothing. "Chester, get over here. What have I done?"

Chester limped to the console. "I have to get this leg fixed."

"My doctor is upstairs attending to Toomey. When it's your turn, he'll buzz you. What have I done?"

Chester reached to take the mouse. "You just reduced it, is all. Let me fool with it for a second."

New text sprang up. He saw Stride's name. He saw Kessler's. The text looked like excerpts from various reports. At the bottom of the screen there was the edge of a photo. He said, "Bring that up. What's that photo?"

Chester spotted a date among numerous codes. "Couple days ago," he said. "From before this last download." He moved the cursor to it. The photo arose. A group of people. Middle Eastern. A woman among them. A notation on the photo. "Almost certainly Stride." There was an arrow pointing to her smiling profile.

Bourne leaned forward. He asked Chester, "Can this be printed out?"

"Well, yeah," Chester told him. "This thing over here is your printer."

"Make it print then. At once." Damn gadgets, thought Bourne. "Print it all. I want all of this out of it."

"You mean printed, then erased?"

"No, just out," said Bourne eagerly. "I want it where I can touch it."

"That's Stride?" asked Chester.

"Almost certainly, it says."

"Stride's no Arab. That's an Arab."

"But Stride must have been able to pass for an Arab. She must have had the coloring for it."

"Wait a minute," said Chester. "What's this other thing down here? Oh, it's a window. It says *Doodlings*. Let me look."

"Lose Stride's picture, you lummox, for the sake of some doodles, and I'll . . ."

"I'm a lummox? Look at this. You want Stride? Here's where she is."

He'd done something with the mouse and hit a button on the keyboard. What he clicked on spread out and filled the screen.

There were only five lines.

The top line, in bold letters, said "STRIDE IS ALIVE."

The second said "BANNERMAN." Only that.

The third, "HOW AND WHERE?"

Next came "HILTON HEAD ISLAND!!!!"

Then, a few spaces down, "From Chamonix."

Bourne stared. "Is that it? She's on Hilton Head Island?"

"Apologize first."

"I apologize. Abjectly."

"Then I'd have to say yes. It looks like Bannerman said so. Except why would Clew write 'How and where?' after that. And what does 'From Chamonix' mean?"

"The 'How,' perhaps, asks how Bannerman found her. The 'Where' is self-evident. South Carolina. All this time she's been practically a neighbor."

"That's if she's not in France. Isn't Chamonix in France?"

Bourne rubbed his chin. He shook his head slowly. He touched a finger to the spaces separating the two locations. "Chamonix could be on another subject entirely. She came back to this country; she stayed in this country. Let's not muddy the water with France."

Chester was doubtful. "Clew wrote that for a reason."

"But he wrote it less boldly. Why lowercase? And he wrote it without exclamation marks, Chester. Look at those after Hilton Head. What do they tell you?"

"He's surprised?"

Bourne rose to his feet. "Yes, they do connote surprise. When repeated they are an expression of wonder. When repeated four times, they're a shout of 'Eureka.' She's on Hilton Head Island. Go find her."

"We'll look."

"Look? I said *find* her. Leave tonight. Take your thugs. First make some more copies of this photograph."

"Ah, Mr. Bourne . . . are you forgetting my leg? Kuntz is in your kitchen with his knuckles packed with ice and Toomey's upstairs with his hand ripped to shit."

"Toomey was a policeman. He'll know how to look for her. When he finds her, he can point with the hand that's undamaged. As for you, you need only a few mattress sutures and a handful of antibiotics. Oh, and do change your trousers, of course."

Chester started to object. Bourne raised a hand to stop him.

"Need I say it? You've a chance to redeem yourself, Chester. Find Stride; bring her to me; all your sins will wash away."

Well, not all, thought Bourne. You can purge the rest in hell.

Chester grumbled, but he said, "You want speed, we'll need your chopper."

"Helicopters aren't stealthy. It's those noisy rotor things. They call attention to themselves when you're dragging women into them. Take a van, drive all night. Make your plans on the way. Report to me no later than mid-morning."

"You're a prick."

"That may be," said Bourne, "but I'm your prick, dear Chester. I know you won't fail me in this."

21

Elizabeth Stride had not seen the news broadcasts. She'd gone out to the theater with a man she had met at a fundraiser for the Arts Center. The show was Cole Porter's *Anything Goes*. The man was a widower. He'd lost his wife to a stroke. He was a building contractor some twenty years older. He was nice; he was comfortable and he was safe. His name was Gary.

He had taken her home. She had not asked him in. She had offered her cheek at the door. He brushed it lightly. He said, "Soon, I hope." He turned and slid into his car. Elizabeth waited for his taillights to vanish before turning off her own outside lights. She went into her kitchen, checked for messages; there were none. She poured herself a glass of white wine and sat down with a book that she'd been reading. Gary, she imagined, would be doing the same. She should really have asked him in for coffee.

But she'd made it clear to him that she had no intention of entering a serious relationship. His age was one factor, not a huge one, but a factor. The scars on her body were another.

He didn't seem to mind that she kept him at a distance or else he was willing to be patient. He would send her flowers after each evening out with a card that simply said, "Thank you."

He was not the type to call and make a pest of himself. Two weeks might go by before she heard from him again. Or she would call him. Not often, but sometimes. Once she needed a partner for a charity golf tournament. At other times, like tonight, there'd be a show she wished to see and she wanted to go with a man for a change instead of always with Aisha or Jasmine or Nadia.

Jasmine had asked, "Did he get you in the sack yet?"

"Um . . . not that it's any of your business . . ."

"Well, did he?"

"He's not that kind of date. He's just a gentleman friend."

She said, "There aren't any men who just want to be friends, especially when the friend looks like you."

"Well, he is."

Jasmine said, "I happen to know something about men."

"I . . . don't doubt that for a second."

"Don't get smart. The subject at hand is your love life, not mine, and what you know about men adds up to squat."

"Oh, you think so."

Jasmine asked her, "Okay. How many men have you slept with? Grand total from day one. What's it come to?"

"Correction. I am *not* the subject at hand. We're not going to have this discussion."

"How many?"

"A lot. I was a slut."

"My guess is maybe three all through high school and college. Maybe one more, tops, before Kessler came along. And nothing since Martin. Am I right? Yeah, I thought so. I was going to say you need to get back in the game, but, girl, you're not even on the bench."

Elizabeth had brought her hands to her temples. "I'm trying to remember. Didn't you convert to Islam?"

"I converted to Islam. Not the part that's all *His*lam. A woman's natural urges don't get locked away just because she found a new way to live."

"Well . . . you live your way and let me live mine."

"What could it hurt to give this Gary a shot? You know who else is hot for you? Your golf pro."

"Never mind."

"Also that guy who came and re-did your kitchen. And trust me, they're not going to lose any sleep over how those holes in you got there. They'd lose sleep, all right, but that wouldn't be the reason. The only holes they'll care about . . ."

"Jasmine!!"

"Well, it's true. Besides, you can say they're something else. What's that spidery thing that white people get when they spend too much time in the sun?"

"Melanomas. And guess what. You don't have to be white."

Jasmine shrugged. "Whatever. You could say that's what they are. You could say you had a few of them cut out."

"I'm sure that's every man's dream. To bed a woman who has cancer."

"Leprosy, maybe. That might slow them down. But even that would depend on what parts are falling off you. It's like I was telling Aisha . . . she's been asking about boys . . ."

"Say you're kidding," said Elizabeth.

"Hey, she's sixteen, remember?"

"Tell me you haven't had a sex talk with Aisha."

Jasmine grinned. "I haven't. I'm just messing with you now. But the true part is that Aisha has been thinking about boys. She's not about to ask Nadia. She'd get sent to the showers. Guess who she's picked for a facts of life session."

"Me?"

"It was down to either you or some local tenth grader. It depends on which one of you knows more."

Smart-ass, thought Elizabeth.

Shows how much Jasmine knows.

As it happens, she'd had several boyfriends in school. Well, two, if you only count the ones she'd had sex with. Okay, one. The other one lost it too soon. So make that one and a half.

Damn, she's right.

She did have a *fairly* good sex life with Martin. But that was after a dry spell of almost three years. And we won't count what happened in that Saudi prison. We won't even think about that. There were a couple of Israelis who she might have considered. But they were her trainers. They'd been told she was off-limits.

Martin said, *"You were off-limits to all of them, Elizabeth. Not because you weren't Jewish. That would not have stopped them. It was because those who knew you were afraid of you, Elizabeth. You were not all peaches and cream."*

"You weren't afraid of me, were you?" she'd asked him.

"Our first time? No, not greatly. I had put your knife away. You were still weak from your wounds. I was sure that I'd be able to outrun you."

"I'm serious, Martin."

"Then what is it you're asking?"

"That first time was . . . awkward. That was my fault, not yours. I guess I'm asking . . . when I healed, I mean when I was better . . . was I better? Was I a good lover?"

"You were the spectacular Elizabeth Stride. No man could have asked for more than that."

"That sounds like a no."

"Well, it isn't. It's a yes. Most emphatically, a yes. Your performance in bed is the least of your qualities."

She'd looked away when he said that. *"Never mind."*

Martin backed away a step. *"I must have answered incorrectly."*

"You said what you meant. You said, 'the least of my qualities.'"

"Then my English is deficient. It is not what I meant. Your least is the best that most men ever find. In my life, I myself have never been with a woman who comes close to you in that department."

It was sweet of him to say that. It was a lie, but it was sweet. And she had gotten better. More at ease. Less inhibited. And Martin was so very patient with her. It seemed to her that he gave a lot better than he got. He would even kiss her scars. She'd wished he wouldn't, but he did. Even now, though, at night, she would lie in bed alone, remembering how gently he would touch them.

He'd once told her, *"They are part of you. I love you; I love them. They are also a badge of your courage and your strength. You should wear bikinis more. You shouldn't hide them."*

"Now you're asking me to put my scars on display?"

"Among certain other assets. Your breasts come to mind. Even with me, you want the lights out all the time. You have a glorious body. Be a show-off."

She couldn't recall how she'd responded to that. She had probably pretended to be angry with him. She did that a lot. She wasn't always pretending. She had probably made some remark about show-offs. Showing off was an art form with Martin.

Even so. Poor Martin.

She could be such a bitch.

She and Martin never did make love with the lights on. By starlight once or twice, but that was it. How she wished that she could see him. One more time. For one more night. She would let herself go as she never had before. Lights? You want lights? You want to see me displayed? How about Yankee Stadium? In the middle of a night game. We'll run down to center field, strip naked, screw our brains out. Maybe then you'll shut up about my modesty.

Except Jasmine was right. She was way out of practice. If Jasmine had in fact been a hooker, pre-Islam, maybe Jasmine would be game to do some tutoring.

The telephone rang. Who'd be calling this late? Gary, most likely. He'd know she's still up.

She put her book down and got up to answer. Her machine had already clicked on to record. Her machine said, *"Hi. Leave a message."*

A woman's voice said, "Pick up if you're there."

She recognized the voice. Molly Farrell.

Instantly, Martin Kessler popped back into her mind. Molly had said that she'd look into those sightings. She and Waldo had also promised Aisha. She didn't want to hear about more rumors, more sightings. She had just been with Martin. She'd been with him in her mind. She felt her eyes starting to moisten.

She picked up. "Listen, Molly . . ."

"Don't talk. Get out now. Go just as you are. Go to where you last saw me. Adam's place. Do you understand?"

"Yes." Adam's yacht. It must still be docked there.

"Let yourself in. We'll be there in two hours."

Elizabeth knew better than to stay on the phone. She almost expected to hear distant sirens. She said, "I understand." She broke the connection. She walked quickly from her kitchen into her bedroom, where she pulled her blue duffel from its place of concealment.

She was out of her house in thirty seconds.

22

Henderson Quigley of the African desk was attending a conference when he learned of the attack. The conference was held at the Watergate Hotel. Its subject had to do with further oil exploration off the coast of Namibia, Angola's neighbor to the south.

Word of that evening's awful event had spread among those in attendance. It had happened only a few blocks away. All were in shocked disbelief.

Details were sparse. Much was being withheld. The police were still trying to make sense of the scene. Roger Clew. Robbed and beaten. Half to death, by all accounts. Someone heard that he was on life support. His driver shot and killed while coming to his aid. My God, thought Quigley. That's our Alex Rakowsky. He had spoken to Rakowsky that same morning.

Rakowsky had seemed to have much on his mind. He'd been helpful in the search for this Elizabeth Stride. Reluctant and perhaps not entirely forthcoming, but helpful nonetheless in that matter.

A woman also dead, but her role wasn't clear. The police are being closed-mouthed about her. Had she been with Clew? Some illicit relationship? Or perhaps she was simply a resident of the building. Did she stumble on the scene and, being armed, try to help? Several residents of that building very likely carry weapons. All that street crime. Now the terrorists. Who can blame them?

Oil exploration was no longer the subject. The room was alive with speculation. Several were on cell phones making calls to . . . whomever . . . in search of more complete information. Quigley himself had a troubling thought. It was far-fetched. Unlikely. Preposterous, really. Might Artemus Bourne have been behind this?

He knew that Clew and Rakowsky had driven down to see Bourne. He knew that Clew intended to confront Bourne on some matter. He himself had warned Bourne that Clew was coming. But, no, he thought. It could not have been serious. He had spoken to Bourne again after that meeting. He'd told Bourne that he'd failed to find much in Clew's computer. According to Rakowsky, Clew downloaded some files and then had erased the originals. He'd told Bourne that Clew might then transfer those files to Paul Bannerman's system for safekeeping. He'd been thought to be doing that for years. And to be doubly safe, another set to Geneva. That set went to Harry Whistler's system.

Might Bourne have decided to prevent that transference?

No, thought Quigley. Out of the question. Bourne might, but not this way. Not a frontal attack. Bourne is ruthless, to be sure, but far from reckless, far from crude. Besides that, recalled Quigley, Bourne had said it himself. Bourne had said to him, concerning both Clew's files and that woman, "It's no longer a concern."

Quigley had no sooner taken comfort in that thought when one of the oil executives approached him. He was pocketing the cell phone he'd been using. It was a man who had often attended Bourne's brunches. A man whose firm had made billions on Angola's off-shore oil and was himself extremely wealthy thanks to Bourne.

He said to Quigley, "No one's saying very much. They

have a name for the woman. Elizabeth something. No by-stander, that one. She's the one who killed Clew's driver. And they know that at least two other men were involved. Not your ordinary muggers. One was wearing a business suit. Both of them are believed to have been wounded."

Quigley felt himself go cold. He asked, "This Elizabeth. Do they have a last name?"

"They're not sure," said the oilman. "It's all very confused."

"I . . . think I'd better run over to State. Clew's staff might be better informed."

"Let me know, will you, if there's anything I can do. Will I see you at Briarwood on Sunday, by the way?"

"I . . . expect so. I hope so. Please excuse me."

Elizabeth? He wondered. Elizabeth Stride? Bourne had asked Clew to find her. He felt sure that Clew had done so. Is it possible that she so didn't want to be found that she did this to silence Roger Clew? Is it possible that she, with the aid of two confederates, decided to kill Clew and his driver?

Or another scenario. She was with Clew. She was going back with him to his apartment. The attackers came in or were lying in wait. They meant to kill all three. But why? And who sent them?

Bourne, of course. That could be why he was looking for her. He wanted to find her and kill her.

He arrived at State and went directly to Intelligence. The section was abuzz, but sparsely staffed at this hour. Shocked faces, women weeping, others angrily questioning. The section didn't seem to be functioning.

He asked one of the men, a communications officer, "Where are Roger's deputies? Do they know?"

"Sir, they're both abroad. They've been told. They're returning."

"Any word yet on who might have done this?"

"No, sir," he replied. "But the FBI is on it. Don't worry, they will get the sons of bitches."

"If there's . . . anything I can do . . ."

"Thank you, sir. We're just waiting."

Quigley had turned away when the man said, "Um . . . sir? A cryptogram from Liberia came in for Mr. Clew. It's flagged 'Urgent,' but no one here tonight has clearance to read it. You're here, you've got the clearance, and Africa's your beat. Maybe you'll want to see if it needs action."

Quigley almost said that it would keep until morning. But he remembered that earlier message from Liberia. From a General Tubbs. Very vague. It said some matter that he and Clew had discussed was being attended to on Tubbs's end. It said that the "package was already wet." Whatever that meant. Must be some sort of code. In fact, it was the message that he'd mentioned to Bourne. This Tubbs had promised to keep Clew advised, but if he had, Clew had buried those messages.

"Urgent, you say?" The other had not been. Quigley asked, "Can I take it on Mr. Clew's console?"

"No, sir," the man said. "I can't allow that. But I can transfer a copy of just that one message. It'll be on your machine when you get up there."

Quigley found it on his screen. He hit some keys to decrypt it. As he read the words of General Abednego Tubbs, a cold feeling returned to his stomach.

"I have tried to get VaalChem to account for itself as to why they make weapons-grade Marburg. More than this, I wanted vaccines and an antidote. My virologist says that if they make such a virus, they must also make corresponding antivirals, if only for their own protection. But all I get is the run-around. They sound like men who have much on their minds and also they sound very frightened.

"I demanded to speak to their head man, of course. He is an Englishman. His name is Cecil Winfield. I am told that Sir Cecil cannot come to the phone. He is indisposed. In no condition. I ask, does this mean that he, too, is infected? They don't say. I get more run-around. They say maybe I should speak to a biologist named Shamsky. I try. He claims to speak only Russian. This place has many Russians. It has many South Africans. At the top is this Englishman, but he

does not own it. An American owns it. How did you not know this? The American's name is Artemus Bourne. Who is this Artemus Bourne?

"Mr. Clew, I give up. It is your turn to get answers. I give you one day. After that, my president calls the president of Angola and asks him to send soldiers to VaalChem. They are lucky that I can't send Major Scar."

The message went on.

"What VaalChem is making is no longer a secret. I've told my president everything and the Red Cross now knows. They know because I let Major Scar call his wife. She works with the Red Cross herself. He did not tell her Marburg, but he told her enough. Now she intends to join him and help care for the sick. She asked me not to tell him that she is coming because he would surely say no. Nor could I refuse her. This is a good woman. Soon she will be there with a medical team. Get me some vaccines and antivirals.

"One piece of good news. Nobody is sick yet. Major Scar might have fed the only sick ones to the sharks. Oh, the sharks. This reminds me. One more piece of good news. Or perhaps I should say one more pieces. Fishing boats netted what was left of the criminals who came to get Bobik's arms shipment. One of them netted the torso and head of Colonel Mobote himself. He must have come because he knew that his soldiers would steal from him. Identity almost positive, based on description. The tattoo on his forehead is unique. His remains are packed in ice so that we can confirm. Death by sharks, however, was too quick for this maniac. I would rather have given him Marburg."

Henderson Quigley felt his dinner coming up. This was almost too much to absorb. A disaster. Marburg traced to VaalChem? Now to Bourne? No one was to know what VaalChem was making. Marburg is the worst, but one of many.

No, it isn't, thought Quigley. Marburg *spliced* is the worst. My God, what if they have Marburg/smallpox?

Savran Bobik. An arms shipment. So Bobik's in this as well. Quigley brushed the thought aside. That was the least of it.

And where? Where was this happening? Liberia, clearly. But fishing boats and sharks? It must be somewhere offshore. If so, it's containable. Tubbs seemed to be saying that it's been quarantined. But the fact of it, thought Quigley, can't be contained. If it were only Liberia, there might be a chance. A bribe here and there for their silence. But now the Red Cross knows? The Red Cross must advise the World Health Organization. Today, Liberia. Tomorrow, the world. And while all this is happening, where the hell is Cecil Winfield? Why isn't he dealing with this?

Clew, thought Quigley. Clew knows all about this. It must be why he was attacked and left for dead. But it wouldn't end with Clew. That wouldn't make it go away. As he had told Bourne, Clew might well have passed this on.

So Paul Bannerman would know. He'd know at least of the attack. Wouldn't Bannerman, then, employ his long and lethal reach to avenge what has been done to his friend?

Quigley's fingers were trembling as he placed them on the keyboard. The first words he typed were, "I'm on it. Never fear."

He paused to wonder, would Clew say, "Never fear"?

He struck the line out and wrote: *"I'm on it; I'm handling it."* He wrote, *"In the meantime, I need you to resend all cryptograms preceding your most recent on this subject. My computer has crashed and I lost them. I'm using a new computer. Note new address. Will get back to you quickly re next action."*

Quigley signed it, "Roger Clew" and he sent it.

He sat back. He would wait. He'd wait all night if need be. He needed to know what was happening over there if he was to distance himself from it.

He had half a mind to call Artemus Bourne and ask, "What the devil have you gotten me into?" But he knew what Bourne would say. He would say what he always says. "It's under control."

He would say, "You're being an old woman, Quigley. Go home; pop a Xanax; wash it down with some vodka. And keep your mouth shut about this."

Quigley touched a group of keys. A long list appeared. It

dropped down from the top of his screen. The list held some
sixty e-mail addresses. All were powerful men and women
in business and government. Each had been to Bourne's
home for his brunches many times. A dozen or more owed
their positions to Bourne. The rest owed a large part of their
fortunes to Bourne. His own name appeared on that list.

Keep your mouth shut, indeed, thought Quigley. Yes,
you'd like that. What you mean is keep it shut until I've settled with you in the same way I've settled with Clew.

Well, I'm sorry, Mr. Bourne.

Quigley's still trembling fingers paused over the keyboard. A touch of two keys would send these messages, un-
encrypted, to every name on that list. They would be warned
and the source would seem to be Clew if he remembered
how to doctor the routing correctly. It would not be traced to
Henderson Quigley.

But, no. He would wait for the full correspondence. He
would read it first for himself. And then decide.

Mr. Bourne? It is over. Our relationship is ended. I have
worked with you because . . . because I am a public servant.
What I've done was purely in the interests of my country. Of
our national security. In these frightening times. I have
asked for no reward. No . . . *specific* reward. It's not as if I've
taken bags of unmarked bills from you. You've suggested;
I've invested. That was all there was to it.

I have my family to consider. My reputation to protect. So
it's over unless . . . unless you're able to get past this. You're
a clever man. You might.

If you do, then we'll see.

But I will not have this laid at my door.

23

Elizabeth hadn't gone to the boat right away. She hid her car behind an unoccupied house that was five lots away from her own. She dressed in the blacks that were in her blue duffel. She checked her weapons, slid her knife into her boot, and stayed to watch her street for a while.

She would like to have seen who was coming, if anyone. She would not have tried to deal with them. She'd as much as promised Molly. Nor would Molly be pleased that she'd lingered this near. If those coming were professionals, they would expect it. They'd have formed a perimeter and moved in very carefully. They would know her car and be watching for it near both of the gates leaving Sea Pines.

It wasn't smart to stay. But this was her home. The thought of some jackboot kicking in her front door . . .

But nothing happened. No one came. Only one car, a neighbor. Molly'd better have a very good story.

She drove down to the marina, her eyes watching every vehicle. She made a half dozen unneeded turns to make certain that she wasn't being followed. She found that boat. It was no longer at the fuel dock. It had been moved, as she'd expected, to one of the slips where the larger sailboats were berthed.

Molly had told her, "Let yourself in." She used the hilt of her knife to twist the lock from its hasp. She settled in to wait. In the dark.

Almost two hours passed. She heard two taps of a horn. The sound came from the parking lot some three hundred yards distant. She moved up into the cockpit, staying deeply in shadow. She drew up her knees and arranged her abaya. She had become part of the shadow.

She saw a woman's form approaching the ramp. The silhouette, the walk, were unmistakably Molly's. Well behind her was a male shape. A large one. Very large. His head kept turning. He walked with arms folded. That could only be Billy McHugh.

Elizabeth waited. Molly slowly drew near. Molly Farrell had raised both her hands above her shoulders. Her left hand was empty. Her right hand held a pistol. She was holding it aloft so that Elizabeth could see it, but also to be ready for any surprise if Elizabeth was not on the boat. Molly still had not seen her, but she saw the broken lock. She said softly, "Elizabeth?"

Elizabeth answered, "I'm here."

Molly kept her hands raised. She turned her head slowly. She saw the dark shape. It could have been a pile of trash bags. She said, "Nice to see that you haven't lost your touch."

"Nice to see that you haven't either," said Elizabeth. "Come aboard and tell me why I'm not home in bed. Were you unable to keep our little secret?"

"Don't get testy," said Molly. "I'd rather be home, too. And we kept your secret better than you know."

Molly finished relating what had happened to Clew. He might not survive it. They could only wait and see. She told her of the woman, as yet not identified, whom Clew's driver, now dead, called "Elizabeth."

She said, "We still don't know what to make of that part
of it. Overall, though, we think that the people who did it
were working for Artemus Bourne. He's the man, you'll recall, who had asked Clew to find you. We now think it's
likely that he knows where you are. And if he did that to
Roger in trying to find you . . ."

"He might intend to do the same thing to me?"

"He might. It's why I wanted you out of there," said
Molly.

Elizabeth was confused. "Then why didn't we wait for
them? You're here. Billy's here. We could have taken them
and asked them. A corkscrew in the ear . . . wasn't that
Billy's specialty? A corkscrew in the ear, all questions answered."

Molly took a breath. "Will you take off that veil? I feel
like I'm talking to my laundry."

Elizabeth turned it to one side, baring most of her face.
She asked again, "Why didn't we deal with it here?"

"Well, for one thing, we've already done enough to this
island. But that's not the main reason. Something else has
arisen. We think we might know why Bourne's so eager to
find you. Or rather, Paul knows. He wants to tell you directly."

"Up in Westport?"

"Tonight. He sent us to get you. We have a plane waiting
at the airport."

Elizabeth frowned. "I'm not buying this, Molly. Why go
to all this trouble just for me?"

"It's not just about you. There's Roger. And there's
Bourne." Molly paused. "And are you ready? There's Martin."

Elizabeth, wearily, raised a gloved hand and brushed the
cowl of her abaya back from her head. Molly saw that her
hair and her eyes were both black. She would barely have
recognized Elizabeth.

Elizabeth asked, "Well, what now? Another Martin
Kessler sighting? I thought we'd discussed this to death."

"He's alive as of yesterday. Paul confirmed it himself. He
made some calls from Westport, then he called me on the

plane. There's no question, Elizabeth. Martin Kessler is alive. It's what Paul wants to talk to you about."

Elizabeth wet her lips. She had trouble forming words. When they came, their sound was throated. "It's not possible, Molly."

Molly stepped closer. She put her hands on Elizabeth's shoulders. She said gently, "He's alive. There's no mistake."

"Yes, there is," she said stubbornly. Now her voice sounded choked.

"Elizabeth . . . listen."

"That man loved me, Molly. You can laugh, but he did."

Molly said, "No one's laughing, Elizabeth."

"He would never have done this. Not a word? In two years?"

"He must have thought he had a very good reason."

Elizabeth's eyes began to moisten. She could only shake her head.

Molly gave her a squeeze. She said, "I know that he loved you. And I know that you loved him in your way."

She swallowed a sob. She asked, "In my way?"

"You . . . didn't exactly wear your heart on your sleeve."

Elizabeth's color had risen. "Just because I never said it? I didn't have to. He knew it."

"If you say so."

"Unless he was stupid. And he was. He was stupid. You knew Martin. Not an ounce of sense in him."

"I remember Aisha saying, 'You should honor him, Elizabeth.' You were mad at him for dying. Now you're mad because he didn't?"

"And damn it, now you're making me cry over this. Are you happy? You're making me cry."

Molly reached for her arm. "Why don't we go?"

She pulled away. She said, "No. Not again." She got up. She paced the cockpit. She said, "Wait." She waved a hand. She said, "Let me . . . think about this."

Molly's cell phone vibrated. She took it out of her pocket. She looked at the calling number. It was Carla's. She brought it to her ear. She said, "Yes?"

She listened without speaking, occasionally nodding. She said, "Thank you. We should be there by sunrise."

"That was Carla," she said, before Elizabeth could ask. "Susan's gone into labor. Paul has taken her to the hospital. Carla's staying with Cassie at his house." She added, "Elizabeth, we can talk more on the plane."

"Will I see him?" asked Elizabeth. "I want to see him."

"You will. But he'll be busy with Susan."

"Not Bannerman," she said. "Martin. Will I see him? Is he there?"

"Martin's never been in Westport. He's in Africa. Angola. You remember I told you we'd heard rumors about that."

"The diamond thing? Israelis?"

"It turned out to be true. And it turns out that Paul knew about it all this time. I didn't, but he did. I'm not happy about that. You have my permission to sock him when you see him."

Elizabeth heard the words, but she wasn't listening. She asked, "When will I see him?"

"Um . . . are we back to Paul?"

"No, damn it. Martin. How soon can I see him?"

"I don't know. We can try to work something out. I don't know how quickly we can do that."

"He won't see me cry. I won't let him see me cry." As she said this, tears were running down both cheeks. Her hands were on her belly. She was feeling her scars. Her fingers traced over the hard fibrous lumps. She asked, very softly, "Did you know I can't have babies?"

"I know. You told me. Chamonix."

"All my tubes were shot out. There's nothing there," said Elizabeth.

She looked off toward the ocean where she'd thought Martin died. She said, "Martin didn't mind. At least he said that he didn't." She removed one black glove. She brushed a droplet from her chin. "He really didn't seem to mind. He still thought I was a woman. I mean, I know that I wasn't so great in . . . some other ways . . . but he said that I was all any man could ever want. He didn't mind that I couldn't have babies."

"I know that."

"No, you don't. How could you know that?" asked Elizabeth.

"Chamonix," she repeated. "Martin and I had some long talks as well. At your worst, Martin Kessler still could not believe his luck that you had come into his life."

The tears came again. Her chin quivered. She sat. "That was then," she said. "People change."

"They don't really."

"And maybe that's why he went. To find a life. I mean, a real one. To find another woman who still had all her parts."

Molly said, "Okay, enough. You're the one who's being stupid."

"I wish . . . I just wish . . ."

"Do you have any other clothes? If you don't, I'll fix you up when we get to my place. Size ten? I have everything you'll need."

Elizabeth was dithering. She gestured toward the cabin. She said, "I have my duffel. It's below."

"Go get it. Wash your face. I'll go up and wait with Billy. You don't want to let him see your eyes all red either."

"I'm not ashamed of having feelings."

"That wasn't my point. If he sees you, he's liable to start blubbering himself. As you've seen, Billy's full of contradictions these days."

"I *will* kill him, Molly."

"Who this time?"

"Still Martin."

"Let's go. You can practice on Bannerman."

24

"Dumbest thing I ever heard of," Chester Lilly said, grumbling, as their van approached I-95's Exit 8. The signs pointed to Hilton Head Island. The three men had been traveling for almost nine hours. It was a quarter past eight in the morning.

"Must be thirty thousand people who live there full time. How the hell are we supposed to find Stride?"

As Lilly spoke, he was staring at the grainy old photo that he'd printed out from Clew's files. Toomey, who was driving, said, "Not even a good picture. Crowd shot, no enlargement, no full face, only profile. On top of that, they only *think* it's of Stride."

Toomey drove with one hand. He kept his left hand elevated. It was too tightly bandaged; the anesthetic had worn off, and he'd already wacked it a couple of times. It was throbbing all the way to his shoulder. Kuntz was in the backseat. He'd slept most of the way. He'd said his hands were too sore to take a turn at the wheel.

"Well, Bourne wants a plan," said Lilly. "So let's plan. Any ideas on where we should start?"

Toomey shrugged. "Ordinarily, restaurants and shops. Show the picture, see if anyone knows her. I still have cop ID I can flash."

"Say someone does know her. They could call her and warn her."

"They won't if I say suspected terrorist connections. All they'd have to see is who she's with in that picture. Most of them look like Arabs. They won't do her any favors."

Lilly glanced at his watch. "Hardly any shops and restaurants will be open yet," he said. "Maybe coffee shops and diners."

"It's a start. And we could all use some breakfast."

Toomey turned off the interstate onto Route 278. He said, "From here it's a straight shot to the bridge. Twenty minutes."

"The other thing we should do," came Kuntz's groggy voice, "is call Information, see if they have a listing."

"A listing for who? You mean Stride?"

"We could ask."

Lilly said, "Hey, Einstein. Go back to sleep, will you?"

"What's the matter with that?" asked Kuntz.

"It's fucking mindless."

"Hey, we covered for you after you got Claire killed. We don't need your insults, okay?"

Lilly had often wondered whether he could take Kuntz. Not real likely, one on one. Not if Kuntz was ready for him. Cage fighters are the nearest thing to pit bulls. His one advantage would be that Kuntz's hands are a mess. Not just from last night. Not just from pounding Clew's face. It's from pounding a few hundred other faces, heads, and elbows. Those guys try to break each other's hands that way. Catch their bare-knuckle shots on harder bone.

Kuntz had fished out his cell phone. He was using his thumb to punch out a number. His other thick and bent fingers were not equal to the task. Lilly heard him ask, "You got a listing for Stride?" He spelled it out for her. He said, "Yeah, that's right." A recording came on. He slapped Toomey's shoulder. Excitedly, he hissed, "Damn, it's her."

Toomey looked at him through the rearview mirror. He said, "You've got to be shitting me."

Kuntz said, "Write this down." He recited the number he'd been given.

Lilly jotted it at the top of the photo. "She said *Elizabeth* Stride? There's actually a listing for Elizabeth Stride?"

"E. Stride," said Kuntz. "It's listed with an initial. Which means it's a woman or they'd give the whole name. I never understood why so many women do that. I mean, who the hell would it fool?"

"Wait a minute," said Lilly. He was trying to remember. The CIA files. They had Strides from all over. And one of them did live in South Carolina. Was it Hilton Head? Maybe. He hadn't paid much attention. He'd skipped over it because the photo in that file couldn't possibly have been the real Stride.

Lilly said, "That's not her. That's a different one. Trust me."

Kuntz bridled. He said, "What? I have to be wrong? Clew didn't write 'Hilton Head Island' for nothing. I come up with this and you blow me off?"

Toomey agreed. He said, "We should check it out."

"It's coming back to me," said Lilly. "This one's old. Really old." He told them how he'd been all through this for Bourne and had spent hours at a CIA computer.

"Say you're right," said Toomey. "She could still be a relative."

"Sure she could," said Kuntz eagerly. "Like her aunt. Her grandmother."

Toomey said, "Think about it. This could make a lot of sense. Stride's grandmother, say, already lives on this island. Same name, which could be very convenient. Stride comes and moves in. It could be perfect for her. Who would look for two of her at one address?"

Lilly rubbed his chin. He said, "Yeah, that could be. Did you guys bring your Orioles jackets and ski masks?"

"We dumped those," said Kuntz. "I brought stocking masks for all of us." He pulled a wad of cut-up nylons from his pocket. He gave one each to Lilly and Toomey. He said, "I got duct tape, a tarp, and this drawstring bag. The bag's to go over her head if we get her. The tarp's to either wrap her or cover her."

"Whatever keeps her quiet," said Lilly.

"Better than those, Bourne's doc gave me a needle. Pheno . . . pheno . . ."

"Phenobarbital, sounds like."

"Except I never gave a shot. You guys know how to do that?"

"Let's worry about that when we find her," said Lilly. He was silent for a moment. "Hey, Kuntz?"

"Yeah, what?"

"That Einstein crack before. I'm just in a bad mood. It would be nice if something went right for a change."

"Forget it," said Kuntz. "No hard feelings. And it will. I'm getting good vibes about this."

Toomey gestured toward the dash. He said, "We're low on gas. We ought to fill up before we get there."

Lilly nodded. "Pull in the next station we hit. I'll look in their phone book for this E. Stride's address. I'll also get us a street map."

Toomey asked, "While we're stopped, should we check in with Bourne?"

Lilly shook his head. "Let's see what we got first. If this isn't her, we'd just get more shit. If it's her, I'm the one who'll give shit."

Nadia Halaby had looked at her watch. Almost ten after nine and no sign of Elizabeth. They'd made a date for the four of them to play doubles and they only had the court for an hour. Aisha and Jasmine had already warmed up. They were banging the ball back and forth.

She'd called Elizabeth's house on her cell phone. No answer. She got the machine. She thought that Elizabeth might be on her way, but Elizabeth still hadn't shown. Jasmine had said, "She had a date last night. She could have overslept. She went out with this contractor, Gary, again. Hey, maybe he finally got lucky."

"Nice talk in front of Aisha," she'd scolded.

Never mind, thought Nadia. Too late to find a fourth. We'll play some round-robin until she shows up. If she doesn't, we'll drive over there and make her fix us breakfast.

And she secretly hoped that Jasmine was right. She wouldn't mind catching her with Gary.

The address for E. Stride was 30 Marsh Drive. The map showed that the house was in Sea Pines Plantation, a gated community on the island's south end. Toomey had asked, "How do we get in?" Lilly pointed. He said, "Look at the sign."

The sign said VISITORS: DAY PASS $5.00. Toomey smiled. He said, "That's to keep out the riffraff, I guess. I mean, what burglar would blow five whole dollars just to clean out a few of these houses?"

Lilly said, "Yeah, but if you're spotted, you're stuck. These two gates are the only way out."

Kuntz had the map. He said, "Maybe three miles. Straight ahead, then bear right on Plantation Drive. Marsh Drive is just past the golf course."

They found the house. They did two slow passes. Not a big house, one story, set well back from the road. Good-sized lot, an acre or more, lots of trees. It had a circular driveway cutting in from two sides. Venetian blinds on the windows, but none of them were drawn. The front entrance was a fancy wooden door with beveled glass. The house had no garage; just a carport on one end. They saw that the carport was empty. They saw an untouched, rolled-up newspaper at the foot of the driveway. They could see no lights on inside.

Toomey said, "Looks like nobody's home. I guess they could have gone out on some errand except wouldn't they have picked up that paper?"

"They?" asked Lilly. "Who's they?"

"Grandma, remember? Her and Grandma. That's the theory."

"Well, as far as the paper, it could have just come. But you're right. One of them could still be home."

"So what now?" asked Toomey. "We sit and wait for who shows up? Three men in a van might look funny around here. They do have a security patrol."

A neighbor's house two doors up was being remodeled.

Lilly saw a Dumpster and a portable toilet. Lilly said, "Park it there. It'll look like we work there. Leave the keys in the ignition. And then we'll go knock."

"We go knock?" asked Toomey. "That's it? That's your plan?"

Lilly said, "Enough talking. Let's go."

Lilly had decided to send Kuntz to the door. Neighborhoods like this one always have people knocking to ask if there are any odd jobs to be done. Fix your roof, mow your lawn, and, especially with contractors, drumming up business from the neighbors. And Kuntz looked like someone who worked with his hands. Lilly and Toomey would wait out of sight until Kuntz had pushed his way in.

But no answer. No one home. No old woman either. Kuntz tried the front door. It was open. He waved the others forward. Toomey whispered to Lilly, "You go left, I'll go right." They both kept their hands on their weapons. He told Kuntz, "You stay by the door. Watch the street."

He and Lilly did a quick check of the rooms. Lilly had gone through the den toward the kitchen. Toomey's side had the bedrooms; there were three in all, but the middle one was used as an office. It had a computer, some bookshelves, and an oak table desk. Pretty basic, clean and neat. The computer's hard drive should be worth taking with them. People put their whole lives on their hard drives.

He looked in the master bedroom. The bed was made. Unslept in, perhaps, but just as likely made early. He checked the closets, the clothing. It was all of one size. He saw none that had the look of an old woman's clothing. He went into the bathroom to check the cosmetics. He saw nothing suggesting an old woman there either. It was all the sort of stuff that his ex-wife might use and she was about the same age as Stride. And the stuff was all there. Her toothbrush, hair brushes, deodorant, a hair dryer. They were the sorts of things that a woman would take with her if she had packed up and gone elsewhere. She'd be coming back sooner or later.

The second bathroom had only a few basic necessities. It was strictly a guest bathroom. No regular use. Nor did the second bedroom show any sign that anyone slept there on a regular basis. Closets used for storage of seasonal clothing. Same size, same sort of taste as the others. Whoever lived here, he decided, lived here alone. She was tallish, fairly young, a size ten. He was reasonably sure that they'd hit paydirt.

One other clue was the way the house was furnished. Nice things, a few antiques, lots of decorative touches, but nothing that he would have called personal. No framed family photos, for example. The den was an especially comfortable room. It had a TV, more bookshelves, a wood-burning fireplace, and a pair of plush leather lounge chairs. On the end table next to one of those chairs were a book and an unfinished glass of wine.

The book was open, inverted, to where she'd left off. He checked the title. A romance book. That surprised him a little. This woman cuts throats, but she reads bodice-rippers. She must not be getting laid very much. And that half-full wineglass bothered him some. Unless she was a lush and was at it this morning, she might have been gone since last night. And maybe in a hurry. Just the clothes on her back. Not even taking time to lock up.

Toomey heard a woman's voice. It was coming from the kitchen. He realized that he was hearing an answering machine. Chester Lilly was checking her messages. The woman's voice had said, *"Pick up if you're there."* Then a click. Stride must have picked up.

Toomey called to Chester, "What time was that left?"

"Eleven last night. Wait a second. There's one more."

Another woman's voice. It said, *"I hope you're on your way."* It said, *"We only have this court until ten."*

Toomey asked Lilly, "When was that one?"

"This morning," said Lilly. "Half an hour ago. It sounds like she's out playing tennis and that's good. It gives us some time to get organized."

Yeah, maybe, thought Toomey. But did she ever get there? He was about to start looking for her tennis racket when Lilly called again from the kitchen. He said, "Hey, get in here. Here she is."

Toomey heard no alarm in Lilly's voice. The tone was more one of discovery. Toomey asked, "She's where? What are you talking about?"

"Right here. We found pictures. Come look."

He proceeded to the kitchen where he found Kuntz and Lilly. Kuntz had found a red-and-yellow Photomat envelope. Lilly opened it and was sorting through its contents. Lilly said to Toomey, "They were right here on the counter. It looks like she just got them developed."

"A party," said Kuntz. "It looks like a birthday party. This kid in the middle, I bet. See the presents?"

Toomey saw that the shot had been taken in the living room. A young girl, very pretty, had been opening gifts. Sitting on the couch. Discarded wrappings at her feet. A smiling black woman on the couch at her side was admiring what must have been one of the gifts, a techy-looking new tennis racket.

Toomey said to Kuntz, "What are you doing in here? Did I tell you to watch the front door?"

"I came in to get some water. I was thirsty."

"Get back to the door. Don't take your eyes off that street."

"It was me who found the pictures. You might not have found them."

"And for that you get a prize. We'll make a stop at Baskin-Robbins. Right now, though, get back to the door."

Lilly watched him go. He said to Toomey, "Look at this."

In his left hand he was holding that old photo of Stride. His right hand held a snapshot with three females in it. The kid, a black woman, and a darkish white woman. The white woman, lean and fit, was the taller of the three. Lilly said, "This one's got to be Stride."

Toomey looked. Same dark hair. About the right height. Same age, more or less, but it was hard to be sure. He said, "We have Stride in profile. Do you have this one in profile?"

Lilly sorted through the snapshots. "Maybe this one."

He handed Toomey a shot of the two adult women. They were caught in conversation sitting at the dinner table. Their faces were turned toward each other. But the white one had a hand up; she was gesturing as she spoke. Her hand obscured a part of her jaw. Toomey compared it to the printed-out copy. He said, "I wish she was smiling. Stride is smiling on ours. And see there?" He pointed. "Stride has a dimple. In the snapshot, her hand blocks the dimple."

"It's Stride," said Lilly. "Who else would she be?"

Toomey said, "You know what's missing? It's whoever took these pictures. And look at that table. It's set for four people. That fourth one's not in any of these pictures."

"Let me see," said Lilly. He leafed through the rest of them. "Not in these," he said, "but the white one is Stride."

"Yeah, maybe," said Toomey. "So who was the fourth?"

"I don't know. Could be anyone. It could be a guy. It's whoever brought a camera along."

Toomey said, "Wait a second. Let's go look at that table."

He led Lilly from the kitchen and into the dining room. Straight ahead were the sliding glass doors to the porch. He saw the porch table where, according to the snapshots, the birthday dinner took place.

He said to Lilly, "Let me see those again." By looking at the snapshots and the background behind them, he was able to tell where each one had been sitting. The dark-haired one had sat farthest out facing the sliding glass doors. The black woman had to have been on the left, judging from the way they'd been photographed. The girl was on the right in a couple of the shots. The nearest chair was empty in all of them.

Toomey asked, "If you're the hostess, where do you sit?"

Lilly shrugged. "At the head of the table?"

"This table's round, but that's not the point. When you're serving people dinner, you sit nearest the kitchen." He held up a snapshot. "Look where Stride is sitting."

Lilly looked. He shrugged again. He said, "This proves . . . what?"

"I don't know. This just bothers me. That might not be Stride. The one with the camera could have been Stride. It's her house; she's hostess, it makes sense."

Lilly said, "Listen, Sherlock . . ." But he didn't finish. Kuntz had come rushing back from the door. Kuntz told

Lilly, "Same three. They just pulled up outside." Kuntz was stretching out his stocking mask as he spoke.

Lilly patted his pockets. He found his own. He said, "There's a laundry room just off the kitchen. Let's get in there. They're not here to do laundry."

Nadia had swung into Elizabeth's driveway. Jasmine and Aisha were in the car with her, all three still in tennis attire. They saw that Elizabeth's car wasn't there.

Nadia said, "She must have left pretty early. Her newspaper's still in the driveway."

Aisha said, "Well, we're here. Let's leave her a note."

"Not a nice one," said Jasmine. "Not after a no-show."

"You know, she could have been in an accident," said Aisha. "And it's not as if she's ever done this before."

Nadia shook her head. "I bet she simply forgot."

"So let's remind her," said Jasmine as she opened her door. "Anyway, I have to use the bathroom."

Lilly listened as the front door opened and closed. He whispered to Kuntz, "Which one of them was driving?"

Kuntz answered, "The dark-haired one. Stride."

"Shit," he said quietly. "That means it's her car. I was hoping that the other two just dropped her off."

They heard multiple footsteps, more than one voice. They seemed to be coming toward the kitchen.

Toomey said, "So they're either going to hang out here for a while, or Stride will be going out with them again. I say we wait."

Lilly asked, "For what? She's right here."

"For her to be alone. Let's do this quietly, okay? If we wait, the other two won't know where she's gone. We'll have her back up at Bourne's before they miss her."

The loud flushing of a toilet startled the three. Someone had used the half bath off the kitchen. There was only a thin wall between them. A woman's voice from the kitchen asked, "Jasmine? You ready?"

"One sec," came the voice from the bathroom.

Toomey mouthed the word, *"Chill."* He added, *"Wait."*

*   *   *

Jasmine wasn't sure, but she thought she'd heard movement. Something hadn't felt right even when she sat down, but the sound had come just as she flushed. Could be mice, she decided. Maybe vibrating pipes.

She rinsed her hands and stepped out into the kitchen. She saw that Nadia had left a note on the counter. It said simply, "Where were you?" signed "Nadia."

Aisha had added, "New racket felt great. I missed you. Let's play soon." She signed it with a cartoon smiley face.

Nadia was waiting at the front door. Aisha had already gone out. Jasmine still hadn't shaken that uneasy feeling. She said softly, "Go ahead. I want to sign that note myself."

Nadia turned toward her car. Jasmine closed the door behind her. Through the door's beveled glass, she saw that Nadia had stopped, confused by the shutting of the door. She raised a hand as if to say, "Go ahead. It's all right." Walking silently, she moved back toward the kitchen.

She heard a soft squeak as if a doorknob had been turned and she thought she heard the scuffing of a shoe. Her eyes fell on the assortment of carving and steak knives that Elizabeth kept on her counter. She reached and quietly drew the largest of them and lowered it to her thigh. She backed off to the entranceway of the kitchen where Elizabeth's telephone hung on the wall. She took the phone from its cradle, pressed a button, got a dial tone. She asked loudly, "Is someone in there?"

There was no answer. No more sounds.

She said, "Well, guess what? I'm not going to come look. What I'm going to do is hit 911 and let the police come and look."

A man appeared. Then a second and a third. All three had stockings drawn over their faces. Two of the three had guns in their hands. One of them, the burliest, wore leather gloves. The one in the middle had a hand fully bandaged. That one said, "Put the phone down. We mean you no harm. Stay calm and you won't get hurt."

She backed away from them. She said, "Glad to hear it." She punched 911 with her thumb.

The third one said, "Take her."

She said into the phone, "I have intruders. Men with guns," before tossing it into the den. The bandaged one was on her in an instant. He swung his pistol at the side of her head. She ducked it and slashed with her carving knife. He hadn't seen it coming. He was almost too late. He raised the bandaged hand to block it. The knife sliced through tape and gauze. The man gasped and cursed, but Jasmine got no other chance. The second man, the gloved one, was on her as well. He seized the wrist that held the knife and threw a punch at her ribs. A second punch followed to her face, and a third. She felt herself spinning. She crashed to the floor.

She heard a distant voice shout, "Get the other two. *Move*." The voice shouted something else about a van. The last words she heard were, "You like knives, you fucking cunt?" before she felt something cold against her throat.

Lilly and Kuntz raced through the front door. They saw that Stride and the girl were still waiting by the car. Both were frozen momentarily at the sight of two masked men running at them down the entryway walk. Stride was the first to react. She shouted, "Aisha, run." But the warning was barely out of her mouth before Lilly grabbed her hair and clubbed her to her knees, using the butt of his Glock. He said to Kuntz, "Get the kid; I'll get the van."

They had parked the van off the street two houses up. Lilly knew that they had one minute at most before the police would be swarming. He reached the van, turned the key in the ignition, and was alongside Stride's car in five seconds. Kuntz had the girl in one arm. She was limp. Kuntz must have cold-cocked her; that was good. Toomey was coming, cradling his hand. It was dripping all over the walk.

Lilly shouted, "In the back. Throw them both in the back." He said, "Kuntz, get in with them. You stay down."

Twenty seconds had gone by. He heard sirens.

Toomey climbed in beside him, his hand dripping blood, but Toomey was keeping his head. Toomey said, "Don't drive fast. We go slow and easy. Cop cars come, pull over like we're giving them room. Try to look like you're saying, 'Wow, what's going on?'"

Lilly turned off Marsh Drive onto Plantation Drive. He asked Toomey, "The black one. Can she talk?"

"Not anymore."

"Why, what did you do?"

"I cut her damned throat is what I did. Stupid bitch."

Lilly cursed. "What for? She was down. She was out."

Toomey showed his bleeding hand. "Do you see this? She did this. I was in no condition to haul her out here."

What's done is done, thought Lilly. The thing now is to keep moving. The van had fallen in between two other cars. That was good. That could help. And they were both SUVs. The van would stand out a lot less.

He said over his shoulder to Kuntz, "Keep them quiet."

Kuntz answered, "They're quiet. They're both hardly breathing. And the kid . . . I don't know . . . I might have hit her too hard."

"Well, don't let Stride die. Keep her quiet, but alive. You got that duct tape back there? Tape them up. Use that hood."

Kuntz was tearing strips of tape. "Which one gets the hood?"

"I gotta tell you everything? Put it on Stride. Then throw that tarp over the two of them."

He asked, "What about the shot? Where's it go? In the ass?"

"You got enough for two?"

"How should I know?"

"Then save it. Give half to whoever wakes up first."

The first two police cars raced past them, blue lights flashing. The SUV ahead of them had pulled over to the side. Lilly held his breath and did the same. "We get out of here," said Toomey, "it'll be a fucking miracle. Even if we get through the gate before they seal it, they still might set up roadblocks on the bridge."

"Are you saying hole up? Break into a house?"

"Eight minutes to the bridge. I'd rather chance it, I think. We can always turn back if traffic's stopped on the bridge."

"Sounds like a plan," said Chester Lilly.

They did get through the gate. They were waved through. Nice surprise. Two guards were moving traffic out of the way so more cop cars and an ambulance could get in.

Seven minutes, thought Lilly. Don't speed. Our luck is holding. His mind was already on the phone call he'd make once they were well clear of the bridge.

Mr. Bourne? I got her. I got Stride plus a bonus. A little messy, but hey, it's Elizabeth Stride. It's not as if you sent us for some kid.

Except speaking of kids, what's Bourne going to say?

Bring the girl, too?

Kill her and dump her?

If it's "kill her," he's not going to say that straight out. He'll say, *Do as you've been told. Only that. Am I clear?*

Too bad, though, thought Lilly. She's a nice-looking kid. But Kuntz says she might not make it anyway.

25

It was earlier that morning. The sun had barely risen. Molly had brought Elizabeth from the airport to her home, the Victorian that she shared with Anton Zivic. She had shown Elizabeth to a spare downstairs bedroom and urged her to get a few hours' sleep until Bannerman could get back from the hospital.

Elizabeth refused. She did not want to sleep. She asked, "Where is this hospital?"

"In Norwalk. Next town over. Norwalk Hospital."

She turned away from the bedroom. "I'll go see him there."

"No, you won't," said Molly firmly. "He's been up all night with Susan. You can wait a while longer. Go sit down."

Elizabeth chewed her lip. She said, "I know. That was thoughtless."

"I'm eager to hear this story myself, but he's promised that you'll be the first."

"I'll sit," said Elizabeth. "I'll shut up and wait."

Elizabeth took a chair, a rocker, in the parlor. She kept her blue duffel at her side. She stayed there, rocking slowly, staring at nothing, sometimes with an angry, vengeful look in her eyes, sometimes with deep sadness and regret.

Molly was busy. She was often on her cell phone. She had spoken to Anton Zivic several times. He'd said that all of their people were eager to assist in finding who did that to Clew. Those who were traveling were told to converge on the Washington area and then wait. He said that all were accounted for except for John Waldo. He was unable to locate John Waldo.

"Wasn't John at the briefing last night?" she asked Zivic.

"He was. He listened. That's the last that I saw of him."

"He's . . . the ghost of all ghosts. He's doing something. He's somewhere."

"Yes, one would conclude that," said Zivic with an edge. "Coordination, however, is desirable in these cases. And so, by the way, is heightened alertness. Have you noticed any strangers in the complex? Last few days?"

"I haven't. Has someone else?"

"I am informed that two strangers have been to Town Hall and were poring over property records. They showed a special interest in Greens Farms Estates. There is no property for sale there that I know of."

"Me neither," said Molly. "Maybe someone's refinancing. Might they have been bankers or lawyers? A title search?"

"Possible," said Zivic. "Their description could fit either. And you are correct; their intent could be innocent. But one of them asked an unusual question. He asked how often the grass there is cut."

"What, here in the complex? The yard crew comes Tuesdays. Did he ask when the trash is picked up?"

"Only grass."

"Um . . . Anton," said Molly, "I'm not sure I see the threat here."

"I was, perhaps, too long KGB. I see at least six conspiracies before breakfast. But if I were Mr. Bourne and I, in fact, was behind this, and I knew that Paul Bannerman was an interested party, I think that I would want some eyes and ears here in Westport. You might check your surveillance tapes, Molly."

"You think they'll hit us on a Tuesday? Disguised as a yard crew? Submachine guns disguised as leaf blowers?"

"Molly . . . indulge me. Look through the tapes."

"Just kidding," Molly told him. "And I will. Last few days?"

"It would take hours, I know, and it is probably time wasted. Perfect strangers go in and out every day. I fully understand your reluctance."

"Anton, I'll look. Just as soon as I can."

"Where is Carla? Still with Cassie?"

"Until Paul gets back."

"Then when she's free," said Zivic, "ask Carla to do it. She has a good eye and good instincts."

"I will."

"Have Carla talk to me. I will give her their descriptions. And tell Paul that he's had quite a number of calls. I've dealt with most of them myself, but there are some he should return. Among them, our esteemed Secretary of State."

"I know," said Molly. "His office called last night. The call is still on Paul's machine."

"Not his office. He himself. Twice more, he has called. When this man calls himself, it's urgent business."

"I'll tell Paul."

Zivic asked, "And Elizabeth? How is she doing?"

"Very quiet," said Molly. "A little numb, I think. Anton, I've got another call coming in. It's Paul. He must have some news."

The news was of the baby. A son, as expected. It had arrived about two hours earlier. There had been some concern about the baby's respiration. Paul had waited until that concern was resolved before calling. Mother and child now both doing well. Susan especially. It had been easier than with Cassie. He said that she'd urged him to go home, see Elizabeth. She understood the state that Elizabeth must be in. But he'd stayed with her until she had fallen asleep, until the nurse took the baby from her arms.

"He's on his way?" asked Elizabeth.

"We're his first stop. Ten minutes."

* * *

Elizabeth was already on her feet when he entered. She forced a smile and a greeting. "Good to see you again, Paul." She said, "You have a son. You must be thrilled."

"I am. Very much so. Elizabeth, please sit."

"And Susan? She's comfortable? Is there anything I can bring her?"

"She's just fine. And I appreciate . . ."

"Have you chosen a name?"

Bannerman caught a signal from Molly, who was standing, arms folded, at the parlor's far end. He understood the signal to mean, *"She's trying to let you know that she's thinking past herself. It's not easy for her. Let her run with it."*

"Um . . . actually, no. We've ruled out my own name. We don't want him known as someone's 'Junior.'"

"Yours especially," said Elizabeth.

"It does carry some baggage. He should be his own person. We also thought about Raymond, which is Susan's father's name. When he was a cop, the New York tabloids called him 'Raymond the Terrible.' There might be a little baggage there as well."

"That, or he'd go through his childhood called Ray-Ban."

Bannerman smiled. "I never thought of that. Good catch." He paused for a moment before speaking again. He said, "We kicked around several suggestions this morning. Now we're leaning toward Martin. That was Susan's idea."

Elizabeth, for a moment, looked as if she'd been deflated. She rocked on her heels. Her mouth fell open. Bannerman realized that he'd failed to grasp the depth of emotion that Kessler's name might elicit. He turned toward Molly. "Will you give us a few minutes?"

Molly signaled again. She touched a hand to her ear and turned her thumb toward the attic. She was asking, *"May I listen?"*

He gave a faint nod.

She asked, "Want anything? Coffee?"

"Elizabeth?"

"Nothing."

"Well, sit down, please," said Bannerman. "We'll talk about Martin."

He said, "That baby's name business; that was clumsy of me. This wasn't the right time to mention it."

She had not regained her color. She asked, "Why would you do that?"

"Do what? Name him Martin?"

"No, I mean . . . in his memory? Would this be in his memory?"

"Oh, gosh, no," said Bannerman. He realized why she'd seemed faint. "That was more than clumsy. Martin's not dead. I understood that Molly had told you."

A sigh of relief. "She did, but for a moment I thought something else had happened. I guess I'm still having trouble coming to grips with him being alive in the first place."

"Alive as of this morning. There has been direct contact. He has not, however, been told that you know or that you're here in Westport with us. . . . Elizabeth, I can't give you the time that this deserves. I've got to pick up my daughter and get back to Susan and I need to make some calls before that. I'm going to try to encapsulate this. Oh, and because I'd rather not go through it twice, Molly's listening in from upstairs. Do you mind?"

"Not so far."

"If we get to an area that you'd rather keep private, say the word and she'll switch off at once."

Elizabeth nodded. "It's okay."

"Do you need to hear how they got Martin off that boat?"

"The Israelis?"

"Navy divers, but at Tel Aviv's request. The Mossad had been trying to find Martin for months. They'd heard about that terrorist attack on your island and they knew, by whatever means, that Martin was involved. Do you need to know how they found out?"

"I can guess. The same people who kept our names out of it."

"Correct."

Elizabeth asked, "But why did they want him? I mean, I would have thought . . ."

"That they'd want you? Not for this. It was Martin or no one. Do you know the name Jonas Savimbi? Angola?"

She nodded. "Rebel leader. He's dead now."

"Replaced by a man named Dumas Duganga, but it's Savimbi who got this ball rolling. Savimbi was a Marxist when it paid to be a Marxist. He was trained in both Russia and East Germany. The Russians trained him in Communist doctrine. The East Germans trained him in insurgency tactics and in how to set up an Intelligence network. For the latter, Martin Kessler was one of his instructors. Meeting Martin was a long-awaited thrill for Savimbi. You'll recall that Martin was a national hero in the GDR and beyond."

She made a face. "Martin's comic books. I know."

Bannerman's eyes went hard for a beat. He said, "Elizabeth . . . Martin was never a joke. He's one of the best men I've known."

She had to look away. Her eyes were moistening again. She said, softly, "I know that. I do."

"So did Savimbi. He admired Martin Kessler. Kessler wasn't one of those turgid ideologues that could put half the trainees to sleep in ten minutes. Kessler thought for himself; he didn't go by the book; he was always refreshingly honest."

She made a feeble gesture with her hand. "Could we go on?"

He pulled out a handkerchief. He handed it to her. "Skip ten years. Savimbi runs eastern Angola. He's made a deal with the Israelis. The Israelis want his diamonds and they want his arms business. Savimbi doesn't trust them. He's learned not to trust anyone. He's been cheated and exploited by just about everyone who wanted a piece of Angola. If this sounds like sympathy for Savimbi, it isn't. He was intelligent, charismatic, but he killed on a whim. In any case, he said that he'd deal with the Israelis if they could produce the one white man he *did* trust. He would only deal with them through Martin Kessler."

"But a German? Why a German? There must have been other . . ."

"He wanted Kessler. He wanted the man. Being German,

however, was apparently a factor. Jonas Savimbi had been heard to remark that the Germans knew how to deal with Jews."

Elizabeth squeezed the handkerchief. This was going too quickly. She reversed that same gesture. She said, "Wait, please. Back up."

She asked him how Martin could have possibly survived a bullet and all that radiation. Bannerman said, "There are only three hospitals in the world that specialize in radiation sickness. One's in Oak Ridge, Tennessee, one's in Kiev, Ukraine, and the third is outside Tel Aviv. The Israelis didn't think that he could survive either, but they wanted to take their best shot."

Elizabeth shook her head. "He had a measured exposure of a thousand rads. No one can survive a thousand rads."

Bannerman shrugged. "Then he didn't have a thousand. It might have been a misreading; he might have been partly shielded. The Israelis think it was more like four hundred, but even that level is usually fatal. Elizabeth, he nearly died several times. The bullet was the least of his problems."

"But then he got well?"

"Not entirely, no. But he got well enough after six or eight months that he could get around on his own. His hair grew back in; he regained some weight; he had some dental work done for the teeth that fell out. He thanked the Mossad for saving his life, but he had no interest in this thing with Savimbi. He left. He said he wanted to go skiing."

She remembered. "Davos?"

Bannerman nodded. "He was strong enough to teach. He wanted to do it and he needed to work. He was broke. I'm told he'd left you all his diamonds."

Elizabeth brought her hand to her mouth as if to stop herself from asking the question that was forming. "John Waldo said that one of the twins . . ."

"Saw him there? Yes, he did. Martin ducked him."

"He said that Martin was seen with a woman."

"I heard that," said Bannerman. "He'd have had women students." He said, "Let's not get off the track."

She looked at him. "Paul, was he there with a woman?"

"Elizabeth . . ."

"Was he?"

"It was not what you're thinking. The woman he was seen with could indeed have been some student, but, yes, he was there with a woman named Sara. She used the name Sara Latham. She pretended to be English. She pretended to be in Davos on vacation. She was actually Mossad; her real name was Sara Gleissman. She'd been assigned to befriend him and stick close to him until the Israelis could come up with a package that might change his mind about Angola."

"So, you're saying she seduced him."

"I can promise you, she didn't."

She flared. "You can promise? How the hell would you know? Is it because you think he'd stay faithful to me? He dropped me out of his life."

She stood up. She was embarrassed. She had not meant to blurt that. She glanced toward the ceiling, knowing Molly had heard it. She turned away, hiding her face.

Bannerman rose with her. He placed his hands on her shoulders. He said, very gently, "Now you listen to me. She'd have tried that, sure, but it wasn't going to happen. Martin would have known that she was Mossad from the moment that she made her first overture. Martin Kessler wasn't new at this, Elizabeth."

"Was she attractive?"

"I assume so. They wouldn't have sent . . ." He paused and heaved a sigh. He said, "This is ridiculous. Sara and Martin? Put it out of your mind. Why her and not you? The answer is neither. Martin was impotent, Elizabeth."

She didn't speak for a moment. "The radiation," she said softly.

Bannerman turned her. He sat her back down. "And as to why he never got word back to you, it was not just his loss of that function. I would guess that there were any number of factors. Your new life was one. You'd made it clear that his presence was destructive of that life."

She had started to deny it. "That was only until . . ."

"Until the day you thought he died?"

Her chin came up. "You wait just a damned minute."

"Elizabeth, I'm trying to explain where his head was. I'm not making a judgment about it."

"And anyway . . . destructive? Destructive is right. You know Martin. He's a train wreck. He can't help it; it's his nature. But he was sweet . . . and he was loyal . . . and . . ."

"I know you had mixed feelings. You made that clear to Molly. But Martin has his pride and that was just as clear to me. He'd have liked to have had a future with you, but he knew that he probably didn't have one at all."

Bannerman briefed her on the long-term effect of ionized radiation at that level. A probable depletion of red and white blood cells. Irreversible damage to various organs including bone marrow and kidneys. A high likelihood of developing leukemia, among any number of cancers. The impotence may be treatable, but he's almost surely sterile.

He said, "Elizabeth, he would never be a burden to anyone. Not even to me, although he could have come here. Not to Harry Whistler; he could certainly have gone there. Most of all, not to you. He had nothing left to offer."

"That's what you think?"

"That's what *he* thinks, Elizabeth."

The tears came again. "Then he's a damned fool."

"So am I, then," said Bannerman. "I'd have done the same thing."

"No, you wouldn't. You'd leave Susan?"

"If I thought she'd be glad to be rid of me, yes. That's what Martin thought and don't lay this all on him. You never gave him much reason to think otherwise."

It was not the gentlest thing that he could have said to her. But he was tired. They all were. They had a lot on their minds. He knew she didn't mean that "damned fool" the way it sounded, but he chose not to let it go unchallenged.

She'd had to leave the room. Use the bathroom. Settle down. Molly came back in, disapproval on her face. She said, "Not smooth. Martin's name for the baby? Did you expect her to smile and say, 'Oh, how nice'?"

A sigh. "Did you come down here just to dump on me, Molly?"

"No, you had a phone call." She flashed a slip of paper.
"It's the Secretary of State. He's now called four times. You
can reach him at these numbers. He says they're all secure."

"He can wait," said Bannerman.

"He sounded pretty upset."

"He has reason to be. He can wait."

Molly's hands went to her hips. "Does that go for me, too?"

He said, "Molly, what I know, I've only known since you
left. Keep listening. You're about to hear most of it."

She softened a bit. "There have been other calls. Lesko
and Elena will arrive here tomorrow. Actually, almost all of
them have decided to come early. It's not just the baby. It's
Roger."

"Can you stop them?" he asked. "It could get busy around
here."

"I think they've doped that out. It's why they're coming."

He grunted.

"And as for Elizabeth, stop trying to jump past it every
time she shows some emotion. Do we need some sensitivity
training?"

"Don't start."

"You tell her, 'Oh, Sara? Don't worry about her. Kessler
couldn't get it up if he tried.'"

"I don't recall that I put it quite in those terms. In any
case, she seems to be handling it so far."

"No, she's not. She will. But it will take her some time."
She said, "That's not a woman who cries easily, Paul. She's
Elizabeth Stride. She hates showing weakness. And she
hates that Paul Bannerman is seeing it."

"That's not weakness. Those are feelings. None of us are
machines."

"Then act as if you know that. Slow down, take your time.
You can't do two years in twenty minutes."

"Well, I'll have to."

Molly asked, "By the way, why hasn't Kessler been told?"

"That she knows? Because she might decide to leave
things as they are."

"Trust me, she won't. She *will* want to see him. She might
clobber him, but she *will* want to see him."

He said, "Besides, I'd rather tell him myself. I had given him my word and I've broken it. But the real question is, will he want to see her? Keep in mind that from his point of view, nothing's changed."

Molly understood. She said, "I know, and that's sad. But don't expect Elizabeth to leave it at that."

"As you say, let's give her some time."

"Speaking of people who've disappeared on us, we can't find John Waldo. Nobody's seen him."

"John's okay," said Bannerman. "He took a trip. He'll be back."

Molly narrowed one eye. "You can't mean to Angola."

"Not that far. And not for long. He should be back sometime tonight."

"You sent him?"

"He just went. You know John. He comes and goes."

"Mostly goes," said Molly. "Paul, what are you up to? Are you going to make me guess where he is?"

"Molly, it can wait. Let me finish with Elizabeth."

"Are you getting to the part about Artemus Bourne?"

"Kessler first. Then Bourne. We'll deal with Bourne later."

"I think you just told me where John is."

26

Bourne's morning had not been without its annoyances, but no matter; it had ended up brilliantly. It had started off badly with those telephone calls. First there was Quigley of the African desk excusing himself from tomorrow's Sunday brunch. He gave some tepid excuse, an illness in the family, as if family had ever stopped him before. He'd have come if his mother were dying.

Two more calls followed. Both from oil executives. Both were men whom he had made rich. These two also claimed illness; one had the flu, the other had wrenched his back playing squash. Neither sounded the least bit convincing.

Bourne was sure he knew the truth. They were going to ground. They were distancing themselves, for a while at least, until they saw which way certain ill winds were blowing.

The whole of Washington seemed abuzz with what had happened to Clew. And word had spread that on that very day, Clew had charged down to Briarwood and provoked a confrontation over some grievance between them. No one knew quite what about. Speculation was rife. But one doesn't trifle with Artemus Bourne. Within hours, Clew's reduced to a vegetative state. Surely, there must be a connection.

Well, of course there is, you cowards, but let someone try to prove it. In the meanwhile, talk it up. Tell anyone who'll listen. It'll make them less likely to trifle with me. No one trifles with Artemus Bourne.

He had half expected that some of the buzz would concern that damned VaalChem container. He'd heard nothing, however. Clew certainly isn't talking. Apparently no one else had yet heard about that freighter. And what of it if they had? Who can tie that to him? Who will testify as to the source of that container? Martin Kessler? Don't be stupid. Kessler put it there himself. What's more, he murdered three men to get it. You want evidence? Go look in my freezer.

Do you want to find more of whatever's on that freighter? Look no further than Kessler, but don't take too long. Can you doubt that he's planning some further atrocity? Go get him. Scorched earth. Turn them all into salt. He's in league with al-Qaida, you know.

Bourne paused. Strike that last one. That might be stretching it a bit. Let's try to stay closer to home.

You ask where did Kessler get it? I don't know. Not a clue. He certainly didn't get it from VaalChem. You say you want to visit VaalChem? Check it out for yourselves? I'll agree to that, of course, but you know those Angolans. They'll stall you until they get something in return for letting you traipse through a national asset. Well, not national perhaps, but an asset nonetheless. Every one of them collects a monthly stipend. By the time you get permission, the place will be so well scrubbed that you'll wish you'd brought your children for a picnic.

That is to say, of course, the parts that you can get into. The serious work is done four levels down. The hot zone, they call it. But you'll never see it. The blueprints only show two levels down.

No, thought Bourne. None of this need be a problem. But Kessler . . . ah, Kessler. There's a problem.

If he put Marburg on that freighter, he can surely put it elsewhere. And the foremost *elsewhere* on the Kessler list of elsewheres would surely be the VaalChem complex itself. One might ask, *But why hasn't he done that already?* Well, you don't just fling the stuff over the fence if you hope to survive it yourself. You need a means of delivery. Some aerosol device. You need experts in this field. You need planning. You need time.

One might ask, *Wouldn't Briarwood be next on his list?*

The answer, Bourne realized, was an almost certain "Yes."

But if that's so, why didn't he add it to those coolers? Let it rise up with the fumes from Bobik's putrefying head.

Bourne shook his head. Same answer. Too dangerous. And besides, he would have thought that I have the antivirals. And I do. But it would have been too late.

One might ask, *Even so, shouldn't you . . . like, not be here? Kessler, after all, now has your address.*

Bourne brushed that thought aside. What, go hide? Leave my home? When I have a basement that's a bunker in itself and armed guards wherever you look? Not a chance. Besides, who'd look after my bees?

One responds, *Your bees? If you're not careful, he will. What if Kessler should spritz it all over your beehives? You'd have a thousand Marburg missiles buzzing all over Briarwood, not to mention the whole of Shenandoah.*

That's the trouble, thought Bourne, with imagined conversations. The straight man within you always wants better lines. Would Kessler hurt his bees? Would he be so cruel? Never mind. He wouldn't. But not because they are blameless. He wouldn't because he would have to consider the comfort and safety of my guests.

What guests? asks the straight man. *Are there any left?*

That shows how much you know, thought Bourne with a smirk. For among those sniveling phone calls that I took this morning was one that was exceedingly welcome. It was Lilly. He's found her. He's got her.

Elizabeth Stride. The great love of Kessler's life. Her abduction was a somewhat untidy affair, but one has come to expect that from Chester. No matter. He's bringing her. She'll be here in time for supper. And, as a bonus, he's bringing a girl who seems, says Chester, to be dear to her heart. A child who has just turned sixteen.

Supper, thought Bourne. But who's going to prepare it? We can't very well have the household staff on hand to see our two guests being hauled to the basement. Best to dismiss them. A night on the town. Have them come back on Sunday morning after Stride and the girl are tucked away. For tonight we'll rustle up something for ourselves and eat it while we're getting acquainted.

Chester had asked, "Should I dump the kid, or what?"

"Dump her how? Set her loose?"

"I think you know what I'm asking."

"Certainly not. She's an innocent. You will do no such thing."

"Mr. Bourne, she's out cold, but she still was a witness."

"We'll deal with her later." It won't matter. You'll be dead. "For the present," he told Chester, "she'll be added insurance. If Stride is to be my hedge against Kessler, the girl may come in handy as a hedge against Stride. A guarantor of Stride's good behavior."

"If you say so."

"This is excellent, Chester. This is better than lamb's blood."

"How's that again?" asked Chester.

"It's a biblical reference. An apt one at that. Moses' seven plagues of Egypt. Or was it six? I don't recall. A smear of lamb's blood kept the angel of death from one's door. In this case, we have our own angel of death fended off by the infamous Black Angel." Bourne paused. "You do grasp the irony, don't you?"

Chester didn't, of course. "Mr. Bourne, are you okay?"

"A little giddy, that's all. You've brought very good news. Drive carefully, Chester. Safe home."

27

"Where were we?" asked Bannerman when Elizabeth returned. Her eyes were dry, but they were softer and more distant.

"You were telling me that Martin is a mess."

"I was telling you what he thinks his future will be. For the present, he's in reasonably good shape."

Elizabeth leaned forward. "Are you saying you've seen him?"

"No, I haven't. I've had no contact with him. But I've spoken at length with Yitzhak Netanya. He now heads the Mossad. I know you've met him."

She nodded. "Years ago. He was with the Shin Bet. I wasn't very nice to him either."

"A problem between you?"

"More of a pique. Someone snapped a photo of the two of us in a group. It shouldn't have happened. There should have been no photographers. It's the only clear photo of me in existence. I was angrier than I should have been. I looked differently then. You'd find it hard to identify me from it."

She brushed that thought aside as being of no consequence. She said, "You're telling me that Martin did go to Angola. What made him change his mind, if not this Sara?"

"Being spotted by the twins, I think, was part of it," said Bannerman. "Or at least that made him want to get out of Davos. He knew the word would spread. He knew it might get back to you. The thought of going someplace where he could get lost began to have some appeal. The Israelis were willing to pay him quite well if he could stabilize the traffic in diamonds and weapons. He could offset the influence of Artemus Bourne, who was trying to control that same traffic. Molly's told you about Bourne?"

"That he wanted me, you mean?"

"He'd been looking for you for maybe six or eight months. I'd heard that he was looking. Then I heard he'd given up. I thought he'd accepted the fact that you're dead. I kept quiet about it because if I'd inquired, people would have wondered what my interest was and the search for you might have intensified."

"You . . . still haven't said what Bourne wanted with me."

"Well, it wouldn't have been any paid consultation. If he'd found you, you would have been a hostage."

"To control Martin Kessler?"

"That would have been his hope. If it worked, he would have a double agent in place. But it got much more urgent in the past week or two. I'll get to why in a minute."

"And Bourne, all this time, knew that Martin was alive. He knew it from the beginning?"

Bannerman shrugged. "I don't know, but I doubt it. Bourne would have had no interest in Martin until Martin showed up in Angola."

Bannerman, having said this, looked away, smiling softly.

Elizabeth asked, "Why is that funny?"

"Oh, it's nothing. Well, yes. Just a story Yitzhak told me. Not only did Bourne know it, he'd met him, had a drink with him. It was at some social event in Luanda. Martin had somehow bluffed his way in and they had a nice chat about diamonds. Bourne, of course, never dreamed that he was talking to Kessler. He found out later. He could not have been pleased."

Bannerman saw the start of an answering smile tugging at the corners of her mouth. He could see that she was thinking, "That does sound like Martin." He said, "Let's skip over what sold him on going."

She said, "You've already told me. It was to get away from me."

"Elizabeth . . . that is not what I said."

"Well, it wasn't for money. It was not to save the world. It certainly was not to help a whimsical killer. Why else would he do anything so dumb?"

Bannerman tried to sneak a glance at the clock. She saw it. She said, "You're not moving. Let's hear it."

In his mind, he heard Molly. She was saying, "Same here. No two years in twenty minutes, remember?"

The Israelis, he told her, appealed to his conscience. They argued that Kessler, and Kessler alone, could help curb some of Savimbi's excesses. These included burning witches who Savimbi suspected of trying to work magic against him.

"He believes in witches?"

"Probably not," said Bannerman, "but he knew that his men did. Every tribe, apparently, has its resident witches. They're used to cast spells on enemy tribes. If one of those tribes should come down with some sickness, it's presumed to be magic, the work of a witch. Savimbi had a lot of sickness . . . for reasons I'll get in to . . . but the short term solution was to burn a few witches to prove that he was stronger than they were."

He said, "Another of those excesses, although Savimbi denied allowing it, was chopping the arms off young children. These machete amputations were done as a warning to anyone who finds diamonds and tries to sell them on their own. The practice is, however, not limited to Angola. It's especially prevalent in Sierra Leone. It's a terrible thing, but neither country invented it. The Belgians and the Portuguese introduced that practice during the colonial era. It was a punishment for lazy field workers."

She cleared her throat. She said, "I guess I'd call that excessive. The Israelis I knew would have called that excessive. They would have killed Savimbi themselves."

"No, they wouldn't," said Bannerman. "That would only lead to chaos. Savimbi was the devil they knew and he was strong enough to keep things fairly stable. He was no dummy either. He was articulate and well read. Even Kessler gave Savimbi high marks for intelligence after meeting with him in Tel Aviv."

"Not Angola?"

Bannerman shook his head. "Savimbi and Duganga flew to Israel to see him. The Mossad snuck them out of Angola. They went to the hospital maybe three or four times and Savimbi renewed their acquaintance. They both tried to sell Kessler on coming to Angola. Kessler still had no intention of going, but the Israelis had asked him not to shut the door entirely so that they could keep Savimbi on the hook. Savimbi, meanwhile, kept sweetening the pot. He already had workers restoring a house that had belonged to some Portuguese slave trader. It would be Kessler's, he'd have servants, and he'd have the rank of general. He'd be given a uniform that would be the envy of every other general on the continent."

"He'd . . . never get Martin in a uniform," said Elizabeth.

"The fact is, he did. Netanya's seen it; I haven't. Netanya says that I'd have to see it to believe it. Savimbi dressed him up, had him photographed in it, made posters, and hung them all over Angola. It was so everyone would know him. No one would dare harm him. He gave Martin a new name. He'd be known as Alameo. The word is simply Portuguese for the German with the spelling changed a bit so that the Bantus could pronounce it. When Savimbi was killed, Duganga printed up new ones with Duganga's own symbol on the poster. By then the rationale was to let it be known that Alameo supported Duganga."

Elizabeth had lost interest in uniforms and posters. She asked, "Did he go there by himself?"

"I know what you're asking and yes, Sara went with him because the Israelis insisted. She spoke Portuguese; he didn't, nor did he object. He liked her; she liked him. There were no other Europeans. I'm sure that he was glad for the company."

"I'm sure," said Elizabeth.

"Um . . . Elizabeth, there's something I should tell you about Sara."

"How long?"

"How long what?"

"How long have they been in Angola together?"

"Elizabeth, there's no 'they.' Will you please let that go?"

"Platonic. I heard you. Let's not beat it to death. How long has *he* been in Angola?"

"Kessler has been there well over a year. That's after spending the first eight months recovering and wandering. But he'd had no intention of staying this long. He figured a few months at the most. When he got to Angola, he began with an inspection. He was appalled by the conditions he saw there. Amputees everywhere. The world's highest percentage. And not from machetes; it was mostly from land mines, the highest concentration on the continent. Kessler told Savimbi that he wanted them mapped and the maps distributed everywhere. Savimbi objected. His enemies would find them. Kessler told him, 'Of course. Make sure that they do. They'll be sure it's a trick. Wouldn't you be?'"

This time she smiled fully. She could almost hear him saying it. She said, "His mind works in wonderful ways."

"He's unconventional, certainly, but he does know his craft. He reminded Savimbi of what he'd taught him in East Germany. No insurgency succeeds without support of the locals. He cancelled an Israeli shipment of arms and had them replaced with twenty thousand prosthetics plus technicians from the Red Cross to fit them. Savimbi may or may not have condoned the amputations, but he agreed that they needed to be stopped.

"Kessler told Savimbi that 'stopped' was not enough. Either round up those who did it or he's gone. Savimbi agreed; twelve soldiers were arrested and identified by several of their victims. Kessler handed machetes to the parents of those victims, but they were too frightened to use them. So Kessler had all of them dig their own graves. He had them buried alive, the parents watching."

Elizabeth seemed startled. "He had that kind of power?"

"He did, at least while the honeymoon lasted. But then suddenly Jonas Savimbi was dead and Dumas Duganga took his place. Savimbi was killed in a government raid, caught out in the open by two helicopter gunships. Those gunships didn't happen to be just passing by. Someone had set Savimbi up. Netanya denies that it was either him or Kessler, but he admits that the timing was convenient. Killed with him were a dozen or so of his commanders. Their names 'just happened' to match a list that Kessler had given to Netanya. It listed those whom he'd found to be thoroughly corrupt. They were there to get rich; they'd tried to undermine Kessler; he was cutting into their action."

"But Savimbi, you said, was the devil they knew."

"Not anymore. By that time, the Israelis knew Duganga pretty well due to Kessler's assessment of him. And Duganga, when this happened, needed Kessler more than ever because he was not as strong as Savimbi."

"Does he still?"

"He'd say yes," answered Bannerman. "But no, not as much."

"Then Martin's work there is finished. Can Netanya get him out?"

"If that's Kessler's wish."

"He'll come out or I'll go in. Either way, I'm going to see him."

"First there's more for you to know. Let me finish."

He said that Kessler found people even sicker than he'd been. The medicines helped, but not nearly enough. Subtropical diseases, all native to Africa, but also some strains that they'd never seen before. All of them viral; penicillin was useless. Always in out-of-the-way villages and farms or in isolated outposts of troops.

"It was as if somebody was testing these strains, but at first no one took that thought seriously. Enter a man named Savran Bobik. He's a major dealer in weapons and drugs. The Mossad got a report that Bobik had boasted that he could wipe out *Savimbi*'s army at will. They knew that Bobik had some connection with VaalChem, a biotech firm owned by Artemus Bourne. Before Bourne, it had been a

South African company. South Africa had a secret bio-warfare program until Nelson Mandela took power. Bourne bought it, dismantled it, and moved it to Luanda where its charter was strictly to develop vaccines.

"The Mossad had a number of operatives in Luanda. They had them report on both Bobik and VaalChem. They also asked Sara if she would volunteer to try to get close to Savran Bobik. They didn't realize that Sara had already been made. Bobik assumed, as you have assumed, that Sara was Alameo's woman."

"He took her?" asked Elizabeth.

"And he tortured her," said Bannerman. "While she was still fully conscious, he sawed off her head. He sent her head back to Kessler."

Elizabeth paled. She couldn't speak for a moment. She said, "Paul, I can be such a shit."

"You didn't know. I should have told you up-front."

She realized that he'd tried to just minutes before. She said, "I am so very sorry."

"Would you like to take a break? You're sure you wouldn't like some coffee?"

"What I'd like is to find Savran Bobik," she said.

"You won't have to. Kessler did. He did the same thing to Bobik. Let's take five while I make a few phone calls."

28

Bourne's Briarwood phone had been busy as well. There were more cancellations, one after another, by those who'd been invited to his brunch. Only one, another oil man, was honest enough to say why he thought that he'd best stay at home.

Yes, what happened to Clew was part of it, he'd said. But it's mostly that business with the freighter.

"What freighter?" Bourne had asked him, as if he didn't know. The point being that this oilman should not have known either.

"Mr. Bourne, I got an e-mail. A very long e-mail. I'm looking at it right now. It's an exchange between Clew and some Liberian general. I don't know what you've been doing at VaalChem and I'd rather keep it that way."

From Clew? How could that be? Bourne had the only record of that correspondence. He had Clew's disc, but of course he couldn't say so. Could Clew have distributed it before he downloaded it? Not likely. Not to this man. Why send it to an oilman?

He asked, carefully, "What is it that you think *they've* been doing?" After all, the only reference to VaalChem on that disc was the mention of the name on that container. In itself, that meant nothing. It was easily explainable.

The oilman replied, "Look, I don't want to know. I've never heard of Marburg, but I think you have a problem. This general names you as the owner of VaalChem. He says he's tried to get through to that Brit, Cecil Winfield, but everyone there's ducking him. He's threatening to send troops. Clew told him he'd handle it, but that doesn't seem likely. Is Clew even still alive? I haven't heard."

Bourne was stunned. Sending troops? Tubbs looking for Winfield? There was nothing about that on the disc that he had. Could Clew have had a further exchange that he'd failed to download with the rest of it?

Bourne asked, "This long e-mail. Can you forward it to me?"

The oilman said, "You mean you didn't get it? Looks like everyone else did." He said, "Wait, I'm looking." There was a short pause. He came back and said, "No, you're not on the list."

"The list? This was broadcast? To whom and how many?"

He said, "I just told you. Looks like everyone you know. At least everyone who I've ever seen at your brunches."

"And you say that Clew sent it?"

"Here's his name. And it's from State." He paused, then said, "Hold on for a second. Let me take another look when this was sent."

Bourne heard a clicking as of keys being tapped. It took only a few seconds; it seemed so much longer. The oilman came on again.

"This is interesting," said the oilman. "It could not have been Clew. This e-mail was sent at almost midnight last night. Clew got hit when? Around seven? And the last one from this general also came after that. If Clew didn't send these, who did?"

"I want to see them."

"Mr. Bourne, I would say that someone's out to embarrass you. Either that, or someone is covering his ass. But my ass is clean. None of this touches me. As I said, I think I'll keep it that way."

"I said I want to see them. Are you going to send them?"

"Let me check with my lawyer," said the oilman.

Bourne placed a call to the Secretary of State. He was told by an aide, "He's in conference, sir."

"Have you told him who's calling? That it's Artemus Bourne?"

The aide only repeated, "He's in conference, sir. I'm sure he'll get back to you presently."

"You will please interrupt him. Go tell him I'm waiting."

"Sir, I'm sorry. He'll call you when he can."

Bourne heard a certain coolness in the voice of the aide, not his usual snap-to-it deference. There was no *"Can I help you? Is there anything I can do?"* There was more of a *"You're poison. Get lost."*

Steady, Artemus, he said to himself. Howard Leland knows better than to try to brush you off. Perhaps another war has broken out somewhere. Perhaps a UFO has touched down on the Mall. Let's give him the benefit of the doubt.

Bourne tried several more calls. Everyone he called was "out." He finally got through to a congressman who was willing to forward that e-mail. Actually, he wasn't really willing at all. He lied through his teeth. He denied having seen it. He said to Bourne, "I know nothing about it, but I'll have one of my interns take a look."

And of course the intern sent it. The expendable intern. She would probably be fired within the week for "poor judgment and exceeding her authority."

See how the rats run, thought Bourne darkly.

He had waited at his basement computer for the light of its mailbox to wink on. It did, and he opened the entire correspondence. Sure enough, at the top, there was Clew's name as "Sender." It was followed by a screen-full of computerese gibberish. He wished that Chester were here. Chester knows what all that means. But Chester was still several hours away, driving carefully so as not to get stopped and so as not to bruise his valuable cargo.

Next came the list. Sure enough, it was everyone. Bourne
hit a key to scroll down to the content. It consisted entirely
of those frantic exchanges between Clew and the Liberian,
Tubbs. But this included Tubbs's last one, the one that Clew
could not have seen. It was the first one that named him
specifically. It named Shamsky, who apparently no longer
spoke English. And it named Winfield, who it said was "indisposed." A towering understatement, thought Bourne.

And then came the threats. Perhaps military action. Perhaps even a visit from the storied Major Scar although Scar
was almost equally indisposed. Most disturbing of all was
the Red Cross involvement. If the Red Cross had been
tipped about weapons-grade Marburg, they'd have promptly
notified World Health in Geneva and the CDC in Atlanta.
Small wonder that his friends are suddenly unavailable or
speaking only through their attorneys. Never fear, though,
you scaredy-cats, you shirkers, you quitters. VaalChem will
survive this. Its good work will continue. And I will exact
retribution on all those who have declined to partake of Eggs
Florentine with me.

The last entry was the unlikely message from Clew that
had asked General Tubbs to resend all the others. It clearly
wasn't from Clew, but who wrote it? It was someone at
State, but not the secretary surely because there was his
name on the recipient list. Quigley? Not Quigley. He was on
the list as well. And Squiggly Quigley was the first to run for
cover.

An impossible thought struck him. Could Kessler have
done this? Ridiculous. He knew that. But for God's sake,
who else? He certainly had the motive, but he could not have
had the means. How could Kessler get into State Department
computers? Could he hack them? Could anyone? Highly
doubtful.

Except . . . what of Bannerman? They say that he can hack
anything, that his tentacles reach everywhere. There's been
talk that Bannerman might even have access to the NSA's
Echelon system. And some FBI system. Magic Lantern, or
whatever. Could Bannerman have done this at Kessler's be-
hest?

You say no. You say impossible. You say I'm grasping at straws.

Well, someone did, damn it. But how to find out?

His two moles up in Westport wouldn't be of much use. They wouldn't know where to begin. And just as well. They are there to reconnoiter, to observe, and to be ready in case Bannerman and his crew become a bother.

They'd already reported. They've done some good work. They've located Bannerman in some cozy little enclave that he shares with a number of his cutthroats. They found a hotel that had set aside blocks of rooms, apparently for those who'll be attending that "conference." Our two moles have been unable to discern its agenda, but its purpose, we'll assume, is less than innocent. Several more will stay at homes within Bannerman's enclave. Cleaning crews have been busy preparing them.

Conference, thought Bourne. Howard Leland is "in conference." Is it possible, he wondered, that the two are the same? No, of course not, you idiot. They're at least three days apart. But do you see how you're letting this mess with your head? Have a care, Artemus. Deal with one thing at a time. Our moles have identified some significant vulnerabilities. Bannerman's wife, among them. She's given birth just this morning. We assume that she won't have round-the-clock gunmen patrolling the halls of the maternity ward. And there's Bannerman's daughter. She's not guarded at all. Takes the school bus every morning unescorted. While at home, her sole companion is a local baby-sitter. "Just some skinny little redhead who lives down the street. We could take her really easy," said his mole.

But there won't be any snatching. Having Stride will be enough. What he'll need from his moles will be simplicity itself. "They are well equipped, believe me," he had said to Chester Lilly. Another understatement. It gave new meaning to the term. For he'd equipped them with a weapon of mass destruction. Well . . . mini–mass destruction was a more apt description. Not enough for a city. More than adequate for a town. A future ghost town if this Bannerman isn't careful.

He'd equipped his two moles with one of his "puppies."

One of his little glass ampules, Marburg/smallpox. They're the ampules whose contents do that cute little dance every time he opens his safe. Toss one on any lawn, have a mower run over it, and none of them will be a bother much longer.

Bourne cleared his screen of the Clew and Tubbs missives. A temptation had come over him. He asked himself, "Do I dare?"

He asked, "Should I wait until Chester gets back? Shall I wait until Stride is in her new quarters and safely strapped onto her bolted-down cot? What if Chester gets stopped for something stupid, like speeding?"

On the other hand, the fat is already in the fire. What the hell. Let's tell Kessler we've got her.

He hit another key. It opened his address book. It held hundreds of names from all over the world. They were listed by country. Angola was first. The names were grouped by their field of interest. Diamond dealers, arms dealers, business executives, and, of course, Luanda's leading politicians. He clicked on the name of one of the ministers. Jose Matala. Minister of the Interior. The title was a joke. The interior was Savimbi's, now Duganga's, Alameo's. Not that it mattered in this case, however. Matala worked both sides of the street and above all for Artemus Bourne. It was Matala who had helped to bring VaalChem to Angola after the South Africans shut it down.

Bourne looked at his watch. Early evening in Luanda. Matala should still be more or less sober, but let's hope that he's carrying his cell phone. Bourne used his thumb to tap out a thirteen-digit number. The call went through. Matala answered, spoke his name. Bourne could hear many voices in the background. He said, "This is Artemus Bourne."

"Oh," exclaimed Matala. "I am most eager that you called. Wait one minute while I find a private place."

The crowd noise clicked off. Matala's voice came back on. He said, "I am hosting a party in our president's honor. He has awarded himself two new medals. But much of the talk is of you and of VaalChem. Big trouble from Liberia, big trouble with Red Cross. I have been trying to get through to Sir Cecil about this, but no one will say where he is."

"He's on ice for the moment," Bourne answered him dryly. "And as for any trouble, I will deal with it shortly. Are you able to locate Alameo?"

"I know where he is. Very near. He is in Cuanza. I know because Duganga gave safe passage to some Jews who wanted to meet with Alameo. These Jews, I believe, are Mossad."

"I don't doubt it," said Bourne. "You say he's in Cuanza. Isn't that just up the road? Isn't that rather bold of Alameo?"

"Not much danger. Things are quiet. No one's shooting so much now. If you are thinking to capture him, this cannot be permitted. Safe passage is safe passage. Good for business. We must honor it."

"As it happens," said Bourne, "I have no need to capture him. But I do need to speak to him. Can you patch this call through?"

"Not by cell phone," said the minister. "They never use cell phones. I can try him by radio and give him a message."

"I would much prefer to give it directly," said Bourne. "No cell phones? Why not? They're most useful."

"Duganga's officers had them, but Alameo destroyed them. He said it's too easy to tamper with cell phones. Too easy to plant a listening device or even an explosive device, so no cell phones."

Damn, thought Bourne. An unforeseen disappointment. Half the fun of this would have been hearing his reaction.

"You can reach him by radio? You can speak to him directly?"

"I can reach him with a message. He might not wish to speak."

"Oh, he'll speak. Say the name, 'Elizabeth Stride,' and tell him that the message is from Artemus Bourne."

"Wait. I write it down. You say Elizabeth Stride?"

Bourne spelled the name for him. "You may tell him that I have her. You may tell him that I have Stride's young birthday girl as well. She's sweet sixteen and if she's never been kissed, she may be in for a crash course on the birds and the bees."

"Forgive me. This I do not understand."

"He will," said Bourne, "and tell him this above all: I very much look forward to reaching an agreement that not only ensures their continued good health but that eases the pain they're now enduring."

"You are . . . torturing these two?"

"On a vivisecting table."

Matala hesitated. "This is true? This is bad. Alameo will put *me* on such a table."

"Oh, I'm joking, Jose. But that would get a quick response. Simply say that they are not kept in comfort."

"Still bad."

"On the contrary, it's splendid. It will bring immense benefits."

"To me?"

"Yes, to you. You'll be richer than your president."

"Please stay on the line," said Matala. "I try now."

29

Bannerman had called Carla to say that he was running late. Carla said, "It's okay, but don't come here; we'll come there."

"With Cassie?"

"Might as well. If Elizabeth's going to be around for a while, Cassie ought to know her on sight. On the subject of strangers, I need to spend a few hours there checking some of Molly's surveillance tapes. Anton thinks someone might be poking around."

"Has Anton put together that package on Bourne?"

"He has," Carla answered. "I'll bring you some copies. You told him to do all this in the clear. Don't you think that was tipping your hand just a tad?"

"It might cause a little scurrying. We'll see."

"Except this guy owns whole countries and a good part of this one. This might not be one we can win."

"I know that. I won't ask you . . ."

"You won't have to. I'm in."

He said, "Actually, I was hoping that you'd look after Cassie if I have to go out of town."

"She'll be fine. I've been teaching her how to handle an Uzi. The kid needs a little work. She took out your TV. I guess I should have started her on knives."

"On second thought . . ." said Bannerman.

"I'm kidding. Relax."

"Carla, just get her up here."

"We're on our way."

His next call was to the hospital, the nurses' station in Maternity. The floor nurse told him, "She'll be sleeping for a while. We were going to let her sleep right through lunch."

"I'll swing by. We'll just look in. And my daughter's very keen to see her brother."

"Little Martin?"

"I . . . guess so," said Bannerman. "But how did you know?"

She said, "We heard you and Susan. Martin Bannerman sounds cool. Oh, and no one likes Raymond. All the kids will call him Ray-Ban."

Settles that, thought Bannerman. "Good point. We'll go with Martin."

"While I've got you, Mr. Bannerman, she's got too many flowers. Twelve bouquets in there now, another twenty or so coming. Would you mind if we spread them around the other wards? Of course, I'll hold on to all the cards."

"Absolutely," said Bannerman. "And thank you."

He hung up. The phone buzzed. It was Molly again. She said, "Our Secretary of State isn't easy to discourage. Howard Leland's helicopter just touched down in Bridgeport. Tomorrow morning, he's attending a prayer breakfast at Yale. He says he flew up early just to see you. He's traveling light, two Secret Service agents, and he's brought some kind of scientist with him."

"Secret Service?" asked Bannerman. "Since when do they guard Leland?"

"I asked. He said he borrowed them. He said they're more discreet. It's also sending you a message that the White House is behind him. He says he won't leave without meeting with you. He says it will be private, man to man."

Bannerman grunted. "About Bourne, I assume."

"On a matter that's vital to our national security. Those were the words; it's all he would say. He hit the word 'vital' pretty hard."

"Tell him I'll see him, but ask him to sit tight. I'll tell him when and where in thirty minutes."

That would give him enough time to finish up with Elizabeth and to look through the package that Anton had assembled. Not that he didn't have more than enough after talking to Yitzhak Netanya.

Elizabeth had returned. She asked, "Your daughter's on her way?"

"Carla Benedict's bringing her, yes."

"Then tell me quickly about this guy's head. It's not a subject that a child should walk in on."

Bannerman told her that it took Kessler a month, but with help he caught up with Savran Bobik. Netanya's people and Kessler questioned him for three days. Bobik told them that those outbreaks were indeed caused by VaalChem. They'd plant a little glass container where some villager would find it and open it, maybe taste it or sniff it. They were using the Angolans as lab rats.

"Bio-weapons?" asked Elizabeth. But she asked it almost absently. He felt sure that in her mind she was envisioning Kessler looking down at the head of Sara Gleissman. Bannerman himself had imagined the fury that must have erupted within him.

Bannerman cleared his throat. He said, "Let me go on. Bobik had an arms shipment . . . not bio . . . conventional . . . that was destined for Sierra Leone. It was one of many things that Bobik gave up in the hope of saving his life. I'll get to its significance; bear with me. Netanya's people, led by Kessler, staged a raid on VaalChem's offices. They brought Bobik's head with them. It loosened some lips. When Kessler was finished, he took two more heads."

Elizabeth blinked. "This was Martin? You're sure?"

"His . . . natural good humor had deserted him some time ago. Stop me now if you don't want to hear this."

"No, I want to."

"If it eases your mind any, they were already dead. Netanya says Kessler shot both of them first. I mean, it's not as if he's turned into some . . ." He stopped himself. He grimaced. Bannerman wasn't really sure what he'd turned into.

He said, "The heads were of the two men Bobik had named as being responsible for the testing in those villages. They'd have taken still another, but the third man wasn't there."

Elizabeth asked, "The third man would be Bourne?"

He shook his head. "The third is Chester Lilly, Bourne's top man in that region. But Lilly wasn't there. He was back in this country."

"Beating up on Roger Clew?"

"We assume so. I believe so. Roger's stable, by the way. Not good. In a coma. But there's reason to hope that he'll pull through."

"Is this Lilly the one who Molly thought might be coming to Hilton Head for me?"

"Yes."

"I look forward to meeting him," she said.

"You're not alone. But he's a goon. Let's keep our focus on VaalChem. Lilly knew about the testing that VaalChem was doing. He knew that Bobik's boasts were more than just talk. He knew that Bobik had killed Sara Gleissman. Bobik claimed, in fact, that it was Lilly's idea to send her head back as a message."

He told her how Kessler had boxed those three heads and had sent them to Artemus Bourne. He had added them to a shipment that Bourne was expecting. Three containers of assorted vaccines and some diamonds. He made room for the heads by removing most of the vaccines and crushing those that remained. He kept those vaccines and several weapons-grade toxins that he found in the safe of VaalChem's managing director. He kept all the documents, the research protocols, and refused to let Netanya's people have them. He might have shared them with Netanya, but not with his agents. He knew that some of it could disappear in transit. He said that he would decide what to do with them.

Elizabeth asked, "What did he decide?"

Bannerman answered, "I'm not sure that he has. This was

only a week to ten days ago. But one flask of it went with that arms shipment I mentioned. It was bound for some rebel group in Sierra Leone whose leader, says Netanya, is a horror. Kessler planted it himself. He knew that this man would open it. That would have been the end of his group. But something went wrong. It was opened in transit. It was opened on a freighter that was well out to sea. It was opened, apparently, during a raid that Roger Clew had arranged."

"Roger knew it was there?"

"He had no idea. Here's the irony, though. Roger learned of that shipment from Artemus Bourne. Bourne had offered it in trade for Clew's promise to look for you. Bourne could not have known that the virus was there either."

He said, "The raid was intended to interdict that shipment. It was arranged through a Liberian general named Tubbs. When the virus was found and inadvertently opened, it apparently infected everyone on board including twenty children who'd been taken as slaves. I don't know their status. Netanya's not optimistic. He thinks that none of those aboard will survive. For that reason, he's kept this information from Kessler. The Martin Kessler I know could not live with the knowledge that his action had killed twenty children."

"But . . . if it was a mistake . . ."

Bannerman shook his head. "He wouldn't give himself that out."

She said sadly, "No, he wouldn't. Not unless all this has changed him."

They both knew that he would never put a gun in his mouth, but he'd find a way to get himself killed.

Bannerman glanced out the window. He saw Carla approaching. Cassie was skipping along at her side, a ribbon-wrapped teddy bear under her arm. The bear, he assumed, was a gift for her new brother.

He said to Elizabeth, "Okay, here's where we are. I haven't decided what I'll do about Bourne. We're making plans in the event that we're forced to take action, but it's possible that we will do nothing. I have people to consider who've made lives here in Westport. Whatever Bourne's done, it hasn't touched them. Until it does, Bourne is someone else's problem. But I *will* find Chester Lilly and we *will* have a talk."

"Like Martin's talk with Bobik?"

"I'm sure that he'll answer any questions we have. If he's responsible for Roger and he acted on his own, he will answer for that, I assure you. If he acted for Bourne, Bourne will answer as well, but I need to be sure of my ground."

He said, "I'd like you, in the meanwhile, to stay here with us until we know that it's safe for you to go home. I know that you have a life there as well. As for Martin, I suggest that you give this time to settle. Consider what I've told you about his state of mind. You might decide that it's best to leave things as they are. If you don't, and he's willing, I'll set up a meeting. Face-to-face, if possible, but by radio at least."

She said, "I *am* going to see him. And it *will* be face-to-face."

"Elizabeth . . . please sleep on it. Promise?"

"One day."

"Well, don't brood by yourself. Talk it over with Molly. Whatever you decide, that's what we'll do."

Carla, leading Cassie, had come through the front door. She met Bannerman's eyes first. She held up two folders. She said, "This is Bourne. One for you and one for Molly." She set them down near his chair.

She said to Elizabeth, "We never got to talk. But at least I got a chance to meet your daughter."

"My daughter?"

"Aisha," said Carla. "Well, I know that she isn't. But she said that you're like a second mother to her. I think it's great that you have someone like Aisha."

"She . . . told me that you filled her in some," said Elizabeth.

"A little. I told her that you were the best. She said that she already knew that."

Elizabeth waved that off. Her attention turned to Cassie. She said, "Introduce me to this lovely young lady."

Carla smiled. She said, "Sorry. Where are my manners? Cassie, this is Elizabeth Stride. Elizabeth Stride, meet Cassie Bannerman."

Elizabeth had totally and visibly softened as she rose to take Cassie's proffered hand. She said, "I'm pleased to meet you. And your father's very lucky. Are you going down now to see your mom?"

"Uh-huh. And my brother. Have you met my mother?"

"No, but I'm told she's pretty special," said Elizabeth. She said to Bannerman, "I can see why you'd rather stay out of this."

"Out of what?" asked Cassie.

"A little problem. It's nothing."

Cassie asked Elizabeth, "Why don't you come with us?"

"Come where? To the hospital? Oh, I don't think I should. But I'd love to meet your mother when you bring her home." She heard Molly on the stairs. She said to Cassie, "Besides, I have some things to finish up with Ms. Farrell."

"That's Aunt Molly," said Cassie. "She's not really my aunt. It's like you and this girl who's not your daughter."

"And I also have a little reading to do." She glanced toward the folders that Carla had brought. She looked up at Bannerman. "May I?"

He said, "Sure." He reached to take a copy for himself. He said, "Elizabeth, you'd be welcome, but you're right; you'd better stay." He asked Molly, who had entered, "You've heard all of this?"

She nodded. She said, "Quite a mess."

He said, "Let's see if Howard Leland can shed any light. Please call him and tell him that I'll see him at the hospital. There's a parking garage. Have him drive up to the roof. I can see the whole roof from Susan's room."

"Him alone?"

"He can have his security, but not within earshot. I expect it to be friendly, but . . ."

"I'll handle it," said Molly.

"Tell whoever you send that if they see me leaving with them . . ."

An exasperated sigh. "Maybe I should write this down."

He smiled. "My apologies. You . . . know how to do this."

"Get out of here. Hug Susan for me."

Molly called Anton Zivic to inform him of the meeting. Zivic, as expected, said what she'd said to Bannerman. "I'll handle it. You stay with Stride."

She next called Leland's aircraft on the tarmac at Bridgeport. She told Leland when and where and recited the conditions. She said to him, "Sir, don't try anything foolish."

He said, "For God's sake, I'm the Secretary of State. I do not go around abducting people."

"Sir, we're mindful of what happened to Roger Clew. If this is a setup, you will not survive it."

"Need I . . . tell you again who you're speaking to, young lady?"

"Sir, with respect, I know who you are. But it's best that we understand each other."

Elizabeth had heard Molly's end of both calls. She asked, "This is *the* Howard Leland?"

She nodded.

"Did you just tell him that you'd kill him if he didn't behave?"

"It seemed worth the reminder. Leland's too close to Bourne. And some of them have tried to take Paul in the past. They've learned better than to set foot in Westport itself, but Norwalk Hospital might be a temptation."

Elizabeth said, "I should have gone with them."

"You're dead, remember? You stay out of sight. But you're in good company. Quite a few of us are dead. We have ghosts all over the place."

Elizabeth said, "I'm not sure I get you."

"We call them ghosts. Or floaters. We rotate them a month at a time. They keep moving. We've let everyone know that if we're hit, they're still out there and they'll hunt down anyone who even *might* be responsible. It was actually Harry Whistler's idea. It started with the twins. You see one, but not the other. Nothing scares people quite as much as the knowledge that someone unseen means to kill them."

Elizabeth said, "Have you needed them?"

"Not lately. We've been left alone."

Molly's phone chirped again. She picked it up. She said her name.

She heard heavy static. She could barely hear the caller. She heard random words. She heard "Bannerman." She heard ". . . speak to . . ." She heard the voice say ". . . need his help . . ." The voice itself was hoarse, its tone almost frantic. She realized with a chill that the accent was Germanic. She said, "I can't hear you, but stay on the phone. Let me get to some better equipment."

Martin Kessler? She stopped herself from saying his name. If this was Kessler, he was looking for Paul and he seemed to want to speak to him privately.

She said to Elizabeth, "I need to take this upstairs."

"Trouble?"

"No, just some bad atmospherics."

"Go ahead. I'll be fine. I'll catch up on my reading."

"Five minutes," said Molly. She hurried toward the stairs. She was halfway to the attic, beyond Elizabeth's hearing, when she paused to ask, "Martin? This is Molly. Molly Farrell. Is this Martin Kessler on the line?"

The voice said, "Yes, Molly. I [static] speak to Paul. It's Elizabeth . . ." More static. "Bourne [static] . . . abeth and Aisha."

"Keep talking, Martin. You'll clear up in a minute."

Molly climbed one more flight. She stepped into the attic. Carla was already at one of the consoles, reviewing the past week's surveillance tapes. Molly placed the phone in the cradle of what looked like a scanner. She adjusted several toggles and played with a dial. She said, "Martin, keep talking. Try again."

"It's Elizabeth," he shouted. "Elizabeth and Aisha. Bourne [static] Elizabeth and Aisha."

Molly said, "Martin, you're still breaking up. Say again about Elizabeth and Aisha."

"Bourne has them [long static] . . . Paul [even longer] . . . I cannot get there in time." These words faded under a crackling screech and a series of electronic pings.

"Martin, listen. It's not true. He does not have Elizabeth."

She got only a few random syllables in response. She tried again. She said, "Elizabeth is safe. Bourne does not have Elizabeth. She's here."

"I have lost you. [static] hopeless. I will [static] Tel Aviv."

"Martin, she's safe. She is downstairs right now."

"Bourne [static] hurt them [static] cut them to pieces."

"Martin? He will not. Can you hear me? She's safe."

He snarled in frustration. "[static] . . . try the Mossad."

The line went dead. There was nothing but noise. Molly said, "Damn." She asked, "What's going on here?"

Carla asked, "That was Kessler? He's really alive?"

"He's alive. In Angola. I'll fill you in later. He thinks Bourne has Elizabeth Stride and young Aisha."

Carla shrugged. "Maybe someone's just busting his chops. You think Bourne? Why would he? All that would do is piss Kessler off and the story's too easy to check."

"Easy if you're not in some Angolan jungle using landlines that are probably all rotted out. You'd think he'd have access to a satellite phone. I bet you that's where he's going right now."

"Then maybe he's been suckered. Someone wants him at that phone. If he doesn't calm down he'll be easy to take. Someone knew how to push the right buttons."

Molly nodded. That was possible. It might even be likely. She said, "I'll call Netanya. He has people with Kessler. Tel Aviv must be in contact with them. Maybe they can warn him in time."

"If you're calling Netanya, put Elizabeth on the line. Let Netanya hear first hand that she's with us."

"Good idea. Will you go get her? Bring her up here."

30

Bannerman lifted Cassie to the nursery window for her first look at her new brother. A young attendant had brought the bundle to them. The baby stirred, but not much. He was smacking his lips. Cassie did not seem greatly impressed. She said, "He looks like a fish."

"He does not," said Bannerman. "He's spectacularly handsome."

"Like a guppy in a fish tank when the water gets too warm."

"Probably just hungry. He's due to be fed."

"Fed how? From a bottle? Can I do it?"

"Your mother wants to nurse him. The bottles come later."

"Boob food," said Cassie. "Was I breast-fed?"

"Sure were. That's why you're so healthy and smart."

"Were you?" Cassie asked. "Did you do that with Grandma?"

"I'm not sure, come to think of it. I guess probably."

"It's a little hard to picture."

"I was a lot smaller."

"Very funny," said Cassie. "Not just you. Grandma, too."

"Yeah, I know. I really wish you could have known her."

She had never met her grandma, for whom she was named. She had only seen photos and newspaper clippings. Her grandmother had been murdered almost twenty years before. Her grandfather had died several years before that, but in his case the cause of death was natural. The elder Cassie Bannerman had been an art buyer for several European museums. Or so Bannerman had thought while he was growing up. It turned out that she'd been better known as "Mama." She'd been a contract agent, not a spy, but something like it. She ended up running a group of such agents. John Waldo and Billy McHugh were among them.

He'd been in school in the States when his mother was killed. He flew to Europe at once. He met Billy. Long story. He ended up being sort of adopted by them. They let him help them in the search for her killers. It was the start of his real education.

Cassie nudged him. She asked, "What are you thinking?"

"About you. And your brother. And especially your mom. And how lucky I am to have each of you."

"Let's go in and see if she's awake yet."

She was, but not fully. He leaned over and kissed her. She purred softly in response and then she drifted off again. He turned toward the window and looked down at the garage. Its roof was unoccupied the last time he looked. Now he saw two cars, both nondescript rentals. One was parked by the ramp, its engine left running; one man was at the wheel, a second was on foot. He was speaking into his lapel. Those two would be the two Secret Service agents.

The other car had stopped in the center of the roof. The driver and passenger were leaning forward, peering, no doubt wondering where he would be coming from. The passenger was a woman, bespectacled, fiftyish. She seemed very nervous, perhaps out of her element. This, Bannerman assumed, was the scientist Molly mentioned. He hadn't expected a woman. The driver was Howard Leland himself. Leland seemed equally skittish.

He couldn't see any of the Westport people whom either

Molly or Anton had sent. Nor would he have expected to see them. But one or more would be positioned to block the ramp, one or more would be watching his back as he approached, one or more would be either on the hospital's roof or on the roof of a neighboring high-rise. Had he not been with Cassie, he'd have told them not to bother. This was Leland, in person, on a wide-open roof. The meeting was a meeting, nothing more.

He said to Cassie, "I need to run out for a while. You stay with your mom. Do not leave the ward. When I come back, we'll have some lunch here with your mother."

Cassie asked, "Can I be here when she nurses the baby?"

"Your mother might want the first time to be private. If she wants us to stay, she will say so."

He walked from the hospital to its covered garage. He took the farthest set of stairs to the level below the roof. He waited and watched, saw nothing suspicious, and proceeded to the last stretch of ramp. As he reached the roof level, the man on foot intercepted him. The driver had also climbed partially out. Neither man's eyes had long rested on him. They were constantly scanning their surroundings.

"Sir?" said the first one. "I must ask you to stop. I must ask you to submit to a search."

"Of course," said Bannerman. He approached and spread his arms. The agent ran his hands across his arms, legs, and torso. He scanned Bannerman's body with a metered device. As this was being done, he glanced up toward the hospital. He saw Cassie at the window. She was watching all this. He reassured her with a smile and a wave of his hand. He motioned her back from the window.

The man who'd searched him stepped away. He asked, "No electronics?"

"No wires, no weapons. This is friendly."

He said, "Sir, will you tell me who I just saw you signal?"

"The signal's meaning was, 'Stand down. They're just doing their jobs.' The signal was entirely in your interest."

"I understand. Thank you."

"My pleasure," said Bannerman.

"Um . . . actually it's mine. We know someone in common. In college, Southern Cal, I had a crush on Molly Farrell. I still might. Would you give her my regards?"

"I'll make a point of it. Your name?"

"Brian Moore, sir."

Bannerman had no doubt that his daughter was still watching, probably peering through a flower arrangement. He offered his hand to Agent Moore and then stepped to the car to shake the hand of Moore's partner. He said to Brian Moore, "Look her up if you'd like. But don't come without calling. That's important."

"I will, sir. May I say, though, that I *will* shoot you dead if you seem to be endangering Mr. Leland, sir."

"I'd expect that of you, Brian. Call me Paul."

Secret Service, thought Bannerman. Nearest thing to the Jesuits. He'd yet to meet one who wasn't thoroughly professional. They must have a high boredom threshold, however. Years on end of nothing but watching and waiting. But the handshakes may have eased his daughter's misgivings at seeing her father being searched.

The woman with Leland had stepped out of their car. He thought he'd seen Leland direct her to do so. She seemed entirely willing to comply. She left the passenger door open and, without looking back, walked to the far edge of the roof. Leland had flipped both sun visors down, the better not to be recognized. He said, "Mr. Bannerman, please get in if you will. I'd like a few minutes, just the two of us first. My associate will join us if needed."

"Who is she?"

"A virologist. A good one. And she's frightened to death of you. If you insist, I will tell you her name, but she would much prefer that I don't."

"Is she someone who I might have reason to harm?"

"On my word, she is not. She's as straight as they come. She's here to address any technical questions that I am not competent to answer. Please get in."

He did, after turning and blowing a kiss in the general direction of the window.

Leland said, "I'd just heard. Roger Clew now seems stable. He came out of his coma, although only briefly. He could answer simple questions. He responded to his name. He did not seem to know what had happened to him. I'm told that's not uncommon at this stage."

"Thank you," said Bannerman. "That's encouraging news."

Leland paused for a moment before speaking again. "Roger has told me that your word is your bond. Can there be no lies between us, Mr. Bannerman?"

"Why don't you tell me what you want of me first? We'll see which of us tells the first lie."

"Is it your intention to go up against Bourne?"

"I haven't decided. That's the truth."

Leland said, "Well, I know that you're certainly preparing to do so. I know that you've been in contact with Yitzhak Netanya regarding Bourne's Angolan activities. I know that you've assembled a dossier on Bourne and that you've made no secret of doing so. I know that you've been scaring off every friend he has by distributing Clew's exchange with General Tubbs. Bourne's Sunday brunch tomorrow will be sparsely attended. I'm not sure that I can make it myself."

Bannerman tried not to show that he did not understand the reference to distributing some Tubbs/Clew exchange. He knew, of course, that there had to have been communication between them, but he'd never seen it, let alone passed it on.

"A prayer breakfast at Yale should take precedence," he replied.

"Quite impressive, Mr. Bannerman. That e-mail in particular. I don't suppose you'd tell me how you penetrated our system. How you got the full text; I know it wasn't from Clew. How you got a list of names that was encoded and most secret. It makes me wonder why we bother with encryptions."

Bannerman could only guess what he was talking about. The list must be of those who had attended Bourne's brunches. But as for who was on it, who sent it, and why, Bannerman was at a loss.

But I'll take it, thought Bannerman. Believe what you will. He said, "We have some capable people."

"I dare say," said Leland. "Quite a reach as well."

"Let's put General Tubbs aside for the moment. Let's skip over the list and the text. Tell me how this is *vital* to our national security."

"I'm relieved that you said 'our.' I hope you mean it."

"I'm listening."

"You're correct that VaalChem produces bio-weapons. By law, we cannot. Someone has to. Bourne does. But VaalChem is infinitely more important than that."

The Secretary of State began counting the ways in which VaalChem's contribution was essential.

"Many nations have biological weapons," he explained. "VaalChem has samples of all of them. *All* of them. He's gathered them by hiring the virologists who've developed them. Mostly Russians, South Africans, a few Chinese, the odd Iraqi. Some have defected and were spirited to Angola bearing spores or master seed strains of whatever they'd been working on. Do you know how small a virus spore is?"

"Invisible," said Bannerman. "I'd take that to mean small."

"And I'm talking weapons-grade. Not your garden variety. One hundred spores of weapons-grade Ebola or Marburg wouldn't measure the width of a hair. And of course we're talking trillions of spores in a container not much bigger than your thumb. Inhale no more than three and it's ninety percent fatal. Compare that to anthrax which is twenty percent fatal and requires the ingestion of thousands of spores. And anthrax is treatable. The others are not. Or at least they were not until recently."

"And you're about to tell me that Bourne has a treatment?"

"He has several," said Leland. "And others in development. As to why he's developing weapons-grade toxins, bear in mind that you must first have the virus in order to create the antiviral. You must have bacilli like anthrax and typhoid in order to create their vaccines. Bourne has everything at VaalChem, but he has much more. These samples he's collected. Each one has a signature. No two processes of making them are ever quite the same. Therefore, any outbreak can be traced to its source. A few blood tests and we instantly know who to bomb. Even better, we can bomb them with their own bio-weapon. We can make it look like an accidental explosion at their own bio-weapons facility."

Bannerman said, "We would do so reluctantly, of course."

"We will do what we must for our survival, Mr. Bannerman."

Leland paused. He knew that he had sounded almost eager. He said, "None of us takes any pleasure in this. But it's here. It's a fact. Someone sooner or later will use this sort of weapon. We can't very well take the Israeli position, so we need to be one step ahead."

Bannerman understood the reference to the "Israeli position." It was a nation within missile range of four hostile states that were known to have developed bio-weapons. They'd put all four on notice that any bio-attack, whether by a state or by a terrorist group, would result in a nuclear reprisal on all four. They wouldn't wait for proof of guilt. It would no longer matter. Most of Israel's population would be dying.

Bannerman nodded. "Fair enough, but why Bourne?"

"Because he is . . . free from restrictions."

"Not bound by our laws? It's not just that, am I right? Bourne is testing them on human subjects."

"One . . . suspects so," said Leland.

"One would rather not know."

"That part of it is really my associate's field. But I hasten to tell you that she'd never consider the use of human subjects herself. In her heart, though, she's glad that someone's saved her the anguish. As I've said . . ."

"No one likes this. I heard you," said Bannerman.

"We blanch at the thought of such testing," said Leland. "But do you suppose, for a moment, that Iraq has not done so? The Soviets have, but at least *they* called them 'accidents.' The Iraqis have been blatant about it. We, in this country, have our own research facility. It's at Fort Detrick, Maryland. Do you know of it?"

"Of course."

"They develop vaccines and a few antivirals. They're

hardworking, dedicated, but their task is quite hopeless, no matter how well they are funded. For one thing, they're too slow, but that isn't their fault. They are bound by inflexible research protocols that require endless clinical testing. They are also subject to political influence. They, therefore, do things that are of no earthly use except to comfort and quiet the voters. You're aware, are you not, that our government is stockpiling two hundred million units of smallpox vaccine?"

"So I've read."

"Well, it's useless. It won't prevent a damned thing. My associate—and she's worked at Fort Detrick, by the way—can tell you why better than I can. Have you been vaccinated against smallpox yourself?"

Bannerman nodded. "I have. Years ago. I'm aware that I've outlived its protection."

"Almost no one is protected. Fifty million might die, and that's just from smallpox. Combine it with Marburg, Ebola, West Nile, and that number could easily triple. We are playing for very high stakes here, Mr. Bannerman."

"One question," said Bannerman. "Why State, not Defense? More specifically, why you? Shouldn't weapons be the Pentagon's job?"

"National security is everyone's job, but I realize that's not what you're asking. The simplest answer," said Leland, "is that I know Bourne. I've known him for years and I know how to work with him. Bourne has a great many interests abroad, several much grander than VaalChem. We have aided him in those interests when they coincide with ours. That is one of the State Department's functions."

"How closely do you monitor these interests?" asked Bannerman.

"We try to learn everything that we need to know. We avoid learning things that we don't want to know. It's not so unlike hiring you or Harry Whistler. You get hired because you can do what we cannot. You are able to focus on the job at hand, unencumbered by legal or political constraints and with no careers to protect. You are how things get done that need to be done. There really ought to be a monument in your honor."

"I'm flattered," said Bannerman dryly.

"Sarcasm again, but you know that it's true. Bourne goes you one better. He's an entrepreneur. We like to speak with great reverence of our Founding Fathers, but this country was built by men like Artemus Bourne. We speak of the great Robber Barons with disdain, but they built the railroads, the steel mills, the ships. They extracted the oil, the coal, and the gold. You don't have to like them; most were utterly ruthless, but they made us the richest nation on earth, the envy of the whole world."

Leland paused. He said, "I don't like Bourne either. He's a sociopath. He sees people strictly in terms of their usefulness. He sees all ideologies, all religions, as childish; he sees loyalty as self-delusion. As I've said to Roger Clew, yes, the man is a criminal. But he is our criminal. Better ours than someone else's. And like the Robber Barons, but unlike that Enron crowd, the man is a builder, a creator."

"You don't like it, but you need him. I get that," said Bannerman.

"What would it take to get you to back off?"

"If he's responsible for Roger, will you still protect him?"

"I've been . . . wrestling with that question. I still am."

"Very well," said Bannerman. "I'll give it more thought myself. First, I'd like a few words with your virologist friend."

"To complete your education? Yes, you should, but be gentle. She's an excellent scientist; she is blameless in all this, but I've made the mistake of summarizing your history. She nearly wet her pants at your approach."

The woman stiffened visibly as Bannerman walked toward her. She began to back way, but thought better of it when she realized that would put her near the edge of the roof.

Bannerman showed his palms. He stopped several feet short of her. He said, "Leland told me that you don't want to be here. I wish that I knew how to put you at ease. I have a wife; I have children; I have many women friends. Not a one of them has ever been afraid of me."

She swallowed. "I am . . . told that others are."

"Howard Leland is, I think. It's why he's talking so much. By the way, I hear an accent. Is it German? Low German?"

She wet her lips. She shook her head. "I am Swiss."

He smiled. "Yes, of course. From the north, though. Near the border?"

Her features softened slightly. She seemed impressed by his ear. "I grew up near Basel, but more years were in Zurich."

"Zurich? I have friends there as well. Perhaps we know people in common."

"I would doubt . . . very much . . . that we would have the same friends." She rushed to add, "By this I mean no offense."

"One of them, in fact, is my father-in-law. He married a Swiss. He married one of the Bruggs."

Her eyes widened. "The big American? His wife is Elena?"

He grinned. "Don't tell me that you know Elena."

"Everyone in Zurich knows of Elena. Not everyone has met her, but yes, we have met. Also Willem Brugg, her cousin, who is chairman of the board. And once Urs Brugg, her uncle, while he was alive. I know them because my education was by scholarship. The Brugg Foundation paid for my two advanced degrees. They gave a fine dinner for all those who earned doctorates. They were wonderful to us. Very kind."

She paused. A blush had come to her cheeks. She said, "Now it is me who talks too much out of nerves."

"Do you ever have occasion to speak to Elena?"

"I write. She writes. We speak not so often. Once she sent a plane ticket. Not to Zurich. To Basel. She did this when my mother was ill. A great lady."

"Well, do me a favor. When you can, call Elena. Unless you think she would lie, ask her about me. You might get a very different picture."

She looked this way and that. She didn't know quite what to do. But she decided, and, abruptly, she thrust out her hand. She said, "My last name is Kirch. My first name is Greta. More formally, I am Doctor Greta Kirch."

"I'm Paul."

She said, "You have questions? This man said that I may answer." She gestured toward Leland, who was watching intently.

Bannerman was getting the germ of an idea. It had to do with Elena. It had to do with VaalChem. The thought seemed so far-fetched that he dismissed it from his mind. For the moment, at least. He'd reflect on it later. And then he might take it up with Elena.

He said, "I have only one or two questions. Leland said that your work at Fort Detrick was useless. Do you agree with that assessment? If so, why?"

"Not useless. It has value. Our vaccines have great value. But only if applied to a virus that we know. I think if we are attacked, it will be with something new. A mutated virus. Or one spliced with new material. Worst of all is a chimera virus."

She explained that a virus must first find a host. When it does, it begins to reproduce. But a virus, like a human, doesn't make exact copies. That is why there are so many strains of flu.

A researcher may isolate the mutated copies, grow them in a different host, produce further mutations. She said, "The public is told that we have smallpox vaccine. Enough for everyone. Plenty. This is not the truth. Even if we had such a quantity of vaccine, it would only be effective against the virus as we know it. You are familiar with the terms 'genetic splicing, genetic sequencing'?"

Bannerman rocked a hand. "Not in depth."

She said, "You know DNA. It's like a twisted beaded necklace. There are several places, beads, in the smallpox genome where foreign genetic material can be added. You take the DNA from Marburg. Marburg is a good example. You isolate the disease-causing parts and you graft these onto the smallpox genome. This is splicing. This is known as recombinant DNA. We call this a chimera virus. You get Marburg's catastrophic mortality rate and the very high contagion of smallpox. You can isolate Marburg if that is all it is, but not if you're dealing with a chimera. It will have already spread before symptoms appear. It will overwhelm all efforts to treat it."

She said, "I am told that this is already happening. An accident on a ship off the coast of Liberia. I am sad for those aboard, but I thank God it is a ship."

Bannerman frowned. "You make this sound hopeless."

"On land? Larger scale? It might be hopeless, yes. But you must understand about these weapons. They cannot be concocted in some Afghan cave or in the kitchen of some lunatic fanatic. It takes years, it takes billions and enormous facilities. You have hot labs four levels below the street surface. You have space suits, many airlocks, many chemical showers. You have fermenter tanks that are two stories tall and dozens of bio-reactors. In case of an accident you need several rings of bio-containment zones, all enclosed. These alone can and should be a half-mile wide. And accidents happen. Even in such facilities. You want to make bio-weapons? You better know what you're doing. They are as likely to bite you in the ass."

Bannerman laughed.

Greta bridled. "You find this amusing?"

He bit his lip. "Not at all. But you've learned English very well." He asked, "What of Bourne? Do you believe in what he's doing?"

"Some of it, yes. Genetic signatures, yes. Antivirals, if he has them, of course I do, yes. There is no antiviral drug that works like penicillin. Each of them must be specific. But this man believes in nothing. He has no humanity. Do you know how he sees us? He sees us as bees and not even as good. We don't make honey for his tea and his toast. But he is doing what no one else is doing."

"Would you if you could?"

"It is useless to say."

"I might ask you again very soon."

He stopped at Leland's car. He said, "I'll be in touch."

"Do you have a better feel for our problem?"

"I think I do," said Bannerman. "Thank you for coming. And I'm glad that you brought Greta with you."

"I see that you've charmed her. You're an interesting man. You are not what I would have expected."

Bannerman asked, "Will Greta be attending that breakfast?"

Leland shook his head. "She'll be going back shortly. My helicopter will take her. It will be back to pick me up tomorrow morning. If you'd like to talk further between now and then . . ."

"You'll be leaving from New Haven?"

"From Bridgeport. It's quieter. This is sensitive business, Mr. Bannerman."

"So I gather."

Leland glanced in the direction of the hospital building. "Who is that little girl watching us from that window? Is she, by chance, yours? She's very sweet."

Bannerman didn't turn. He spoke very softly. "You have two of your own, do you not?"

"Oh, for heaven's sake, Paul. I meant nothing by it."

"Perhaps not, but as you say, there's a great deal at stake. Your oldest is married. She is an attorney. Your youngest is in her first year of residency. Pediatrics, correct? At Johns Hopkins?"

"Look, Paul . . ."

"Grown women, so I don't suppose they still believe in ghosts. Hmm, I don't know why I said that. I meant nothing by it either. I will be in touch, Mr. Leland."

31

He reached Susan's room. He was surprised to see Molly. Cassie was no longer there. Susan was awake, her lunch in front of her untouched. Instead she was nursing the baby, unabashed.

She smiled; she said, "Hi," but her eyes were not smiling.

Molly said, "I had to come. You didn't bring your cell phone with you. I called here. You were busy with Leland."

He hadn't brought his cell phone because it might have rung. He'd wanted this time with his family. "Where's Cassie?"

Susan said, "Billy took her downstairs for an ice cream. Something's happened. Molly's told me about it. Don't tell her she should not have. By the way, I'll be going home with you."

"No, you won't."

"So is the baby. I've already booked a nurse."

"Susan, you could hemorrhage before we even get there."

"I'll sit on a towel. Molly, tell him."

Molly began with the broken-up call that had come in

from Martin Kessler. "Apparently, Bourne got word to him that he has Elizabeth. Never mind that she was down in my parlor at the time. Bourne claimed that he had Aisha as well. She's the girl . . ."

"The one close to Elizabeth. You told me."

"I brought Elizabeth to the attic; I called Yitzhak Netanya. I put Elizabeth on so he'd know it wasn't true. Netanya didn't know what to think either. Netanya said he'd have his people find Kessler. Reassure him, protect him, and help get him out. Elizabeth told Netanya to put him on a plane."

"To Westport?"

"With an escort. Netanya said he'd try."

"Slow down," said Bannerman. It was as much said to Susan. She was starting to climb out of her bed. "If it's not true, what's the urgency? Why go to this trouble?"

"Just listen," said Molly. "It gets worse. Elizabeth called Hilton Head, the Tennis Academy. It's where Aisha and some other Muslims live. Aisha's definitely been kidnapped. So has Nadia Halaby. Halaby is Aisha's legal guardian. They both were taken from Elizabeth's house. We don't know why they were there, but they were. Another woman, another Muslim named Jasmine Rashad, was found dead at the scene, her throat cut. One of them had managed to call the police, probably the one who's now dead. She told the dispatcher, 'I have intruders. Men with guns.' The police responded; they must have missed them by seconds. All this happened this morning at around half past nine."

Bannerman blinked. "Bourne thinks Nadia is Elizabeth."

"Whoever took them sure must have. I asked Elizabeth why they would. Elizabeth said there's not much of a resemblance except that they have the same build. But remember, there's only that one photo of Elizabeth and in that one, she's dark head to toe and in profile. The Elizabeth in that photo could be Nadia, and vice versa. Add to that, she was found in Elizabeth's house. Yeah, I'd say that Bourne thinks he has Elizabeth."

Bannerman asked, "Were there witnesses? Descriptions?"

"Men with guns is all we have. No one in the neighboring homes saw a thing."

"Not even their vehicle?"

"Not as far as I know. I'd guess an SUV or a van, but the Highway Patrol can't stop and check every one. And someone's cut pretty badly; we don't know who. Maybe Nadia, maybe Aisha, maybe one of the men. There's a trail of blood leading to the driveway."

Bannerman asked, "Where's Elizabeth? How's she dealing with this?"

"She's with Carla. She's hog-tied. We had to. She lost it. Carla will stay with her until she calms down. Meanwhile, they're waiting to hear more from Netanya."

Susan had begun to gather her things while cradling the blanket-wrapped baby in one arm. Bannerman, carefully, took the baby from her arms.

She said, "Thanks, but watch it. He's got a burp coming."

"You can burp him yourself when you get back in bed. Look at you; you're waddling. You can't walk a straight line."

She said, "Paul, those men took a sixteen-year-old girl. Forget what I said to you last night."

Molly grabbed a towel. She laid it over his shoulder. She asked him, "Where's John Waldo. Is he at Bourne's house?"

"I think he was. He still might be. He hasn't checked in."

"You think?" Molly asked. "Did you send him or not?"

"Molly, I would have, but I didn't have to. He knew we'd need someone to look the place over. That's what he does, so he did it."

Bannerman, in fact, thought that Waldo should have waited for the plot plan and blueprints that Zivic had obtained. Waldo wouldn't have said, "They're for amateurs. Too easy," but that's what he would have been thinking. Zivic calls it the arrogance of the gifted.

Molly asked, "He'd stay reachable, wouldn't he? Otherwise, there's no use in him being there."

"He knows that. He'll reach us when he's ready."

"Except for all you know, he could be taken or dead. You don't seem to have a very good grip on this, Paul."

"Molly . . ."

"Delete that. I'm sorry. I should not have said that."

"She's upset," said Susan. "She met that girl. She liked her. So did Billy; he was in here and he's just as upset. You won't get him to sit still for very long."

He said, "I'll talk to Billy. And Waldo knows what he's doing." He asked Molly, "How long ago did you speak to Kessler?"

She glanced at her watch. "A little over an hour."

"You said the abduction took place at nine-thirty." He looked at his own. "It's now almost two. Bourne must have called Kessler by noon or so, our time. Could Bourne have physically had them by then?"

"Not by car. Not from Hilton Head. That would take him until this evening. But that's assuming they didn't have an aircraft waiting for them. And it's assuming that they're not being held someplace else."

"And assuming," Susan added, "they don't realize their mistake. Wouldn't Nadia or the girl have corrected them by now?"

"They might have," said Bannerman. "If they're able to speak."

"Would they kill them?" asked Susan. "I mean, if they knew?" She was struggling to step into her shoes.

"They might want to. They won't. Not without Bourne's approval. Bourne won't give it because they're birds in the hand. Not the hostage that he wanted, but they'll have to do. Bourne will want to keep them alive. He'll especially want young Aisha alive if he learns that she's close to Elizabeth."

"Paul," said Susan, "Bourne sounds nuts; he sounds desperate. You're telling us what you think a sane man might do."

"No, he's telling us," said Molly, "the only thing we can act on. Bourne has either ordered them both brought to Briarwood or he'll know where they're being held."

Bannerman had walked to the window of the hospital room. He was gently burping the baby. He looked down at the roof of the parking garage. It was empty of cars. Howard Leland was long gone. But Leland had seen Cassie at this window, this room. He knew that Leland would never make a move against his family, but Leland might share that knowledge with someone who would. That was reason enough to go home.

He turned to Molly, "Leland's staying the night."

"I know that. His prayer breakfast is tomorrow."

"So Leland will have eaten. I don't think he'll want brunch."

Molly's eyes widened slightly. "Are you thinking . . ."

"We'll see."

He said to Susan, "You're right. You'll be safer at home."

Molly's cell phone vibrated. She snatched it from her purse. She flipped it open and said "Farrell." Her eyes widened. She sputtered. "You listen to me. If you ever . . ."

She stopped. She exhaled. She closed her eyes. Her body language said, "What's the use?"

She handed Bannerman her phone. She said, "It's Waldo."

32

Chester Lilly nudged Toomey, who had fallen asleep. "We're almost out of gas. We need to stop."

Toomey stifled a yawn. He saw farmland outside. He asked Lilly, "Where are we now?"

"A few exits past Raleigh. Forty miles to Virginia. Another hundred or so up to Bourne's."

Toomey sat up. "And I need to take a whiz. Look for a station with the rest rooms outside."

"Why outside? You get bashful?"

"Yeah, that's it; I'm bashful. I also would rather not walk in past the clerk with blood all over this hand and my clothes. Do you have enough cash to fill up? Don't use plastic."

"Don't leave a paper trail. Is that your advice? You thought I'd pay for the gas with my credit card?"

"Well, you didn't dope out why I couldn't go inside. Don't get cranky. Reminders never hurt."

Lilly gestured with his chin toward an upcoming station that was also a convenience store and gift shop. "No cars at the pumps. Nice and quiet. We'll stop there. You can walk around and whiz in the back."

Toomey turned in his seat to check on Kuntz and their passengers. Stride and the girl were still under the tarp. Kuntz was stretched out with them to one side of it. He'd been using the girl for a pillow.

"Hey, Kuntz. You awake?"

"What? Yeah. How much longer?"

"Three hours, more or less. How are they?" asked Toomey.

"They haven't moved since I gave them their shots."

Lilly pulled in to the farthest pump. Toomey said to Kuntz. "You climb out, fill the tank. You got enough cash in your pocket?"

Kuntz reached in to see. "Yeah, I'm good. Fifty bucks."

"Get a bag of ice, too. And buy some towels or T-shirts, some kind of cloth. I need to wrap up this hand."

"Yeah, all right," said Kuntz, whose right hand was still swollen. "I could use some more ice myself."

"And some coffee," said Lilly. "Some sandwiches. Something."

Kuntz said, "I'll see what they got."

He rolled off the young one and climbed over Stride to reach the sliding side door of the van. He yanked it open, swung his legs, and got out. As he did so, one foot got caught on the tarp. It pulled most of the tarp off the bodies of both women, exposing their white tennis dresses. It also snagged on Stride's legs, bound together with duct tape, dragging them almost to the door. He quickly gathered the tarp and spread it over both bodies. He reached under it to push Stride's legs back inside. Her skin was cold to the touch.

He said, "Oh, shit."

"What's wrong?"

"I'm not sure. Wait a minute," said Kuntz.

He peeled the tarp back and reached to feel for her throat. He slipped his fingers under the drawstring bag with which he had covered her head.

He said, "I get no pulse. I think this one's dead."

Lilly straightened. He turned. He asked, "Which one? The kid?"

"No, Stride. She feels like she's dead."

Lilly cursed. "Before you said the other one. You said the kid."

"That was before. I said she wasn't breathing good. She's still not, but she's warm and she's breathing. Stride isn't."

Lilly said, "Well, do something. Try mouth to mouth. Get that damned bag off her head."

"I told you. Did I tell you?" He groped for the strings. "I told you I don't know how to give shots."

Kuntz tugged the bag off. He stripped the duct tape from her mouth. He said, "I don't know CPR either."

Lilly said to Toomey, "You do. You were a cop. Get back there and both of you work on her."

It was Toomey's turn to curse. He began to climb out. He saw two other vehicles pulling into the station. He said to Kuntz, "Hold it. Shut that door."

The first vehicle to turn in was a pickup truck with a confederate flag on its bumper. It had a big German shepherd in the passenger seat, its head sticking out of the window. The pickup stopped at the set of pumps behind them. Next came an RV, Ohio plates; it towed a boat. That one pulled up adjacent to the van, separated by no more than five feet. Both drivers climbed out and prepared to pump gas. The RV's side door opened and two small boys emerged. They had a little terrier with them on a leash. They were headed toward a patch of dirt and grass.

The pickup truck's dog began snarling and barking. The smaller dog yapped in response. In a flash, the German shepherd was out through the window. The RV's two children were screaming for their father. The father ran toward them; he kicked at the shepherd. The shepherd was trying to get at his dog. One of the boys got tangled up in the leash. A bump from the shepherd knocked him down.

The pickup driver kept on pumping as he whistled for his dog. He was a big, beefy man in overalls and a cap. The father from the RV was still kicking at the dog, shouting. The driver called to the father, "You kick him, I'll kick you."

Kuntz said to him, "Hey. Don't just stand there. Grab your dog."

The driver threw him a sneer. "Butt out, asshole."

Toomey hissed to Kuntz, "Never mind them. Get in."

Kuntz said, "One second. I'll just pull them apart."

Lilly said, "Get in, damn it. We'll get gas up the road."

But Kuntz was already halfway to the shepherd. He reached it and he seized it by the neck and the tail. The shepherd gave a yelp of pain and surprise. Kuntz turned toward the pickup. He told the driver, "Open up."

He said, "I'll open *you* up if you don't put him down."

Kuntz ignored him. He released the dog's tail but kept his grip on its scruff. He reached for the pickup's door himself. The pickup's driver made a grab for Kuntz's collar. Kuntz slapped the arm away and opened the door. The driver threw an overhand right at Kuntz's face. Kuntz lowered his head into it; he took it on his skull, and otherwise seemed to pay no attention. He threw the shepherd into the cab. The shepherd spun, showed his teeth, and was snarling at Kuntz, but seemed to think better of attacking him. Kuntz said, "Good dog. Just relax. Not your fault," as he reached to roll up the window.

The pickup's owner, enraged and nursing sore knuckles, kicked the door into Kuntz. It slammed his hip. He kicked it again with a heavy work boot, but Kuntz had backed out and it missed him. The driver ran around him to the back of the pickup. He grabbed a coil of chain that he'd probably used for towing. He swung it at Kuntz and he missed a second time. He swung it again and this time Kuntz stepped inside it. Kuntz jabbed at his eye, kicked his legs out from under him, and dragged him out of sight between the pickup and the pumps.

He called to Lilly, "Two more seconds. Be right with you." Kuntz went to work on the driver.

They had driven a few miles and had made several turns before Lilly was satisfied that there was no pursuit. In that time, Lilly had not said a word except those he'd been mumbling to himself. Toomey had climbed into the back of the van. He'd confirmed that the woman was dead.

"Suffocation," he said. "Her lips and ears are all blue. She's probably been dead for two hours."

Kuntz had picked up the drawstringed bag that he'd used to cover her head. He pressed it against his own nose and mouth and said, "You can breathe through this easy. Look, I'm breathing."

Toomey said to Lilly, "It wasn't just the hood. Take that whack you gave her, the injection Kuntz gave her, the tape across her mouth . . . it added up."

Lilly said, "Do you remember . . ." He wet his lips before finishing. "Do you two remember, we were on our way down there, I said I'd like just one fucking thing to go right?"

"One thing did," Toomey answered. "Bourne wanted her; we got her."

Lilly said, "Hold that thought. We'll get back to that thought. There is one other thing I'd like to vent."

"Venting's healthy," said Toomey. "Get it out of your system." Toomey struggled back into the passenger seat.

"Do you also remember, pulling into that station, some discussion about trying not to stand out? Paying cash? Your bloody hand? Do you remember all that?"

"This shouldn't have happened, but it did. Shit does happen."

Lilly glanced back at Kuntz. "Is that two now? Two dead? Did you leave that cracker with the pickup truck dead?"

"Uh-uh. He's not dead. I just stomped his face some. Look, it's not like I had a whole lot of choice. All I asked him to do was go grab his dog. He wouldn't; someone had to, and I was right there."

Toomey said to Lilly, "Kuntz did try to walk away. He didn't want to fight him with his hands all messed up. The other guy was out of control."

Lilly asked, "What was wrong with just *driving* away? You couldn't let the cracker and the father fight it out?"

"You saw the kids' father. He would have got creamed. His kids would have seen it. They'd never forget it. And that little dog would have got eaten."

Lilly lifted his eyes toward the heavens. "So *what*?"

"Not everyone's as big a prick as you are," said Toomey. "But how about we drop it. We've got more urgent problems."

Lilly made a calming gesture. It was meant for himself. He took a breath. "Yes, we do. Now we're back to that thought."

Toomey said, "What I meant was we still need gas and I still need to piss even worse. But you're talking about Bourne. He wanted Stride, now she's dead. Keep in mind that we're the only ones who know that," said Toomey.

Lilly squinted. "You're saying?"

"Bourne would have killed her in the end, no matter what. You didn't think he'd let her go, did you?"

"Yeah, but . . ."

"The only thing he's lost is he can't put her on the phone. She might have told him to go fuck himself anyway. But he still has this girl. He can put *her* on the phone. And as long as the girl thinks that Stride is alive, Bourne still holds a pretty good hand."

Lilly nodded slowly. He was remembering Bourne's words. He called the kid insurance. A hedge against Stride. He'd said she's a guarantor of Stride's good behavior.

"Think about it," said Toomey. "Say they were both still alive. Bourne would have kept them separate anyway, right? He'd have told each one that the other was okay, and would be as long as they both behave. He still can. This doesn't change anything."

Maybe, thought Lilly. But Bourne wanted more than that. He wanted time to get to know Elizabeth Stride. Lilly had seen it. The gleam in Bourne's eye. He wouldn't be surprised if Bourne had jacked off when he heard that they had her and were bringing her. The famous Black Angel. The beautiful killer. The thing is, she's not really all that beautiful, thought Lilly. Not bad, but she's no Claire. Built more like a jock. Himself, he'd have thought she was a lesbo.

They were on a rural road, two lanes running through pines. He said, "Dirt road ahead. I could use a leak myself. We'll get gas when we get back near the highway."

"Yeah, good."

Lilly made a right turn. He drove in two hundred yards. The road curved around a dark scummy pond that had stumps of old trees sticking out of it. He pulled over near the edge of the pond. He said, "Let's make it fast. We're running late as it is. Hey, Kuntz? You need to go too?"

"I can wait."

"Do it here," said Lilly. "When we get gas, you stay put, and that's going to be our last stop."

"Yeah, okay."

Three doors opened at once. All three men stepped out. Kuntz followed Toomey to the algae-covered pond. Both men had some trouble undoing their zippers. Lilly waited until both men had succeeded in spite of their damaged hands. He drew his Glock from his belt and thumbed off the safety. He fired at the back of Kuntz's head.

Shock and surprise caused Toomey to whirl as Kuntz pitched forward on his face. The side of Toomey's own face was splattered with blood. He was unable to interrupt his stream.

He croaked, "What was that? Why the hell did you do that?"

Lilly lowered his weapon. "I could give you a list. Finish pissing, then empty his pockets."

A part of Lilly was surprised that a single shot had done it. He'd seen how that cracker broke his hand on Kuntz's skull. But maybe it wasn't so thick in the back. He had aimed just above the spinal cord.

Toomey did finish. He shook himself off. Lilly told him, "Like you said, Bourne might see the silver lining. But when I have to tell him all the ways Kuntz screwed up, he'd tell me to get rid of him anyway."

"Jesus."

"Get his stuff. Roll him in. Then let's get out of here," said Lilly.

Toomey grimaced, but obeyed. He started going through Kuntz's pockets. He said, "This isn't right. You shouldn't have done this. It's not like you didn't fuck up yourself."

"How me? I told him to keep her alive. How many times did I say that?"

"Yeah, you did. But last night. We were all done with Clew. Except for my finger, we were out of there clean. But you, you just had to go look."

Lilly darkened. He said, "That was Claire."

Toomey's eyebrows went up. "Now you believe your own bullshit? You went in there to scalp him over your fucking hair. Why was this? Because he pulled it? He messed up your perm? Your fag hairdresser should have fixed your whole head while he was at it."

Lilly glared. He said, "One time. Shut your mouth."

"A simple mugging and a beating. That was all Bourne ever wanted. What would he say if he ever heard the truth about how he lost Claire because of you?"

Toomey knew, in that instant, that he'd made a mistake. He knew what Lilly's next question would be. It would be *"Who's going to tell him. You're the only one who could."*

But that was not what Lilly said. He said, "Empty your pockets."

"Hey, hold it. Just wait. You don't need to worry."

"You did a bad thing back at Stride's house, you know. You cut that spade's throat. You turned a snatch into murder. That was contrary to my clear instructions."

"Just wait," said Toomey. "Look, I'm emptying my pockets."

Chester Lilly still held his Glock at his side. He asked, "Do I look stupid? You're going to try for your gun. So go for it. What can you lose?"

Toomey raised both his hands. "I'm not doing this," he said.

"Then I guess we're done talking."

Lilly fired.

33

Susan's obstetrician had come in with the charge nurse to argue against her going home. Molly was using the bedside phone to check up on Carla and Elizabeth. Bannerman had taken Molly's cell phone to one corner and had covered one ear so he could hear.

He said to John Waldo, "I assume you've been to Briarwood."

"Still here," he answered. "There's not much going on."

"Is Bourne on the property? Have you seen him?"

"He's here," said Waldo. "He's been down in his basement. Right now there's just him and nobody else. Two hours ago, the whole staff started leaving. It looks like they got the night off."

"No bodyguards? None of his personal assistants?"

"If you're asking about Lilly, the guy who you think did Clew, there's been no one like that since I got here. If you're asking about gate guards, there are four, two each gate, and two more patrolling the grounds. They patrol it in Jeeps; they got rifles; they got dogs."

Bannerman asked, "Have you been in the house?"

"Well, yeah. Since the staff left. I've been mostly all through it. Right now I'm upstairs in one of the maids' rooms. The guest rooms are all wired and the biggest ones have cameras. This guy likes to know what's going on."

Oh, really, thought Bannerman, although he wasn't surprised. But that tidbit might turn out to be useful.

"Cameras everywhere," said Bannerman. "But you haven't been seen?"

"Cameras aren't a big help if there's nobody watching. The recorders and monitors are all down in the basement, but no one is at them; I looked. Bourne's been on the phone or he's been on a computer except once he went upstairs to talk to a book and . . ."

"A book?"

"This big atlas. He leafs through it. On some pages, he talks to it. And twice he went outside to talk to his bees."

Bannerman closed one eye. "These are actual bees?"

"There's this row of hives, yeah. Behind the stables."

Bannerman remembered what Greta had said. He'd thought it was a figure of speech.

"They seem to calm him down. This guy has big mood swings. The first time, he looked like he was mad at the world. The second time, he's smiling and clapping his hands. It's like he couldn't wait to share good news with the bees."

"What time was the smiling and clapping?" asked Bannerman.

"I logged it . . . let me look. At ten thirty-five this morning."

About the time, thought Bannerman, that Bourne would have learned that Elizabeth Stride had been taken.

"Well, we think we know what pleased him. It'll keep for the moment. Zivic's blueprints say that basement had a fifties' bomb shelter. Are we talking a bunker? How secure?"

"Secure? I got down there."

"I meant for normal human beings."

"That sounds like a crack that Molly would make. Molly is sore at me, right?"

"So is Anton," said Bannerman. "You can mend those fences later." He used his free hand to open Zivic's bound dossier. He said, "I'm looking at the blueprints of that basement."

"Those blues must be old. Bourne made all kinds of changes. You go through his wine cellar, it's like thousands of bottles. One rack, all dessert wines, slides open like a door. It seals like a bulkhead, but only from inside. After that, there's what must have been the shelter apartment. There's two bedrooms, one of which has a kitchen and pantry. The other's now used as an office and a lab. Whatever they work on has to be hot. I saw two HazMat space suits and, out in the hall, there's a de-con chemical shower." He added, "Oh, and there's this cot in the lab. It's not for sleeping. It has tie-down straps. That room is where Bourne is right now."

Bannerman said, "I see it. It's the same basic layout. What other changes have you seen?"

"There's a walk-in vault that's been converted to a freezer. It's a big one, a Mosler Class 3. The lab and the bedroom have heavy steel doors with little glass windows like you see in a nuthouse. The ventilation system seems to be the original, and it's separate from the rest of the house."

"Because of the HazMat?"

"Well, originally," said Waldo, "it's from when it was a shelter. It cleans and recirculates its own air supply. Otherwise you'd be down there breathing fallout."

"Is it functioning?"

"Yeah, it works, but now it's also for the wine. There's a duct he leaves open to the rest of the cellar. Right now, Bourne is sitting down there in a bathrobe. It keeps the whole place pretty cool."

Bannerman said, "Okay, listen. Here's what's happened since you left."

He told Waldo what they knew of the Hilton Head kidnapping and the murder of one of Elizabeth's friends. Three men with guns, almost surely led by Lilly. That Bourne believed, as of mid-morning, that they have Elizabeth. That he might know by now that they took the wrong woman. That they also took Elizabeth's friend, Aisha.

"That nice kid?" asked Waldo. "The one Billy and me talked to?"

"That's the one. We weren't sure where they were being taken. But if Bourne has dismissed all his household staff, the way to bet is that they're being brought there. If so, they'll turn up sometime this evening."

"You don't have to bet. I'll go down now and ask him. There's a stove there. I'll hold his face over it."

"No, you stay away. Observe and report. This thing goes beyond simply rescuing those two. I need you to sit tight for a while."

"What's a while?" asked Waldo.

"It could be overnight. I have arrangements to make. And some of us need to get a few hours sleep. Will you check in with Anton every two or three hours?"

He said, "Yeah, but Paul, I could end this when they show. I can tell from your voice, real quiet and calm, that they're going to be dog shit regardless."

"Move too fast and a great many people might die. As I've said . . ."

"It goes beyond. Yeah, I heard you."

"Are you okay alone?"

"I got the run of the house. But maybe I better make a couple of calls. I don't want to be alone and asleep."

"Calls to whom?" asked Bannerman.

"People nearer than you. We got floaters who could be here in a couple of hours. We could use someone watching the gates and the dogs. Don't worry. They'll stay in the weeds."

"One more thing. Bourne's two hostages. If you think they're endangered . . ."

"I know how to do this," said Waldo.

Bannerman's broke the connection. He reached into his pocket. He withdrew the slip that contained Leland's numbers. Two were marked "home" and "cell." Two others were marked with an "S" for "secure." He knew that Leland would still be in transit to Bridgeport in order to send Greta Kirch home. He punched out the number of the cell phone.

"Yes?" came Leland's voice. He answered on the second ring. Bannerman could hear highway sounds.

"It's Bannerman," he said. "I have a message for Bourne. All interested parties are willing to negotiate. Martin Kessler will agree to listen to reason and you, Mr. Leland, may get what you want. No harm, however, can have come to Kessler's friends. If they are harmed in any way . . ."

"Wait a minute," said Leland. "Who is Kessler?"

Bannerman said quietly, "I think you know."

"And I think you're mistaken. That name rings no bells. If you think you know better, kindly give me some context. Where, how, and when would I know it?"

"Angola."

"Well, thank you," said Leland. "That narrows it down. But, damn it, I still do not recognize the name and, damn it, I will not have my integrity impugned. And if I ever hear one more threat from you people . . . "

"One more. It's the last. There are no more after this. It's directed at Bourne, not at you, sir."

"Or my daughters?"

"Neither you nor your daughters have anything to fear as long as my family and friends are not threatened. But understand this. I am seen as a leader. If harm should come to them and I don't respond, I'll have lost all credibility with them. In the end it won't matter because *they* will respond. They'll go killing on their own. They won't do much sorting out."

The line was silent for a moment. "I do understand."

"I would think so," said Bannerman. "It is precisely what your . . . what *our* government has done when its citizens came under attack. I would think you'd feel the same about Roger."

A longer silence followed. "Was it Bourne? Can you prove it?"

"What will you do if I can, sir?"

"On my honor . . . on my *honor* . . . I will see him in prison after personally shoving my fist down his throat. But that doesn't mean I'll throw VaalChem to the wolves. My wife and daughters will be just as dead as the rest of us if we are attacked with bio-weapons."

Bannerman asked, "Is Greta still with you?"

"Right here at my side."

"May I speak to her, please? I'll be brief."

"He wants you," he said to Greta.

She had taken the phone from him. "Yes, hello, Mr. Bannerman."

"It's Paul. You've been listening. Is he telling the truth?"

"You . . . ask me to look into his heart. I cannot."

"His eyes, then. His manner. Don't think. What have you felt?"

"I have felt that he knows what is right and what isn't. I think that his choices are not always so easy. I think he is not a bad man."

"Thank you, Greta," said Bannerman. "Let me speak to him again."

Leland came back on. He sounded bemused. "An intuitive character reference? You're serious?"

"I like her and trust her," Bannerman answered. "I'm still working on whether to trust you. Regarding VaalChem, it's possible that I might be of help. I'll need a few days; we'll talk then. But for now, please call Bourne and give him my message. If Kessler's friends are harmed, he won't live out the week. And neither will many on his list."

"I . . . must have misheard you. Now you're threatening mass murder?"

"I'll do *some* sorting out," replied Bannerman.

"These friends of this Kessler. Do they have names?"

"Just say friends," said Bannerman. "Bourne will know who I mean."

He heard Leland taking a long tired breath. "I'll get back to you as soon as I can."

34

A small motorcade made the ten-minute trip from the hospital in Norwalk to Westport. One car took Susan and Cassie and the baby. The car was driven by Viktor Podolsk, the former KGB major. He would stay with them until he was relieved. The nurse that Susan had booked was en route.

The second car was Molly's. She drove directly to her home, anxious to look in on Elizabeth. A third took the Westporters who had watched over Bannerman during his meeting with Leland. He had never seen who they were.

Bannerman drove his own car. He took Billy McHugh with him. They were headed for Molly's house as well. He used the time to brief Billy on all that had happened, including his last call to Leland. Billy listened without speaking, without visibly reacting, except that he'd stiffened at the part about Aisha. At the end of it, he said, "I should get down there with Waldo."

"I need you to stick close to Elizabeth."

"Whatever they done to her . . ."

"To Aisha?"

"Yeah, Aisha. Whatever they done to her, I'm going to do worse."

"You may well get your chance very soon."

Billy asked, "What's this list? The one Leland thinks you got."

"It's the names of all those who've attended Bourne's brunches. It might, in fact, be a useful thing to have. It shouldn't be hard to construct."

"We're going after them all?"

"Oh no," said Bannerman. "Most are none of our business. Most have no knowledge or involvement in this."

"You think the rest of them are Boy Scouts?"

"That's not what I said. We'll focus on the Angolan connection. Our plate will be full as it is."

Billy mouthed the word "plate."

"Beg pardon?" said Bannerman.

"Heads on a plate. Didn't they used to do that?"

"There's a . . . biblical story. John the Baptist and Salome. Is that what you're thinking about?"

"Yeah, I guess. Is that where Kessler got the idea?"

"No, Kessler's inspiration was firsthand; it was personal. A woman named Sara. She was Mossad. Someone sent her head to Kessler."

"That someone was one of the heads he sent Bourne?"

"After Kessler was through with him, yes."

Billy fell silent. Then, "I got a bad feeling."

"Aisha again?"

He nodded. "What if Bourne . . . ?"

"Beheads her?" asked Bannerman. "Waldo won't let that happen."

"Waldo won't unless it happened already. I have such a bad feeling about this."

"Billy . . . for Pete's sake, don't say that to Elizabeth. She's probably going crazy as it is."

But she wasn't.

When they reached Molly's attic, they found Elizabeth in a daze. She was lying with her eyes partly closed. Her hands and feet were bound with extension cords. Molly or Carla had spread out some seat cushions in an effort to make her more comfortable on the floor. Her wrists and her ankles were rubbed raw from the struggle.

Carla was busy printing out stills that she'd taken from Molly's surveillance tapes. There were joggers, bicyclists, deliverymen. There were roofers, house painters, men in slow-moving cars. A car moving slowly meant nothing in itself. The posted speed limit was twenty. But none of the faces were familiar to her. That was her only standard for the moment.

Bannerman noticed bite marks on one of Carla's wrists and he saw that her upper lip was swollen. Molly, who had been the first to return, was busy at one of her radios. She sat with a headset held against one ear as she played with her toggles and dials.

Carla looked up at Bannerman and Billy who were standing over Elizabeth. She said, "I had to force-feed her some pills." She rolled her arm at them, displaying her bite mark. "She tried to swallow part of me instead."

Bannerman lowered himself to Elizabeth's side. He spoke to her. "Elizabeth? Can you hear me?"

Her eyes moved, but they could not seem to find him. Her breathing seemed shallow and irregular. Bannerman asked Carla, "What have you given her?"

"Seconal. Sleeping pills, mashed up in water while Molly had her in a headlock."

"How many did you give her? What strength?"

"I'm not sure how much of it she actually swallowed, but I gave her a pretty good hit. About ten."

"You don't consider that dangerous?"

"Not as dangerous as she is. She could use a nice nap. She'll be down for anywhere from eight to twelve hours. You could do with some shut-eye yourself."

"Why was this needed? What was she going to do?"

"Grab her duffel, go to Bridgeport, hijack a small plane. I'm not sure she thought it out beyond that. There's a silenced Mac-10 in her duffel, by the way, along with her blacks and her knives. We tried to tell her we're not sure where they were taken. She didn't care. If she had Bourne, she'd have them. She'd have cored out one of his eyes with her knife and saved the other one for her next question."

Bannerman touched her sore wrists. "Does she still need these cords?"

"They'll make it easier," said Carla, "to haul her downstairs without whacking her head too many times." She said, "Billy, can you stash her in one of the bedrooms? Bring back the cords. They're not spares."

Billy said to Bannerman, "I could take her to my house. That way me and my wife can watch her together. I got too many bad thoughts to sit alone."

Carla rose from the printer. "I'll give you a hand." She flashed a handful of photo lifts at Bannerman. "I have to get to Town Hall. They close early on Saturday. I need to see if they recognize the two guys who were in there checking out when we cut our grass."

"Our grass?"

"Not to mention where all of us live and our floor plans. Someone in records tipped Anton. He put me to work."

"But our grass? Why would anyone ask about that?"

Molly raised a hand before Carla could answer. She said, "I'm getting it. They've found Kessler. But he's not coming here."

Bannerman glanced at Elizabeth. She didn't react. He asked, "Who was that on the radio?"

"He's still holding. It's Netanya's agent in charge. He was with Kessler when Kessler called earlier. He got Kessler to a radio and put him on with Netanya. But he doesn't think the call reassured him."

"Did Netanya tell him that Elizabeth's with us?"

"He did, but then Netanya tried to patch him through to Westport. I wasn't here to take it. Carla couldn't work this radio. Kessler lost patience and took off again."

"Took off to where?"

Molly made a grimace. "This part isn't good. They say he's called up a company of Duganga's troops and they're moving toward Luanda with Katyushas, Russian rockets. They say he plans to drop a few dozen on VaalChem. They won't have to go far to be in range."

"Are you saying that Kessler wouldn't take Yitzhak's word?"

"I guess not. Wait a second. Let me ask."

She had a further exchange with the agent in charge. She turned again in her seat to face Bannerman.

"He says Kessler wasn't buying that they couldn't get through to us. See what happens when we have these little lapses? Kessler decided that Netanya was stalling him to keep him from hammering VaalChem. An attack like that on VaalChem won't just flatten VaalChem. It could wipe out half of coastal Angola if the rockets spread that stuff VaalChem makes. It's also because Netanya couldn't give him an answer when he asked whether Aisha was safe as well. Remember, we didn't know that Aisha had been taken when I first got through to Netanya."

"Are they still trying to get Kessler to talk to us directly?"

"They're trying," said Molly, "but then what? He'll want to talk to Elizabeth. He'll believe you if you tell him why we had to calm her down, but what will you say about Aisha?"

"That we're handling it," said Bannerman.

"But that we're taking our time?"

Bannerman glared at her. "I thought we'd been through this."

"Sorry. Frustration. Look what it's done to Kessler."

He said, "Kessler, for the moment, is the more pressing problem. He's either bluffing about VaalChem or he isn't. If he is, he'll be contacting Artemus Bourne to threaten VaalChem's destruction. If he isn't bluffing, he's gone over the edge. Netanya will have no choice but to stop him."

"Kill him?"

"Stop him," said Bannerman. "One way or the other. Netanya might hope that it's only a bluff, but what happens if Bourne calls him on it?"

"Then he'd have to show that the bluff has some teeth." Molly asked, "What would you do in his place?"

"I might launch a few Katyushas to get his attention, but I'd drop them around the perimeter."

He paused, then grimaced as he recalled Greta Kirch's description of such a facility. Especially the bio-containment rings and their width.

He said to Molly, "Put me through to Netanya."

"Are you thinking what I'm thinking."

"Netanya's right," said Bannerman. "He'll need to know that I agree. He might well have to kill Martin Kessler."

35

Aisha's mother had come to her twice in her dreams.

In the first one, her mother had slipped into her bed and snuggled up with her and kissed her. That wasn't unusual. She'd done that many times. She would lie there with Aisha, not saying a word, just smiling and stroking her hair.

Two things were different about the first dream. The first was her bed. It didn't feel right. It was hard and it vibrated and it pressed on her ribs. That made it hard to breathe and her face had been hurting. But the hurt went away at her mother's first kiss and the bed soon began to feel softer.

The second thing that was different was that her mother seemed sad. Aisha asked her, "Is something wrong?"

Her mother said, "Oh, it's nothing. It's just that I miss you. And I've been a little selfish about it."

"Selfish how?"

Her mother sighed. "Never mind. Go to sleep."

Aisha nudged her with her shoulder. "No, tell me."

"It's just that . . . well . . . for a little while, earlier, I thought you were coming to be with me."

Aisha didn't understand. "Mom, I'm with you right now."

"No, I meant . . . something different. Something more than a visit. For a while there, I thought you'd stopped breathing."

"It's this bed. It got hard, but it's much better now." Aisha paused. "Wait a minute. You mean dying?"

"No one dies."

"Moving on, then."

"Uh-huh. That's what was selfish. I almost found myself hoping. But your father reminded me that you're only sixteen. He said he misses you too, but we can wait."

"Were you both at my party?"

"Uh-huh. You drank wine."

"Mother, I had two tiny sips."

Her mother nudged her back. She said, "Oh, I'm kidding. The holy book never says that you can't touch the stuff. All it says is that alcohol does more harm than good and it warns against getting sloshed."

Aisha said, "Hmmph. I don't think that's verbatim."

"Close enough. It's in 2:219. Check it out."

Her mother wasn't really a Muslim. Well, she was, but not from the beginning. She was Lebanese by birth and a Maronite Christian. She'd embraced Islam, or rather she added it, when she agreed to marry her father. The gentlest parts of both religions were essentially the same. They were the parts that most Muslims live by. One God, a loving God, a giver of blessings who expects all who get them to pass them along. And one who doesn't take kindly to sleazes.

Her mother suddenly stiffened. She said, "I have to go." She said, "Oh, my gosh. I'll take care of them. Don't worry. I'll be back very soon."

Aisha had no idea what she meant. Her mother left. Her bed went hard again. She would have been more comfortable sitting in a soft chair, but her body didn't seem to want to move. And other dreams came. They were angry dreams. Confusing. Two men running at her out of a house. In the dream it seemed to be Elizabeth's house. Running at her. Someone shouting. That was all she remembered.

Except later, before her mother came back, she had a dream in which those two men were shouting at each other. No, wait. There were three of them. Three different voices. She thought that she heard them say Elizabeth's name. And in that dream one of them was almost on top of her. He was partly in the space that her mother had left and he was resting his head on her butt. It wasn't nasty or anything. He wasn't nuzzling her or touching her. She just wished that he would find another bed.

Her wish came true. He got up and went out. She heard a door slide open and close, so he must have gone out onto the balcony. Soon after that, she heard two loud noises. There was one, like a door slamming shut, and then silence. A minute later, she heard a frightened male voice and again, the loud slamming sound. After a while, a smaller door opened and she felt her bed vibrating again. But at least there wasn't any more arguing.

Her mother came back. This time she just sat. Her mother rubbed her shoulders and hummed very softly and soon the bed was soft once again. And this time her mother wasn't alone. Jasmine was there. And Nadia was there. They'd never been in one of these dreams before this. It had always been just Aisha and her mother.

They both looked confused. More so Nadia, than Jasmine. Nadia was looking all over the place as if she'd taken a wrong turn and gotten lost. Jasmine seemed to have gotten there first, but still hadn't figured it out.

She heard her mother say, "I'm Leyna. I'll be with you in a minute." Leyna was her mother's Christian name.

Jasmine moved closer. She was squinting at her mother. Then her eyes popped wide open. Jasmine asked, "Did you say Leyna? You . . . look just like Aisha."

"I'm Leyna Bandari. Aisha's mother."

"If . . . you're Aisha's mother, then we're in deep shit."

"No, you're not. You're just not in Kuwait . . . never mind. You're both okay. Really. It gets better from here. Give me just another minute with Aisha."

"Where is Aisha?" asked Nadia, who was suddenly alarmed.

"She's right here. But not like you. We're just visiting."

Nadia said, "I can't see her. Why can't I see her?"

"Well, it's something that you sort of have to work your way up to. She can see you because she's only dreaming. I don't understand the distinction myself, but it's how things seem to work around here."

Jasmine asked, "If she's dreaming, she's still alive, right?"

"She's alive," said Aisha's mother. "She's in trouble, but alive."

Aisha asked, "I'm in trouble? What trouble?"

"I'll stay with you. Don't worry. So will Jasmine and Nadia. And Elizabeth will be coming to help you."

Jasmine asked, "So she's cookin'? Those three bozos didn't get her?"

"Wait a minute," said Aisha. She asked Jasmine, "Are you dead?"

"They can't hear you," said her mother. "But they have moved on, yes."

"Oh, wait. Wait a minute. Is this just in my dream?"

"No, it's true," said her mother. "I just found out myself. Their lives were taken, but there wasn't much pain."

Her mother's tone was sympathetic, but toward Aisha, not her friends. From her mother's point of view, a life was not a great loss. She had surely felt differently before she was murdered, but she now saw life as a preparatory interval. A life wasted was a far greater tragedy than one shortened.

Aisha had not yet subscribed to that view. This particular shortening seemed terribly unfair.

She said, "It's too soon. They're too young."

"Well, your father and I weren't in our dotage either. But you've learned that we're not really gone. Same with them."

Aisha didn't ask who had killed them and when. In these dreams, that would seem an incidental detail. Nor were their deaths necessarily final. She asked, "Can you help them come back?"

"I'd like to, for your sake," said her mother.

"But can you?"

"They can't come back, honey. And very soon, they won't

want to. At the moment, they'd both like to shorten a few lives, but they're much more concerned about you."

Aisha persisted. She said, "Claudia came back. How come Claudia was able to come back?"

"Um . . . who is this Claudia?" asked her mother.

"She's a woman I met. She got shot and she died. But she came back as a guardian angel."

"Is she one of the women you met on that boat? On the night you snuck off with Elizabeth?"

"Yes."

"She talks to animals and such? She knows things before they happen?"

"Yes, and . . . well, she throws knives," Aisha told her.

"Give me a minute. I'll ask. Be right back."

Her mother didn't actually leave. She never seemed to have to in these dreams. She would only close her eyes and roll her head a few times. She did the same thing when she was alive and would be thinking, as now, about the answer to a question. But alive, she wouldn't say, "Be right back."

She was only gone for a moment or two. She opened her eyes. She said, "That would be Claudia Geller, correct?"

"Yes. That's her name. So she *was* there?"

"Not all the way, no," said her mother. "She was sent back; quite a few people are. But she wasn't sent back with any wonderful new talents. Whatever gifts she had, she'd had all the time. The big difference is that now she believes in them, Aisha. Belief can do remarkable things. You've been blessed with some special gifts yourself."

Aisha understood. It's what Elizabeth had said. She said it was enough that it was true in her mind. But Elizabeth had also said that dreams weren't real.

"While I was away, I asked about your other friend, Martin. There's good news. We were right. He's alive."

"Martin Kessler?" Aisha beamed. "I *knew* it. Where is he?"

"Far away. But he's alive. He is most certainly alive."

"Does Elizabeth know? Can Elizabeth find him?"

"It's Elizabeth who told me. That was my other stop."

"Wait a minute," said Aisha. "You can do that?"

"Do what?"

"That. Make these stops. Popping into people's heads."
"More or less. Isn't that what I'm doing with you?"
"Yes, Mother, but I'm dreaming."
"So was she."

36

It was one in the morning, Angola time, when Jose Matala was awakened by his phone. The interior minister switched on a light and dragged the receiver to his ear. He looked at his alarm clock and asked, speaking Portuguese, "Why am I called at this hour?"

An accented voice said, "Wake up. Clear your head. This is Alameo calling. Speak English."

Matala gasped in surprise; he glanced at his wife. She appeared to be still sound asleep. He whispered, "Alameo? What . . . what is it that you want?"

"You will extend my courtesies to Artemus Bourne and then you will give him this message. You will tell him that I am coming for him. But first I will set VaalChem ablaze."

Matala said, "Listen . . . that message he sent you. I have only passed it on. I know nothing of this woman and this girl."

"His message did reach me. It disturbed my rest briefly. But then I soon learned that Mr. Bourne is a liar . . ."

"Oh yes. A liar. He cannot be trusted."

"Nor can you, you toady. But you will do this for me. Bourne's threat was empty. More than that, it was stupid. But the mere fact that it even entered his mind to harm that innocent child . . ."

"This was bad," said Matala. "I said that to him. When he told me, I said, 'This is bad. Very bad.' You can ask him. This is what I told him."

"Make the call."

"It is . . . true that you are going to set VaalChem ablaze? Might I ask when this is intended?"

"What you're asking is whether you have time to pack your bags and get to the airport in Luanda. What you're asking is whether it is time to go abroad and visit the money you have stolen from your people."

"Stolen? Not so. I am a modest civil servant."

"Oh, shut up, Matala. Make the call."

Bourne answered the ring when he saw the name of Jose Matala on his readout. He listened as Matala gave an account of his stalwart performance against Kessler.

"He called you a liar. I said *he* is the liar. He said your threat was empty. I said *his* threat was empty."

"Yes, yes, yes," said Bourne. "I'm sure that put him in his place. He said he's about to set fire to VaalChem?"

"He will not get near. I have dispatched tanks and soldiers. Six tanks and also two fire trucks."

"And he seemed to be saying that I don't have Stride?"

"This name was not mentioned. He only spoke of a child. He refers, I assume, to the birthday girl female that you said you would cut up on your table."

"Cut up? Oh, vivisection. I was teasing when I said that. You didn't tell him that, did you?"

"No," said Matala. "I told him, however, that I would cut *him* if he did not treat you with more respect."

"I am touched."

"When I return," said Matala, "this will be my priority."

"You're about to take a trip? Why am I not surprised?"

"It is my wife who must travel. I had promised to go with her. She requires facial surgery. This was long ago planned."

"Facial meaning cosmetic?"

"One's wife must be presentable."

"I'm sure that she'll be stunning. Bon voyage."

Bourne used the same telephone to call Chester's pager. Chester returned the call almost at once.

Bourne said, "Ease my mind. Do you have them or don't you?"

"Absolutely. They're . . . both right behind me."

Bourne caught the slight hesitation in his voice. He said, "No names. We'll avoid using names. But give me some hint of who they are."

"You already know. But, okay. Big long step."

"Uh-huh." Very clever. A stride. "And the other one?"

"Um . . . I don't know. Candles?"

"Well chosen," said Bourne. "When might I expect you?"

"Depending on traffic? A half hour."

"And all is well? I'll have reason to smile?"

"This trip hasn't all been a barrel of laughs. I'll tell you when I get there. Thirty minutes."

A banner day for the telephone company, thought Bourne. His own phone had hardly stopped ringing. More cancellations. More unwanted Eggs Florentine. Not a good day for the bloody mary mix people or the makers of fresh-squeezed O.J.

Not long after Lilly, Howard Leland called and canceled. He called from Connecticut of all places. He had taken it upon himself to confer with Paul Bannerman in the interest of preserving VaalChem's good work.

"Well, jolly for you," Bourne responded. "Any luck?"

"Some, I think," said Leland. "Let me ask you straight out. Did you order the attack on Roger Clew?"

"In truth? And this *is* true. I was aghast."

"I'm . . . not sure that you've answered my question," said Leland.

"Oh, for heaven's sake, Howard. Would I admit it if I had? If I did, it was something that got out of hand in a way that was contrary to my wishes. If I did, it has cost me more than

you know. Get over it. Move on. Water under the bridge.
Let's get back to saving the world."

"Thank you," said Leland.

"Have we put that to rest?"

"We may need to discuss it. Tomorrow, perhaps?"

"Don't expect to be fed. You're scratched off."

"One more question," said Leland. "Who is Martin
Kessler?"

"You don't know?"

"I'm asking."

"Don't you ever talk to Quigley? Do you read his reports?
Martin Kessler is a mercenary, a murderer, and rude. Martin
Kessler has played hob with our Angolan interests. Martin
Kessler is a Kraut, former Stasi, former Communist.
Martin Kessler is a trickster and a practical joker. I could
show you three examples of his lighthearted whimsy. Mar-
tin Kessler's better known as Alameo."

"Alameo . . . is Kessler?"

"I could not have said it better."

"And what is Paul Bannerman's interest in Angola?"

"I don't know," Bourne answered. "Perhaps none at all.
His main interest seems to be in Martin Kessler. They are
very much cut of the same cloth, you know. They and Roger
Clew, whom we're no longer discussing, and others I could
name of that ilk."

"You mention 'others,'" said Leland. "Do you refer to
Kessler's friends?"

Bourne hesitated. "Which friends are you speaking of?"

"I don't know. None in particular. But Bannerman has
asked me to give you this message. If any of Kessler's
friends should be harmed in any way, he assures you that
you will not live out the week. And neither will *'some'* on
your guest list."

Bourne grunted. He asked, "And you don't know which
friends?"

"I do not. But clearly, he has someone in mind. He believes, and I suspect, that you know who he means."

"Well, I don't, so don't trouble your head."

Damn, thought Bourne. Bannerman knows that I have

Stride. Kessler must have called him in a dither. Well, no matter. Let him bluster. This is doubly why I have her. To ensure the good behavior of both of them.

"And you say that he's threatened some of those on my guest list? So it's him. He's the one who distributed the exchange between General Tubbs and Roger Clew."

"He's as much as admitted it," said Leland.

"How could he have gotten it? To say nothing of that list?"

"I don't know," said Leland, "but while we're on the subject, what are you going to do about that ship?"

"What ship? Tubbs's death ship?"

"Yes, Artemus. That one," said Leland, his words dripping. "The one that the Red Cross is screaming about, as is World Heath in Geneva. The one that's brought VaalChem to their attention. The one that has twenty children on board. What help can you offer? Can you save them?"

"Why should I?"

"I don't know. Common decency? You do have the antivirals."

"That ship is Kessler's doing, not mine," said Bourne. "He broke it; he can fix it. I'll watch."

"You'll do nothing?"

"I said that I'll watch. We may learn something useful. Controlled, isolated, it's the best sort of field test."

Leland didn't respond. There was silence on his end. Then, "You really are a son-of-a-bitch, aren't you."

"Big picture," snapped Bourne. "Big picture. *Big picture*. Must I remind you that you are the Secretary of State? Think global. Worldview. Not of one stupid ship. Put that rust bucket out of your mind."

"We'll speak again soon," said Howard Leland.

"What was Bannerman's threat? That I won't live out the week?"

Leland had broken the connection.

"What have you turned into? His messenger boy? Are you there? Did you hang up on me?"

Dead air.

"Well, let me tell you something. Are you there? No,

you're not. I don't care. I'll tell you anyway. No, I won't. Yes, I will. We'll just see who lives out the week and who doesn't. I'll show you a field test you won't soon forget."

Bourne slammed his phone onto its cradle.

He rose from his chair. He said, "So mad, I could spit."

He said, "That's it. No more calls, no more weasels, no more cowards."

He said, "Calm yourself, Artemus. They're beneath you, every one of them. And you've spent too much time in this basement. Go upstairs to your study, put on some music, have a brandy. Strike a match to the fireplace, a nice cozy blaze. Take your atlas from its stand and peruse it, caress it. Your atlas never fails to smooth your brow. The big picture. The world. Your personal oyster. But calm down lest you spill your brandy on it."

Bourne left the room. He passed his bank of monitors. Motion on two of them caught his eye. It was only his guards on patrol in their Jeeps. He was about to turn away when he saw new activity. A guard at his north gate, the one approached through dense forest, had stepped out into the road and was raising the barrier. And there was Lilly's van coming up the dirt road.

Oh, bless you, Chester Lilly, thought Bourne.

His joy was short-lived. He thought he might go insane. Lilly had driven the van into the stables. Bourne had gone outside to await his arrival. He still was dressed in his robe.

He wanted to tell Lilly to pull right up front. The household staff had been dismissed; there was no need to be furtive. Are they both still unconscious? All well and good. Have Toomey and Kuntz bring them into the house. You and I will drag them down to the basement and show them to their new quarters.

Lilly emerged from the stables by himself. He said, "I didn't want to say on the phone. We had a few problems on the road."

He began his recital of how his man Kuntz had managed to suffocate Stride. Soon after that, Kuntz got into a brawl with a family of tourists looking on. "All we did was stop for gas. There was this thing with some farmer. We got out of there before the cops could be called. But they would have described Kuntz and the van he was in. Kuntz had to go. I had to use my best judgment. Besides, he deserved it for Stride."

Bourne was barely listening to Lilly's account. He was in his own mind. Stride is dead?

"As for Toomey, not only did he slit Stride's friend's throat, he left his own blood all over Stride's house. It's the same blood he left in Clew's parking garage. He had to go. I took their IDs. I dumped them in some swamp. They're both alligator food. With luck, they won't ever be found. I drove up the road a little. I found some parked cars. I couldn't dump the van, but I stole some new plates. The cops would have been looking for a van with three men in it. They would have been looking for Virginia plates, which is why . . ."

"Stride is dead?" asked Bourne softly. "Did you say Stride is dead?"

"Yeah, she is, but hold on. That might not be all bad. Anyway, that van still has Toomey's blood in it. We have to torch it and junk it real quick."

"You . . . see an advantage to Stride being dead? You assured me that she was alive."

"She was. But then Kuntz . . ."

"Never mind about Kuntz."

"Okay," said Lilly, "but what's done is done. Stride's dead, but no one else knows that she's dead. The kid doesn't know either. It was good we kept the kid. We take Stride to the basement, we strap her down like you planned. We lock the kid in Winfield's old room."

"Um . . . and then?"

"The kid wakes up, we let her look in through the window. We tell her Stride's drugged. She's not going to know different. You get word to Alameo, you tell him we have them. He wants proof? Let him talk to the kid."

Oh, how I hate you, thought Artemus Bourne.

"I know you're pissed," said Lilly. "My guys let me down. But with Clew, that was Claire. Claire was yours.

She wasn't mine. Even so, I took care of it. I cleaned up their mess. The question is what to do now."

Make the best of it, thought Bourne. And plan Lilly's slow death. Something rectal. On a tall sharpened pole.

"Bring them," said Bourne. "Carry them to the basement."

"Another thing I was thinking . . . that basement's pretty cool. Turn the thermostat down a few degrees more and Stride's body will keep for quite a while."

"See there? A silver lining already," said Bourne. "Whatever would I do without you?"

"Longer term, you've got your freezer. Stick her down with the heads. The thing is, longer term, you don't want to keep her here. You want to make them think you've got her stashed somewhere else, but you ought to hold on to the kid."

Bourne moistened his lips. The thought actually had some merit. That's assuming that the girl was . . . "She *is* alive, isn't she?"

"Oh, yeah. She's okay. I heard her talking."

"She's awake?"

"No, in her sleep. For the last forty miles. Phenobarbital does that, I guess."

Bourne nodded. "It would. It's a hypnotic."

"Hallucinating, right? Just as well. Kept her quiet. I don't think she even realizes we took her. She thinks she's someplace else with her mother and two, maybe three, other women she mentioned. It didn't sound like Stride was one of them, but she talked about Stride. She definitely thinks Stride's still alive."

"Thank pheno for small favors," said Bourne.

"The only time she got excited was just now when I pulled in. Her mother found some guy named Martin Kessler."

"Say again?"

"She was still out; don't worry. She settled right down."

Bourne said, "No, back up. Her *mother* found Kessler?"

"Yeah, that's how it sounded. Who's this Kessler?"

"Why would the girl's mother be looking for Kessler?"

"You're asking me to make sense of a dream? Anyway, who is he? You know him?"

Bourne's eyes had narrowed. "No, no, stay with the mother. Is it possible that the mother is Elizabeth Stride? Did it sound as if Stride could be her mother?"

Chester shrugged. "I didn't really get that impression. But it's possible, I guess. By their ages, just barely. And the coloring's the same. I never thought about that."

"And therefore might it follow that Kessler is her father?"

"Someone has to be, I guess. So who's this guy, Kessler?"

"Martin Kessler happens to be Alameo. Alameo is Martin Kessler."

"Hold it," said Lilly. He raised his hands. He stepped back. "Let's stick with one who's-who at a time. You knew right along what Alameo's real name was? How come you're only telling me now?"

"I told you that Alameo is one of his names. That should have suggested that he might have others. He was only of interest in his present context. What do you care what his name was before? What would you have done with that knowledge?"

"I could have known him a hell of a lot better," said Lilly. "Maybe had a lot more leverage against him. I could have found out where *his* mother lives. I'd have snatched her long before this."

"I'm ahead of you. He has no one. Only Stride."

"And now a daughter?" asked Lilly.

"Perhaps. If God is good. How long will she be unconscious?"

"I don't know. Ask the doctor who gave us the shots."

"No need. I can wait. We'll let her sleep it off."

"I'm going to need some sack time myself. I've been up two days and a night now. You want me to stay here or sack out at my own place?"

"You may stay," said Bourne. "Take the smaller of the guest rooms."

"With the cameras? No thanks. I might want to take a shit. I'll use one of the maids' rooms, top floor."

"As you wish."

Bourne could not have cared less where Lilly bedded down. His mind was on the near-miraculous gift that may have been dropped in his lap. Was it too much to hope for? Kessler's daughter with Stride? Even Kessler's without Stride or Stride's without Kessler. And Chester Lilly found her by the purest of chance. Even imbeciles get lucky now and then.

"Get the van," he said to Lilly. "Let us get them downstairs."

He could scarcely wait for the girl's head to clear. They would have a nice chat. Just the two of them.

37

It was five in the morning, Angola time. Kessler stood on the heights near the waterfall at Cuanza looking out upon VaalChem, some three miles distant. He watched through his night-vision scope. He had watched the arrival of the tanks and the soldiers and the gathering of fire trucks, a score of them.

He'd prepared his troops for the counterattack that would surely follow the rain of fire that he would soon visit upon VaalChem. Its destruction would begin at first light. He had fewer Katyushas than he'd wanted. Only twenty. He could have had more if he'd asked Duganga for them, but he had not consulted with Duganga. In addition to the rockets, he had six heavy mortars manned by crews that he had trained himself. They would pound through the roofs and then one floor at a time until they reached those that were well below ground. The fires would take weeks to extinguish.

The Mossad agent Yoni said, "Don't do this. I beg you."

He answered, "It should have been done long ago."

"You spoke to Netanya. He has given his word. Netanya

spoke to Bannerman. You have Bannerman's word. Your lady is safe. She is with Bannerman."

"Paul Bannerman has given his word before this."

"What, to not tell your lady that you are alive? How can you say that he was bound by that promise after Bourne found out where she was?"

"I believe that she's been taken. I do not believe she's safe."

The Mossad agent said, "I must tell you three things. I, too, will break my word as I tell you the first of them. Netanya had asked me to keep it from you. It's about Savran Bobik's arms shipment."

Kessler listened as he heard what had become of that freighter when the vial that he'd added was opened at sea. Most of the crew dead. All of Mobote's men dead. Mobote himself torn apart by the sharks. Twenty children on board, most of whom will surely die. The Liberians who boarded. Most of them will surely die.

Kessler didn't believe him. "So many dead already? It's been what? Three days? Four? What kind of virus works that quickly?"

"Not the virus. Not yet. They were shot, drowned, or eaten. Those shot or drowned were the lucky ones."

Kessler answered, "You told me. The sharks."

"It is true about the children. This is not an invention. You can call the Red Cross, World Health; they will tell you. You can call America's CDC in Atlanta. You can call the Liberians, a general named Tubbs. Everyone knows of this but you."

Kessler was still doubtful. "I would have been told."

"We kept you from knowing. For your own good and ours. You would have done something crazy."

Kessler's hand went to his chin. He said, "If this is true . . ."

"Now you're thinking, so let's get to the other two things. Those on the ship have a chance to be saved. What will save them is down there." He pointed at VaalChem. "We need what is down there to save them."

"Antivirals?"

"Precisely," said Yoni. "Unless you already have them. I refer to what you took from Winfield's office."

Kessler shook his head. "I don't know which is which. Most are marked with colored tape, nothing more."

"Did Winfield not tell you as he begged for his life?"

"He identified the worst of them. The Marburg. The smallpox. He said there were treatments, that he had antivirals. I took what he had, but as I've said, they were coded. Also, this was a hit-and-run raid. We didn't have all day to sort them out."

"Yet you took time to send three heads to Bourne."

Kessler looked away. He was silent.

"And it's hatred that is driving you now, Alameo. It's making you forget who your friends are. Who to trust."

Kessler remained silent. He was staring toward VaalChem.

"And now," said the agent, "we get to the third thing." As he spoke, he drew a pistol from his belt. He pressed its muzzle against Kessler's neck. Several troops were nearby. They shouted warnings to Kessler. They all turned their weapons on the agent.

The agent said, "I have been ordered to stop you from doing this. I asked, 'Yes, but how? How am I to survive?' All Netanya could do was repeat this hard order. He knew very well that I would die seconds later. So I ask, as a friend, would you please save my life?"

Kessler turned his head. He said a few words in Bantu. The soldiers eased their grip on their weapons, but slightly. He asked, "This is true? Netanya ordered my death?"

"With the greatest reluctance, I assure you," said Yoni. "This reluctance, I should tell you, is shared by Paul Bannerman. We won't even get into how reluctant I am, but believe me, I will shoot you right now."

"And Bannerman knows? He has given his approval?"

"Only if I'm unable to persuade you to wait."

"Wait for what?"

"One more day. He asked you to give him one day. Look at VaalChem. It's moving? It will be there tomorrow. I also wouldn't mind one more day."

Kessler turned. He paced. "Is Elizabeth truly with him?"

"He's your friend. How are you able to doubt him?"

"Because Bourne says he has her. It's possible that he's lying. But even if Bourne does not have Elizabeth, he has a certain young girl who owns part of my heart."

The agent shrugged. "If you don't mind a personal suggestion, why don't you stand down long enough to go see?"

"Go how? Through Tel Aviv? When I'm on your hit list?"

"Reluctant, Martin. That's the key word. What you're mostly on is a don't-blow-up-the-plant list. You're also on a don't-go-nuts-again list like you did when Bobik cut up Sara Gleissman. You'll recall, however, that I went nuts myself. I did worse than you to Savran Bobik."

Kessler took a breath. He rubbed his chin.

"This gun is getting heavy. Can we make a decision?"

"Put it down for the moment. Wait here."

Kessler walked to a soldier who wore captain's bars. It was the captain who went with him after Bobik. Kessler spoke to him quietly. The officer seemed troubled. But the officer nodded and reached into his collar. He extracted a small leather pouch that he wore hung from a thong around his neck. He pressed the pouch into Kessler's hand and embraced him.

He turned back to the agent. "You won't have to shoot me."

"That's a magic pouch he gave you? Then this gun won't work anyway."

"Three days," said Kessler. "You asked for one; I'll give you three. This officer is to assume that I'm dead if I am not back in three days. This officer will then lead the attack and he will obliterate VaalChem."

"Deal."

"After that he will execute the first ten Mossad agents that he's able to find in Angola."

"That's no good. You're not heading for a weekend in the country. You're going where someone is bound to get killed."

"Then I'm sure that you'll do your best to protect me. You're going to get me to the States in one piece. You're going to be at my side every moment."

"That does what? I wear a sign saying that this guy's with us? We're not all that popular either," said Yoni.

"Netanya will have known that I won't do Tel Aviv. He'd have given you options. What are they?"

"Small plane to Lagos, Lagos to Lisbon, Lisbon to Dulles, D.C. Better and quicker is direct from Luanda. An International Aid flight, nonstop, JFK. It's going back with doctors who've finished their tour. About a third of those doctors aren't doctors at all, but nobody messes with Aid flights."

"When?"

"Three hours," said the agent. "I can have papers waiting and I'll get you the right clothing. You will be Belgian, a researcher of AIDS. There is always a risk that you'll be stopped and detained, but we've done this before. Money talks."

"I'll be armed," said Kessler. "I will not be taken."

"You want extra insurance? I will give you my advice."

"Which is?"

"Don't walk in with that hat."

38

Bannerman was at home in his kitchen, fixing dinner for Susan and Cassie and the nurse. Bannerman and the nurse, a former combat nurse, Gulf War, had set up Cassie's old layette and crib after washing them down with disinfectant. The nurse had brought a wheelchair and made Susan use it. They'd have dinner out on the terrace.

Carla had stopped by, announced by her *Jaws* tone, with some of the photographs that she'd brought to Town Hall. They were down to only three. The same two men were in each.

In one they were joggers trotting together. In another they were cyclists riding on bikes that had probably been rented in town. In a third, they were driving together in a car. The face of the man in the passenger seat was obscured by a camera; he'd been taking pictures, but there was no mistaking the driver. They were both in their thirties, both lean and fit. They would not have stood out in Westport.

She said, "These are the two who were digging through records. They must like our little neighborhood a lot."

Bannerman asked, "Do we have anything more?"

Carla said, "I've made copies. We have people out looking, checking all the area motels for a start." She touched a finger to the photo of the two on their bikes. She said, "This one I remember. I saw them in the flesh. I was walking down the road from my place with Cassie. These two were pedaling from the opposite direction. They looked at us and one of them said something to the other. I didn't think anything of it at the time."

Bannerman asked, "Might they have known who you are?"

She shrugged and shook her head. "No, I didn't get that feeling. I thought they were paying more attention to Cassie, but that wouldn't have set off any alarms. People smile at her every day."

"Were they smiling on that day?"

"No, they weren't. Hey, we'll find them."

Bannerman said, "I expect to be busy tomorrow. Normally, I'd ask you if you'd care to be part of it."

"I told you. I'm in. For whatever."

"I'd rather have you here." He gestured toward the photos.

"Yeah, I figured. Don't worry. I'll stay close."

"There's this, and then our guests will be starting to arrive. Lesko and Elena should be here by noon. Harry Whistler and his crowd could show up any time. He never announces in advance. You'll know he's here when you see one of the twins."

"I know Harry's act. I'll take care of it," she said. "Have you heard any more from John Waldo?"

"He's late. It's been more than three hours."

"He's okay. Don't worry."

"I'd like to hear that from him."

Carla was dismissive. "I know his act, too. He'd see them before they'd see him."

"Would you like to stay for dinner? We have more than enough."

She said, "Thanks, but Viktor's made a pot of lamb stew. His mother's recipe; it sucks and it stinks up the house. But he thinks it's to die for. I pretend."

Not well, thought Bannerman. Viktor knows she gags it down. He's still getting even for her shooting him.

Waldo called as Bannerman was just sitting down. He excused himself from the table.

Waldo said, "Well, they're here. The Chester guy brought them."

"You saw them? What condition are they in?"

"Out cold, but no real damage from what I could see. Aisha's face is swollen. She has a black eye. The one they think is Stride . . ."

"They still do?"

"Oh, yeah. That's what I heard them call her. Right now they got her strapped to a cot. I got one look, but I had to be quick. Aisha's in the next room; it's like a regular bedroom. She was taped, but not now. They're letting her sleep. Bourne peeks in through the glass now and then."

"She's locked in?"

"Both of them. I told you. Heavy steel doors with windows. You need a key card to get in. I'd try them, but I think they're both rigged to alarms and I need time to dope out the system. I found the one on the freezer, but that Mosler door's tough. I told you it's a vault? I can't open it."

"It'll keep."

He said, "Listen, there's Bourne and there's the Chester guy; that's it. They were saying something happened to the other two guys, but I couldn't hear much of that part. So there's only these two. This is not a big deal. Tell me why I don't finish this now."

"John, as I've said, there's more to it than this. I'm trying to work several strings."

"One of them's Kessler?"

"He's the most urgent, yes. We might not be able to save him."

"Could he be Aisha's father?"

"Kessler? Of course not. That's not possible, no."

Waldo asked, "Then could Stride be her mother? I mean, I know she can't have kids. But maybe before her insides got shot up . . ."

"Out of the question. We know Aisha's history. Lebanese mother, Egyptian father. You're not asking this idly. What's happened?"

"Well, I'm not clear on this. I only overheard parts. But Bourne has got it into his head that her parents might be Kessler and Stride."

This gets more bizarre by the moment, thought Bannerman. "If he thinks so, he'll be sure to keep her healthy."

"Trust me, she's good. I won't let anything happen. I might spend the night down there anyway."

"In the basement?"

Waldo grumbled. "Yeah, there's a closet I can use. That pain in the ass, Lilly, took one of the maid's rooms. I thought I'd have the third floor to myself. Second floor, there's the peep shows, but I better stay out of them."

"You're referring to the rooms with the cameras?"

"The guest rooms, yeah. I found cameras in the big ones. I didn't check the others, but I shouldn't take a chance. This closet in the basement has two shelves full of tapes. I can't sit around and watch them, but I looked at the labels. Lots of names that you'd recognize with some woman named Claire. Looks to me they got taped playing whoopee."

Bannerman asked, "Is Howard Leland's name among them?"

"I didn't see that one. I don't think so."

"Bourne might get a visit from Leland tomorrow."

"Just from Leland?"

"And whomever. Get some rest."

Bannerman heated his plate in the microwave oven. Once again, he was about to return to the terrace when heard the first bar of "Pretty Woman." Molly Farrell knocked and entered minutes later, looking pleased.

She said, "Kessler's okay. They stopped him in time. They're sneaking him out. He's coming here."

A sigh of relief. "Coming when?"

"Netanya says barring any unexpected problems, sometime tomorrow, not before mid-afternoon. One of Netanya's top agents is escorting him. He's been told about the freighter. He had no idea. Netanya *thinks* he's been persuaded that Elizabeth is safe, but even Netanya's in the dark about Aisha. I promised him that Aisha will be fine. Will she be fine?"

"She seems to be now. Waldo saw her."

"Well, why doesn't he . . ."

He stopped her. "One thing at a time. Finish what you were saying about Kessler."

"Kessler has to be back in three days. If he isn't, VaalChem gets flattened."

A soft smile from Bannerman. "He's no fool."

"And Netanya wants to know if his agent can stay for the conference we're having this week."

"Did you tell him that it's only a gathering? Friends and family?"

"Sure, but we both know he'd never believe it. He knows that people aren't coming from as far away as Moscow just to grin and make faces at a baby."

"Netanya's not so dumb either," said Bannerman.

"He says he knows that you won't let his agent sit in. But he asks if we can give him an hour to discuss what ought to be done about Angola."

"I think everyone's been doing quite enough about Angola. But I owe him one for Kessler. We'll listen."

Molly nodded. "On to Bourne. What do we do about Bourne."

"I won't ask you . . ."

"Oh, stop that. Who's hitting him and when?"

"I was thinking that I might drop in by myself. He and I need to have a quiet talk."

She glared at him. "When?"

"Tomorrow morning sometime. Can you keep Elizabeth under control until I can resolve this with Bourne?"

"Yes, I can, but I won't. I'm coming. So is Billy. And so, by God, is Elizabeth Stride. By yourself? What the heck are you thinking?"

"Waldo's there. He's in place. I don't need to go in blasting."

Her hands went to her hips. "Paul, what time?"

"You're not listening."

"I asked you what time."

"Okay, but not Stride. All she'll want is blood. She should stay here and wait for Martin Kessler."

"This is Aisha. Her Aisha. Stride's in it."

"Besides, all that Seconal. She might still be in a fog. I'll want nothing but clear heads around me."

"Paul . . . when and where? Or I make my own plans."

"Bridgeport airstrip at six in the morning."

39

Bourne had overslept. His bedside clock read almost nine. He was usually awakened with his breakfast tray at seven. He reached for his intercom and pressed the button for the kitchen. There was no answer from the kitchen. He pressed for his butler. No answer there either. Next he pressed the button for the gatehouse.

A guard answered, "Sir?"

"Have any staff been through yet?"

"No, sir. We haven't seen them."

"Have any at least called to say they'd be late?"

"No, sir. Not to the gate."

"Well, damn it, they did not get the whole weekend off. Get on the phone. Round them up. I want them all here. They have a brunch to prepare."

"Right away, sir."

Except it might not be much of a brunch, thought Bourne. We'll see who shows up. It will be a good test. It will separate the wimps from the chaff.

And where's Lilly? Bourne wondered. Ah, yes. Servants' quarters. He started pressing all the buttons that called the third floor. One of them found Lilly. His voice was befogged. He managed a "Yeah, what?" through a yawn.

"Get up. It's late. Go down and put on some coffee."

"You woke me up for that? Call the kitchen."

"I did. No one's there. There's been some sort of a mix-up. Get cracking. I'll be down in the basement."

Bourne, still dressed in his robe and pajamas, pulled the rack of dessert wines aside. He closed it behind him and sealed it. He stopped first at the monitors that scanned the exterior. The main gate and the north gate were both manned, two guards each. He saw one Jeep, then the other. They were both on patrol. All seemed quiet. All seemed normal. All the guards seemed alert. Not the dogs, though; they were napping. Bourne took that to be a good sign.

He went to the door of Cecil Winfield's laboratory. He looked in through the glass. Stride was just as they'd left her. She was on her right side in a slumbering pose. There had, of course, been no need to strap her down. Bourne had covered her with a blanket taken from the next room. He had brought her left hand up under her chin and entwined the blanket's edge in her fingers. It had seemed a nice touch. Very natural.

He stepped to the door of the bedroom adjoining and peered through its eye-level window. He was startled to see that the girl's bed was empty. He leaned closer to scan the rest of the room. He saw her. She was there after all.

She was sitting very quietly on one of Winfield's leather chairs, a duvet wrapped around her for warmth. Tanned bare legs protruded from her short tennis dress. He'd see later about getting her some suitable clothing. His wife must have left a few things scattered somewhere. Or perhaps from one of the maids.

A lovely girl, isn't she, he thought to himself. She'll become a real stunner if she lives to grow up. And she might, but she'd have to grow up in this house. He couldn't very well let her go while he lived. But with some patience, the

right tutoring, she might learn to like it. She might even
learn to like him.

He drew an electronic key from his pocket. He slid it into
a slot that disabled the alarm. He withdrew it, inverted it, and
slid it in again. A loud click and the bolt fell away. He pulled
the door open. She turned her head and looked up at him.
She did not seem especially frightened. Only sad.

He said, "Have no fear. I will not harm you in the slightest. My name is Artemus. And yours?"

She said softly, "My name is Aisha."

"I . . . know how upsetting this must be for you. In good
time, I'll explain to you why you're here. I'll explain how
terribly important you are. If you're as bright as you look,
you'll understand."

She asked, "Where am I? What day is today?"

"It's a Sunday. You haven't been here very long. A good
friend of yours is here. Elizabeth Stride. She's sleeping in
the next room."

Her eyes widened. She said, "I don't believe you."

"Oh, she's there. I'll let you look. But you must tell me
the truth. She's your mother, is she not? I want the truth."

She started to rise. "Let me look."

"First the truth."

"Let me look," she said calmly, "or I will not speak
again." She drew her knees to her chest.

"Very well," said Bourne. "But we mustn't disturb her.
We've had to sedate her. She's sleeping."

Chester Lilly had dressed and spent five minutes on his hair
before going down to the kitchen. He found the makings of
coffee, put it on, and as it dripped, he looked to see what he
could find in the fridge. There were several carafes of assorted
fruit juices. He chose orange, took the carafe, and walked
toward the front hall, sipping from the carafe as he went.

He, too, thought it strange that the help had not arrived.
He stepped into Bourne's study and went to Bourne's desk.
Bourne's big atlas was on it as usual. There was also another
intercom unit, one of several that were scattered through the
house. He pressed the button that buzzed the main gate.

The guard's voice said, "Sir?"

"This is Lilly. What's happening?"

"It's all very quiet down here, Mr. Lilly."

"Who's this?"

"Lawson, sir."

He asked, "What's with the help?"

"Mr. Bourne was right. There was some misunderstanding. They'll be here just as soon as they can get here."

Lilly broke the connection. He stepped to Bourne's window. It looked out on several acres of manicured lawn. He blinked when he saw a man standing there. An older man, white hair; he was dressed in dark clothing. He stood, arms folded, looking up at the sky. Lilly turned away and went back to the intercom. He pressed the same button as before.

"Yes, sir?" came Lawson's voice.

"Who's this guy on the lawn?"

"Sir, I'm not really sure. He's some kind of security. He's waiting for some of your brunch guests to arrive."

"Some kind of security? That's all you know?"

"That's all he was willing to say, sir."

"Jesus Christ," said Lilly. "You're a shit-head, you know that? Do you at least know which guests he's waiting for?"

"No, sir. I'm afraid I've neglected to ask."

I don't believe this, thought Lilly. I'll go ask him myself. And then I'll get Lawson's ass fired.

Aisha had to stretch to look through the small pane. She saw Nadia on the cot. She did appear to be sleeping. But she knew, mind and soul, that Nadia was dead. She'd seen Nadia and Jasmine with her mother.

She knew that they were well and that her mother would care for them. Tears spilled onto her cheeks all the same. She asked Bourne, without turning, "Where is Jasmine?"

"Jasmine?" asked Bourne. "I don't think I know the name."

"She was with us. There were three of us. A black woman. We played tennis."

"Oh, that one," said Bourne. "No, she's perfectly fine. My men had to tie her up, but she's surely free by now. We're going to let her know that you're safe."

"Yes, she'd worry."

"You haven't answered me yet. You've seen Elizabeth. And you've promised."

"What are you going to do with her?" asked Aisha.

"Well, before she wakes up, we're going to move her someplace else. I understand fully that you'd like to be together, but it's better for me if you're not."

"I see."

"Is Elizabeth your mother?"

Aisha wet her lips. She nodded.

To lie was a sin. She would do penance later. But to tell this kidnapper, this murderer, the truth, seemed to her that it would be helpful to him. That would be a greater sin than her lie.

She kept her eyes fixed on Nadia's body. She wished that she was able to dream right this moment. Perhaps by now, she'd be able to speak to her. The man's breath had quickened in response to her nod. She heard him swallow before speaking again.

He said, "She must have had you at a very young age. Have you been with her ever since. All your life?"

Aisha shook her head. "She took many long trips. Sometimes for years at a time."

"Were these trips . . . with your father? Martin Kessler?"

The name, and that question, took her by surprise. She had very nearly answered with the truth. She steadied herself. She said, "Sometimes."

"So, he *is* your father?"

"He's been away, too."

She felt, rather than saw, that this man had pumped his fist. These answers had pleased him for some reason.

He said, "Oh yes, he has. He has been away indeed. Your father's been in Africa. Did you know that?"

"No, I didn't."

"Well, your father has threatened to do something naughty. You and I are going to save him from himself. I'm going to put you on the phone to a man named Duganga. You'll tell him who you are. He'll get a message to your father. I think your father will call back very soon after that.

When he does, you can speak to him as long as you like. So, you see? I'm not such a bad fellow."

Aisha nodded. "I would like that. Very much."

"Now go back in your room while I call."

"Hey, you," called Lilly as he strode across the lawn.

The man glanced in his direction, then back at the sky. His arms were still folded on his chest.

"Hey, you, you old fart. I'm talking to you. Who said you could stand here like this?"

The man said, "Name's Waldo. I'm waiting for Leland."

"You say you're with Leland? Let me see some ID."

Waldo said, "You're Lilly, right? I knew from the hair. You got a really nice head of hair."

"Yeah, well . . ."

"Roger Clew's was okay, but he didn't take care of it. Some mousse, a good stylist . . . he'd at least be in the game. But even before someone tried to peel off his scalp, he didn't belong in your league."

Lilly's fingers had crept to the butt of his pistol. Waldo said, "Don't do that. Check my armpit."

He raised his left elbow so that Lilly could see the silenced Beretta that was leveled at his chest. But Waldo was no longer looking at Lilly. He gestured with his chin toward the northeast horizon. He said, "Chopper coming. Just stand there. Don't move. If you move, I shoot off both your kneecaps."

Lilly did move, but carefully. He reached for his cell phone. He said, "I have to tell Bourne Leland's coming."

"Yeah, you should."

Lilly saw the helicopter. It had State Department markings. He felt a measure of relief, but this still felt wrong. He tapped out two digits. He whispered, "Code One."

Waldo asked, "You're calling Bourne? I don't think that was Bourne."

"More security," said Lilly. "This is normal."

Waldo said, "The thing is, you said you have to call Bourne. You should do what you say you're going to do."

Lilly broke the connection. He tapped two more digits. He

waited. Bourne answered. Bourne's voice sound distant and crackled. He said, "Mr. Bourne, we have company. It's Leland." He lowered his voice. "Don't come out here just yet."

The helicopter came in low. It hovered over the lawn. Before setting down, it made two full revolutions, clearly scouting its surroundings before landing. During one of the turns, it had paused as if pointing. A Jeep had appeared, an armed guard and a dog. The aircraft paused once again, this time pointing toward the forest. A second Jeep was emerging. Again, an armed guard. Both had scope-mounted rifles. The two Jeeps paused at either end of the lawn. Both guards slung their rifles into firing position, sighting in across the tops of their windshields.

Lilly said to Waldo, "Hey, dick-face, look around you. Now tell me who's going to shoot who?"

Waldo said, "Yeah, I see them. So you won't need your gun." He reached with his left hand. "Put it here."

"Kiss my ass."

Waldo shattered the first of his kneecaps.

Howard Leland had asked to come to Briarwood with Bannerman. He'd come close to insisting, or no deal. He said that he wanted to make good on his promise to slap Bourne's face raw before arresting him. It was more than just Clew. It was kidnapping, murder, and depraved indifference to the plight of the people who were still on that quarantined freighter. To a lesser extent it was those peep shows that were found. The betrayal of Bourne's guests by making videotapes of whatever had gone on in those guest rooms.

"Might you be on them?" asked Bannerman.

"Those who know me wouldn't ask. But feel free to look. If I'm lying, destroy me. If I'm not, destroy the tapes. That's unless you're a blackmailer. Are you?"

"Oh yes," said Bannerman. "I am, indeed. But not over this or anything like it. I will destroy all the tapes."

"I *will* go with you," Leland said once again. "I've lost interest in saving my political ass. I will bear any cost that comes with it."

"And you've been a welcome surprise to me, sir. Your air-craft and your pilot will suffice."

He knew that he and Waldo could have done this by them-selves. Waldo, in fact, had already done most of it. The rest could be minimally violent. But neither Molly nor Billy would be denied, nor would they deny Elizabeth Stride.

Elizabeth had awakened from her enforced sleep to find Molly sitting astride her. Awakening, she remembered who had put her to sleep. She bucked and she tried to bite at Molly. Molly slapped her and said, "We are going to get Aisha. You'll agree to do *only* what you are told or we'll put you under again and we'll leave you."

Elizabeth stared with murderous eyes. Molly Farrell slapped her again.

She repeated, "Elizabeth, we're going to get Aisha. Paul doesn't want you with us. I insisted. Was I wrong?"

Her eyes softened slightly. They blinked questioningly.

Molly told Elizabeth, "You'll come as you are. No blacks, no blue duffel, no weapons; you won't need them. Aisha's safe. So is Nadia. Waldo's found them. Say you hear me."

"I hear you," said Elizabeth quietly.

"Kessler's coming. Not with us. He's coming here. You'll see him later. Would you rather wait for him here?"

Her eyes began to moisten. She seemed overwhelmed. She swallowed. She said, "Get Aisha first."

"Swear to me. Promise. You'll do only what you're told."

She whispered. "When?"

"Right now."

She said, "I swear it."

It was a three-hour flight to Bourne's sprawling estate. Eliz-abeth and Molly wore dark jumpsuits and boots. Elizabeth's had been borrowed from Molly. Billy McHugh wore loose-fitting leathers that made him seem even more massive than he was. Bannerman was dressed in a gray suit and tie not un-like the suit that he'd last seen on Leland.

He'd told Elizabeth what he'd learned from John Waldo as early as six o'clock that morning. All was quiet. Nadia still slept. Aisha could be heard up and moving about. Neither seemed at immediate risk.

She asked, "They're in Bourne's house? And you know where, exactly?"

He nodded. "But first I need to have a talk with Bourne. He is not to be harmed by you or anyone."

"Until then?"

"Until whenever," said Bannerman. "He is not to be harmed."

"Are . . . you telling me that you might let this man live?"

"We'll see. We might need him. But be clear on this, Elizabeth. It's not going to be your decision."

She was silent for a moment. "Are you testing me, Paul?"

"You've always worked alone. I do not. We do not. You've worked out of hatred. We try not to."

Molly told him, "She swore. She'll do as she's told."

Stride answered, "As long as . . ." She thought better of finishing. She'd seen Bannerman's eyes. She lowered her own eyes and nodded.

Bannerman had a map of Bourne's estate in his hand from the package that Zivic had prepared. He asked the pilot to pass low over all approaches before proceeding to the house and outbuildings. Two roads seemed to be the only access. First they buzzed the main gatehouse. They saw two guards looking up at them. They stood at parade rest, in their uniforms, wearing side arms. Their faces wore sullen expressions. They flew on to the north gate a half mile distant. Two more uniformed guards. They seemed equally unhappy.

The pilot said, "I think I saw some other movement down there. Bourne might have called in some reinforcements."

"He hasn't," said Bannerman. "Let's get up to the house."

They followed the north road. The pilot gestured with his chin. He asked, "Is that your man on the lawn?"

Molly looked. She said, "That's John Waldo. What's he doing?"

"He's waiting for us. And he's waiting for that one." Bannerman nodded toward the wavy-haired man who was crossing the front lawn toward Waldo. He said to Elizabeth, "That would be Chester Lilly. Your forbearance is about to be tested."

McHugh said, "Here's trouble. Two Jeeps moving fast. Sniper rifles and dogs. They'll have Waldo between them."

Bannerman showed no concern. "I'm surprised at you, Billy."

McHugh squinted. Then he got it. "Oh, yeah, sorry."

Elizabeth asked, "What is all this 'don't worry'? I count six armed guards and that's only what's in sight. Those rifles can knock us out of the air and we have three handguns between us."

Bannerman asked Molly, "Is Elizabeth armed?"

"Two knives, boot and sleeve. She thinks I don't know it."

"You will leave them where they are, please, Elizabeth."

As he spoke, they saw Chester Lilly go down. He was on the lawn writhing. He was gripping his knee. Elizabeth's head turned toward the two Jeeps, expecting those guards to turn their weapons on Waldo. They didn't. The men in the Jeeps made no move. Their attention was fixed on the front of the house. Nor did the dogs react to the shot. Even silenced, they still should have heard it.

"They're ours," Billy told her.

"Which are ours?" asked Elizabeth.

"These two in the Jeeps. Not the ones at the gates. But the ones at the gates must have our guys close by making sure that they do what they're told. The two who used to be driving those Jeeps are sitting around somewhere in their shorts."

"And the dogs?"

"Darts, I hope. No one's mad at the dogs. No one likes it when we have to kill dogs."

The helicopter settled. The engines were cut. Bannerman was the first to alight. He extended a hand to Elizabeth, who ignored it.

Elizabeth asked Bannerman, "You knew all this coming down here?"

"As I've told you," he answered, "we work as a team. No, I didn't know it, but I did expect it. John had told me that he'd gather a few people."

"Why the suit, by the way?"

"We have business to discuss. And it seemed a good idea to have Bourne think I'm Leland until we were safely on the ground."

"So, what now?"

"Down to business. I will meet with Mr. Bourne. You will join me, but you're not to speak."

"I'll join you after I find Aisha and Nadia." She stepped to the lawn unassisted.

"Look at me, Elizabeth. You've just had your last chance. You won't get another warning from me."

She did look at him. It was a different Paul Bannerman. The Bannerman that she'd described to Aisha was gone. It was all in the eyes and the voice; they'd gone cold. They were telling her that if she said one more word, it would be the last thing she'd remember.

Waldo approached Bannerman. He handed him a cell phone. He said, "This is Lilly's. He just used it to call Bourne. Bourne will be looking out a window by now. Hit Redial if you want to say hello." He said to Elizabeth, "You're along for the ride. You won't get another warning from me either."

Her hand almost went to one of her knives. She struggled to remain still and silent.

Molly said to Bannerman, "You're calling it. Who does what?"

"You stick with Waldo. Follow John's lead. Billy, I would like you to interrogate Chester. Do it up near the house. Do it where Bourne can hear him. But don't let him die; I might need him."

Billy nodded. "You want this guy loud; he'll be loud. First Clew. We'll talk about Clew."

"Let's do this," said Bannerman. "I'd like to get home. I think we're going to have a full day."

40

Bourne had wondered why Chester Lilly would say, "Leland's coming, but stay in the house." He'd come up from the basement and looked out a front window in time to see Lilly go down. He was holding his knee in obvious pain and Bourne could see blood on his hands. Bourne had heard no loud report; he'd not seen a weapon, but Lilly was behaving as if he'd been shot. A smallish older man had been standing there near him. Now the smallish older man was ignoring him.

Moments later, he'd seen the helicopter arrive. It was Leland's helicopter. He'd said he might come. He'd seen a man emerge from it; he'd thought it was Leland, but this man was considerably younger than Leland. He was followed by two women, also young, wearing jumpsuits and at last by a huge man in leather. He recognized none of them. Where was Leland?

He had seen the two Jeep guards. They had come, but they'd done nothing.

Nor did their dogs react to the activity.

Bourne rushed to his study. He buzzed the main gate.

"Yes, sir?"

"Who are they? What is this? What is happening?"

"Sir, I don't think we can be very helpful. We've got our own problems down here. We'll get shot."

"Shot? Shot by whom?"

"They haven't told us who they are, sir."

"Have you called the police?"

"Sir, I said we'd get shot. We've . . ." He paused. "Sir, hold on please."

Another brief pause and the guard came back on. "Sir, he says you're welcome to try calling them yourself. He really does not seem to mind, sir."

Bourne snarled in frustration. He broke the connection. He turned and stepped to the window again. The small man who'd been waiting had Chester by the hair. Chester was struggling to reach a pistol that he must have dropped on the grass. The man holding him didn't seem to be paying much attention. But each time Chester reached, the man would give his head a shake. The idea that an older man could do that to Chester . . .

Now the man released Chester and approached the new arrivals. He addressed them, especially the two women. He handed something—a cell phone?—to the man in the suit. He and one of the women, the one with dark hair, turned away and began to walk toward the house. The man in the suit and the blond one remained. The big one in leather took Chester by the collar and was dragging him up toward the stables.

The police, thought Bourne. You're damned right I'll try. I'll have a Swat team up here in ten minutes.

Bourne did try. He used the phone on his desk. There was nothing, no dial tone. His desk phone was dead. It was true. The lines had been cut. But they can't cut a cell phone. Lilly'd called him on his cell phone. Where is it? thought Bourne. Oh, right here in my pocket. Bourne fished it out. He punched 911. He got a recording, very faint, broken up. It said something about limited range. He stared at the phone. Its low-voltage light was flashing. The LED readout was dim.

"You're welcome to try," said the intruder at the gate who must have known that no phone would function. But how? And when? When could this have been done? His cell phone had never been farther than his bedside. Could a prowler have already been in the house? Standing over him? While he was sleeping?

It rang. The sound shocked him. Bourne nearly dropped it. The police perhaps. They might have traced his 911 call. He fumbled with his thumb for the button.

He sputtered, "Hello? This is Artemus Bourne."

"And this is Paul Bannerman," said the answering voice. "We have a few things to discuss."

He had wanted to hide, but it would be of no use. It would also be beneath him. Demeaning. He might have wanted to fight, but he had no weapons except for a few antique swords above the mantel. He put them out of his mind. He'd look ridiculous.

Above all, he was Artemus Bourne, for God's sake. He owned half the government. They needed him. They owed him. And Bannerman was nothing. More legend than substance. Bannerman would be hunted for the rest of his life if he touched one hair on his head.

Well, he's more than nothing. Let's be honest about that. One should never undervalue an opponent. Just look at what he'd already done. Holding gate guards at gunpoint. Holding Briarwood hostage. Turning away any guests that might have come, turning away household staff.

And the guest list, somehow getting it, and distributing Clew's exchanges regarding that damnable ship. It's now abundantly clear how he got it, thought Bourne. He got it from Leland, the coward, the traitor. Leland even provided transportation.

Even so, remember, you are Artemus Bourne. Be cool. You're a giant. You are dealing from strength. They have Chester, but Chester will keep his mouth shut. Chester Lilly won't cut his own throat.

He'd said to Bannerman, "You may enter. You will find me in my study. Be good enough to wipe your feet first."

And he did. Bourne could hear them outside the front door. Two pairs of feet entered. A man and a woman. He expected to see Bannerman appear at his study, but it was the other one, the one who'd shot Lilly, and the darker-haired of the two women.

The woman entered first. She saw him seated at his desk. She said to him, "Please show your hands." The man with her told her, "Don't worry. Room's clean."

"His desk?"

He said, "Trust me. Room's clean."

Two more pairs of feet. This time it was Bannerman. Bannerman and the much lighter-haired of the two. Bannerman surprised him. He had rather a nice face. No hint of malevolence in his expression. Not so, the blond woman. A quite beautiful woman. Or she would be in some other circumstance. Her expression seemed frozen, lips pressed tight together, eyes that bored into him unblinking. A strange color, those eyes. A curious amber. He'd only seen that color in animals.

Bannerman said, "While you and I talk, my friends would like to look around. Do you mind if they do a little browsing?"

"I leap to the assumption that they already have. That and this," said Bourne, "is criminal trespass. Not to mention felonious assault."

"Might you have a secret room that they haven't yet found?" He gestured toward the ceiling, toward Bourne's upper floors.

Bourne was instantly relieved. He'd gestured upward, not downward. They may have been to his basement, but they'd not found his shelter. They knew nothing of what stood beyond the wine racks.

Bourne glanced toward the ceiling. He pretended discomfort. "I forbid any further violation of my home. I forbid you to poke about rapping on walls. State your business, then vacate at once."

He saw Bannerman nod toward the one who shot Chester. A toss of his head asked that man to proceed with a search of the upper floors. The dark-haired woman seemed confused by the instruction. Bannerman said to her, "Molly, go with him, please." She obeyed, but still with misgivings.

The blond woman with Bannerman seemed ready to burst. She was looking into Bannerman's eyes; she seemed to be pleading with him. She didn't speak, but it was clear that she wished to search with them. He said to her, "Soon. Stay with me."

From nowhere came the sound of a shriek. Then another, and a third. They were coming from outside. Then the sound of a man bawling, a hysterical bawling. Then the bawling became muffled. As if a door had been shut. But the shrieks, although muted, reached an even higher pitch.

Bannerman had led the blond woman to a chair. He said, "That would be Chester Lilly."

Bourne turned ashen. "What are you doing to him?"

"I don't know exactly. Shall we go see?"

Bourne shook his head. He sank into his chair. He put his hands to his ears.

Bannerman walked to a window. He said, "I'm curious myself. Your man Lilly has been making some very odd sounds."

He opened the window. The shrieks became louder. Bannerman leaned his head out and looked off to his right. He said, "Oh, my." He pulled his head back inside. He said to Bourne, "You really should see this."

Bourne closed his eyes. He kept them squeezed shut. He refused to move from his chair.

He heard Bannerman say to the woman who'd stayed with him, "Where those screams became muted, but then hit some new notes, Billy had found a row of beehives back there. He picked up one of the hives and slapped it down on Chester's head. Chester's wearing the whole hive on his shoulders."

Bourne looked. Her eyes had widened, but she still hadn't spoken.

Bannerman said, "I'm being rude. I haven't introduced my friend. We'll get to that in a minute." He said, "Chester's being asked about Roger Clew. I would assume that he's incriminating you."

"I . . . had no role . . ."

"Do you like bees, Mr. Bourne?"

"I had . . . wanted to know what was in certain files. They were to be borrowed. All I asked for was his briefcase. Chester . . . I don't know . . . he had some personal grudge. I was horrified to learn what had been done."

"Two men and a woman were also involved. The woman is dead. Where are the men?"

"Those two . . . have been punished for that terrible act. As I've said, I was horrified . . ."

"I heard you. Dead as well?"

"I'm assured that they won't be seen again."

"And no doubt you intended the same fate for Chester?"

Bourne leaned forward. "Rely on it, sir. Believe that if you believe nothing else."

"Well," shrugged Bannerman. "Then that seems to be that. Are you of a mind to do me a favor?"

"If there is . . . any other way in which I can make amends . . ."

"There's a freighter off Liberia. I think you know the one I mean. And you know they've had a problem with one of your products. I know that Howard Leland asked if you'd care to help. You declined. I'm asking you to reconsider."

"It *isn't* my product. It *might* be VaalChem's product. If someone at VaalChem is making such poisons, they certainly haven't told me."

"Uh-huh. Well, it's Marburg. And probably smallpox. Your phones aren't working, so you can use mine." He placed his cell phone on Bourne's desk. "I'd like you to call VaalChem now as I sit here. Have them rush a supply of antivirals to that freighter. It must be specific to both Marburg and smallpox. Assume fifty treatments to be safe."

"You are assuming that these antivirals exist."

"Uh-huh," said Bannerman. "Make the call, please."

"And are you aware that I have no guilt in this? No role, whatsoever. That was Kessler."

"Why don't you and Kessler hash that out some other time? Please make the call now, Mr. Bourne?"

Bourne, once again, felt a surge of relief at his use of the phrase, "some other time." He said, "Gladly." He reached for the phone.

Bannerman said, "Have them flown by air courier to Liberia. From Liberia, deliver them by seaplane to that freighter. Send them to the attention of a certain Major Scar. I'm not sure that's his name, but he's known by it. If he should be ill, give them to Scar's wife. She's Red Cross, and I'm told that she's with him. They must be on that freighter by this time tomorrow. If they get there, and they work, you'll have my thanks, Mr. Bourne. Please call VaalChem this minute. We'll wait."

Molly was listening from the top of the stairs. She asked Waldo, "Why did he send us up here?"

"He knows what he's doing. Sit tight."

"Bourne thinks we don't know what he has in his basement. He thinks this is all about Roger and that ship."

"One thing at a time. There's a rhythm," said Waldo.

"Don't you think it might be helpful if you filled me in on it?"

"No offense," said Waldo, "but what would have been helpful was if you and Stride stayed in Westport. Paul and me could have done this ourselves."

"Listen, John . . ."

"Right now it would be me who was out there with Chester. Chester would be making the same kind of noises. Bannerman would be in there; he'd be messing with Bourne's head, without worrying whether Stride would blow his act."

"John . . . why didn't we just take him to the basement door and kick his loathsome ass down the stairs?"

"Because Bannerman thought this out. He's not like you and me."

"Did you . . . just then, forget to say, 'No offense'?"

Waldo rolled his eyes. "I should have said, 'in this case.' Right now, you and Stride just want Nadia and the kid. After that, all Stride wants is to cut this guy up. You heard Bannerman. He's getting a few things off the table. He just covered Clew and now he's doing that ship. He's also deciding whether he can trust Stride."

"Trust her to do what?"

"To play well with others. Not just for now. Now and later."

"Are you saying that Paul has other plans for Elizabeth?"

Waldo shrugged. He said, "It's more like, where else is she going to go? She can't just waltz back to Hilton Head Island. Her house is a crime scene and she's disappeared. Also she's no longer dead. Nadia and Aisha; they can go back, but Elizabeth's life there is finished."

"I suppose," said Molly. "But at least she's found Kessler. He won't stay, though. He's got to go back."

"You mean he's coming?"

"Not for more than two days."

"No, I mean coming here. Could he show up here?"

Molly shook her head. "Not to this place. To Westport. Sometime today. That's one reason why Paul said he wants to get back. I thought we'd be in and out by now."

"All we'd need," said Waldo, "is him showing up here. It's bad enough you and Stride . . ."

"Oh, shut up."

Bannerman had listened as Bourne made his call. The noise from outside had subsided into moans. Bourne had to ask for several scientists by name before he found one who had remained at his post. The one he spoke to, a virologist, had also tried to leave, but VaalChem was encircled by Angolan tanks, by fire trucks, and by several hundred troops. The virologist was in a state of near panic. An attack by Alameo might be imminent.

Bannerman grimaced inwardly. He had forgotten. Kessler had aborted the rocket attack, but no one told that to the Angolans.

"You may tell him," said Bannerman, "that he needn't be afraid. You may tell him that there will be no attack. Get him started preparing the package."

Bourne asked, "Are you saying that you've called Kessler off? You can do that? One word from you?"

Bannerman flicked a hand as if the answer were obvious. He asked, "What exactly is he sending and when?"

Bourne asked. He listened. He reached for a pad. He scribbled several notations. Bourne tore off the sheet. He handed it to Bannerman. He said, "These will be ready in an hour at most. He wants to know how he gets them past the tanks."

Bannerman glanced at the sheet. He raised an eyebrow without comment. He slipped the sheet into his pocket. He said, "Tell him that someone will come for them shortly. End the call and give the phone back to me."

Bourne did as he was told. He slid the phone back toward Bannerman. Bannerman took it and punched out a number. He waited; a voice answered: He said to the voice, "I must ask you to hold any questions for now. I need the United States Embassy in Luanda to facilitate a shipment from VaalChem to Liberia. The contact's name is . . ." He raised an eyebrow toward Bourne.

Bourne said, "Shamsky. Doctor Nikolai Shamsky."

Bannerman repeated the name to his listener. He said, "VaalChem has been quarantined by Angolan troops. You may tell their commander that he can stand down, but either way, that shipment must get out of VaalChem."

Bannerman listened and replied, "No, not yet, but shortly. I'll advise you as soon as I can."

He'd completed the call. He saw Bourne staring at him. Bourne asked, "Who was that? Will you tell me?"

"Howard Leland."

Bourne's mouth fell open. "I suppose I might have guessed. And those antivirals. You recognized them? You know them?"

The hand flicked again. Like the last, it was a lie. The only word he recognized was "lipid," a fat. He would, however, ask Greta Kirch to explain what the other scribbles meant.

Bourne asked, "And is it true that you forestalled that attack?"

"It's a valuable facility. Not entirely well used. That's why you're going to sign VaalChem over to a management group of my choosing."

"I . . . confess to being greatly impressed by you, sir. But you will, by God, not have VaalChem."

Bannerman cocked his ear. Lilly's moaning had stopped. He said, "We seem to be giving Chester Lilly a rest. Is there anything that you'd care to tell me?"

Bourne said nothing.

Bannerman turned to Elizabeth. He said, "I'm proud of you. Thank you." He asked Bourne, "Can we now have a look in your basement? This lady has been more than patient."

"My basement?" Bourne tried to show no reaction. "There is nothing for you in my basement."

"Well, actually there is. Will you get to your feet, please?"

Elizabeth was already standing.

Bourne started to speak. He paused to wet his lips. He asked, "Who is this woman? Why is she here?"

"Ah, forgive me," said Bannerman. "I did say I'd introduce you. This woman is Elizabeth Stride."

Bourne didn't believe it. He would not. He could not. He said, "This one's not even close."

"We'll still need to see your basement," said Bannerman.

"There's a furnace room and an extensive wine cellar. There is nothing else in my basement."

Bannerman turned to Elizabeth. "You may show him your knife. You may take out one of his eyes."

She had seemed to barely move and yet the knife was in her hand. With a gymnast's grace, she sprung and vaulted his desk. One whipping foot knocked Bourne and his chair backward. She followed him down; she was straddling him. Her hand clamped down against the right side of his face. She had chosen the eye that she would take. "Wait, wait," shouted Bourne. He brought his arms across his face. "If you harm me, you'll die. Every one of you will die."

"We'll discuss that. But we'll do so in your basement."

"Sounds like show time," said Waldo. "Let's get down there."

Molly asked Waldo, "John, does Paul ever scare you?"

"Scare me, how? I don't get what you mean."

"I mean the way he is when he does things like this."

"What way?" asked Waldo. "He's the same. He's like always."

"Yes, he is."

"And this rattles you?" asked Waldo. "Why all of a sudden? Who it rattles are people who aren't expecting it. Look what it just did to Bourne."

"You think it's his act. I'm not sure it's an act. I'm not sure he feels anything at all."

"You know better."

"I do?"

"Yeah, you do. A lot of years. You're suddenly bothered that he's being polite. Would you rather see him lose it like Stride?"

"Now and then. Yes. I'd like to see that now and then."

"You saw it once," said Waldo. "When they almost killed Susan."

"He didn't get mad. He was ice."

"Ice is mad."

"Ice is also very scary," said Molly. "I remember."

"So now you're saying it bothers you, him being so cool, what with Aisha down below scared to death all this time. Don't you think that's a female thing maybe?"

"Let's go down there."

"Now, you're what? Mad at me?"

"Let's get down there."

Waldo asked, "Molly, what comes after cool?"

"I'm in no mood for riddles."

"I'm telling you anyway. The answer is ice. Ice is what comes after cool."

41

Bourne, even in the basement, although visibly shaken, made a final attempt at concealment. "You see? I told you. Nothing but wine."

Waldo reproached him. He said, "This gets offensive. Haven't you doped out why nothing works in this house? You think we'd come down here not knowing what's here? You think Chester told Billy there's nothing but wine?"

"The dessert rack," said Bannerman. "Slide it open if you will. Do you have the key cards to those rooms on your person?"

Bourne's hand, involuntarily, moved toward his robe's pocket. Bannerman saw it. "Will you hand them to me, please?" He took them and slid the rack open by himself. He turned to Elizabeth. He handed her both cards. He said, "Go get your friends. We'll wait here."

They heard the sound of a muted alarm. "Forgot to tell her," said Waldo. "Those cards go in twice."

But Elizabeth had apparently figured it out. The alarm

stopped abruptly. They heard the bolts sliding open. They heard a joyous shout. They heard Elizabeth's name. They heard rustling and running and a soft crunching sound that they took to be bodies colliding.

Bourne said to Bannerman, "That really is Stride?"

Bannerman, enjoying the moment, ignored him.

Bourne lowered his voice. "Just remember what I've told you. If harm comes to me, you'll all die and quite horribly. Your wives, your children, your friends. They'll all die."

"Yes, I got that," said Bannerman. "Please be silent."

He couldn't hear much of what was being said. Their voices were muffled, perhaps by their embrace. He heard Nadia's name. It was spoken by Aisha. He heard Elizabeth's voice say, "Oh, honey. Oh no." Then Aisha again. Her voice was comforting, soothing. He heard her make some reference to her mother. He heard footsteps, rapid footsteps, moving away. He heard the click of a second door opening. They must have gone in. Nothing more could be heard.

Several more minutes passed before Elizabeth appeared. She had an arm around Aisha. She was holding her closely. Aisha was startled when she saw them all waiting, but she smiled as she recognized John Waldo and Molly. Molly answered her smile. She said, "Hello again, Aisha."

"Elizabeth didn't tell me. It's so good to see you."

Her eyes went to Bourne. Her face darkened. The smile faded. They next fell on Bannerman. Molly said, "This is Paul."

Aisha looked up at Elizabeth. "Paul Bannerman? Really?"

Elizabeth's eyes had never left Bourne's. She said to Bannerman, "I've told her about you."

He smiled. "Hello, Aisha."

"Hello, sir."

Elizabeth said to Bannerman, "Nadia's dead."

He took a slow breath. "She's still in there?"

"She's in there. She's dead. They brought her here dead. First Jasmine, now Nadia. They're both dead."

Her gaze stayed with Bourne, who had taken a step backward. His expression was more one of confusion than of fear. He clearly did not know who this Nadia was if this new one was Elizabeth Stride. He said to Bannerman, "It was Lilly. It was Lilly's incompetence. The last thing I wanted was any of them dead. But the girl. I did save the girl."

Elizabeth asked Molly, "Would you take Aisha, please? Would you take her out to the lawn?"

Molly understood. She wanted Aisha well away. She didn't want Aisha to witness or hear what she intended for Artemus Bourne.

Bannerman approached them. He touched Aisha's cheek gently, careful of the bruise and the swelling. He said to Elizabeth, "I'd like both of you to go. You and Aisha ought to talk. Just the two of you."

She said, "Later." She mouthed, *"Do not ask me."*

He said, "I know what you want. Think about what you need. Think about what the both of you need."

Elizabeth mouthed, *"I will not let him live."*

Bannerman turned to Molly. He took her aside. "I was trying to be subtle. I'm not sure I got through. Elizabeth is all Aisha has now."

"She heard you," said Molly. "She knew that before you did."

"Get them out of here, Molly. Take them upstairs and . . ."

"No chance. Not this time. I want Bourne myself."

"Will you please let me finish? You'll be back in ten minutes. Wait until they're both well away from the house, then ask Billy to bring Chester Lilly down here. Aisha doesn't need to see Chester Lilly."

Molly nodded. "I'll find some ice for her cheek."

"I'll be looking for you in ten minutes."

Bannerman watched them go. He said to Bourne, "After you. You and I will have that talk you've been wanting."

Their first stop was the room in which Nadia had been kept. He knew that Elizabeth would have checked for a pulse, but he wanted to do so himself. He saw quickly that there was no need. Her skin was cold to the touch and her muscles had stiffened. The undersides of her legs were discolored reddish-blue because of the settling of her blood.

Bourne said again, "It was Lilly."

"Uh-huh."

"Lilly blamed the others. He shot them both for it. He was right to do so. This was shockingly stupid. In the end, I would have had Lilly put down for going against my instructions."

"Uh-huh. Mr. Bourne, what is this laboratory for?"

"It's . . . merely a convenience. It is hardly ever used."

"There are straps on this cot. Have you watched people die here?"

"Die how? You mean tortured?"

"Experiments," said Bannerman.

"Nothing of the sort. That's ridiculous."

"I find myself doubting you. Would you open your vault, please."

"No, I won't. And it's time we had our talk."

"About what? Killing us and our families and our friends? Would the cause of our destruction be the two men whom you've sent to scout our community?"

Once again, an involuntary tic gave the answer.

"Would the date of our destruction be this coming Tuesday, coinciding with the cutting of our grass?"

Bourne kept his face immobile, but his shoulders seemed to wilt.

"And would the means of our destruction be a fine pinkish powder that is similar to the substance on that freighter?"

Bannerman had expected Bourne to deny it. But Bourne said, "I commend you. How vigilant of you. You're telling me that you have taken those men. But there are *thousands* of men. There are *tons* of that powder. All I need to do is pick up the phone and . . ."

"Um . . . how would you manage that?" asked Bannerman.

Waldo had found a supply of quilted foil bags of the type used for hazardous materials. He was filling them with the collection of videos that Bourne had kept stored in a closet. Next, he would take the hard disk from Bourne's computer and some notebooks from Bourne's laboratory.

Billy appeared with Chester over his shoulder. Molly Far-rell preceded him, showing the way. John Waldo saw that Billy had red welts on his face. He asked him, "You need a hand?"

"I'm good," said Billy. "Where do you want him?"

Waldo shrugged. "Just dump him. This room over here." He gestured toward the bedroom where Aisha had been kept. Molly saw the bank of monitors that scanned Bourne's house and grounds. She saw movement on one of them. Elizabeth and Aisha. They were walking hand in hand. They had passed the helicopter. Elizabeth in her jumpsuit, Aisha still dressed for tennis. Aisha was holding a cold compress to her cheek, her head on Elizabeth's shoulder.

She turned to ask Waldo, "Will you help me with Nadia? We should wrap her before we take her out of here."

Waldo said, "Sure. Soon as Bannerman's ready." He turned back to Billy. "What's with Chester? He dead?"

"No. Paul said don't. I even tied off where you shot him."

"He talked to you, right? You get anything useful?"

"He cleared everything right up. None of this was his fault. Every single thing I asked him, someone else did it. He said he didn't even know that this place was down here. I saw Aisha with Stride. They okay?"

"Yeah, I think. Throw Chester on the bed in that room."

Billy did as he was asked. He almost literally threw him. The bed collapsed under his weight. Waldo got his first look at Chester Lilly's face and his head. He asked Billy, "This was keeping him alive?"

"Hey, he's breathing."

Lilly's face and his head were a mass of red welts under-neath a thick coating of honey. His eyes were swollen shut, his lips and cheeks seemed inflated. His nose was broken, pushed to one side. He had hardly any hair except at the edges. The rest of his scalp was all blood. There were bees crushed and dead on Chester's collar, down his shirt, and at least one was visible in his mouth.

"What's this?" asked Waldo. "You scalped him for Clew?"

Billy said, "That's not scalped. That's just no hair."

Waldo said, "See? This is why you got that image. You don't like it when someone calls you Bannerman's monster, but you go and keep doing stuff like this."

"I'm not a monster." Billy almost seemed hurt. "That thing where I'm a monster was a long time ago. You talking the corkscrew?"

"In the ear. A good example."

"That was then. I got a wife. I got friends. Things are different."

"Yeah, well tell that to Chester. I think given a choice, Chester would have taken the corkscrew."

"I didn't bring a corkscrew and I didn't do his hair. This guy did that mostly by himself."

Waldo curled his lip. "Self-inflicted, you're saying."

"Yeah. When he tried to rip the hive off his head. He's punching at bees. He broke his own nose. The worst was when a lot of them got stuck in his hair, glued in by all that honey that came loose. I already got stung, so I stepped back and watched. He ripped out his own hair with the bees."

"Has Bannerman seen this?"

"Just the start. From the window."

"Oh, right," said Waldo. "And Bourne wouldn't go look. Let's go see if he'll open that vault now."

Seeing Chester didn't have its desired effect. Bourne did reel backward when led in to view Chester, but he almost seemed vaguely amused. He said to Bannerman, "You were serious, weren't you? Did your man have to kill so many bees?"

Bourne stepped closer, the better to view Lilly's scalp. He shook his head slowly. "Poetic justice, you know. Chester once put a bullet through one of my hives. I'm not making that up. He really did."

Bourne clapped his hands. He asked Bannerman, "Well, what happens now? Shall I swoon? Beg for mercy? Give you anything you ask? You don't dare hurt me. We both know it."

"I know that because . . . ?"

"I'm a national treasure. Kill me and you'll doom millions who might otherwise have lived, thanks to me and the work that I alone have been doing. Kill me for what? Because two women died? You've avenged them. There's the culprit. There is Chester."

"Please open your freezer," said Bannerman.

Bourne raised his chin. He said, "You know what? I will. I'll show you what's worth not two lives, but a thousand. You tell me if you don't agree."

He worked the combination, hiding it with his body. One loud click, two loud thunks, and the heavy door swung open. A wave of frigid air washed over their faces. Lights blinked on revealing a well-ordered interior more than twice the size of most bathrooms.

Bourne said, "Step right in. I have nothing to hide."

Waldo said, "He means all of us. We should all go in first. He's going to hold the door like a gentleman."

Bourne stepped in. He muttered, "Well, it *was* worth a try."

The freezer was lined floor-to-ceiling with shelves except for one panel with its temperature controls. The shelves were filled with containers, all coated with frost. Bannerman guessed there to be two hundred or more. The containers were red with white lids and white handles. Only three of them displayed the VaalChem logo.

Bourne said to Bannerman, "These are largely vaccines. A few dormant seed strains; miscellaneous bacilli. You'll find nothing that's especially lethal."

Bannerman asked, "Vaccines against what?"

"Against any number of viral diseases. You may ask why so many. One likes to be prepared. And one likes to have enough on hand for one's friends should there be a bio-weapon attack."

"These friends . . . do they know that you've provided for them?"

"It is more that they know who to ask."

Bannerman said, "And I bet that if there should be an outbreak, you'd make even more friends very quickly."

"I dare say."

"Are you planning an outbreak any time soon? I mean, other than in Westport, of course."

"I respond to them, sir. I don't plan them."

"Yeah, he does," said Billy. "Chester says he's got one cooking."

"That's a lie."

But Bourne wondered whether Chester had actually said it. He recalled that, not a week ago, Chester had asked him what all these vaccines were for. *"In case of an epidemic,"* he'd answered. Chester had asked, *"An epidemic of what?"* His reply was, *"I haven't decided as yet."* But of all the misdeeds to which Chester might confess, why would he volunteer that one little snippet? There, in fact, was no such plan. It was more of a notion, an "if and when" sort of thing. Nothing major, but enough to produce screaming headlines. Perhaps a hundred dead or dying in some Washington suburb. Perhaps a congressman among them. A few journalists.

"You don't plan them," said Bannerman. "You only respond. And yet, twice now you've threatened to kill everyone I know. Which of these containers holds the virus that you'd use."

"None of them. Too dangerous. Wouldn't have them in the house."

"If I were to pick a few containers at random and dump their contents on the floor at your feet, would you find that unnerving, Mr. Bourne?"

"I'd find it wasteful, Mr. Bannerman. But amuse yourself, do." He pointed. "Start with that one, why don't we?"

"One of your choosing?"

"We'll take turns. You choose next."

Bourne took one of the containers that were nearest the door. He chose one of the three that bore a logo. He held it, sniffed it, and put it back on the shelf. He took and sniffed another. This one caused him to recoil. "A little ripe," he said to Bannerman as he peeled off the lid and allowed its contents to spill on the floor. There was a clatter of stones followed by a hairy mass that narrowly missed Molly's feet.

Bannerman looked down. "That would be . . . ?"

"Savran Bobik."

"And the stones?"

"Angolan gravel. Not diamonds, I assure you. If you doubt me, help yourself; be my guest."

Bourne pointed to two of the other containers. "There's Winfield and Kruger. I forget which is where. These were sent by your friend, Martin Kessler."

"So I've heard."

"These three, between them, did everything I'm blamed for. These three and, of course, Chester Lilly. Revive him, if you can, and ask him this question. 'Did Artemus Bourne have any knowledge whatever of some testing they'd been doing in Angola?'"

He stepped to Bobik's head and rolled it over with his shoe. "See that carving on his forehead? It spells the name Sara. Ask Lilly whether I had any foreknowledge of that woman's existence before this showed up here."

"I'm inclined to believe you," said Bannerman.

"Those four are your culprits, Mr. Bannerman, not I. Take their heads back to Westport. Mount them on pikes. Then turn your attention to your friend, Martin Kessler. He is the butcher, not I."

"Do you blame him?"

"Not for these three beheadings. I don't blame him in the slightest. I condemn his assumption that *I* am to blame. You are looking at an open declaration of war against a man who was totally ignorant of his grievance. So, what does one do in the face of such a threat? Does one escalate the violence or does one try to reason? But to reason, one needs to be holding some cards. I went after Stride. Wouldn't you in my place? You've been doing the same thing for years."

"Taking hostages?"

"No, you use your wandering ghosts. Shall I assume that they now guard my gates? I'd always thought they were a myth, a clever bluff on your part. They are said to be all over, always ready to strike, should anyone in authority be emboldened to attack you. In effect, you hold them hostage, do you not?"

Waldo didn't seem to be paying much attention. Not to Bourne or Bobik's head or to the containers. He seemed to be more interested in the vault's configuration. He was at a metal box, about two feet square, that had several instruments on it.

He asked Bourne, "What's this panel?"

"Those are temperature controls. Which reminds me, these vaccines mustn't thaw."

Waldo asked, "But why here? I mean, why not outside?"

"How should I know?" said Bourne. "I didn't design it."

He said to Bannerman, "These containers are starting to sweat. If you're going to examine them, please do so quickly. This much temperature change isn't good for them."

Waldo said to Bannerman, "This box is a dummy."

Bannerman looked up. "What else is it?"

"I don't know. One second." Waldo felt around its edges. He found a release. The panel swung out. He told Bannerman, "It's a safe. Not a Mosler, however. This one's typical hardware store crap."

Bannerman said to Bourne, "Please open it for us."

"I don't know the combination. Cecil Winfield installed it. I don't even know what he kept in it."

"Why then were you trying to get us out of here just now?"

"This looks easy," said Waldo. "Five minutes."

42

Aisha and Elizabeth had walked almost aimlessly, each of them lost in quite different emotions. They made two stops. One was at the helicopter. Howard Leland's pilot was anxious to depart and, with luck, to resume the secretary's flight schedule without his absence attracting too much notice. Elizabeth told the pilot that it shouldn't be long now. She told the pilot that Nadia was dead. They'd be bringing her body back to Bridgeport.

The pilot had asked her, "What about Bourne?"

"Mr. Bourne will be staying," she told him.

The pilot had said, "Yeah, but . . . there's staying and there's staying."

"I'll be seeing Mr. Bourne before we leave."

The other stop was at one of the Jeeps. Aisha had seen the dog in the back. It wasn't moving and its mouth was hanging open. The man with the rifle said that she needn't worry. He said, "Bring your hand to his nose. He can smell you." She did and the dog did react, but just barely. It licked its lips once. It made the sound of a sigh.

The man said to Elizabeth, "You won't remember me, Miss Stride. Chamonix. Harry's place. We only spoke once or twice."

"I wasn't very sociable then."

He said, "Kessler made up for it. Glad to hear he's alive. And I'm glad to see the girl not much worse for wear." He lowered his voice. "Does Bourne still have his hands?"

"I'll be seeing him shortly," said Elizabeth.

Aisha had heard. She said, "Walk with me."

She'd already told Elizabeth that she'd known she was coming. She told her of her dream in which her mother had stayed with her. She'd told her in response to Elizabeth saying what a very brave girl she had been.

"I was never awake long enough to be scared. I didn't do anything brave."

She would miss Nadia. She would especially miss Jasmine. But her mother had promised to look after them. Jasmine had never met her mother before, but she noticed the resemblance right away. Only then did Jasmine realize that she might be dead. She was looking around. It was not what she'd expected. She'd said to Nadia, "We're in deep shit." But her mother calmed them both and told them to stay close.

"They couldn't see me, though. That's the only sad thing. But my mother says they will after they've settled in. She'll try to bring them the next time she comes."

Elizabeth listened. She was letting her talk. Aisha knew that she thought it was only a dream.

Elizabeth might have said, *"Aisha, honey, here's what happened. You were drugged and you were floating in and out of being conscious. You heard them talking in the van. You heard one say he killed Jasmine. Later on, you heard them say that Nadia had died. You might not remember, but it stayed in your brain. That explains how they could show up dead in a dream that you were already having of your mother."*

But Elizabeth didn't say that. She said, "I'm glad you got to see them," even though she didn't believe it.

Aisha had told her about the other two men. The one named Chester called them Toomey and Kuntz. They were dead now. Chester killed them. This wasn't exactly part of the dream, but she was pretty sure that it happened.

Elizabeth might have said, *"Same thing. You were drugged. You heard them climb out and you heard two loud noises. After that, there was only the one they called Chester. Your brain told you that those were shots. They were probably just dropped off somewhere."*

But she didn't say that either. She seemed to know better.

Aisha had told her that her mother found Martin, or at least she knew that he was coming as well. And that he was thinking of her. And he was thinking of Elizabeth. And that he was coming from Africa.

Elizabeth might have said, *"You thought we were coming because you wanted us to come. You knew that we both would be worried about you."*

She didn't. Or she started to. She stopped walking. She said, "Hold it."

"What's wrong?"

"Martin Kessler *is* coming and I knew that. How did you?"

"I told you," said Aisha. "My mom said so."

"Your mother told you that he was coming from Africa? The same woman who couldn't find him for two years?"

"Oh, wait. That was Artemus. The man in the bathrobe."

Elizabeth seemed relieved. Perhaps a little disappointed.

Rats, thought Aisha. Now she'll never believe it. But this wasn't why she had wanted to keep walking after seeing that man in the Jeep.

"Elizabeth," she said, "I don't want you to kill him."

Elizabeth looked away. She said nothing.

"Nadia and Jasmine are okay. They really are. And if I'm wrong, which I'm not, that won't bring them back."

"You're enough of a reason," said Elizabeth.

"No, I'm a reason for you not to do it. I don't want to think of you that way. And I watched Mr. Bannerman. Even he knew you shouldn't."

"Aisha . . . Paul Bannerman has his own agenda. I don't think that saving my soul made the list."

"Nobody's talking about saving your soul. And nobody expects you to stop being you. Elizabeth, I know that you would kill to protect me. But you mustn't kill just because I got a black eye. I need to know that about you."

"Aisha . . . honey . . . what do you want from me?" It was all that Elizabeth could think of to say.

"I don't want you to kill him, or cut him, or anything. I don't want you to even go back in that house. I want us to go and wait for Martin to come and then I want us to go home."

"What, the three of us?"

"Yes."

"That's a pretty thought, Aisha. But I won't *have* a home. And Martin isn't staying. I don't think he wants to."

"Do you want him to stay?"

"It's not up to me."

"Oh, of course it is, Elizabeth. It was always up to you. And my mom, by the way, maybe didn't mention Africa, but she did say that he'd been far away. Elizabeth, look at me. How did she know that?"

"Aisha, I have no idea."

"She knew because you told her. Now did you, or not?"

"No, of course not," said Elizabeth. "How could I?"

"She said you were dreaming. Did you dream of her, or not?"

"Aisha, I had a whole jumble of dreams. About you, about Martin, all random, no context. In fact, you weren't even you anymore. You were older, grown up, your hair was much longer . . ."

"Don't stop. Keep remembering. What did you say to me?"

"That . . . Martin was coming."

"Did I ask you where he'd been?"

"I said that he'd been . . . I didn't say far away . . . I said that he'd gone as far from me as he could."

"And you say I was older? A little older than you?"

"Aisha, you shouldn't make too much of dreams."

"You were talking to my mother. Get used to it."

*   *   *

Bannerman had timed Waldo. It took him longer. Eight minutes. Bourne was forced to stand watching. He'd started perspiring. The freezer's temperature had risen no higher than forty, yet Artemus Bourne was perspiring. Even so, Bourne had made no real effort to leave, as he would have if a trap had been rigged.

Waldo was less certain. He proceeded with care. He listened when the last of the tumblers fell away for the sound of a switch being thrown. There was nothing. He opened the door no more than an inch. He used a penlight to look for connections that normally should not have belonged there.

He said, "Think it's clear." He opened the door slowly. He was startled by an unexpected movement.

"What is it?" asked Bannerman.

"Some of this stuff looks alive."

Bannerman moved forward. He saw vials in racks. There were ten padded racks, four vials in each. All their contents were pinkish in color. The vials in each rack were wrapped with colored bands. The color for each rack was different.

Most different of all was the nearest of the racks. It held not four vials, but three. The three that remained seemed almost excited, as if at the prospect of being released. Their contents were a powder so exquisitely fine that they almost seemed to have no substance at all. At the edges, the powder would erupt in small streams that seemed to be trying to reach the vial's seal. The streams would cling for a moment and then they'd recede, leaving room for others to try. The colored band on those vials was yellow.

Bannerman said to Bourne, "Tell me what these are, please."

"Never seen them before. Those are Winfield's."

"They have yellow bands like the one on the freighter."

"I wouldn't know. I had no part in that."

Bannerman asked him, "Why only three? Is one missing? Has one been sent elsewhere?"

"I don't know."

"Not to Westport, by chance. No, of course. You wouldn't know." Bannerman said to Waldo, "Toss me one of those vials."

Waldo reached; he removed one; he turned to face Bannerman; he started an underhand toss.

"No, no," shouted Bourne. "I mean . . . not knowing what's in them . . ."

Bannerman turned to Molly. "Have you finished with Nadia?"

"Best I could. She's ready when we are."

Bannerman said to Billy, "Will you lift her off that cot? Bring Mr. Bourne with you. Put him on that cot. And see that he's strapped down securely."

"About time."

"Just a moment," said Bourne. "You will do no such thing."

"I'll be with you, Mr. Bourne, in a very few minutes. I need to make a phone call. Excuse me."

He'd asked Molly to come with him while he made his call. He said, "Molly, I know that this is driving you crazy."

"It was, but you were right. You and John could have done it. John and I have had this discussion."

"And?"

"I'm not being so professional. *And* I'm a woman. I don't react well to men who hurt women. Left to me or Elizabeth, Bourne would have been dead long before he opened that vault."

"Yes, I know that."

"You're still calling it, Paul, but when this is over. . . . Never mind. This isn't the time."

"Molly, if you're saying that you want someone else . . ."

She squinted. "What?"

"Then you'll have it," he told her. "I'll step down in a heartbeat."

She seemed shocked. "Are you nuts? You think *that's* what I want? If anyone is going to step down, it will be me."

"Um . . . help me with a reason. Because you let this thing get to you?"

"No, because I've got to get some kind of a life. Everybody seems to have one but me."

He asked, "Is that it? That's why you've been . . ."

"A nag."

"Asking questions isn't nagging. Impatience isn't nagging. Molly, how can I help you? Name anything."

"Not now."

"Then starting tomorrow, we'll make it a project. We'll make this priority one."

"A project? Don't you dare. You'll do what? Call a meeting?"

He said, "Well, no. That's not exactly . . ."

"A group conference on how to get Molly laid? Don't you know a damned thing about women?"

"Revelations . . . occasionally come out of the blue."

"Make your call."

"Stay with me."

"Make your call."

He had reached Greta Kirch at the number she'd given him. A cell phone. She was probably at home. He had placed the call from the wine cellar proper where Bourne's struggles, howls of outrage, would not be a distraction. He told her of the drugs that were en route to the freighter. He read to her from the slip on which Bourne had written. She asked him to repeat it, more slowly.

She understood. She said, "Yes. We are testing something like it. That drug is cidofovir, but substantially improved. The lipids are fats. You need fats for a pill. Otherwise it must be taken intravenously."

"Will it work?"

"It should. It works by preventing replication of the virus if taken before the first symptoms appear. Once the symptoms are pronounced, there is no hope."

"It will have been four days. Will that be soon enough?"

"This begins to get close, but most likely. Also tell them to drink all the water they can. That drug is not so good for the kidneys."

"Will the Red Cross know that?"

"Assuredly, yes."

"Then let's leave that to them. I won't burden you by telling you where I am, or my intentions, but I do want to tell you what I've found."

He described what he'd discovered in Bourne's freezer and his safe. He described the dancing powder in detail.

She said, "Same as the ship. It must be Marburg with smallpox. And I am no fool. You are with Bourne at his home?"

"I will ask you to keep that thought to yourself until . . ."

"I cannot. This man keeps a private supply? And of chimeras? Many? And he keeps them at his home? I have told you of the need for bio-containment. An accident would be catastrophic."

"How quickly would it spread if it were released?"

"How quickly? With the speed of the wind."

"And if there were no wind. No movement of air?"

"The speed of . . . I don't know . . . tobacco smoke, perhaps. The speed at which it rises from an ashtray."

"And the symptoms?" asked Bannerman. "Please describe them in detail."

"Mr. Bannerman . . . with respect, I must terminate this discussion. I must notify the authorities at once."

"Which authorities?"

"The FBI, the CDC, and of course the military."

"Well, they can arrive and find Briarwood in flames, or you can give me one hour's grace and you'll find it all here for the taking."

"All of it? You'll keep none of it?"

"Not a molecule. I promise. Nor will there be a need for extraordinary measures. Just walk down to his basement and start gathering."

"His vault is open?"

"We'll close it," said Bannerman, "but it won't be locked. It's also a freezer. Must it not be kept cold?"

"Absolutely. The colder, the safer."

"Now describe the symptoms, beginning to end."

She did. He listened. He thanked her.

He asked, "Will you accompany the authorities you send?"

"If permitted. It is not up to me."

He said, "I want you to come. I want you to coordinate. Tell them that I said, without you, the house burns."

She was silent for a moment. "Sir, why do you do this?"

"I will tell you, Dr. Kirch, but later," said Bannerman. "I will call you in an hour at the most."

He broke the connection. Molly Farrell had heard most of it. She said to him, "No movement of air?"

"Let's wrap up here."

She said, "I think I see what you have in mind. And now you're going to say you need to do this alone. Are you trying to get yourself killed?"

"Just this once, trust me, will you? Get out of this house. John and Billy will be right behind you."

Bannerman made one more stop at the safe before going to the laboratory room. Waldo was there. The cot was not. The bolts that had fastened it had been ripped from the flooring.

Waldo said, "I told Billy, put him next door with Chester. I'm trying to look around here in peace."

"So Billy ripped it out?"

"With Bourne strapped to it, yeah."

"John, the point of having a bolted-down cot . . ." Bannerman tossed a hand. "Never mind." He said, "Tell me again how the vent system works."

"These two rooms, the kitchen, the pantry are all separate. They make up the original apartment."

"These metal doors are airtight?"

"They'd have to be, yeah."

Bannerman asked, "Are these rooms shut off now?"

"No, there's a control this side of the wine racks. Right now it's all open, like I told you, for the wine."

"Please shut it off. Isolate the apartment."

"Okay, then what?"

"Take those videotapes, whatever else you've collected. Molly's waiting upstairs. We'll be leaving."

Bannerman left the laboratory. He paused in the hallway. He walked over to the de-con chemical shower and the two HazMat suits that hung next to it. He stopped to read the directions for the de-con shower's use. They were printed, large type, in both English and French. The directions boiled down to "Step in, push a button." The designers had great haste in mind.

He stepped into the room where Bourne had been taken. Billy stood, his arms folded, watching Chester and Bourne. Chester was conscious, not alert, but conscious. He'd managed to cover his head with a pillow and was shivering; he was going into shock.

Bourne's cot had been placed beside Chester's collapsed bed. Bourne seemed exhausted, disbelieving, his stare vacant. This couldn't be happening to him.

He swallowed. He asked, "Are you going to kill me?"

Bannerman didn't answer. He turned to Billy. He said, "Billy, if you will, carry Nadia upstairs. I'd like to be alone with these two."

"You sure?"

Bannerman said, "I'll be fine. Make sure that John goes with you. I don't expect to be long."

Bourne strained against his straps. He said, "He is. He's going to kill me." This plea, unaccountably, was directed at Billy.

"A lot easier than I would," said Billy.

43

Bannerman had pulled a chair up to the cot. He leaned forward. He paused before speaking.

"You have no idea," he said to Bourne, very quietly, "how badly I'd like to end this right now. One bullet behind Chester's ear, and then yours."

Bourne blinked. He swallowed. Once again, he felt hope.

"I won't do it," said Bannerman. "I'll be leaving you here. I'll be leaving you locked in this room. You and Chester."

Bourne's face drained of color. He said nothing.

"You won't be alone long. You'll have visitors soon. They'll want to arrest you. I don't think much will come of it. It would not be in the national interest."

"I . . . *will* make amends for any harm . . ."

"No you won't," said Bannerman. "Not even if you mean it. You've effectively orphaned an innocent girl. This makes twice in three years that she's been orphaned, Mr. Bourne. How would you ever make that right?"

"That was Chester. I told you. I was horrified . . ."

"Yes, you've told me. Clew as well. Now be quiet and listen. You've threatened my wife, my children, my friends, and thousands of innocent neighbors. You would have caused them to sicken and die in a painful and horrible way."

Bourne lifted his head. "That was only a threat. You have your ghosts; I'm entitled to have mine. And you've led me to believe that you've already prevented . . . whatever they might have done."

"We're still working on it," said Bannerman.

"Well, then let me make certain. I can stop it with a phone call right now."

"Yes, you will," said Bannerman. "But let's say that you didn't. The sickness would begin on the fourth or fifth day. First there would be headaches and an itching of the eyes, a cough and a thickness in the throat. They would think it's the flu, an inconvenience. Within hours, however, they would look in a mirror and they'd see that the whites of their eyes were turning red. Next, they'd have nosebleeds and they'd notice bruises that were caused by no bumping that they could recall."

"Did you hear me?" asked Bourne. "I can stop it."

"They would soon become nauseous. They would vomit; they'd see blood. Then they'd have diarrhea. It would be mostly blood. A day later, they'd see blood from every orifice on their bodies. Add a day, and it's oozing through their skin. They would notice that the blood flows in spidery patterns. It would do so because it can no longer clot. They would bleed through whatever clothes they have on. The blood would collect in their shoes."

"I am . . . fully aware of how terrible it is. It's exactly why I've been working so hard to . . ."

"Do you have a cigarette?"

"A what? No, I don't."

"A cigar?"

"Will you listen? I'm trying to tell you . . ."

Bannerman asked, "Is Chester a smoker?"

"Oh, for God's sake. Yes. His shirt pocket."

"It will keep for the moment," said Bannerman. "Where was I?"

"You were telling me things that I already know."

"I'm sure, but I want it to be fresh in your mind. And please indulge me, Mr. Bourne, because it's newer to me. It is also a good deal more personal. When we say 'epidemic,' we think about numbers. We don't think in terms of people who have faces, who have lives. They watch each other suffering. It gets worse by the hour. Their children are too sick to even cry anymore or to ask for water to relieve their awful thirst. They just lie there turning black. Black all over. Many will pray; some will curse the same God, and a few will decide that they mustn't prolong it. They'll start by ending the suffering of their children by whatever means might be at hand."

"Why are you doing this?" asked Bourne. "What's the point?"

"I'll get to it shortly," said Bannerman. "Bear with me. The CDC would, by then, have been alerted. Reports of bleeding would have told them that it isn't the flu, that it's some kind of hemorrhagic fever. But they wouldn't know which one and the symptoms would confuse them. This is because we would also have smallpox. Add great swelling pustules to our hemorrhaging bodies."

"Mr. Bannerman . . ."

"Even then, the CDC won't be sure of what we have because the virus will be a variant that they haven't seen before. They will know, however, that it's too late to help us. The CDC would order all of Westport quarantined as well as parts of the neighboring communities. They would be too late because many would have left before the worst of the symptoms appeared. Anyone who tried to leave after that would be told to turn back or they'd be shot. Not that it would matter. At least not for long. Most of us would be dead by day eight from the Marburg. A small percentage would survive. Some are naturally immune. But then, of course, they'd all die of smallpox."

Bannerman paused. He looked over at Lilly and then back at Bourne. "You've done this in Angola, have you not?"

"I have not."

"I am informed to the contrary, sir."

"If any such thing has been done in Angola, it was Lilly

and Winfield and Bobik. I had never even heard Bobik's name until last week. Until then, I had no reason to suspect it."

"Uh-huh."

Bannerman reached to release the velcro strap that had fastened Bourne's right arm to the frame. "Don't undo the others quite yet, Mr. Bourne." He handed Bourne his cell phone. "Make the call."

"I don't have their cell phone number. It's upstairs in my study."

"Do you know where they're staying?"

"At a Marriott hotel. On the Post Road, they said."

"Try them there. It might save us some time."

Bourne called Information. A voice gave him the number. He dialed it and another more cheerful voice said, "Marriott Hotel. How may I help you?" Bourne said, "Connect me with Room 224." The operator asked him to hold.

He waited on hold for almost a full minute. A male voice came on. It spoke a terse, "Yeah?" Bannerman could hear the voice plainly.

Bourne said, "Richard?"

"Who's this?"

"Do I have Room 224?"

"Richard went down the hall. I'll go get him. Who's calling?"

Bannerman reached to take the phone. He broke the connection. He said to Bourne, "That would have been the police." He hit a two-digit code for Carla Benedict's number. She answered on the first ring. She said, "Bingo."

He asked, "Both of them?"

"Yep. Two hours ago."

"You found them in their room?"

"I left them there, too."

"They'd have had a glass vial. Three inches. Pink powder."

"They did. It would have been tossed on your lawn unless they got word to abort. That's Marburg and smallpox, did you know that?"

"I knew it," said Bannerman. "How did you?"

"From Kessler. He just got here. We showed it to him. Are you going to be where you are for a while? He's hot to get his ass down there."

"No point. We're just leaving. Where is that vial now?"

"With Anton. He says not to worry."

"Thank you, Carla. Good work."

"Always glad to pitch in."

Bannerman broke off the call. Bourne was staring at him. "Once again, I commend you. I am most impressed."

"Getting back to Angola . . ."

"No, let's finish with Westport. I'd have stopped them. I *would* have."

"And that's noted," said Bannerman. "But getting back to Angola . . ."

"What possible interest could you have in Angola?"

"Well, the subject at hand was the effect of VaalChem's products and your use of them on innocent people. You did test them in Angola. I know that."

"If . . . there has been live testing, it was for a greater good."

"And they're only Angolans. They don't count for much. I think I'll have that cigarette now."

He found a crushed pack in Lilly's shirt pocket. He didn't find matches. He lit it on the stove. He drew on it lightly and blew the smoke gently. He watched as it eddied toward the doorway. He found a small dish that would serve for an ashtray. He carried it to the far end of the kitchen. He left the burning cigarette there. He watched how the smoke rose. It seemed to want to stay at that end.

He said to Bourne, "I have one more thing to ask you."

He reached into his pocket. He produced several vials. Each vial had a different colored band. He said, "I have six. Are all of them chimeras?"

"Only the yellow," said Bourne. "And be careful."

"And this blue one?" he asked.

"The blue is Ebola. The red is bubonic. The orange is either Lassa fever or dengue. I'm not sure; I get those two confused. The gray and green are similar. They are both encephalitics."

"Sleeping sickness, correct? And they cause widespread blindness?"

"Of a sort. The brain swells. The eye muscles are paralyzed."

Bourne reached to undo the strap on his left wrist. He sat up to start on his ankles. "Mr. Bannerman, you appear both well versed and intrigued. Are you about to propose some sort of partnership?"

"No, in fact, I'll say good-bye now, Mr. Bourne."

He stepped to the door and he tossed the six vials. They sailed over Bourne's cot and over Lilly's smashed bed on a line toward the hard tile floor of the kitchen. He heard them shatter, at least some, perhaps all. A counter blocked his view of their impact. To be certain, he did not close the door until he could see a mist rising. If he'd closed it and waited to look through the glass, the mist might have been invisible by then. He saw the mist; he stepped out; he closed the steel door.

He almost hadn't realized that Bourne had been screaming until the closed door changed Bourne's pitch.

44

He made good on his promise to call Greta Kirch. He called
her from the lawn, where he stood in the sunlight, waiting for
his suit to dry somewhat. He had used the chemical shower.

He told her of Artemus Bourne's situation. Bourne and
Lilly were locked in a sealed-off apartment whose air supply was discreet to that unit. The air was contaminated by no
fewer than six of VaalChem's weapons-grade viruses. He
presumed that the apartment would need to be quarantined
until those contaminants could no longer replicate. Until
they ran out of flesh to consume.

He presumed that Bourne might possibly be saved before
the symptoms begin to appear. But by whom? And with
what? What infection to treat first? And who would dare au-
thorize opening that door, no matter how well equipped they
may be for the task, and risk the escape of that cocktail.

Greta asked, "You say the rest of the basement is clean?"

"As far as I know. But take precautions."

"I assure you," she said, "we'll take heroic precautions.
His vault and his supply are intact?"

"Except for those in with Bourne and one other in West-port. The one in Westport is Marburg with smallpox. If you'd care to come to Westport, say on Wednesday or Thursday, that vial will be surrendered to you. And I mean you, Dr. Kirch. It will be placed in your hands only."

"Are you saying come alone? I cannot come alone. We'll need a bio-hazard vehicle and surely an armed escort."

"I understand," said Bannerman. "They'll come and they'll go, but I'd like you to stay. I will have a few things to discuss with you. Until then, you'll have much to discuss with Mr. Bourne before he realizes that he's beyond hope."

"And you?" she asked. "Were you not exposed?"

"I tried to be careful. I don't think it's likely. And I took a chemical shower at once while dressed in the clothing I was wearing."

"Clothing? Only clothing?"

He said, "I know. There are HazMat suits down there. But I needed to have a discussion with Bourne and I thought that he might have been less forthcoming if I'd walked in wearing a space suit." He added, "Besides, the gloves are too bulky. You can't use a phone with those gloves on."

She said nothing for a moment, but he could read her thoughts. She was calling him a damned fool.

She cleared her throat. "You are going back to Westport? Have blood drawn at once. Watch for symptoms. Watch for headaches. Watch for burning in the eyes."

"Actually, they're burning a little right now."

"Burning? *Burning*?" She could no longer help herself. "You walk into a de-con chemical shower and you tell me that it made your eyes burn? Do not look to me for sympathy. I have none."

"I look forward to your visit, Dr. Kirch."

45

It was four days later. It was Thursday.

VaalChem's antivirals had reached the freighter. They arrived not a day too soon for Major Scar. He had begun to show the first symptoms. The better news was that no one else on board had. The rotors of Scar's attack helicopter had blown all the particles sternward. Beyond the stern, they were dispersed to the ocean. Greta Kirch said that any that had not found a host would have died in the heat of the following day.

They would have found hosts in the captain and crew. They had been held at the stern. Bobik's man on board had told Scar that they were doomed. Scar had to make a decision. He saw little use in keeping them alive to infect, among others, their kidnapping victims. Scar had them all shot and washed over the side by means of the freighter's bilge hoses. Scar had hoped that he himself, having been upwind, might not have ingested any particles. It was a vain hope. It would only take a few. Two to five out of billions of particles.

But his blood, taken three times a day, showed improvement. Replication of the virus had been stopped. The ship would remain quarantined for at least two more weeks before being towed to Liberia.

Bannerman had learned, to his mild surprise, that Major Scar's true name was an Irish one, Thomas Mitchell. His Red Cross wife was named Sheila. They had both placed a ship-to-shore call to Howard Leland, thanking him for procuring the medicines. Leland told them that the credit should go to Roger Clew. But for Clew, the twenty children would now be enslaved and the cannibal, Mobote, would still be alive and making good on his terrorist intentions. Leland told him that the credit, in almost equal measure, belonged to the efforts of one Paul Bannerman. Perhaps the Mitchells would care to thank him as well.

Leland set up the call. Bannerman spoke to them by satellite. Bannerman told Scar that it was Scar and his wife who were most deserving of credit in this matter. He told Scar that they would speak again soon, that he might have a proposition of interest to the both of them. He told Scar that, in fact, it might be of interest to all those who served in Scar's Second Commando.

Bannerman had also called Roger Clew. Bannerman kept it brief. Clew had difficulty speaking. Bannerman had no need to tell Clew very much of what had transpired since he was attacked. Clew had heard it all from Leland. Leland had gone to see him. He'd briefed him and he had apologized abjectly for not listening to him about Bourne.

Clew would face a good deal of surgical repair. Five or six operations, a few months of healing, but he ought to be as good or even better than new. Mercifully, Clew had no memory whatever of the terrible beating he took. Bannerman told him that he'd fought back very fiercely, managing to wound at least one of his assailants. He further brightened Clew's day by conveying a promise that he had extracted from Elizabeth Stride. It wasn't much of an extraction. She was more than willing. She said to tell Clew that, when he felt up to it, she would be pleased to go out with him for dinner and a movie. Just the two of them. She might even cook for him.

*   *   *

Artemus Bourne hadn't waited four to five days before showing serious symptoms. He'd started hemorrhaging on Tuesday morning. Until then, he had tried to bluster and to threaten the federal officials who had come there to question him, speaking through the door that entombed him. He demanded instead to speak to their superiors, men who had often attended his brunches.

None of these would respond. He threatened to ruin them. He'd demanded his attorneys. They wouldn't go near him. The senior executives at his Houston headquarters had scattered to wherever their money was kept. Hundreds, worldwide, ran for cover as well, after the atlas in Bourne's study was found with Bourne's damning notations in its margins.

Elizabeth had asked Bannerman, "Was this why you didn't end it?"

"It was not the only reason," he'd told her.

Chester Lilly was dead. He hadn't lived through the night. There were those who thought the bee toxins had killed him. There were others who thought that he'd died of embarrassment soon after he'd managed to limp to a mirror and see what remained of his hair. So, Bourne, for whatever time he had left, would remain in that room with a corpse. The pantry held ample food, but he'd eaten almost nothing because nausea had set in so quickly.

Dr. Greta Kirch, at Bannerman's suggestion, had a camera set up, trained through the small window, to record the onset and progression of his symptoms.

"There are people who should know what they've supported," he told her. "There are people who should be made to watch it."

Bourne saw the camera. He realized what it meant. He'd become a test subject, like a monkey or a rat, or like the many human subjects that he'd probably observed. He tried to smash the glass with a leg torn from his cot, but the glass was too thick and he was weakening. Soon he could only sit, his mind almost gone. This had been the other reason for not ending it.

*   *   *

Waldo had taken those other recordings, the tapes of the bedroom antics at Briarwood. Molly had told Waldo, "We're not keeping them. Destroy them."

This discussion took place in Howard Leland's helicopter. It had crossed Long Island. Bridgeport's airport was in sight.

She said, "We're not going to watch them. We're not going to release them. They're jerks, but they have families. Destroy them."

Waldo said, "We got some big names on these labels. This is leverage. They could come in handy."

"If that day comes, it's enough that they'll think that we have them. Save the labels and jettison the tapes."

"Yeah, okay, but we ought to lift a shot of this Claire. I bet you she's the one who they found dead with Clew, but who didn't have much of a face left."

"Okay, one," said Molly. "Toss the rest."

"Yeah, I will."

"Do it now," she said. "We're over Long Island Sound."

"You could kill some poor stiff on a sailboat down there."

"It could have been worse for them. Toss them."

Speaking of Molly, her mood hadn't improved. It was surprising, more than troubling, because this was Molly. She'd always been outgoing and unfailingly pleasant, except, of course, when she had to be otherwise. She was not at all like Carla, who was prone to black moods and who'd always had a hair trigger temper.

In fact, Carla had been positively sunny of late. All that damage that she'd done on Hilton Head Island had probably served as an overdue fix. And then there were those two at the Marriott. She hadn't done that by herself. It turned out Viktor had been with her. And then, having done it, she'd had Viktor to go home with. Molly went home alone. She had no one. She'd said so. She'd never expressed such a sentiment before. Bannerman wasn't sure where it had come from.

It didn't seem to help matters much when she saw Adam Whistler arrive with his beautiful angel. It was the first time Bannerman had seen Claudia in the flesh. He'd only heard her described. Seeing her, meeting her, feeling her touch, he could almost believe that she'd undergone some extraordinary change in the netherworld. Molly greeted her warmly because Molly is Molly, but one could feel a slight tinge of jealousy there. It was not because Claudia was a beautiful young woman and not because she seemed to be singularly gifted. It was because she had Adam and because Adam loved her. Everybody had someone but Molly.

Well, not everyone. There was Waldo. At least Molly had a home; she ran a business; she had roots. No one really knew what sort of life Waldo had. He comes, then he goes. He might vanish for weeks. Then he pops up out of nowhere when he's needed. But on that day when Molly spoke of it, by Bourne's rack of dessert wines, he'd known better than to offer that comparison.

Harry Whistler came with Kate. Kate was Claudia's mother. Bannerman had not met Kate before either. A surprising bit of news was that he'd asked Kate to marry him. Harry's wife, Andrea, the spectacular Andrea, had died years ago. Cancer took her. Kate, very wisely, said, "Let's take our time. Ask me again in two years." But that hadn't stopped her from moving in with him. She'd asked him, however, whether she could redecorate. He'd said, "Ask me again in two years."

Even so, they were a couple. Molly saw them as lovebirds. It was the same when Lesko arrived with Elena. An unlikely couple, but totally devoted. Both in late middle age, but they'd had a son together.

Their little son was named Willem. They had brought the boy with them. He was roughly the same age as Cassie. They'd named him after Elena's cousin, an excellent man, Willem Brugg. The elder Willem was chairman of the board overseeing the Brugg business empire. Elena was vice chairman and unspeakably rich. Lesko ran the Brugg Foundation, endowments worth billions, aside from being overall chief of security.

And then there was Kessler and Elizabeth and Aisha, but they were a whole different story. The subject at hand was Molly Farrell.

Bannerman had done something he should not have done. Even Susan had warned him against it.

She'd said, "Paul, it's one thing for a woman to say that she wishes that she had a man in her life. It's quite something else for a man to decide that a woman needs a man in her life."

"That makes no sense at all."

"You know nothing about women."

He asked, "Why does everyone keep saying that to me?"

"Because you know nothing about women."

Very well, he decided. He would try to be delicate. He'd called Howard Leland to ask him about the Secret Service man who'd been guarding him. Brian Moore. The sharper one. The good-looking one.

"What sort of fitness reports does he get?"

"Exceptional," said Leland. "I just hope we can keep him."

"He's considering leaving?"

"He's been getting a bit restless. You're not thinking of stealing him, are you?"

"It's nothing like that. Is he married?"

"Divorced," said Leland. "I believe for some time."

"Do you happen to know why? Has he ever said what led to it?"

"Um . . . why are you asking?"

"Just curious. I liked him."

"Well, he certainly hasn't discussed it with me, but I gather it was one of those mutual things. Two people simply realizing that they've made a mistake and had married for the wrong reasons."

"Or maybe that they've married the wrong person?" asked Bannerman.

A brief pause. "I don't suppose . . . that you know the *right* person. He did mention, in my hearing, after you and I met, that he had once known Molly Farrell."

"Oh, had he?"

"Ah," said Leland. "So you didn't know that. For a moment there, I thought that you'd begun a dating service."

"Nothing like it," said Bannerman. "Not at all."

"Then of course you'd have no use for his telephone number."

"Not unless you have it handy."

"I'll e-mail it."

Bannerman reached Moore at his apartment that evening. Moore thought at first that it was a prank by some friend, some other agent, who had been told that Moore had actually frisked *the* Paul Bannerman.

"No, this is no joke. It's deadly serious," said Bannerman. "In fact, you just might save my life."

"How is that, sir?"

"You'll recall that I invited you to drop in and see us?"

"I'd . . . concluded that you were just being polite. What is this about saving your life?"

"Brian, are you able to get some time off?"

"Um . . . actually, I'm off now through next Tuesday."

"Would you care to come visit? This weekend would be good. We have a guest house that should be available by then. It's just two doors down from Molly Farrell."

A pause. "Mr. Bannerman . . ."

"It's Paul."

"If there's something that you hope to get out of me . . ."

"On my word, not a thing. This is entirely social."

"I did say that I'd like to see Molly again. Is she behind this invitation?"

"She is not. She doesn't know. I haven't mentioned you to her."

"Should I . . . come armed?"

"No, of course not. Why would you?"

"Sir . . ."

"It's Paul."

"I'm confused about the part where I'd be saving your life."

"Okay, here's the truth. Molly's been a little down. Do you think that she might be pleased to see you?"

Moore's voice took on a smile. "Is that really all this is?"

"There is no hidden motive, I promise."

"Well, then yes. I'd sure like to give it a shot."

"It's me who'll get shot if she finds out I called you for the purpose of getting you together."

"We are . . . trained to throw our bodies in the path of a bullet. I'll see you on Saturday," said Moore.

He had also asked Greta to fly back from Briarwood to renew her acquaintance with Elena. Well, actually, that wasn't his sole reason either. Bannerman had sat the two of them down and put a thought that he'd had on the table. Simply put, the Bruggs should buy VaalChem.

The Luanda government still had VaalChem under guard and they were frightened to death of it. The first step would be to get them to seize it. They can do so under international law and keep it or sell it as they choose. They would probably be glad to be rid of it.

Bourne had purchased VaalChem when it was in Johannesburg. He'd had it dismantled and moved to Angola where the government not only gave him the land, but promised no interference. If it was moved once, it could be moved again. The Liberian government, now reasonably stable, was aware of VaalChem's strategic value in the eyes of nearly all Western governments. The Liberians would entertain VaalChem's presence in their country, provided it is tightly controlled.

"But who would control the Liberians?" asked Elena.

"Western aid. Western oversight. They'd have far more to lose than they'd gain," he told her, "if they were to break their agreements. Their biggest benefit would be the international prestige that would come with having such a facility. But it mustn't fall under any government's control. It ought to be privately owned."

"Why by me?"

"Because the Bruggs are already in similar businesses. You control two large pharmaceutical firms and, I believe, a biotech of your own. You understand the safeguards, you have the trained specialists. I would suggest, however, that you recruit Dr. Kirch here as senior researcher and director."

Greta Kirch raised her hand. "Wait one minute," she protested.

"Dr. Kirch would go to Luanda at once. Howard Leland will guarantee her security. He'll provide all the help that she needs. She will seize all weapons-grade bacilli and spores in the name of the CDC. She will seize all existing documentation. It's not all there because Kessler took much of it, and I have a good deal of it that we took from Bourne, including his computer's hard drive. Those we'll keep, but we'll make them available to her. She'll return, but she'll soon be going back to Luanda. Assuming that we're able to work this out with Liberia, she will then supervise the dismantling of VaalChem."

Greta, once again, raised a hand to demur. Elena reached for that hand and gently lowered it. She said, "Tell me again. Why Liberia in particular?"

"We've discussed it," said Bannerman. "We've conferred with our people. Our own, Harry Whistler's, Leo Belkin's from Russia, the Israelis, and, of course, Martin Kessler. When I say the Israelis, I mean the Mossad. Yitzhak Netanya sent his top Angolan agent who, incidentally, helped save VaalChem from destruction. The consensus was Liberia. We already have a relationship with them, primarily through Roger Clew. He considers that Liberia is likely to become the most stable nation on the continent. He says that in Liberia there's a national pride that he hasn't seen anywhere else."

"And your stake in this would be?"

"Not financial. Not control. But we'll be seen as the people who *are* in control. Our influence will be considerable."

"I see."

"Greta Kirch, if she accepts, will be seen, in short order, as the foremost virologist on the planet. She'd be free to choose her own personnel, but I might make one or two suggestions."

"Such as?"

"Her security staff. Major Scar from the freighter. And Major Scar's men. They're the best in all Africa. And Major Scar's wife, now with the Red Cross, who would serve as their liaison and watchdog."

"You trust them?"

"I do. It's mostly instinct, but I do."

"And I trust you," said Elena. "And I trust Greta Kirch."

Greta said, "Wait. I have not agreed . . ."

"Nor have I," said Elena. "I'll discuss it with my husband. Then, back in Zurich, I'll discuss it with Willem."

Bannerman said, "But we should start this ball rolling."

Elena nodded. "I agree." She put a hand on Greta's arm. She asked, "Will you go to Angola?"

"That much . . . I will do. But as for the rest . . ."

"We'll take it one step at a time."

EPILOGUE

Kessler had not yet flown back to Angola.

Before the third day, when he was to have returned, he had used Molly's radio to contact the captain whom he had left in command. The captain was to stand down, but not to withdraw. The captain was to contact the government commander and say that he would not fire on VaalChem unless government troops entered VaalChem itself. If they did, he would assume that they were looting the complex. He would turn it into a furnace.

Kessler had to promise that he would return within a few more days at the most. He gave his word that he wouldn't abandon those soldiers who had chosen to serve at his side. He'd told the captain that Artemus Bourne could no longer work his mischief in Angola. With Bourne's influence non-existent and Savimbi long dead, an honorable truce with Luanda might be possible. Kessler promised that he would do all in his power to end the rape of this country.

"A tall order," said Bannerman.

"One must try," Kessler told him.

"You'll do what you can. And we will help you where we can. I know you understand that you can't change the world. What you *can* do is try to make your own."

"As you have? Fortress Westport? This place is unique and it is only for a few. There ought to be a place for the many."

Bannerman shrugged. "We're not so unique. There must be a thousand neighborhood watch groups that have been organized all over this country. Not gated communities. I mean inner cities. Neighbors who've decided to take care of their own."

"In terms of lethality, take my word; you're unique."

"Granted," said Bannerman, "but the principle's the same. They let the criminals know that the pickings would be easier in some other neighborhood, on some other street. It takes courage, but they do it and they see that it works. They'd be out there with bullhorns and baseball bats in areas that even the police wouldn't enter except in considerable force.

"The police would say to them, 'You're not solving the problem. All you're doing is shifting it. You are ordered to surrender your bullhorns and bats. Violence isn't the answer.' The men with bats would say, 'Go tell that to the criminals. Let us know when they've handed you their guns and their drugs. That's when we'll give up our bats.'"

Kessler nodded. He said nothing. He got up and he paced. Then, finally, "I don't know what to do."

"About Angola?"

"No," he said, grimacing. "About Elizabeth and Aisha. What can I possibly offer them, Paul?"

"Everything that's worth having," said Bannerman.

Bannerman had witnessed their first encounter when he drove back to Westport from the airport. Elizabeth and Aisha were with him, as was Molly. John Waldo was gone. He had vanished again. This was normal. No one bothered to remark on it.

Kessler had been waiting with Carla and Viktor. Their home, their Cape Cod, was the first house one encountered on passing through the pillars of Greens Farms Estates. Carla said later that he'd been a wreck. She said she'd been forced to threaten to cripple him if he didn't stop pacing and wringing his hands. He'd been watching through the window for Bannerman's car ever since he'd gotten word that they had touched down in Bridgeport.

Bannerman had driven past Carla's house. He hadn't been told that that's where Kessler would be. He saw sudden movement in his rearview mirror. He saw that it was Kessler. He'd run out into the street. But then Kessler had stopped. He stood there frozen. He seemed shaken. He didn't know what to do next.

Bannerman slowed and had not quite stopped when he gestured toward the mirror and said, "There he is." He had barely completed that very short sentence when Aisha exploded from the car. She ran to him, squealing and shouting his name. She reached him, leaped at him; he lifted her bodily. Kessler was smothering Aisha with kisses, but he quickly broke off, again unsure of himself. He told Bannerman later that it had suddenly struck him that the child he had known was now a young lady and kissing should perhaps be more restrained. But if this had troubled Kessler, it did not trouble Aisha. She threw herself at him once more.

Elizabeth had made no move to get out. She had turned her head once to see the first of their embraces, but then quickly turned again to face forward. Bannerman saw that her face was flushed. He saw that her shoulders were trembling.

Molly asked Elizabeth, "Are you just going to sit here?"

Elizabeth seemed unable to move. She almost seemed unable to breathe.

Molly punched her shoulder. "Get out of this car. Don't you dare make him look at the back of your head."

Bannerman said to Molly, "She just needs a moment. Remember, he's been dead for two years."

"A moment to do what. Check her makeup? Fix her hair? Elizabeth, you'll either step out of this car or I'll . . ."

"Um, Molly . . ."

"Paul, butt out."

"I don't think she hears you."

Molly said, "Elizabeth, I'm counting to three." She said, "And another thing. Don't shake his hand. Elizabeth, if I see you stick out your hand . . ."

Elizabeth seemed only vaguely aware that what Molly was saying had some relevance to her. She had started to climb through the door that stood open. She moved very slowly as if still in disbelief that the man in the road could be Martin. She turned toward Molly; she blinked as if to ask, Did you say something?

"Never mind. Just get up there," said Molly.

Bannerman watched her through his rearview mirror. He was watching a different Elizabeth Stride. She walked slowly, faltering, her hands covering her mouth. Kessler saw her coming. He'd been smiling, but it faded. Bannerman couldn't know what he was seeing in her eyes. He saw Elizabeth's hands come away from her face. He saw her right hand reaching out to him.

"I'll kill her," said Molly. "She's doing it. I'll kill her. She's going to shake his hand and let him kiss her damned cheek."

But Molly was wrong. The hand rose to his face. Aisha's lips were moving; she was speaking excitedly, but Elizabeth didn't seem to hear Aisha either. Her fingers brushed his lips and his chin and moved up his cheek to his brow. At the corner of one eye she found a V-shaped scar that he'd had long before she first met him. She touched it as if to make sure it was real. She leaned her head forward, not to offer her cheek, but to lean it against Kessler's chest. Aisha did the same. He kissed the tops of their heads. He buried his own face between them.

As far as Bannerman could see, no more words had been spoken. He had watched them for the better part of a minute. He realized that he was intruding.

He said to Molly, "Let's be getting on home."

She said, "I'd better get them. We can't leave them on the street."

"They'll move when they want to. Let's go home."

*   *   *

Elizabeth and Aisha stayed with Molly at her house. Molly had expected Kessler to join them. She had offered her bedroom to Kessler and Elizabeth if that was what the both of them wanted. Elizabeth looked at Kessler. Kessler declined. He said he thought it best to stay with Carla if he might. He said to Elizabeth what Elena had said. They should take this one step at a time.

Molly took him aside. She said, "You ought to be together."

He told her, "It's better to wait."

She said, "Martin, I'm aware that you have certain limitations. She's been told. I don't think she cares."

"I care. Not for my sake. I've grown used to it now. I care because she deserves better."

As for Bannerman, he'd be glad when the weekend came and Molly, for a change, might have her own life to manage.

Kessler did stay with Carla, but only to sleep. He spent most of his free time with Elizabeth, or with Aisha, most often with the two of them together. And together they would stop by to visit the baby, taking turns holding him, cooing at him. Kessler had been stunned when he learned that the baby was going to be named after him. More than stunned, he was speechless. He could find no words. Or else he did not trust himself to speak.

He was kept busy otherwise when his input was welcomed on issues that this group had assembled to discuss. Few were surprised that he'd turned up alive. This was, after all, Martin Kessler. What *did* surprise some was that he was Alameo. Most had heard of Alameo and they'd heard that he was white, but none of them had dreamed that Alameo might be Kessler. Bannerman had offered to provide them with proof in the form of the poster that Netanya had sent him.

Kessler said, "Show them that and I burn down your house."

"How about just the head with your pretty blue cap?"

"For that, I only burn your garage."

Elizabeth had been patient for the first three days. More than patient, she was even deferential. She gave no sign of wanting to lace into Kessler for the two years of anguish and regret that he'd caused her. She would think before she spoke or she would listen in silence, all the while holding either his hand or Aisha's. This alone caused some in attendance to wonder whether she was the real Elizabeth Stride. This Stride was, perhaps, a more even-tempered twin of the Stride who had been the Black Angel. Some conjectured that she must have been lobotomized.

On the fourth day, late evening, Kessler came to the house. The children were upstairs asleep. Bannerman had expected that the visitor would be Carla. The chimes from the "Jaws" theme had sounded. But it was Kessler alone. Carla merely had alerted him. Kessler came to the door with a small bag in hand. It contained his few personal effects. He told Bannerman that he had made up his mind. He would slip away quietly. He would not be returning.

Bannerman asked him, "Does Elizabeth know this?"

"She'll be all right. She has Aisha."

"So, you're saying that you haven't said good-bye to either one."

"It is cowardly, I know. But in the long run, it's better. I'll go to Angola. I have obligations. After that, I think I will go back to Europe. I am happiest when I ski. I would like to ski. And I'll teach to put food on the table."

"You'll have no money when you leave Angola?"

"I'll have a little," said Kessler. "Enough."

"You might be the first white man in the history of that country who ever walked away broke."

Kessler shrugged. He said, "There's nothing there that is mine."

"Their diamonds might not be, but you have your own. You have the diamonds that you left for Elizabeth two years ago. I'm sure that she'd say they're still yours."

"She'll need them more than I will. She must make a new home."

Susan entered the room. She had overheard some of it. She asked Kessler, "What has happened? What is making you leave?"

He said, "You must excuse me. It's a personal matter. It's not a thing that I'm comfortable discussing."

She said, "No, what's uncomfortable will be us in the morning when we try to explain this to the people who love you. And don't try to tell me that you don't love them. Everyone who's seen you knows better."

"I must go. Will you tell little Martin about me?"

"He's going to see for himself. He needs godparents, damn it. You're elected. You and Elizabeth."

Kessler blinked. "You want us? For moral guidance? Stability? Forgive me, but you are insane."

"For courage," said Bannerman. "For honor. For loyalty. The christening is this coming Sunday."

Before Kessler could speak, the chimes sounded again. It was Molly's theme, "Pretty Woman." But, again, it wasn't Molly who came to the door. It was Elizabeth. She had Aisha with her. Elizabeth's eyes went to Kessler's small bag. She said to Bannerman, "Carla told us he'd packed." She said to Kessler, "I just don't believe you."

Kessler couldn't look at her or at Aisha. He kept his eyes on the floor. Elizabeth apologized for the intrusion. She asked Bannerman and Susan, "Did he tell you what caused this?"

Bannerman answered, "I think it's been building. He's told me that he has nothing to give you. I told him he's wrong. He has everything."

"What brought it on tonight is that I asked him to sleep with me. Nothing sexual, just some holding until we fall asleep. I was careful to say that I had no expectations."

Kessler had reddened. "Elizabeth . . . please."

She said to Susan, "And yes, I did tell him that I love him. I didn't blurt it out. I didn't say, 'By the way.' I had my hands on his cheeks; I looked into his eyes. I said, I might not have known it, but I've loved him from the start. I said that I love him now more than ever. I said that I would love him for as long as he lives. That last part, I think, was the problem."

"Elizabeth," said Kessler, "Aisha shouldn't be hearing . . ."

"Which part?"

"The intimate parts. About sleeping together. About certain physical deficiencies."

Elizabeth asked Aisha, "Were you raised in a bubble?"

"No, I wasn't," she said. "I know how babies get born." She said to Kessler, "And I know about cuddling and loving. I know that you don't need sex to do that."

Kessler took a breath. "There'll be no babies from me."

Elizabeth said, "Well, guess what. From me either."

"That would seem to take fertility off the table," said Susan. She said to Kessler, "That leaves impotence and it's treatable these days. Have your doctors not told you that it's treatable?"

Kessler covered his face. He begged, "Will you stop?" He gestured with his shoulder toward Aisha.

Aisha said, "Impotence isn't news to me either. There are ads on TV every day."

Elizabeth told Susan, "His doctors said that it's hopeless. But those doctors were Israelis. They were Mossad. And Kessler, who *knows* the Israelis can be tricky, was too dumb to get a second opinion."

Susan asked her, "They lied to him?"

"Or they let him believe it. The Israelis needed him to want to go to Angola. The less future he thought he would have, the better. The bleaker it looked, the less likely he'd be to turn up on Hilton Head Island again. Even when Martin took off for Davos, they had loaded him down with a cocktail of pills that they said would delay the development of cancers. Do you see his little bag? It's still loaded with pills. Martin, to my knowledge, has shaved twice since he's been here. What will you bet that there's something in that bag that shuts down his testosterone pump?"

Kessler threw up his hands. He said, "Enough about this."

Bannerman asked, "Except what if it's true?"

"What is true," said Kessler, "is that I have five years. This is at most. This is if I am lucky. Five years before leukemia, liver failure, kidney failure. The doctors did not lie about that. When I got there, I had lost all my hair, half my teeth. Do you think this was caused by some Israeli pill?"

Aisha said to him, "We'll take it."

"You'll take what?"

"Those five years."

Elizabeth said to Kessler, "Look. I'm through being nice. You're going to beat this because you're Martin Kessler and nothing has ever beaten you yet. We're going to find you some new doctors. But even if the Israelis were right, I'm with Aisha; I want those five years. We'll take care of each other; we will love each other, so stop whining and get with the program."

Kessler sighed. He said to Susan, "This was so close just now. From Elizabeth, this was almost a tenderness."

"She's right about the doctors," said Susan. "What else?"

"I must go to Angola. I have given my word. I must go for two months, maybe three."

"Then I'm going with you," said Elizabeth. "What else?"

Kessler shook his head. "It is no place for you."

"It was good enough for Sara and I'm meaner. What else?"

"And leave Aisha? What of Aisha? Without you, she has no one."

Aisha said brightly, "Oh, I won't be alone."

Elizabeth said quickly, "She means she's among friends."

She warned Aisha, with her eyes, that she'd best not elaborate. Keep your mother and Nadia and Jasmine to yourself until Bannerman's crowd has had a chance to get used to you. They already must be wondering how you could be so chipper a day or two after your guardians were murdered. We don't want you saying, *"Oh, I'm fine; so are they. I'll probably see them tonight."*

Aisha knew that look. She understood what it meant. She said quietly, "Not just them. I have new friends. Still alive."

Not quietly enough. Susan asked her. "Still alive?"

"Well, there's Claudia. She's an angel. But she's still flesh and blood. We've been having some wonderful talks and she's staying."

"Aisha's not nuts," said Elizabeth to Susan. "She just has a broader view of what's real and what isn't."

Susan answered, "She's told us that her mother stays in touch. That's nothing to explain or apologize for. As for Claudia, she's right. She'll be staying for a while. Claudia is almost as new to this as Aisha. She and Adam will be spending a few months with us."

Aisha said, "Claudia's not so nuts either. She has this one great idea that really could change the world. It's about an old prophecy that I never knew about. It seems that my namesake, the original Aisha . . ."

"Later," said Elizabeth firmly.

"No, this could be good. It could be great for Muslim women."

"If enough of them live through it," said Elizabeth. She'd been told of it.

"This could save them, Elizabeth. Claudia says . . ."

"Aisha . . . later. Put a lid on it. Thank you."

Susan caught Aisha's eye and gave her a wink. The gesture said that she'd like to hear it herself. But Elizabeth was right. It would keep.

Elizabeth said to Kessler, "Here's where it stands. You and I are going to buy a home here together." She paused. She said to Bannerman, "That's assuming we're welcome."

He smiled. "We'll look at houses in the morning."

She lowered her eyes. She moistened her lips. She said to Aisha, "It's going to happen."

"I know."

Bannerman told her, "We'll get your possessions shipped up here. Go to Africa, come back, and we'll get you settled in. Don't leave before Sunday, however."

"What's Sunday?"

"Martin will tell you. You can talk it over later."

"We'll line up some tutors for Aisha," said Susan. "She won't fall behind while you're gone."

"By the way," said Bannerman, "there's a rumor that you're dead again. Roger's driver killed a woman who was working for Bourne. He called her Elizabeth. He even tried to say Stride. All we know about her is that her name was Claire. The police, apparently, don't even have that. No prints of her on file, and her face was disfigured. There are some who think you died in that garage."

"You're saying?"

"I'm saying you can probably stay dead if you wish. You might want to think about changing your name. Or at least don't slap Stride on your mailbox this time."

Kessler frowned. He asked, "You are Paul Bannerman, are you not?"

"Well, yes, but I haven't tried to be dead."

"Up the street is Molly Farrell, Carla Benedict, Anton Zivic. Not much farther away is Billy McHugh. Somewhere else, God knows where, is John Waldo. I don't even mention Harry Whistler and the twins and about fifty others who are here for your meetings. Name one who has not had a price on his head by one angry government or another."

"Just a thought," said Bannerman. "Up to you."

"She is the incomparable Elizabeth Stride. And I am Martin Kessler, now that I have stopped whining. We will both keep our names, if you please."

"I'm sorry I mentioned it," said Bannerman.

"Do you have wine? What wines do you have?"

"Um . . . the normal assortment. Reds and whites. A few nice ones."

"Champagne?"

"I don't think so."

Susan said, "Yes, we do. Harry brought us a Dom and a Cristal."

"I'll replace them," said Kessler, "but not before morning. Tonight they must turn a lady's head."

Elizabeth had her hands on her hips. She glared at Kessler. "What do you think you're doing?"

"I intend to make approximate love to you."

"Well, forget it. I come on to you and you're ready to skip town. You had your chance, Kessler, and you blew it."

Kessler said to Bannerman. "Woman scorned. She'll get over it." He said to Susan, "Baby powder. Do you have some? You must."

"My parents," said Aisha, "always kept some in the nightstand. And you know what else they liked?"

"Not one more word," said Elizabeth.

Susan said, "And some music. You can have our CD player. We're a little light on porn films, but I've got *Cosmopolitan*."

"Wait a minute," said Elizabeth. "Every one of you. Wait. Now it's gone to committee? Next you'll ask us to tape it."

Kessler winced. He said, "She's right. We are making this a joke."

"Sorry," said Susan. "I got carried away."

Kessler said to Elizabeth, "It is nerves. I am frightened. I've been frightened since I knew that I would see you again and a wreck when I feared that I might not."

"Then walk with me, Martin. We'll just take a walk. We'll go sit by the shore and watch the water."

He said, "In two years, there has not been a day when you were not in my heart and in my mind. In two years there has been hardly a night when I didn't visit you in my dreams."

She reached for his hand. She said, "Tell me as we walk."

He said, "You never came to me. You didn't know where I was. But I came to you. I knew where you would be. You would be working in your garden. Sometimes you were cooking. Sometimes you were sitting with your glass of wine, reading. I would watch you for a while. I wouldn't disturb you. But sometimes I would feel that you were thinking of me and remembering more good things than bad."

Elizabeth said nothing. But her eyes took on a shine.

Susan had tugged at Bannerman's sleeve. She reached to touch Aisha's shoulder. She whispered, "Let's go." She cocked her head toward the kitchen. She eased them both from the room.

Kessler gave no sign that he had noticed their departure. Nor did Elizabeth. She was frozen in place.

"And then I would lean very close to your ear and I would whisper, 'I love you, Elizabeth Stride.' And sometimes, not always, I would see your lips move. You would not return the sentiment, not in so many words. You would say, 'Damn you, Martin,' but it meant the same thing. I would know this because I'd see the pain in your eyes."

From the kitchen, Aisha saw that Elizabeth seemed in shock. Her legs seemed unable to support her. She began to wilt. Kessler took her in his arms. They held each other tightly, not speaking.

"She knows he was there," Aisha whispered to Susan. "She knows that he did come to her all those times because she knows that she did say, 'Damn you, Martin.'"

They watched as Kessler turned her toward Bannerman's front door. She did not resist him. She almost seemed to melt into him.

Susan said to Aisha, "You'll be sleeping here tonight."

Aisha answered with a smile. She said, "Thank you."

Susan said, "The baby powder would have been a nice touch."

"I don't think they're going to miss it," said Bannerman.

**Follow *New York Times*
bestselling author John Maxim
into the World of Bannerman**

A team of once deadly government assassins led by Paul Bannerman has "retired" in the quiet, affluent town of Westport, Connecticut. All Bannerman and his people want is a normal life—but there are those who refuse to live and let live . . .

The Bannerman Solution

When Paul Bannerman and his highly trained group are thought to be too dangerous and must be terminated, Bannerman is lured to Westport, Connecticut, with the intention that he never leave alive. Bannerman, however, has other ideas. Electrified with suspense this is truly an unputdownable thriller. In stores now . . .

"If there's no other business," Paul said rising, "the bar's open."

"Paul? Aren't you going to tell us about Palmer Reid?"

"What about him?"

"Anton says you met with him at Windermere."

Paul made a face. "I did not meet with him. He learned I was there and he came uninvited. I warned him not to do that again, especially at Windermere."

"So? What did he want?"

"Just more of the same. He wants us to surrender Anton, he wants me back in the field, or so he claims, and he wants the rest of you scattered and relocated individually. The only new thing he offered was that we can keep the funds we seized and, if you don't want to trust him, he'll put your relocation under the FBI's Witness Protection Program."

"We're supposed to trust the FBI?" Carla smiled.

"It's academic. I said no."

"Reid's not a man to be brushed off," Russo warned. "You don't think he's cooking something up?"

"Reid's always cooking something up."

"I don't know why you don't let us scratch that son of a bitch once and for all," Carla said. "He's going to hit us sooner or later."

"Look . . ." Paul stepped to the bar and poured a glass of wine. "Let's not even think in those terms. Reid's people will never come to Westport in force because they'd never be able to get all of us. He probably isn't even sure how many there are. I don't think he'll try to infiltrate again because I've told him I'll be obliged to kill any agent he sends in. He won't try a snatch on Anton because he knows we'll retaliate—against his family if we have to—and all he'll end up with is a swap. Palmer Reid is frustrated, humiliated and angry, but as long as we keep our heads he has no acceptable options.

"So," Anton Zivic chose a cognac, "your assessment is that he will do nothing, Paul."

"He'll watch us, try to contain us, and keep looking for a crack he can exploit. In the meantime, I think his immediate concern is making sure what we did here can't happen in his other towns."

"Perhaps it would not be a bad idea to stir up some trouble in one or two of them," Zivic suggested. "Take his mind off Westport."

Paul answered with a pained expression. It was not a new suggestion. It seemed to come up every time one or more in the group felt restless. None of them and especially Anton, were accustomed to taking static defensive positions and leaving all initiative to the opposition. But the point was, they were no longer a tactical action group. They were retired. They had new lives, each of his own choosing. As far as other towns were concerned—there were five other "Westports" across the country that he knew of—what was happening in them was none of their business. So far, Paul had declined even to name them.

Anton Zivic accepted the cue and dismissed the subject

with a wave of his glass. Perhaps over a quiet drink one day he would tell Paul that his government—his former government—had knowledge of at least two. One was certainly Wilmette, Illinois, a Westport-like suburb just northeast of Chicago. Another was Palo Alto in California. Suspected were Framingham in Massachusetts, and Fort Worth in Texas.

It would not be very difficult, were Zivic so inclined, to compile a list of towns that were likely candidates. Paul had long ago told him how Westport was chosen. It followed that the same criteria would apply to all. They would be upper-middle-class communities. Not conspicuously affluent, but comfortable, offering a lifestyle that was at least the equal of what the agents had enjoyed in the field. Like Westport, they would all be commuter towns, towns with more or less transient populations where newcomers attracted little notice. No company towns. No one-industry towns such as those in Silicon Valley. No socially competitive towns such as nearby Greenwich or Darien. A primary consideration would be finding places in which people tended to respect the privacy of their neighbors. Westport had that reputation, and for that reason it had attracted many celebrities over the years, particularly those in the arts. People left them alone.

A computer would narrow the list further. First there were all the ordinary quality-of-life considerations. Recreation, cultural activities, affordable housing and so on. Schools were not a factor. Agents were not supposed to have been there long enough to conceive, let alone raise, children. Romantic relationships with the locals were, in any case, forbidden. The computer would also exclude any towns that had career intelligence officers or retired State Department personnel in residence. It would not do to encounter a former case officer while standing in line at the supermarket.

The concept, Zivic supposed, was sound enough in theory. It was like the halfway house, but on a grander scale. Halfway towns. A way to depressurize and rehabilitate certain agents who were being retired from the field. A year or so of learning to live, under close supervision and tutoring, like normal citizens. Then relocation elsewhere under more relaxed supervision but with continued counseling. Then eventually, a more complete reabsorption into ordinary American life. A sound enough concept. It might even be called benevolent. It gave some of these people a chance to save their lives.

The halfway towns were not intended, Zivic knew, for the ordinary CIA or NSA or military intelligence field agent. Not even for those Operations Branch agents of whom so much cloak-and-dagger nonsense is written. Such personnel usually retired to become authors, lecturers, local police chiefs, registered foreign agents or lobbyists, private corporate spies, and, occasionally, whistle-blowers. Those meant for the halfway towns were different. Nearly all were contract agents, freelancers who were bound by no official constraint or code of conduct. Nor were they, like career agents, immune to criminal prosecution by informal convention among NATO countries. Many were operatives who had spent half their lifetimes in deep cover and high-stress situations. These were assassins, kidnappers, expert interrogators, even torturers. These were people who would think nothing of robbing a bank or trafficking in arms in order to finance an operation too sensitive to be funded through identifiable channels. Most were living, breathing weapons. Cocked weapons. Some were borderline psychotics, likely to choose an enemy of their own if one were not regularly provided for them. A few, like Billy, could never be allowed to retire to any environment short of a maximum-security mental institution.

The halfway town concept, first envisioned by Allen Dulles and later expanded under President Jimmy Carter, provided some with at least the chance of being salvaged. But the rehabilitative process was also an evaluative process. Though President Carter was unlikely to have known it, fully one third did not survive the relocation. They simply vanished en route to their promised new locations. Nor was there ever a need to explain their disappearance. They had, after all, been relocated with new identities. It could truthfully be said, to anyone who might inquire, that they no longer existed. Of those who did survive, few of any value were left in peace.

Anton Zivic sipped his cognac, his expression thoughtful as he studied the faces now standing about Paul's conference table. Not one of them, he was certain, would be allowed to retire to private life.

The Bannerman Effect

Bannerman's group has been chosen as a test case for a new State Department toy—a computer program called the Ripper Effect. Its purpose is to destroy criminal organizations through strategically chosen assassinations. Yet in picking Bannerman and his band of deadly operatives, they may have made the biggest mistake of their lives. In stores now . . .

Roger Clew reached for the Toshiba's "power" switch and flipped it. A soft blue light filled the screen. He followed this procedure with the IBM. A title appeared. JTR EFFECT, Fuller thought it said. The younger man quickly advanced past it to what seemed to be a short list of instructions. From his tote, he produced a single sheet, covered in plastic. This he placed beside the keyboard.

"These are some special commands." He pointed. "Otherwise, the system is interactive. It's basically self-explanatory."

"Am I going to hate this, Roger?"

"My hope is you'll. . . ." He pulled out Fuller's chair. "Sir, if you'll just—sit."

An hour later, Barton Fuller had still not moved from the IBM machine. Nor had his eyes left the screen except to consult the list of commands or to glance up, blinking, at Roger Clew.

The younger man watched him in silence, his hands wrapped around a mug of coffee that had long grown cold. He'd watched the secretary's expression change from one of confusion to one of disbelief to one of horrified fascination. But he did not see rejection. He began to hope that, come Monday, he would still have a career after all.

Fuller, a large man, a full head over six feet, leaned back in his chair and stretched. With one huge hand he kneaded the muscles near his neck. His head turned toward the little Toshiba that Clew had set up within arm's length of his machine. Curiously, to no purpose, he reached out to touch it. He found himself reflecting on its size. One of his hands, spread wide, could easily cover the entire keyboard. Such a little thing. Somehow he'd always thought of laptops as more toy than tool. Not any more. This was no toy. This, in theory at least, was a machine that killed.

In the past thirty minutes alone, Barton Fuller had snuffed out the lives of eight men and two women. He had kidnapped three others. He caused four more to vanish without a trace. He made a shambles of two known terrorist organizations, one Libyan, the other Irish. He had paralyzed them, caused defections from their ranks, and caused member to turn on member.

Fuller muttered something. Clew leaned forward. "Sir?" he asked.

"I said it's a game." Fuller's eyes remained fixed to the screen. "It's still only a game."

"No, sir," Clew answered. "I don't think so."

Fuller waggled the fingers of one hand in a signal to be still as his other hand searched the keyboard and his eye returned to the list of commands. At the top of the sheet was that legend again: JTR EFFECT. He'd asked what it meant at the outset. Clew, he thought, had avoided answering. He'd apparently forgotten it was there. "When you're finished, sir," he said. "Please."

An index of organizations appeared on the screen. He scrolled past those of known terrorist groups. There were more than 200 in the Middle East alone. A similar number throughout Europe. More in Africa. More everywhere. A few, even, in the Soviet Union.

Next came the drug traffickers, another long list. Then Mafia families. Then came corporations. Barton Fuller frowned. Corporations?

Then he understood. He recognized the names of a German firm that had helped Libya build a chemical weapons factory, a Danish company that had illegally sold submarine detection devices to the Soviets and an American defense contractor whose greed and shoddy standards had resulted in the deaths of several flight crews.

Fuller returned to the drug traffickers. He was more comfortable there. He selected one at random, a drug distribution network based in Mexico. He touched a key and an organization chart appeared. He touched another and the names became faces. Fuller chose one face at random. A brutish looking man, hooded eyes, thick lips. Fuller ordered his execution, using the keyboard to type in the means. He chose a car bomb. Next he asked the computer to predict the effects of that assassination. A list of consequences appeared on the screen, in order of probability. The primary effect was a relatively peaceful reorganization and a redistribution of the dead man's property among his associates. Fuller then killed his replacement. Another car bomb. Now the effect was panic. He killed two more. The effect was chaos. Incredibly to Fuller, the computer predicted six additional deaths, all men and women who were likely to be suspected of the original killings. The drug distribution network was effectively destroyed. In theory.

Fuller folded his long arms. He nodded in the direction of the laptop. "Who knows about this? Who programmed it?"

"Basically it's the TENET program adapted to the new Cray-3 computer system. I asked some of the Cray programmers to experiment with a few refinements. No one person has seen all of it."

Fuller nodded.

TENET, an acronym for Terrorist Network, was a data bank that collected and continuously updated all available information on known terrorist organizations. It included estimates of capability, political orientation, and even psychological profiles from the world's leading experts on terrorism.

"Roger," the secretary asked quietly, "by any chance, are we talking about government death squads here? Argentine style?"

"Absolutely not."

Fuller gestured toward the screen. "But I see a great many unpleasant people dying in many exotic ways. How else does this come about?"

"The actions I have in mind do not necessarily involve killing. And I do not propose to use government personnel."

Fine distinctions, thought Fuller. Perhaps young Roger is a closet lawyer after all. "What, then, do you have in mind?"

"Sir, at this time I'm still really just exploring potential. But these actions would not be unlike many of the covert operations, past and present, of our intelligence services."

"Those operations fall, for better or worse, under a legally constituted charter. Does this?"

"No, sir. It can't work if it does."

"Do I gather, then, that I have just been lured into a criminal conspiracy with you, Mr. Hagler, and Mr. Kaplan?"

"Not at all. We're just . . . talking."

"Funny, you don't look hypothetical," Fuller said, deadpan. "But as long as we're just talking, what does our expert on counterterrorism think about all this?"

"You know what Hagler wants. He wants his hands untied."

"Who among us does not? But I'm asking about this." He turned his thumb to the laptop.

"In Harry's words, he would like the freedom to hit those fuckers so hard and so often that they'd be afraid to come up for air. Any way he could. Legally or not."

"That's Harry, all right. Where would he draw the line?"

"I asked him that. He said he'd let me know when he reached it."

"Surely he'd stop at murder."

"Naturally. If that's what it was."

"What else could it be and still have the same effect?"

"Punitive action. Preemptive strikes. Pest control. Whatever works for him."

"And Irwin?"

"He was—uneasy in the beginning. He's coming around. It was Kaplan who insisted that I expose this to you before we go any further."

"In search of a godfather, I take it."

"On the contrary, Kaplan doesn't think you'll have the stomach for it. Frankly, I think that's what he's hoping for."

"He might be right. What are you hoping for?"

"That we can all, the four of us, put our minds together. That we can come up with a way to use this technology that is both morally defensible and effective. Above all, sir, I'm with Hagler. I want the enemies of our country to be afraid. TENET can show us how it hit them with random but strategic—*countermeasures*." He'd almost said *brutality*. "But they will have no idea who is hitting them or why."

"No idea?" Fuller raised an eyebrow. "Does TENET say these people are all stupid? You don't think they'll make some gesture in our direction such as blowing a few more of our airliners out of the sky?"

"Not if our strikes appear to be the work of rival factions. We can have terrorists killing each other off at two or three times their current rate. We can start wars between drug lords, drive them undercover, paralyze their traffic."

"And gang wars between mobsters?"

"Eventually, yes."

"In any case," Clew continued, "after these—surgical strikes—our own legally constituted agencies would be employed to move in and pick up the pieces. The computer would have told them exactly—"

"I get the picture."

"The beauty of it is," Clew pointed out, "that no one else has to be in on this. Just Kaplan and Hagler. They'll go on directing operations just as they're doing now. No one's going to ask them how they got so smart all of a sudden."

"No CIA?" Fuller asked.

"Not while Palmer Reid is there."

Fuller's eyes narrowed. "Which, I gather, means that your chief surgeon is to be your old friend Mama's Boy."

"There is no more Mama's Boy. He's just Paul Bannerman now. But yes, he'd be my first choice."

"Are you ready to tell me what JTR EFFECT means?" Fuller asked.

"It's not important." Clew seemed faintly embarrassed. "Just a name I gave it."

"Well? Tell me. That way we'll both know."

Clew took a breath. "I had to call it something. I call it the 'Ripper Effect.' "

"As in Jack the Ripper?"

"Yes."

"Melodramatic." Fuller raised an eyebrow. "But apt. Random terror. Tied up an entire police force. Kept people at home nights."

"And," Clew added pointedly, "the Ripper was never identified."

Fuller sipped thoughtfully from his mug. "No one else, beyond you and me, Kaplan and Hagler, would have to know?"

"And Bannerman, if he'll do it."

"No records would be kept?"

"None."

"No accountability?"

"You might wish to tell the president. That's up to you."

Fuller threw him a look. He did not bother to comment. "When Hagler and Kaplan arrive, we will play platform tennis. That's all."

"Can I tell them you'll . . ."

"You can tell them I'll think about this. If you wish, I'll say something cryptic to that effect. But the four of us will never sit down and discuss it."

"I understand." A sigh of satisfaction. Relief.

"It's a fascinating premise, Roger. Not just counterterrorism. Terrorists, America's own, striking back, taking the initiative for a change. But it's hardly the answer to all the world's problems. And your friend Bannerman is just one man. I assume you do not expect him to eradicate both the terrorist threat and the drug problem single-handedly."

"Of course not. But he can start giving us the experience we need. Let me work with him. A test. Find out if what works in theory will work in the field."

"And if he refuses?"

"I won't let him. He owes me."

Fuller didn't doubt it. Palmer Reid had, however uncharacteristically, tried to harass Bannerman by legal means. Getting his passport lifted; trying to interest the IRS in his financial affairs; and demanding the arrest of Anton Zivic, a former colonel in Soviet Military Intelligence, in the country illegally and now, apparently, Bannerman's second in command. Roger Clew had blocked him at every turn. A thought struck him. "That computer of yours . . ." He pointed with his mug. "Is Bannerman's organization in it?"

"Yes."

"And is Reid's?"

Clew hesitated.

"I thought so."

Clew remained silent.

"No further action, Roger. No experiments. No computer games. Do nothing at all. I've said I'll think about it, and I will."

"Yes, sir."

"Why aren't you arguing?"

"The truth? This is already more than I'd hoped for. I was afraid you'd ask me to resign."

"I still might. You're a very good man, Roger, but you may have spent too many years with Mama's Boy. I hope it hasn't damaged you."

"He says the same thing about my years in Washington."

Fuller frowned. "You took an oath. He didn't."

". . . Yes, sir."

"May I hold on to that laptop for a few days? I'd like to become more familiar with some of these groups."

"Sir, if someone should get into this room—"

"Take the list of commands. I've memorized them."

"Yes, sir."

"Yes, Bart," Fuller corrected him. "The meeting is over."

*　　*　　*

The Ripper Effect, indeed, mused Barton Fuller, returning to his painting. The Ripper was small potatoes compared to some of Bannerman's crowd. As Roger knows perfectly well. Why not call it The Bannerman Effect and be done with it?

The Bannerman Effect.

Bannerman's Law

Bannerman and his entire group have been trying to retire and blend into the community. But when Lisa Benedict, the younger sister of one of the group, is brutally murdered after stumbling onto a government secret, Carla Benedict sets out to find the truth, and soon Bannerman and his operatives become both hunter and hunted.

On a cool and perfect California morning, on the last day of her short life, Lisa Benedict parked her Fiero in a quiet residential area several streets away from the gate house of Sur La Mer.

She had come by a different route this time, using only back roads and residential streets. She avoided Tower Road, which ringed the grounds on all but the ocean side. It had been tempting to make a quick pass of it, to see that all was quiet, but that would have meant driving past the surveillance cameras. Better, she decided, not to let them see her car again. The car was white, with a USC Trojans decal across the rear window, a student parking sticker on the windshield, and a crumpled left front fender. They were likely to remember it from the previous Sunday. But without the car, she felt sure, they would not recognize her at all.

On that first Sunday she had worn a skirt and blue blazer, and a pair of heels, which she'd ended up ruining. This time she was better equipped. She wore a borrowed running suit, dark green and hooded—to hide the shine of her auburn hair—and she had muted her new white Reeboks with a bottle of Kitchen Bouquet which, she hoped, would wash out. The suit was three sizes too large and shapeless, all the better for camouflage. She would blend nicely into the thick forest of sugar pines that ringed the asylum.

She locked the car, then strapped a bulky tote around her waist, adjusting it so that her Nikon and recorder would not chafe her spine. She began jogging. Upon reaching Tower Road, where it bordered Sur La Mer to the north, she turned right, away from the gates, and paced herself with another runner some fifty yards ahead of her. *That's good,* she thought. *Not being the only one out here.* The other jogger, a man, faded red sweatshirt and shorts, visored tennis hat, glanced back over his shoulder but kept on.

He'd seen her. It meant she would have to keep this up for a while. She couldn't very well have him look back again and see that she'd vanished. But now he was turning, reversing his direction, heading back toward her. As he drew near, he nodded. A brief, polite smile, a flicker of eye contact. He was a man in his forties, well tanned but fleshy, not very fit.

That face. Did it seem familiar? No. Just a face. Don't get paranoid. She bobbed her head in response, then continued on, keeping the Sur La Mer estate to her left. She counted off two hundred paces and then pretended to trip as if over a shoelace. She stopped, pretending to tie it. Glancing the way she'd come, she saw the other jogger was gone.

Rats, she thought. She'd prefer to have seen him peel off toward his home. Or at least to be sure that he wasn't from Sur La Mer. Not that it should matter necessarily. She wondered what her sister would do in this situation. Better to make sure, she decided. She turned in the direction he had taken.

Keeping a steady pace, she approached the main gate, the only gate, and its video camera. The camera's stare remained fixed, not tilting or turning as she went by. Morning dew still covered the driveway. It showed one set of tire tracks but no footprints. Satisfied, she slowed to a walk, then reversed her field once more.

All was quiet now. No people in sight. She heard no sound but the distant yap of a small dog.

She reached the place where, seven days earlier, in heels, she had struggled over the low fence and scurried for the cover of the trees that formed a living moat around Sur La Mer. She did it again, this time smoothly vaulting the fence and promptly blending, green against green, not the forest. Just inside the tree line, she lowered herself into a squat so that it would seem, if anyone came, that she had paused to relieve herself. She waited for five minutes, listening, then she checked her watch. The climb to the main grounds, she estimated, would take twenty minutes. Last Sunday it had taken nearly an hour. But this time she was dressed for it. And she had a map. She knew where the trip wires were. She would not have to feel her way.

Not bad, she told herself, for someone who'd never done anything like this before. Her sister, Carla, would be proud of her. Well . . . maybe after bawling her out first. Lisa had asked herself, all that week, how Carla would have gone about it. Careful preparation, came the answer. Slow and easy. Except Carla, being Carla, would probably have brought a weapon of some kind. And her heart would not be pounding this hard.

"Who am I kidding?" she muttered aloud.

Carla wouldn't have done this at all. She would have thought the whole thing was dumb. Seen too many movies.

On the other hand, Carla never cared much about her grades. She had never even finished college, let alone earned a masters at the toughest film school in the country. Let alone graduating third in her class, if she could lock in an A for Mecklenberg's course.

And if Nellie Dameon, up there, isn't worth an A . . . heck, an A *plus* once Mecklenberg learns that she, Lisa Benedict, actually got her voice on tape, then nothing is.

Lisa took a breath and began her climb.

Bannerman's Promise
(formerly *A Matter of Honor*)

Carla Benedict is Bannerman's most ruthless agent—but she's also a woman in love. And she's just had to eliminate her new lover—a smooth, lethal spy. It doesn't take long for Bannerman to realize that Carla's call will have deadly and far-reaching implications. But even he could not predict they would all become unwitting pawns in an underground civil war involving hard-line Communists, devious reformers, drug smugglers, and a new and brutal Russian Mafia.

The man in the tam-o'-shanter stood on the edge of the pit, looking into it. He was shaking his head, wearily. The others joined him there.

He nodded toward his chauffeur, who turned the flashlight on and shined it where he pointed. The man from the Zil could see better now. Before, they had been only shapeless mounds, glistening under a glaze of sleet. He seemed confused.

"Only animals?" he asked. "Where are the villagers?"

"Underneath," said the one who had been in charge. "This way, if anyone should ever start digging . . ."

"Good idea." The older man nodded. "Well done."

"This is a sugar beet field," said the younger man, "but the soil of this whole collective has been exhausted. It is not scheduled to be worked again for at least two years. Even so, we'll plow it up and plant alfalfa to hide all the tracks."

Another nod. "How many dead?"

"Not as bad as we thought. Ninety-two."

"You're sure that you have all of them?"

"We've combed this whole valley. Every building, every vehicle, even the privies."

"Some will have relatives elsewhere. How will you deal with inquiries?"

"An outbreak of anthrax," the younger man answered. "The dead, we'll say, have been cremated to destroy the bacillus. Their clothing and personal effects with them, for obvious reasons. Their livestock burned in pits. We'll quarantine their homes as well and restrict all access. Anyone who knows anthrax will understand the need for these measures."

"Anthrax kills like this? No survivors?"

"It can. Not as quickly, perhaps, but in a day or so. Without treatment, the pulmonary form is always fatal."

The man in the plaid hat seemed doubtful. He put that question aside. "What have you learned about the accident? How it happened, I mean."

The younger man blinked. "Accident? Who told you it was an accident?"

The lorry driver watched them through the flap.

He could hear little of what they were saying. Only a word here and there from the man who had just come. He had one of those voices that carried.

But all would be well, he told himself, because the man in the Scottish cap looked so very sad. Now he was hugging the one from around here. Giving him a squeeze.

The lorry driver turned to the kerosene heater, lighting one of his Marlboros off the mantle.

When he looked back, the two men were heading toward the truck again. The one in the cap stood with his chauffeur, watching them go.

Suddenly, the silent one halted. He was looking toward the pit as if something there had caught his attention. Now he was walking toward it. He stopped at the edge, scanning it. Now he called out to the nice one.

"He has a tongue after all," remarked the lorry driver. The others, busy eating sandwiches, were not so interested.

The one who called out ran back toward the chauffeur. He reached out a hand, came away with the flashlight. Now he called again to the other.

"It's a woman," the lorry driver heard him say over the growl of the bulldozer. "She's still alive."

Impossible, thought the lorry driver. Did she climb up through dead livestock? But the other man rushed over to look.

"Where?" he seemed to be saying. "Shine the light on her."

The first one did so. The nice one leaned closer. Suddenly, a dull pop. The nice one went rigid. He staggered for a step or two, then turned to the other, disbelief on his face. Another pop, sharper this time. The lorry driver saw the pistol. He saw the nice one fold up and sink to the ground, his whole body twitching.

The one who shot him swung his beam toward the bulldozer. At the same time, he aimed his pistol. He held both of these on the driver, but the driver, it seemed clear, had neither seen nor heard. He kept working. Now, with the beam still blinding the driver to him, he pressed his pistol against the fallen one's neck. Another pop. Almost silent. He holstered his pistol. He stood erect. With his boot, he pushed the nice one over the side.

At first, the lorry driver felt frozen in place. For a moment, he could not think. A part of him was not even surprised. That's what trying to be decent gets you, it told him.

"We're dead men," he said at last.

The chauffeur hesitated, then ran, dragging his boss with him. The flatbed smashed into the Zil, knocking it aside.

But it did not accelerate. It was slowing. Drifting into the thickest mud. The Afghan veteran must have taken a bullet. The lorry driver wanted to stop. Help him. But he knew that all of them were finished if he did. Even the driver of the bulldozer had finally caught on to what's happening. He was on foot. Running for his life. The lorry driver stepped on the gas.

No question. They would get him.

If not here, then on the road to Kemensk.

If not now, then later.

But he would make the bastards work for it.